The
Sea Wall

The Sea Wall

Leslie Ann Keatley

For more information please visit www.leslieannkeatley.com

Book design by:
Arbor Books, Inc.
www.arborbooks.com

Printed in the United States of America

The Sea Wall
Leslie Ann Keatley

1. Title 2. Author 3. Fiction

Library of Congress Control Number: 2011912111

ISBN 13: 978-0-61551146-7

For Isabelle—may you never know the cruelest side of human nature.
And for Mom, who always dreamed of her own blue bayou.

ACKNOWLEDGMENTS

A huge thank you to:
My personal posse of fabulous women, including:
Vicki, for teaching me the art of southern hospitality;
Michelle and Donna, for your undying enthusiasm,
advice and confidence in me;
Melinda, for answering my endless stream of questions about OLA;
Stacey and Elise, for your keen eyes and editing skills.

1

Torment

I knew I should have stayed in bed that morning. If I'd just pulled the covers up and clicked off the alarm, I could have been dreaming of someplace far away from this hellhole. I mean, let's face it: that's what adolescence is for about fifty percent of us who go through it—the degradation of middle school and the sadomasochistic ritual known as high school. And the same people humiliated me on a regular basis throughout it all. They never outgrew their taste for cruelty, and my march of misery continued unabated.

But part of what happened that day was my own fault too. I should have known better than to squeeze a zit in the open in the girls' bathroom. I should have been safely enclosed in one of the stalls with my compact mirror. I had just come in to wash my hands before lunch and had noticed the small whitehead protruding from my chin. I was leaning forward, close to the mirror, giving it a good pinch when, wouldn't you know, in walked Caroline Riggs and her posse of hangers-on. She took one look at my guilt-stricken face as I backed away from the mirror, and the tirade began.

"Oh my God," Caroline said with a look of supreme disgust on her face. "Please tell me I don't have to look in a mirror smeared with Audrey Kelly's vile face pus!"

A chorus of ewwws erupted from the four girls standing behind her.

"Oh, gross," chimed in Hillary Staunch, her perfectly coiffed chestnut hair bouncing around her shoulders. "Can't you, like, use some zit cream or something?"

"Get bent," I mumbled, dodging them as quickly as I could and heading for the exit. I had just stepped through the door when I heard Caroline make a comment about dogs not being allowed on campus.

Get bent? Jesus, I was pathetic. Tears pricked my eyes, and I clamped down on my anger in an effort to hold them back. Congregating with my friends at the north quad was out of the question—there was no way I could maintain my composure, and I was in no mood to socialize. Instead I left the school and ended up at a small community park two blocks away.

How had things gotten so bad? I wasn't an ugly girl. In fact, I'd been told I was pretty. The Cheerleaders, as I liked to call them though only three of them actually were cheerleaders, were vicious in their taunting. They had singled me out in middle school, ridiculing my scruffy jeans and loose T-shirts and comparing them to their stylish short skirts and tops. As a result I had abandoned my tomboy tendencies long ago, forgoing them for blouses and skinny jeans. Mom let me get my light-brown hair highlighted with blond, and I spent at least thirty minutes each morning meticulously styling it. My smile was white and even, thanks to three torturous years of braces and wearing a retainer every night, and my glasses had been replaced by contact lenses. I didn't have a great sense of fashion, but my best friend, Kara, helped me out with my shopping every spring and fall. Still, the Cheerleaders tormented me.

I was ridiculed for my history of participating in and winning spelling bees. The snide comments continued whenever I was too quick to raise my hand with the correct answer to a teacher's question. I was called "bookworm" and "nerd." I always had my nose planted in a book between classes—anything from Twain and Hemingway to Rice or Rowling.

My friends sympathized when the bullying began but never stepped in to defend me. They would call Caroline and her gang "bitches" and "skanks" behind their backs but were terrified that the cruel banter would be aimed at them should they ever come to my defense. Being marginally overweight, Kara had already suffered at their hands. Caroline had once screamed at her and called her a fatass when she missed a play during volleyball practice.

Lonely sorrow enveloped me as I reflected on the current state of my life. I lived in a cookie-cutter, Southern California suburb that felt as fake as its name—Moss Ridge, devoid of actual moss thanks to years of drought and overdevelopment—and this, my junior year at Moss Ridge High, was not going to be stellar. I usually pulled good grades, managing As and Bs most of the time, but they had been slipping lately. I missed class too much, and when I was there I didn't participate in discussions the way I used to for fear of ridicule. Some days I just couldn't face the possibility of a confrontation with Caroline and her clique, so I would stay home.

On top of that I had only vague plans for college and none at all for work. No plans for anything, really. I asked Mom if I could transfer out to home study, but she wouldn't have it. She didn't consider a GED the same as a high school diploma. She chalked up my anguish to teenage hormones and dramatic exaggeration.

Dad was no help either. They had divorced when I was twelve, and I spent every other weekend at his house in the Valley. I wanted to move in with him and change schools, but Mom wept and moped until I gave up on the idea. I thought that sometimes Mom used me as collateral to punish Dad. I also thought things couldn't get worse.

I was so wrong.

I woke up the following morning and contemplated skipping school. Damn... I had a test in environmental science and one in US history. If I skipped I'd have to stay after school next week and do make-up tests. I decided it wasn't worth it as I climbed wearily out of bed and headed for the bathroom.

Amazingly I was having a good-skin day. The nasty cluster of zits on my chin had faded to near nothingness, and my complexion looked fairly rosy. I went on autopilot to complete my morning beauty rituals, but none of them really helped. I had been so foolish to think changing my appearance would make the in crowd at school accept me. I was seventeen, tall, and stacked, but once you're pegged as an omega, you'll never be an alpha. Not without a fight. I had been forever meek in my torment when instead I should have fought Caroline. Even if I'd gotten my ass handed to me, I should have tried.

I was waiting for Kara in my driveway when she rolled up. The walk to school was only four blocks, but since Kara had a car, we almost always drove to school together. I had been envious of the cute little car her parents had gotten her, but I got over it quickly with the help of Kara's generosity—she let me drive it whenever I wanted.

"Morning, sunshine!" she said, smiling. Her dark hair was twisted and clipped to the back of her head; a few wispy bangs framed her round face.

"Humph," I mumbled listlessly, dropping into the passenger seat.

"Cheer up, Miss Morose. It's another beautiful day in the neighborhood!" Kara's voice dripped with sarcasm. I scowled at her.

By the time the second bell rang I was seated in my favorite class: American lit. Mr. Harris was at the whiteboard, busily scribbling chapters and assignments. He paused, unconsciously rubbing his hairline. By the end of class his temples would be smudged with dry-erase marker. He finished at the whiteboard and turned to launch into a discussion of our latest reading assignment.

"Audrey, what's your opinion of 'Alas, Babylon'?" Mr. Harris asked me.

I snapped to as quickly as I could. I had been only half paying attention while looking at the back of James Ridley's head. James was on the basketball team, and I'd had a crush on him since I was twelve. I paused, trying to decide whether to give Mr. Harris my honest opinion. Just when I had concluded that I should pretend to like the story and give it a flowery review, James turned in his seat and looked directly into my eyes. I felt an electric shock from my feet to my throat; my face flushed deep pink, and my eyes watered. My agreeable summation leapt right out my ear and into the wind. I hastily jerked my eyes back to Mr. Harris.

"I hated it, sir."

I expected Mr. Harris to be irritated or even weary, but instead his eyebrows shot up with interest. "Why is that, Audrey?"

"Because the author makes nuclear war sound winnable. The story ends with the main characters fishing off a pier, for Pete's sake. It's like he's never heard of mutually assured destruction. I felt like I was reading war propaganda."

"That's a valid point, Audrey. What you need to remember is that this book was written in nineteen fifty nine, the height of what we call our atomic society. Most Americans believed wholeheartedly that we would fight an atomic war with the Soviet Union. This book illustrates one author's opinion about what would happen to a particular family and town in such a scenario. Needless to say, our opinions and outlooks have changed somewhat since then, not to mention the increasing number and yield of nuclear missiles."

My face continued to burn. Mr. Harris moved on to discuss the next book assignment as the bell chimed for the midmorning break. I gathered my books slowly, wanting to be the last one to file out. I left the classroom and headed in the direction of my locker. Maybe Kara would walk with me down to the cafeteria for a soda.

"Hey, I liked what you said about the book."

I turned to see James leaning against a column in the hallway. He was wearing his varsity jacket, and my eyes were drawn to the four inches of chest peeking through the top of his button-down shirt.

"You d-did?" I said. "Mr. Harris made me sound like a fool."

"No, he's just making himself feel smart. I felt the same way you did when I was reading the book. Like, aren't these people going to glow in the dark after they eat the fish they're trying to catch?"

I laughed, nodding my head. I was suddenly very conscious of how close we were standing. I was wearing my strappy wedge sandals that day, but even with a three-inch lift I was still a good two or three inches shorter than James. He shared my laugh and unconsciously brushed his dark-brown hair off his forehead.

"Hey, do you want to get a snack at—" His words were cut off by a sing-song voice.

"Jayyymes! Where were you? I thought you were going to meet me at the cafeteria."

My heart sank into my stomach. It was Caroline. She sauntered up, linking her arm with James'. Her perfect face had the russet glow of a spray tan. Her platinum-blond hair was styled into low-slung pigtails. I would have looked ridiculous with my hair that way, but Caroline looked like this month's Playboy Playmate. She cut her eyes to me, and the simpering smile dropped off her face.

"Oh, I didn't know you were slumming," she said to James.

"Jeez, Caroline, don't be a bitch. We were talking about homework."

"Come on. We've got only ten minutes before next bell," she crooned while tugging his arm and leading him off.

James followed, turning his head to silently mouth "bye" while walking away. My face flaming, I stalked off to find Kara.

"Are James and Caroline going out?" I asked her when I found her in front of our lockers.

"They dated for a couple months last summer, but I heard she dumped him for Steve Schubert. After she found out Steve was dating her and Sabrina at the same time, she broke it off, and she's been trying to get James back ever since."

Kara had the conspiratorial gleam in her eye that always came with good gossip.

"In fact, I heard that she begged James to take her back, but he was playing the friend card on her."

"I thought she was dating Dan Taylor." Dan was the varsity quarterback and thought he was God's gift to Moss Ridge.

"She was." Kara sounded gleeful. "But Caroline wants James back. You know what they say—you don't know what you've got until it's gone. Why're you asking? Did they get back together?"

"James and I were talking after American lit when Caroline came around the corner and shot daggers out of her eyes at me."

"Oh man, Audrey, that's bad. If you thought she hated you before, she's going to annihilate you now! If she thinks you're on James' radar, she's going to go ballistic." Now she was breathless.

"Oh screw her!" I said. "I'm so sick of her shit. The next time she gets in my face, I swear to God I'm going to bitch slap her as hard as I can."

"You can't do that, Audrey. Zero tolerance, remember? Hasley will have you suspended in a heartbeat, and trust me, that will not look good on your college applications."

I leaned my forehead against my locker. "I just can't take it anymore, Kara. Every time things start to get better, Caroline starts gnawing on me," I said.

The bell rang, and Kara and I headed to gym class. Our high school was built on a hillside, with the English department and our lockers at the top and the gym at the bottom. From our vantage point walking downhill, the center quad of the school resembled a busy ant farm with students hurrying this way and that, headed toward various classes.

Kara and I reached the girls' locker room and hurried to change into our gym wear. I was pulling my sports bra over my head when I saw a flash out of the corner of my eye. As I quickly pulled my bra in place I saw blond pigtails streaking around the corner. I didn't hesitate. I pulled on my shorts and T-shirt and hurried straight to the gym office where our teacher, Ms. Lake, was sitting at her desk, sipping coffee and reviewing attendance sheets. I knocked hurriedly and cracked the door open. The words tumbled from my lips in rapid-fire succession, my heart pounding so hard my temples throbbed.

"Ms. Lake, Caroline Riggs just took a photo of me while I was changing."

Ten minutes later, Caroline and I were seated in front of Ms. Lake's desk. Short, stocky, and built like a fireplug, Ms. Lake stood behind her desk, gazing down at both of us. Her arms were crossed in front of her, her right fist gripping the silver whistle that dangled from a lanyard around her neck.

"Ms. Lake, I didn't take a photo of her," Caroline said. "I was turning off my cell and I hit the camera button by accident. It took a picture of the floor! Look for yourself."

"I have, Miss. Riggs, and I see there is a picture only of the floor, but that doesn't change the fact that cell phones must be kept in lockers during class hours. Your phone is hereby confiscated, and a note will be sent home to your parents. This is your first violation, but it's your only warning. If you're caught using a cell phone on campus again, you will receive a mandatory three-day suspension. Am I clear?"

"Yes," Caroline said, hanging her head in contrition.

"Please go join your class on the track," Ms. Lake said.

Caroline left the office, casting a smirking look in my direction as she did. Ms. Lake sighed and pinched the bridge of her nose, as if staving off a sinus headache.

"Ms. Lake, you don't really buy that story, do you?"

"Audrey, I checked the phone myself. There's nothing on it except the floor. If she did take a picture of you, she erased it."

"But she might have e-mailed it to someone," I said. "What's going to happen if she e-mails a seminude picture of me around the school?"

"You're worrying too much," Ms. Lake said. "I know Caroline has a...challenging...personality, but she wouldn't risk the trouble she'd get into for that kind of behavior. Here's a hall pass." She handed me a slip of pink paper. "Go ahead and change. You can spend the rest of this period in the library."

I quickly changed in the deserted locker room. My hands shook as I dressed, and I wondered if I would ever feel safe changing my clothes in there again. Ms. Lake was probably right, but the sick feeling in my stomach lasted the whole day and night.

2

A Teenage Girl's Worst Nightmare

My premonition of dread took no time at all to prove horrifically accurate. The ring of my phone woke me on Saturday morning. I reached for it without lifting my head from my pillow.

"Hello," I said groggily.

Kara's voice was tight with anxiety. "Audrey, did you see it?"

I snapped awake. "See what? What's going on?"

"The bitch posted the picture on the Moss Ridge Web site. And that's not all. She altered it."

The Moss Ridge Web was a networking site for students and alumni. The yearbook staff a few years back had created it, but no one seemed to know who currently maintained it.

I scrambled out of bed and went straight to my desk. My laptop was agonizingly slow starting up. I still had the phone pressed to my ear as Kara jabbered away, but I wasn't hearing her. My ears were filled with a ringing buzz, my heart pounded with adrenaline, and my hands shook so badly that I couldn't type the Web address properly. I let out a frustrated cry and took several deep breaths. Finally the page finished loading.

There it was, front and center: the photo Caroline had taken in the locker room. I could see the top part of my face, including my startled eyes, but my arms pulling the sports bra over my head blocked the rest. Photoshop creativity began from the neck down. My breasts had been shrunk, and they sagged. My navel was a bulging outie. The lines of my white bikini panties were overrun by bushy pubic hair. The picture was a humiliating lie, but the forgeries were subtle enough to appear realistic. And the caption above was the clincher: Audrey, Audrey, quite contrary, trim that pussy, it's too damn hairy!

Hot tears stung my eyes, overflowed, and rolled down my face.

"Audrey? Audrey!" Kara's voice sounded far away as I tore my eyes from the screen.

"What?" I asked, sounding like I had given up—because I had.

"She's not going to get away with this, Audrey. She'll get kicked out for sure. You should sue her ass."

"I gotta go. I'll call you later after I talk to my folks."

Kara sounded timid and worried. "Okay, but call me before tonight, okay?"

"I will. Bye."

I hung up the phone, my fingers feeling boneless. My eyes drifted back to the photo and the caption. With a mind of its own, my hand scrolled to the blog below. Seventy-two posts, and it was only nine in the morning on a Saturday. I scanned the postings.

Shreikdude86:   Dang, a dude would need a flashlight to find that clit!

Bubbabeer4U: I think those titties would be classified as flapjacks. I'm digging the full bush, though.

Prettygirl919:   Somebody needs a good plastic surgeon and a Brazilian wax.

Nanuparty: I bet she smells real bad down there…know what I mean?

I stopped reading. I was sweating and panting; black spots swam in front of my eyes. I collapsed on my bed limply and fell asleep crying.

I woke three hours later with a splitting headache. Mom was gently shaking my shoulder.

"Hey, sleepyhead. Are you going to sleep the whole day away?"

"Mom, you have to help me. I'm in trouble."

Her eyes widened as her hand gripped my shoulder tightly. She sat on the edge of my bed next to me.

"What is it, honey? You know you can tell me anything. Are you pregnant?"

"God, no, Mom! I'm a still a virgin, for Christ's sake. It's those girls who have been bullying me. Caroline Riggs posted a…a grotesquely altered nude photo of me on the school's social Web site!"

Confusion and shock flooded my mother's features. "What? What? Who did what?"

I got up from the bed, pulling her by the wrist to my laptop, which still displayed the Web site.

"See for yourself," I said.

Her reaction was immediate and indignant. "That's not you, Audrey. You're body looks nothing like that."

"I know it doesn't!" I screamed. "She Photoshopped it! She made me look horrible! The whole school has seen this by now. I want to die!"

My mother stood up from my desk chair quickly, causing it to topple over. It thumped on the carpet with the sound of a body landing on grass. Her arms wrapped around my shaking torso. I burst into huge, wet sobs. Tears and snot wet my mother's shirt until I could cry no more, and the sobbing turned into coughing hiccups.

My mom released one arm from around me to grab two tissues from the box sitting on my nightstand. She helped me to blow my nose like she had when I was four.

"We're going to take care of this, Audrey. You're father and I will get this fixed."

A half hour later I sat at the kitchen table while my mom prepared to make several phone calls. Before she did, I watched her pour orange juice into one of our big water glasses. Then she pulled a bottle of vodka out of the freezer and poured about two inches of it on top of the orange juice. She added a few ice cubes and stirred it with a cereal spoon. I gaped as she plunked the glass in front of me.

"I know some people would condemn me for giving you this, and I don't want you to think that this is a way to solve your problems, but right now I think you need it," she said.

I looked in her eyes for a beat. Wordlessly, I picked up the glass and took three big gulps. I could taste the heat of the vodka, but the sweetness of the orange juice overpowered it. She nodded silently, grabbed her address book, and approached the phone.

By seven that night the Web site was cleared of any trace of the photo and blog, and I was wedged on the living room sofa with Kara on one side and our friend Lily on the other. Opposite us in the two wing chairs were our friends Jane and Megan. My mom and dad were in the dining room with Principal Hasley and the junior/senior counselor, Janet Davis. Their voices were purposely low, and we couldn't make out the conversation clearly.

I didn't care. I felt like I was surrounded by a warm glow. My friends had spent the last two hours comforting me. Their words soothed me: "Everyone knows the photo is rigged," and "Caroline is going to be expelled for sure." Their sentiments floated over my psyche like warm bath water. It felt so good to be defended, to be consoled, to be championed.

—————

At seven o'clock on Monday morning the school looked deserted. The April morning dawned cool and foggy, white mist swirling in the trees and shrubs surrounding the sprawling campus, hovering low to the ground and muffling all sounds. It made me feel claustrophobic. As I walked through the parking lot flanked by my parents, I wrapped my arms tightly around myself, trying not to bite my lower lip in worry.

Staffers in the administration building were sparse. We sat in the small, windowless conference room, waiting for the Riggses to arrive. The principal, vice principal, two class counselors, the school's psychologist, and Ms. Lake were quietly exchanging good mornings, organizing their papers and folders, and getting coffee at the small table against the wall. I watched silently as Principal Hasley filled a Styrofoam cup three quarters full of coffee. Picking up a canister of powdered creamer, he poured in a small avalanche. He took two stir sticks and began to stir, stir, stir. The powder stubbornly continued to float on top.

He glanced up as the Riggses entered the conference room. I had never seen Caroline's parents before, and they didn't look anything like I'd imagined. Her mother was squat, with a portly middle. Her hair was short and bleach blond, and she favored very heavy eyeliner. Caroline's father was tall and thin, with salt-and-pepper hair and mustache. Neither looked particularly arrogant or cruelly pompous, as I had imagined.

Caroline had come prepared to play the part. Her hair was pulled back into a low ponytail. She was wearing a white linen shirt buttoned all the way to the top, pleated khakis, and plain, white tennis shoes. Bile boiled in my stomach. My jaw clenched as I struggled to control my breathing.

The adults introduced themselves to one another and shook each other's hands—and acted as if Caroline and I were not even there. Principal Hasley was the first to speak.

"I'm sorry to say that these types of incidents are growing at an alarming rate in today's schools. We need to resolve this issue as quickly and painlessly as possible before there can be any further detriment to either of the parties involved. I have already spoken with the Riggs family, and they have agreed to a five-day suspension for Miss Riggs, as well as school service for the rest of the semester. Miss Riggs will be spending a minimum of four hours each Saturday assisting school personnel in projects and improvements. The offending photograph has been deleted and a posting placed on the Web site admitting to the falsity of the photograph, including a full written apology. I trust this is satisfactory to all parties."

He looked expectantly from one side of the table, where the Riggs were sitting, to the other, where we sat.

Mr. Riggs looked grim and tight-lipped. "Yes, we agree to these terms," he said.

"That sounds reasonable," my father replied.

I felt stunned. I was still trying to process what had happened while everyone was gathering their paperwork and saying their good-byes. That was it? It was all done? I'd been made the laughingstock of the entire town, and all Caroline got was a week's vacation and a handful of Saturday detentions? I wanted her expelled! Hell, I had fully believed she would be expelled. All the things my friends had assured me of had fallen through some giant sinkhole. They'd said she'd be expelled and lose her scholarship to UC. None of that had happened.

The next thing I knew my dad was giving me a one-armed hug, telling me to have a good day while my mom gently touched my hair. I stood immobile outside the admin building, watching their backs as they returned to the parking lot. The fog was dissipating as the warm spring sunshine burned it away. A voice at my back startled me out of my trance.

"You think you won, huh?" Caroline said. "You think you got me back so bad. Bitch, this isn't even a blip on my radar." Her voice was nonchalant and bored. "I've already gotten early acceptance to UC.

This little incident on my high school record doesn't mean anything. I'll still be graduating from university in five years while you'll be giving ten-dollar blow jobs on Third Street."

Her parents came out of the admin door just as she finished her speech.

"Let's go," her father said tonelessly.

Caroline flashed a twisted, sneering smile at me and then turned and walked away.

I don't know how long I stood frozen in place. Sometime later I felt a hand gently grasp my shoulder. I slowly turned to see the school shrink smiling at me kindly. She was a tall, dark-haired woman whose name I couldn't remember. Honestly, I hadn't known the school had a psychologist until the previous day. Her hair was soft and curled to her shoulders and did not match the severity of her gray polyester suit.

"Audrey, I'd like us to meet this Wednesday for a discussion about how things are going, okay? Please come to my office after your final class."

"Um… Where's your office?" I asked her.

"I share an office with the junior/senior counselor. Just come to the administration building, and the secretary will show you where to go."

She gave my shoulder another gentle squeeze before she walked back into the building. I continued to stand immobile, trying to think of the shrink's name. It was a color…maybe brown, or green? Finally the bell rang, rousing me from my daze.

During first break I relayed to my friends what had happened. They didn't say it, but I could tell they too were shocked Caroline had dodged the expulsion bullet.

3

Outcast

The following days at school were a living hell. Boys would leer and laugh when I walked by. Girls would stare and whisper behind their hands. The whole school knew every detail about what had happened, including the fact that the photo was a fake, but I was still a social pariah. Even my small circle of friends seemed uncomfortable and distant when we hung out.

Caroline returned to school after her one-week suspension looking tan and happy and, it seemed, convinced that I no longer existed. It seemed like I was invisible to her, although her circle of admirers still looked at me with disgust. The situation was so screwed up I started seeing the school shrink, Mrs. White, every Wednesday.

Heading in for my second session with her, I waved to the school's secretary and entered the counseling office. Mrs. White was seated behind her cluttered desk.

"Audrey," she said, smiling. "Close the door and come in."

She was always so damn cheerful, and it didn't seem at all forced or fake, making her all the more annoying. I sat down in the hard folding chair in front of her desk and rested my arms on my purse.

"So how are things going this week?" she asked. "I'm assuming the hubbub has died down, hasn't it?"

"I guess." I shrugged while studying the peeling veneer of the desk.

"Uh huh." She scribbled notes in a folder. "And you're keeping up with your classwork?"

"Yes."

"And how about your friends?" She thumbed through several papers in her folder. "Kara…and Lily… You've been doing things with your friends?"

"Yeah, I guess."

"Audrey, I can't help you if you won't talk to me," she said, laying the folder aside and leaning forward. "I'm here for you, to make sure you get any help you might need. I can't do that if you shut me out."

I crossed and uncrossed my arms, feeling the anger and frustration building.

"There's really nothing to say, Mrs. White. I get up in the morning, I go to class, I talk to my friends, I ignore the people who laugh at me and point fingers. What do you want to hear?"

"How does it make you feel when people laugh and point?" she asked, clearly eager that she was making headway.

I knew she wanted me to vent, to let it all out in a sobbing confessional. I knew she was doing her job—trying to help screwed-up teenagers who might go over the edge, reach for a razor blade, or worse, grab a gun and head for campus. But to me she was just a nosy, self-important nag.

"It makes me feel lousy, but I'm dealing with it," I said, looking her straight in the eyes.

"How are you dealing with it?"

I shifted in my seat, growing more irritated. "I just am, okay? I don't need to come here and get the Dr. Phil treatment from you. I can handle it myself, with my family and my friends."

"That's good." Her voice was calm, placating. "A strong support system is vital to handling stressful situations. But Audrey, I need you to include me in that system. I need to know what you're feeling so I can help you process these emotions."

"What I'm feeling..." My voice was deadpan. "Hmmm, let's see, where should I start? How about how I felt when I was twelve and Caroline had three boys take turns spitting on the back of my jacket while I was sitting in the cafeteria? Or how about when Hillary and Kylie spent the entire eighth grade mimicking the lisp I had from my retainers? Or—hmmm—here's a doozy: how about when Caroline poured a can of tomato juice down the back of my pants and yelled to everyone that I had my period? The truth is, it doesn't matter how I feel. As long as no one sues the school and there's no blood spilled, the same shit goes on day after day, year after year. You don't want to help me." I shook my head. "You just want to make sure I don't pull a Columbine or off myself."

Mrs. White steepled her fingers and looked at me for several seconds. "I'm glad you told me some of your history with Caroline and her friends. You've helped me understand so much more about the extent of the bullying you've had to endure. If you continue to confide in me, I can help make sure Caroline and her friends never bully you again."

"I'm sorry Mrs. White, but I find that hard to believe."

"Why?"

I grabbed the back of my neck with both hands, squeezing tightly, trying not to scream in frustration. I closed my eyes. "Mrs. White, Caroline Riggs put a nude, distorted photograph of me on the Internet for the whole school to see. She's still in school, enjoying her life. If it had been the other way around and I had been the one who posted a picture of her, I would have been expelled."

"You don't know that. And I can assure you that her punishment was just." She held up her hand to stop me from interrupting. "I know that it doesn't seem adequate to you, but you need to trust that we're doing our best to be fair."

I re-crossed my arms over my chest and looked at the floor. There was no point in going on with this. Perhaps it was time to talk to Mom again about letting me transfer schools. Mrs. White continued to talk, but I tuned her out…until I heard a phrase that caught my attention.

"Have you ever thought about Caroline's motives for bullying you?" She didn't wait for my reply. "People bully others to make themselves feel powerful. Many bullies have been in powerless roles themselves, at home or in other aspects of their lives."

"If you're trying to make me feel sorry for her, forget it," I said. "Everyone has crap to deal with in life, but they don't turn into a…a Nazi tyrant."

"You also need to consider that much of Caroline's treatment of you stems from jealousy."

I stared at her. "Why would Caroline be jealous of me? She has everything—looks, grades, car, clothes… She's a Cheerleader! She can get any guy in the school she wants. I've got nothing in comparison."

"Don't sell yourself short, Audrey. You're a smart, beautiful girl. Stop and think about what sparked the incident with the camera. Weren't you having a conversation with Caroline's ex-boyfriend? That's certainly something for her to be jealous of."

I sat silently, pondering her comments. Mrs. White waited to see if I would add anything else. When it was clear I wouldn't, she stood up.

"I want you to continue coming to our Wednesday meetings and let me know what's happening in your life. Please know that you can tell me anything, whether it's about school or home or your friends. I'll be in your corner."

"Thanks, Mrs. White," I said, though I wasn't sure if I meant it or not.

I grabbed my purse and book bag and left her office deep in thought. I walked out the school's front gate and was cutting through the bus drop-off when I heard a whiny voice call out.

"Hey, Audrey! How's your bush hanging? I heard you got it corn-rowed!"

I turned to see Heather Gibbons sitting on a bench next to her friend Danielle. I stared at her, stunned. I'd known Heather since the fifth grade. We weren't close but had always been on friendly terms, and I thought we understood each other. She had often been a victim of Caroline's taunting as well. The Cheerleaders called her Miss Piggy because she was heavy and had an upturned nose. Once they'd stuffed her locker with Twinkies that tumbled out all over the hallway when Heather opened it. Everyone laughed—especially the Cheerleaders, with Caroline right at the front.

Now, Heather giggled at me and whispered something in Danielle's ear. Danielle smirked. Apparently Heather was seizing her opportunity to move up the ranks of the social ladder, leaving me to take her place at the bottom.

A smattering of students milled around the front of the school. Several turned to watch. I stared at Heather, too stunned at first to retaliate. The names I had heard her called in the past played through my head: mushroom butt, Michelin Man's dream, Krispy Kreme...

"Why don't you go eat a bucket of chicken, Heather? You look really hungry."

I saw the flicker of pain in her eyes, but she quickly smirked and flipped me the finger.

I walked home enveloped in a haze of hatred.

Spring break arrived, heralding the final push to the end of the term. I woke that first Saturday alone—Mom was away for three days at a real estate seminar—but with a heavy cloud of depression hanging over my head. I turned over in bed and went back to sleep.

At noon I got up to use the bathroom and to drink a glass of water. I went back to bed. At two I watched a Grey's Anatomy rerun and a million commercials for personal injury lawsuits, at-home work training, and garden fertilizer. At three I wandered downstairs in the T-shirt and shorts I had slept in. I poured myself a bowl of cereal and ate it. At five I went back to bed.

And I dreamt. I was running, but my feet felt heavy as lead. I could hear the shrieking laughter of Caroline and her girlfriends. They were chasing me, throwing handfuls of cafeteria coleslaw on me. Students and teachers lined the walkways. They watched silently and without expression. Suddenly James Ridley was standing in front of me. He grabbed my upper arms in his hands. "I wish I could help you," he said. "I just can't. You're untouchable."

I woke up crying. It turned into screams of anger. I tore at my pillow and mattress. I punched and kicked until my legs burned and my fingers felt raw. My rage exhausted, I lay still. And in that moment my plan began to take shape.

"I'm going to get you, Caroline. I'm going to make you pay. I'm going to make your friends pay. I'm going to ruin you."

I spent the remainder of spring break plotting. I racked my brain for any and all ideas of how to humiliate, hurt, disgrace, and debase my nemesis. I made lists and then burned them. I could not let any evidence lead back to me.

Revenge is hard work, but I became adept at it. Every new idea was a black seed planted in the fertile earth of my hatred. Those seeds would sprout and bloom, nourished by the heat of my wrath.

4

Fight or Flight

The first week back from break was nondescript. I was too busy plotting to worry about much else, and I went through classes on autopilot. In Wednesday's session with Mrs. White I forced myself to speak with animation about my friends and activities, pretending my life was back on track, the trauma left in the past. Mrs. White seemed to buy my newly cheerful demeanor. She appeared relieved. If she had suspected what I was really up to she would not have been so comforted.

On Friday I stopped to get an iced coffee before I headed home. Proud's Mini-Mart, a popular student hangout, was just two blocks northeast of the school. The parking spaces in front were filled with teenagers leaning on car hoods and doors, but I barely took note of who was there as I walked inside. The glass door resisted my push, but then the whoosh of conditioned air bathed my face as the door sounded its mechanical ding.

Mikey was working the counter. He was a senior at my school; he ran with a very tough crowd. He and his friends favored long hair, ratty T-shirts, and worn-out blue jeans. We had grown up on the same street, but our early childhood friendship faded when my parents divorced and I moved to a new house with my mom. Now I hardly saw Mikey unless it was here at Proud's or at the occasional bonfire party behind the old, abandoned sanitarium.

I set my coffee on the counter and reached for my wallet.

"Hey," Mikey said.

"Hi," I returned.

"Hey, Tawdry Audrey!" a voice behind me sneered. I turned to see Hillary Staunch and Tracy Rhodes, two of Caroline's cohorts. Caroline and the rest of her clique were nowhere in sight. "Maybe you can get a job here selling razors," Hillary went on. "All you have to do is show that picture of your overgrown crotch and I bet you'd sell a million!" She and Tracy laughed.

I had heard of tunnel vision, but had never experienced anything like it until that moment. My sight squashed into a thin, red slit as a wave of adrenaline exploded in my body like a tsunami. I grabbed my coffee, my fingers clutching it convulsively, causing the lid to pop off onto the counter. Barely registering what I was doing, I flung the iced latte at Hillary. It hit her full in the face, splashing sweet, sticky coffee all over her hair and clothing. Ice cubes splattered her, Tracy, and the surrounding floor. I faintly heard Mikey expel a soft "whoa" as I flung the cup aside and lunged for Hillary.

I grabbed double handfuls of her curly hair with such force my fingernails raked her scalp. I twisted my fists as I pulled her head down to her knees. Hillary let out an earsplitting screech, and I released one fist from her hair to pommel her face, arms, and torso. My punches were ill-aimed and frantic. Someone grabbed me from behind; I flung my elbow backward and caught Tracy square on the nose. I heard the crunch as blood exploded from her beak. She immediately grasped her face in both hands, coughing and spitting blood as she backed toward the store's front windows, which were suddenly filled with the faces of all the kids outside the store. I felt a painful scratching as Hillary grasped the front of my shirt, catching skin and tearing it completely open in front. I kicked without thinking. My foot landed directly between her legs. She crumpled like an empty sack.

Another hand gripped my upper arm. I turned to swing but stopped when I saw it was Mikey.

"Get out of here, Audrey. Someone's going to call the cops, and I don't need that shit," he said. He let go of my arm and turned toward Tracy and Hillary. "Get the fuck out of my store! All of you! Get the fuck out!"

I walked toward the door on legs that felt like stilts. People hurriedly backed away from me. Outside I stood swaying for a moment, my shirt fully open. I glanced down to see four angry scratch marks across my chest, oozing blood onto my bra. A girl whose name I didn't know handed me my purse. I took it wordlessly, hugging it to my chest and wrapping my arms around myself to hold my shirt closed.

I headed home in a state of shock, my mind on autopilot. I changed my clothes, ate dinner, and mumbled single-word responses to my mother. I awoke the next morning with only vague memories of what had happened.

Word of the fight spread like wildfire. The school was buzzing with it Monday morning. After an entire weekend of phone calls, e-mails, and messaging, the story had grown to epic proportions. Kara, Lily, Jane, and Megan surrounded me at my locker before the first bell.

"You totally kicked their asses," Jane said breathlessly. "I heard you ripped out a huge chunk of Hillary's hair and then crammed it into Tracy's mouth!"

"Don't believe everything you hear, Jane." I laughed. "The whole fight lasted about a minute."

"But you don't even have a scratch on you," Kara said.

"Look again." I pulled down the neck of my shirt to show her my scratches. A collective ooooohhh rose from the group.

Lily gave voice to what everyone was thinking: "Aren't you afraid of getting jumped now?"

"Not really. I almost hope they do just so I can get a shot at the rest of those snotheads."

They all looked at me apprehensively.

"You're crazy," Kara said.

"Maybe."

My Wednesday meeting with Mrs. White was uneventful as usual; the teachers and school administrators were apparently not clued in to the gossip grapevine. No doubt if she had known about the fight she would have harangued me with endless questions, and Hillary and Tracy would have been brought into it. I thanked God adults were so clueless.

It's truly amazing how fast life can change. Just weeks earlier I'd been gazed upon with pity and scorn; now my classmates stared at me as if I were a celebrity. People still whispered behind their hands, but the rumors were of a wholly different nature.

My first post-melee glimpse of Caroline and company came as I headed to the soda machine outside the cafeteria. They were standing in a tight circle, talking. Tracy and her busted nose were nowhere to be seen, but Hillary was present, sporting a bruised cheek that she'd tried to hide with makeup.

As I approached, Caroline's head whipped around. Her eyes threw daggers at me. Then the whole group walked off without a glance back. I continued to the soda machine, dropped my change in, and pressed the diet iced tea button. Reaching down and extracting my beverage, I saw two legs clad in holey, faded Levis. Straightening up, I turned to face Mikey.

"You scared 'em. You've got them spinning now," he said, grinning, his hands stuffed into the pockets of his jeans.

"There're four of them," I replied. "They could gang up and pulverize me. And they could get a dozen more to join in and help."

"Yeah, probably, but now you're unpredictable. I've seen those chicks target you for years. You always took it. Now they don't know what to expect."

I thought it over. "Yeah, I guess you're right."

"Come on," he said, tilting his head and gesturing toward the parking lot. "I've got something to show you."

I followed, curious as to what Mikey could possibly want to show me. The scared rabbit inside my head wondered if this was another setup—if he was leading me to the Cheerleaders to get jumped. But I dismissed the thought immediately. Mikey and I had been friends. He was broody and tough, but he wouldn't waste his time with that crowd.

In the school's parking lot we walked up to his van—a beat-up 1984 Dodge. It used to be brown, but the sun had faded it to a nondescript beige. Stickers of metal band logos were plastered haphazardly over the door and sides, forming a mosaic.

"Welcome to the Stink Wagon," he said with a grin, sliding the door open.

Inside the van were two captain's chairs in front, a mini-bar with a built-in fridge against the side wall, and a bench seat in the rear. The carpet looked like it had originally been light brown but was a discolored, dirty gray with dark stains. The smell of old bong water permeated the air.

Mikey climbed in and gestured for me to follow. I had one leg on the running board when I heard footfalls approaching. Mikey's on/off girlfriend, Skinny Tanya, was running toward us. Skinny Tanya was just that—skinny as a rail. Her dark-brown hair was straight and baby fine. Her wardrobe rarely varied: halter top, short shorts or miniskirt, and flip-flops. Tribal tattoos circled her ankles, and her hands were stained with henna designs. She arrived breathless.

"Are you showing her?" she asked Mikey.

"Yeah. You're just in time."

"Yes! I didn't want to miss it," she said.

"Show me what?" I asked.

Tanya didn't answer; she simply climbed into the van and pulled me up after her. As soon as I was in, she slid the door shut.

"You're going to love this!" she said with a huge smile. "Mikey and I have already seen it like twenty times!"

The van had a small, boxy television suspended from the ceiling over the mini-bar. Mikey opened a nearby cabinet door, revealing a DVD player and stereo components. Before I could even process what he was up to, he turned on the set and pushed "play" on the DVD. A black-and-white image of Proud's Mini-Mart appeared on the screen. The picture showed a side angle of the counter—and me standing in the area immediately in front of it. This was the store's security camera footage. I watched, barely breathing, as I placed the iced coffee on the counter. In a matter of seconds I was fighting with Hillary and Tracy.

"Play it again," I said without taking my eyes from the screen.

After several viewings, I sat back on the bench seat. My thoughts careened wildly in my head. I looked like a badass in that fight. Who knew I had a brawler inside me? I felt thrilled and anxious at the same time. Tanya and Mikey howled with laughter each time the crotch kick I gave Hillary was replayed. Tanya told me a story about a fight she had been in a year before, but I barely heard her. Then Mikey interrupted her combat reverie.

"So what's your plan now?" he asked. "Are you going back to trying to be invisible, or are you gonna strike while the iron is hot?"

I considered what to tell them. I had vowed to keep my machinations to myself. It was risky to bring anyone else in, but Mikey and Tanya could help me achieve goals that would be impossible to do alone. I looked from one to the other soberly.

"I'm not finished with them yet," I said softly.

Mikey and Tanya listened raptly to my plan, their reactions shifting from amusement to wide-eyed surprise to silent shock. Instantaneously they began discussing how to implement what I wanted to do. The three of us spent the rest of the break and well into the next class bouncing ideas off each other, making suggestions, and discarding elements that couldn't be done. We agreed to meet later that night to begin stage one.

5

Fish Out of Water

The night arrived with a soft, cool breeze. I sat on a low wall bordering one of the endless bike paths that crisscrossed the valley. I was dressed in a black hoodie, jeans, and running shoes. I heard the low rumble of Mikey's van before I saw it, and I hopped off the wall. When Mikey saw me, he slowed and stopped. I climbed in the passenger side and closed the door. Skinny Tanya was in the back, rifling through a plastic grocery bag.

"Did you get it?" I asked.

"Course I got it," she replied. "I didn't even have to go the store. My mom actually eats this shit."

I smiled.

We cruised to the north side of town, and Mikey parked the van two blocks from Caroline's house. I was never sure where she lived, but Mikey and Tanya had been to one of the many parties she hosted when her parents were out of town. I was surprised by that, but as he explained, it was an opportunity to drink for free.

"Yep, there it is," he said, pointing to a tall, boxy McMansion, a Spanish-style tract home with a three-car garage. The windows were dark. One small light glowed at the entrance to the gated courtyard. Caroline's white Volkswagen Jetta—a seventeenth birthday present that still sported dealer plates—was parked at the curb, directly in front of the house; the halogen streetlights cast a yellowish glow on the hood. Mikey lifted his arms at ninety-degree angles in front of us, bringing us all to a halt.

"I don't think they've got security cameras, but I don't want to take a chance," he whispered.

He pulled his hoodie over his face, tying it tightly so that only his eyes, nose, and upper lip showed. Tanya and I followed suit. Tanya reached into the front pocket of her hoodie and extracted three sets of blue latex gloves, which she passed out, and then several flat, silver tins. We each grabbed one, grasping the pull tabs to open them. I heard the soft pop as I peeled back the lid, and, a pungent fish smell wafted through the night air. Sardines. Nothing smelled quite like them.

Tanya and I held on to the fish while Mikey crossed the street to Caroline's car. I saw him lift the back of his shirt and remove a slim jim. He slid it between the window and the door on the driver's side of the Jetta and jimmied it back and forth. Just when my heart began to pound and I thought our plan might be a bust, he grasped the door handle and swung it open. I held my breath and waited for the bray of a car alarm, but it didn't come. The breath surged out of my body. Lady Luck was shining on me.

Tanya and I slowly walked over to Mikey with the open tins. One by one he took them and, using his gloved hand as a strainer, carefully poured the oil in which the fish were packed into the crack between the driver's seat and the backrest. Tanya and I did the same on the passenger side. Mikey then pried off the defrost vent at the base of the dashboard and tipped his tin into the gap, and with a brisk shake of his hand the sardines landed with a wet flop. I handed him the remaining tins to add to it, sending the school of fish from my sea of discontent to their new home.

When we were done, Tanya collected the empty tins and Mikey softly locked and closed the door of the Jetta. We scrambled back across the street on cat feet. I was retracing our path back to the van when Mikey told me to wait.

"Hang on just a sec," he said. He pulled out a palm-sized camera. I watched him, my mouth gaping, as he pressed several buttons on the camera and trotted forward to the house directly across from Caroline's. He crawled headfirst under a hedge between the two houses. After several scuffling seconds he crawled out sporting a huge grin. We walked quickly back to the van. Soon we were all in and the Stink Wagon was rumbling down the road.

"Why did you leave your camera?" I asked. "What if someone finds it?"

"Nobody will see it," he said. "It's totally hidden. Besides, even if someone did, it can't be traced back to me. I wiped my prints off just in case."

"What about sales records?" I asked.

Mikey laughed, looking at me over his shoulder while he drove.

"It's stolen, you dork. I'll have to wait a few days for everything to cool down before I go back and get it. I set the timer to record from six a.m. until it runs out of tape, so I should capture the moment of Caroline's discovery perfectly."

I leaned back against the mini-bar, feeling both elated and fretful. I slowly began to relax, smiling as I imagined Caroline's reaction in the morning.

"Here," Tanya said, passing me a blue plastic bong and a lighter. "You get the first hit."

I hesitated for a few seconds, but then I held the bong to my mouth, and I lit the small protruding bowl. I inhaled deeply, holding my breath as I passed the bong and lighter back to Tanya. She quickly flamed the bowl to toke the remainder of the weed. I exhaled and began coughing uncontrollably. Catching my breath and wiping my eyes, I looked up to see Tanya smiling at me as she repacked the bowl from a small plastic baggie in her lap. She then held the bong to Mikey's lips and lit the bowl for him so he could smoke while he drove.

A few minutes later we were ordering from a drive-through window. With my eyes half closed and a feeling of deep relaxation washing over me, I told Tanya to get me whatever she was getting. Mikey ordered and then parked the van. After several minutes, an employee walked over to us with two bags of food.

"See, the secret is you've got to order the fries with no salt. That way you get a freshly fried batch," Mikey explained. He then dumped the three packages of fries he'd ordered into one of the larger food bags, extracted a canister of seasoned salt from the glove compartment and sprinkled the fries with it.

I laughed and shook my head. "So you order the fries salt-free and then douse them with your own?"

"Yep. It's the best," he said, passing the bag to me.

I grabbed a handful and began eating. Mikey was right. These were the best damn fries I had ever tasted. As we ate, we talked about people we knew, teachers we liked and hated, and cars we wished we owned. Then Tanya and Mikey got into a debate about whether all drugs or just pot should be legalized. I watched their friendly argument with amusement, waiting for it to hit a lull.

"So are you two boyfriend and girlfriend or what?"

Under normal circumstances I never would have asked such a blunt question. But the pot had apparently erased my naturally reserved demeanor.

Mikey was nonplussed by my query. "Yeah, we are…when Tanya's not pissed at me."

"What he means to say is that he's a man-whore who can't keep it in his pants. I should just dump his ass completely, but he's like a bad habit I can't quit." Tanya reached over and mussed Mikey's long hair affectionately.

"You know you can't live without me, baby," he said, leaning over to kiss her neck. Tanya giggled, pushing Mikey off her.

It was four in the morning by the time I collapsed in my bed. How the hell was I going to get up in two and a half hours? I barely had time to fret about it as I fell into a deep sleep.

—————

Kara picked me up at our usual time the next morning. After my fourth yawn she glanced over at me.

"Tough night?" she asked.

"You have no idea," I replied.

I had no intention of telling Kara or any of my other friends a single iota of my new activities. As much as I liked them, I knew they could never keep their mouths shut. Kara and Megan would never understand my new friendship with Mikey and Tanya. I could only imagine the reprimand I would receive if I revealed I had smoked out with them. Christ—Kara would probably give me the "gateway drug" speech.

Kara parked on campus. We slapped out our customary low five and then went our separate ways, Kara to biology and I to US history. In front of the cafeteria I saw Caroline talking to Kylie and Hillary. I caught the tail end of her sentence as I passed several feet away.

"…and the whole fucking car reeks like a Third-World whore-house." Caroline gestured wildly with her hands.

I quickened my pace and turned my head to hide the grin that was breaking through my sleepy haze.

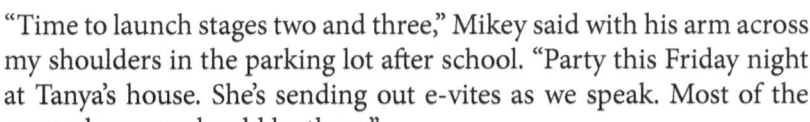

"Time to launch stages two and three," Mikey said with his arm across my shoulders in the parking lot after school. "Party this Friday night at Tanya's house. She's sending out e-vites as we speak. Most of the upperclassmen should be there."

"Her parents are letting her throw a huge bash?" I asked.

"Well, it's just her mom and her. Her dad lives in San Diego. Tanya told her mom a party was the only graduation gift she wanted. Much cheaper than jewelry or college tuition, so…"

"Tanya's going to college?"

"Nope. And her mom is pretty relieved about it, to be honest. She would hate to curb her spending on clothes, travel, and boyfriends. Tanya can't stand her. But it's cool. Tanya and her friend Merry are going to open a magic shop this summer."

"You mean like…supplies for magicians? Like tricks and stuff?"

"No, like witchcraft, the occult, mother goddess stuff."

"Wow! I thought Tanya was just into henna and chanting and hippie stuff like that."

"She's into all that stuff. She even tried crystal healing once. Personally I think it's all bullshit, but she and Merry will probably make a fortune shilling that voodoo crap." Mikey ran his hands back and forth through his hair, making it stick out at crazy angles. "Anyway, the party is a go, and I'm confident that Caroline and her staff will show."

I turned down Mikey's offer of a ride home, preferring the walk to mull over my thoughts. Stage one had gone off without a hitch. I wondered how long my luck would hold out.

6

The Party

Friday arrived with lightning speed. Mikey had been right—the whole school was buzzing with talk of Tanya's party. Kara and I headed straight to her house after school to hang out and prepare.

Kara's tiny bedroom resembled a Bollywood movie set: all orange and pink silks and a mosquito net over the bed. The only thing missing was burning incense—it made Kara sneeze.

She sat at a small brass vanity, carefully using a flat iron to straighten her hair. "So did you hear about Caroline's car?" she asked.

"Yeah, I heard something about that," I said, laughing.

"You didn't have anything to do with that, did you?"

"Of course not. But I think it's funny as hell!"

Kara let out a sigh of relief. "Good, because if they catch whoever did it, they're going to be charged with destruction of property and criminal mischief."

Her words were sobering, a cold lump of ice in my stomach. But then my thoughts drifted back to that awful picture of me on the Web. My loathing quickly vaporized that ice.

"So check out my closet and pick something to wear," Kara said over her shoulder.

"I can't. You know I suck at fashion. Please play designer for me."

Without hesitation, Kara began a thorough examination of her closet's contents. The clothes and shoes were so tightly wedged in there I didn't know how she could decipher one outfit from another. But within seconds she was pulling out shirts and skirts for me to try on, some with the drycleaner's plastic still over them.

Twenty minutes later I was standing in front of the mirrored closet doors. She'd put me in a cream-colored miniskirt—much shorter on me than her, given our six-inch height difference—sheer, pink thigh highs and a delicate, cleavage-revealing pink camisole, and she tied a thin, pink ribbon around my neck. One end trailed down my shoulder, the other down my back.

"I can't wear this," I said quietly. "It's way too risqué for me."

"Don't be such a puss!" Kara said, bouncing on the balls of her feet. "With your hair up, you're going to look like a centerfold!"

"Kara, I'm half naked! I wear more than this to bed!"

"Audrey. It's a pool-slash-pajama party. Everyone is going to be half naked, and it's high time you started showing off that body. Prove to everyone just how fake that photo was. Have some confidence, for Christ's sake. You look hot!"

I sighed. "I don't have any shoes to go with it, and none of yours will fit me."

"Stop whining. I've got just the thing." She jogged out of the room, returning a few seconds later with a pair of pink satin Mary Jane pumps, their four-inch heels tapering to a pinpoint.

"They're my mom's," she said. "She got them for a costume party last year. She and her sisters dressed up as Hugh Hefner's girlfriends."

"I'm gonna break my friggin' neck in these!"

"Stop your bitching and put them on," Kara said, and so I did. Then I let her do my hair. After much twisting, pinning, spraying, and ironing, it sat elegantly atop my head, with heavy bangs and tendrils framing my face. She started on my makeup next.

"Okay. Open your eyes," she said a long while later. I gasped. It took a good ten seconds to believe it was me staring back from the mirror. Kara had smoothed mineral powder over my face, giving it a velvety glow, and had applied lush false eyelashes and soft pink blush that added subtle color to my cheeks. On my lips she'd put delicate pink lip gloss. I didn't look overly made up as I'd feared. A smile slowly lit up my face.

"I think maybe that self-confidence we talked about is peeking through," Kara said.

Lily arrived at Kara's house at seven thirty. The party wouldn't start until eight, and we planned to make our entrance just before nine. We spent an hour speculating who would be there and what they would be wearing, what guys would be wearing swim trunks, and what hookups would be made. My hands began to tremble as nine o'clock approached.

The ride to Tanya's house was quiet. When we got there, the street was already packed with cars.

"Shit. We'll have to park a block or two away," Kara said.

"No, no. Tanya said we could park in her neighbor's driveway," I said.

Lily eyed me. "I didn't know you're friends with Tanya."

"Um, sort of," I said. "I'm friends with her boyfriend, Mikey. You know, the guy who works at Proud's."

"Oh," Lily replied, looking surprised. She and Kara exchanged glances.

Kara parked and the three of us walked to the house. The closer we got, the more we could hear and feel the deep bass of music inside. I opened the front door onto a spacious foyer with a white-marble floor; to the right was a great room with a fireplace and a huge flat-screen TV. Double French doors opened onto the patio and a pool beyond. Everywhere my classmates milled about, most with drinks in hand—guys in board shorts with wild patterns and colors, some paired with loud Hawaiian shirts; girls in form-fitting T-shirts with kitschy designs on the front and boy-style boxer shorts, more-traditional pajamas with cartoon characters or heart patterns on them, or bikini tops with short shorts or grass skirts.

I spotted Tanya on the patio wearing what appeared to be an oversized men's pinstriped dress shirt, her gangly arms and legs protruding like sticks. I made a beeline for her with Kara and Lily on my heels.

As I walked through the living room, my eyes drifted to the television over the fireplace. The video of the fight at Proud's was playing on the screen, followed by a compilation of candid photos of students at after-school events and other parties. The montage faded out, and the video of Caroline approaching her vehicle began to play.

Kara, Lily, and I stared at the television in frozen silence as the video showed Caroline unlocking the door of her Jetta and dropping into the driver's seat. Barely two seconds passed before she leapt from the car screaming. She turned around several times, unsure of what to do. A dark stain was clearly visible on the seat of her pants. Her fingers touched it gingerly. Several people watching the video roared with laughter as it showed Caroline bringing her fingers up to her nose to smell them.

The next shot showed her ducking her head back into the car only to rip it right back out. Her yelling could be heard faintly: "What the hell? God damn it!" The video ended with her storming back into her house.

"Pretty cool, huh?" Tanya had walked up behind me while I was staring at the TV. "All the videos and pictures were downloaded from the Moss Ridge Web." She leaned close to whisper in my ear. "Mikey uploaded all the footage from a cyber café. He even wore his hoodie while he did it just to be extra careful. He looked like the frickin' Una-bomber." She laughed softly. "The fight is by far the most popular. Everyone here has seen it at least five times by now. The guys especially get a kick out of it."

"Tanya, don't you think some people are going to get way pissed at me when they see me beating the shit out of Tracy and Hillary?"

"Hell no!" she said. "Look around, Audrey. You're the belle of the ball tonight."

She laughed and waved for us to follow her out to the patio. The flagstone courtyard stretched to the edge of a curvy, free-form pool with a huge rock waterfall surrounded by lush plants. Steam rose gently from the surface of the warm water. Two guys were waist-deep in the pool, chicken fighting with squealing girls on their shoulders. The rest of the pool was empty. Guess none of the girls wanted to spoil their hair and makeup.

Two long tables sat at the sides of the patio, weighed down with a huge assortment of junk food: a bowl of popcorn, a plate piled high with pink Hostess Sno Balls, sandwiches, three different kinds of chips and dip, and a dozen small bowls of M&Ms. The second table held a gigantic bowl full of punch with sliced fruit floating on the top and a three-tiered chocolate fountain surrounded by bowls of fruit for dipping. Large stainless-steel tubs filled with a variety of iced beverages lined the edge of the patio.

"Wow," I said softly.

"Impressive, isn't it?" Tanya said. "My mom gave me the cash, and I did the rest. I even had enough for a DJ." She gestured to a guy in a sideways hat, popping and locking behind a huge stereo setup at the far end of the yard. "We've got to keep the volume low to avoid any complaints, but Mom told all the neighbors about my graduation party, so I think they'll be cool until about eleven." She gestured to the tables of food. "Go ahead and help yourselves."

Kara and Lily timidly approached the chocolate fountain while Tanya grasped my elbow, leading me to the opposite table.

"The punch is spiked with coconut rum, so watch out. Mikey should be here any minute with a couple of kegs. His friends Jeff and Tony are going to pour out of the laundry room. I'm telling everyone to dump their drinks on the lawn or in the pool if the cops show up. Jeff and Tony are legal, so they can shut the door and claim the keg belongs to them."

"What about the punch?" I asked.

"I'll claim I had no idea it was spiked," Tanya replied. "Don't worry. I highly doubt the cops will show if we keep the noise down and some dumbass doesn't block a driveway or double park. Now back to the fun stuff. Check out the M&Ms!"

The jumbo-sized candies were in our school colors, gold and silver. I scooped up a small handful and squinted at them, then burst out laughing. On each candy, in perfect black-and-white clarity, was the image of Hillary with a face full of coffee. Her eyes were squeezed shut and her mouth was set in a comical cringe.

Kara and Lily walked over to see what I was laughing about. Tanya showed us another candy that had Caroline's yearbook photo on it with devil horns and a pointy goatee. Tanya rooted through the bowl and came up with another M&M sporting a third picture: Tracy with her hands grasping her nose.

I was laughing so hard I had to wipe my eyes to see the fourth photo on a different candy. It was another yearbook photo, this time of Caroline's buddy Kylie with blackened teeth, hag-like hair, and warts.

"How did you do this?" Lily asked Tanya.

"I ordered them from the M&M Web site. I tried getting them with 'Caroline is a ho,' but they wouldn't allow any negative comments or profanity. So I got still shots of the video on the Web, and I artistically altered the yearbook photos and scanned them. Upload, order, done!" Tanya looked cheerfully smug.

"It's so awesome. Has anyone else noticed?" I asked.

"Everyone has. They're all cracking up. They're not even eating them—they're stashing them to keep!"

Tanya was distracted by another group of people arriving at the front door. "See you in a little while," she said as she breezed off to meet and greet.

Kara just looked at me. I smiled and shrugged my shoulders as if to say, "What do you know?" But Kara wasn't fooled by my nonchalance.

"Why is Tanya on the anti-Caroline bandwagon?" she asked.

I looked into her quietly serious face. Lily looked back and forth between the two of us. I juggled thoughts in my brain, trying to decide what to tell them. I sighed. "God, Kara! Big freaking deal—so Tanya is on my side. She knows what a bitch Caroline and her friends are, and she's not afraid to stand up to them! I wish you had my back as much as she does."

The hurt look in Kara's eyes made me regret my outburst immediately.

"I'm sorry, I didn't mean that," I said, gently putting my hand on her shoulder.

"I do have your back, Audrey," she said. "Just because I'm not outrageously demonstrative about it doesn't mean I'm not on your side."

"I know that," I replied, trying to sound gentle.

Lily breathed a small sigh of relief, obviously glad that things were settled again.

I scanned the yard to see if Mikey had arrived. I saw James Ridley talking to a couple of guys by the waterfall and felt a familiar blush creeping from my neck to my face. Stepping briskly over to the punch bowl, I grabbed the ladle and filled a large plastic cup to the rim. Kara and Lily watched in surprise as I drank half the cup in several large gulps. It was absolutely delicious. I couldn't taste the alcohol at all. I wondered if Tanya was mistaken about the rum.

"Here," I said to Kara and Lily, handing each of them a cup.

Kara set hers aside. "I'd better not if I'm driving tonight," she said as she grabbed a soft drink from one of the nearby tubs.

I thought about the next phase of my plan, which would happen later that night. I tossed my cup into the trash, thinking that I'd better be sober as well.

7

Sink or Swim

"God, I'm nervous," Kara said. "I hardly know anyone here."

"You know me," I said, putting my arm around her waist. She smiled at me.

I felt someone touch my shoulder. I turned to see James standing right behind me.

"Hey," he said, smiling.

"Hi." I paused, trying to compose myself. If only my traitorous blush would let me be.

"You look really nice," he said, then glanced embarrassedly at my friends.

Kara and Lily left us, making their way through the crowd, toward the refreshments.

James smiled again, putting his hands in his shorts' pockets while bobbing on his feet just slightly. Was he nervous? Gorgeous, tall, unattainable James? Was I someone a guy could be nervous around? I tried to conjure the image of my reflection in the mirror at Kara's, trying to regain that confidence I'd felt. My limbs grew warm and tingly. I didn't know if it was due to standing so close to James or from the half a cup of rum punch I'd consumed. Either way it felt really nice.

"Those are some M&Ms, huh?" he said with a chuckle. I wasn't sure how to react.

"Yeah, Tanya's got quite the sense of humor," I said, nervously toying with the end of the ribbon tied around my neck. "You're not mad or offended or anything, are you?" I suddenly felt stupid for asking. I mean, jeez, I was plotting ultimate revenge on his ex-girlfriend. What were a few M&Ms compared to that?

"Nah, I thought they were funny. With all the mean shit Caroline's done to people over the years, I guess she's due for a little payback."

I couldn't help but feel relieved. Still, my fingers worked the ribbon around my neck until I accidentally untied it.

"Here, I'll get that," he said, gently grasping the ribbon to retie it. His warm hands brushed my skin, making me break out in goose bumps. My heart pounded and blood rushed through my veins. Just when I thought my knees were going to give out, Tanya burst through the crowd.

"Hey," she said, out of breath. "Mikey and his buds are in the garage." She looked at me, silently communicating that phase two was about to begin. She circled around to place herself between me and James, putting her arms around our waists, leading us in the direction of the garage before dashing off.

James took my hand as we walked. His friends were in a long line outside the laundry room door. Everyone was waiting for beer. James released my hand when we stepped up next to them, and they started talking about who had brought the kegs and how many. I was only partially listening as I leaned my head to the side to peer into the utility room and the garage beyond it. Mikey was in there with the two buddies Tanya had mentioned. One of them was holding the large funnel of a beer bong while the other cheered on Caroline, who guzzled it down. When she finished and removed the end of the long, plastic tube from her lips, a few drips fell on her skimpy bikini top, which matched her equally tiny booty shorts. She held her hands up in the air, accepting the cheers of Mikey and his pals.

I glanced around, looking for her mob. Then I heard Hillary's tittering nearby—she was next in line for the beer bong, Kylie and Tracy behind her. They obviously wanted their share of the attention from the mostly male crowd. I watched, mesmerized, as Hillary chugged down the frothy brew. She wasn't nearly as skilled as Caroline. Foam spewed from her nostrils, and she coughed loudly.

I tried to smother my laughter with my hands, but James noticed and looked to see what was so funny. He made a tsk sound through his teeth.

"Looks like some cheerleaders are going to be taking turns holding each other's hair tonight while they drive the porcelain bus."

I turned around, desperately trying to keep my giggles from turning into guffaws. What was wrong with me? So many things could have gone wrong with my plan, and there I was, struggling with being overtaken by hilarity. The stress had made me giddy and reckless. The alcohol surely hadn't helped.

I spotted Kara and Lily sitting at a poolside table. I turned and placed a hand on James' shoulder.

"I'm going to go talk to Kara. I'll see you later?"

"Yeah, I'll catch up to you after I get a drink," he said, gently sliding his fingers from my neck to the middle of my back. I tried not to tremble visibly as I walked away.

My friends stared as I approached, looking excited and incredulous. Lily scooted to the edge of her chair, gesturing for me to share with her. I sat down, glad to rest my feet. They were feeling the strain of Kara's mom's high heels.

Both of my friends began talking at once.

"Where'd you go?"

"What did he say to you?"

"Did you make out?"

"Are you guys going out now?"

"What base did you get to?"

"Did you see the Cheerleaders?"

"I saw them going in the garage."

"Chill," I said, slipping off one shoe and massaging the ball of my foot. "We walked to the garage and checked out the beer bong. That's it—end of story. The furthest I got was holding his hand for a few seconds. I don't even think that counts as being up at bat."

Putting my shoe back on, I looked up into their slightly crestfallen faces—no doubt they were disappointed by the lack of juicy details.

Suddenly, a familiar, shrill voice echoed through the yard. "What the hell is this?"

Caroline was standing at the buffet, staring at a handful of M&Ms. She flung them viciously; they scattered and pinged off the French doors.

"If you think that's bad, you should see what's playing on the TV," said a girl I didn't recognize, pointing inside the house. Caroline stormed through the doors and then froze in place as she watched the action on screen.

No one else moved either. It was like the entire crowd was hypnotized, waiting to see her reaction. We didn't wait long. Caroline stomped back out to the patio.

"Who's the fucking comedian?" she shouted. Necks craned to see what was going on. The low thumping of the music continued unnoticed. Even the DJ had left his podium to get a better look.

"I think the proper term is comedienne," Tanya said. She was standing only feet from Caroline, and I was suddenly scared for her.

Caroline charged toward her, looking murderous, stopping only inches from her face. Tanya didn't flinch.

"You want to start a war with me, freak? I'll snap your skinny ass like a toothpick!"

I was on my feet and running to Tanya when Caroline's head snapped toward me. She stomped forward, and we stood heels to flip-flops, eyeball to eyeball. Her face twisted into an ugly scowl.

"Oh, I should have known," she said. "Dirty Hippie and Pizza-Face Bush Woman are in league. How unoriginal. And don't think I don't know you're the one who dumped fish in my new car. I had to have the entire interior replaced! You think that mini-mart brawl and this little makeover of yours have made you some kind of half-assed prom queen? You're nothing, and you'll always be nothing. You'll never belong no matter how hard you try. You pathetic wannabe." She enunciated every word as if stabbing me with them.

I heard footsteps behind me and stole a quick glance to find Kara, Lily, and Tanya at my back. Caroline's eyed them with the same contempt in which she held me.

"Ohhh, and now you've got your fat dyke friends here to back you up! After you finish fooling yourselves into thinking you're actually cool, you can go home and stuff your fat faces with nachos and donuts and pop each other's zits."

A collective sigh echoed from the crowd of onlookers. Hillary and Tracy remained by one of the snack tables, looking uncertain of what Caroline wanted them to do.

I was used to Caroline attacking me, but her assault on my friends was something new. I felt hatred flare in my chest, but just as quickly I got a mental image of her absurd insults—the nachos, the donuts—and I was overcome with an unbearable urge to laugh. It burst through my lips with no hope of containment. Caroline's face went from angry to mutinous, which only further fueled my laughter. I doubled over, tears streaming from my eyes. I paused long enough to take a deep breath before I spoke.

"You're the one who's pathetic, you shallow, spoiled, peroxide bitch." I spoke calmly; I didn't shout. But my words carried through the yard. "You and your friends can take that bully stick you carry around and shove it straight up your asses." I crossed my arms, feeling empowered, with a few hiccoughing giggles still escaping.

Caroline's eyes scanned the crowd and came back to rest on me. Waiting for her next verbal assault, I was unprepared when her arms shot out like pistons, catching me squarely in the chest with enough force to knock me off balance. My feet scrambled, but it was too late. I felt my calves and ankles scrape painfully against the concrete edge of the pool as my back hit the water. I came up sputtering, blinking, and pushing my ruined hair out of my face. I looked up in time to see Caroline and her gang leaving through the side gate.

Utter humiliation engulfed me as I struggled to the side of the pool. Then I heard Kara yell out, "Everyone in!" and she cannonballed into the deep end. Lily jumped in too, squealing with delight.

"What the hell," Tanya muttered, and dove in headfirst.

Suddenly it was bedlam. People were jumping in all at once, creating wave after wave that spilled over the edge and onto the patio. Kara's arms were around me, hugging me close. We looked at each other and laughed.

We spent the next hour in the pool, lounging and socializing. All the people at the party approached us at some point to laugh about Caroline's reaction and to say how glad they were to see her put down for once. James and his friends swam with us briefly and then headed out as the crowd began to disperse.

Finally we sat shivering on some loungers by the poolside, trying to dry off before we got into the car. I looked down at my satin Mary Janes. They had a drowned, deflated look.

"Um, Kara… I think I owe your mom a new pair of shoes."

She looked at them. "Yes," she said. "But they died for a good cause. May they find peace in shoe heaven." She looked around as if she had suddenly realized something. "Where's Tanya?"

"It's cool," I said. "She and Mikey planned to ditch the booze if anything went down tonight. She was probably afraid that Caroline would call the cops or something."

Kara accepted my lie without question. But I knew the truth about exactly where Tanya and Mikey were. They were carrying out phase three. I hoped with silent fervor they would find success.

8

A Cold Dish

The hot shower felt like heaven. I stood under the steamy spray until the water began to cool. Wrapped in my plush terrycloth robe, I sat on my bed to towel dry my hair. I kept replaying the night's events in my head: James touching my hand and neck, his obvious interest in me, all of my friends having my back, my schoolmates' admiration. I couldn't have slept even if I had tried, and I didn't try.

I was anticipating a message from Tanya. The fact that I hadn't heard from her yet did not bode well, and I was wondering if something had gone terribly wrong when I heard the soft trill of my phone, signally an incoming text message.

I lifted the phone from my nightstand with shaking hands. The message contained only one word: SUCCESS.

———

I was dressed, sitting at the breakfast bar with a bowl of cereal, before the sun had finished rising. Mom stumbled into the kitchen, her short hair poking out in all directions, and blindly headed for the coffeemaker.

"Nice hair, Mom," I said with a grin. She jumped at my voice and clutched her chest.

"Jesus, Audrey! You just scared ten years off my life. What are you doing up so early? I thought you were going to spend the night at Kara's after the party."

"I didn't feel like sleeping on the floor," I said. "Plus I promised Tanya I'd help her clean up this morning. I have to get going soon."

She stared at me, looking suspicious. I fidgeted and scratched my elbow. God, I hated it when she looked at me with that X-ray vision all moms have.

She contemplated me a moment longer and then scooped ground coffee into the filter. "Oh…okay. So how was the party? Did you and your girlfriends have fun?"

"Yeah, it was really good, actually. Tanya has a sick backyard, and the food was amazing. She even had a DJ."

"Was anyone drinking?" She feigned indifference.

I spoke quickly, my story already prepared and rehearsed. "Some older guys showed up with a keg, but Tanya made them take off."

"That's smart," she replied, buying the story without question.

A half hour later I was perched on Tanya's living room sofa, wedged between Mikey and Tanya. Mikey's hair looked even more disheveled than usual, and he was antsy, chewing on the straw of his soft drink, cigarette in hand. The house was littered with the refuse of last night's party. Tanya laughed at my distress over the mess.

"Don't sweat it," she told me. "You keep forgetting that part of my budget was cleanup. The crew will be here at ten."

Mikey set his drink on the table and his cigarette in his mouth and went to hook the wires from his small video camera to Tanya's big-screen TV.

"Wait till you see this," he practically sang, squinting through the hazy smoke.

I clutched my knees in anticipation as the picture appeared on-screen. The first shot was footage of the party. There was Caroline, downing the beer bong, followed by Hillary's foamy nose spew. All three of us laughed.

"That bitch needs to be on America's Funniest Home Videos," Mikey said.

"Um, I don't think the network would approve of underage drinking," Tanya replied. "But trust me, it will be posted where it counts."

The film cut to a panning shot of the backyard. My heart sped up as I saw myself briefly in the crowd, chatting with James. The picture switched to a shot of the buffet tables and then to a crisp close-up of the M&Ms.

"Tony is a great videographer," Mikey said. "If he could quit dropping F-bombs he could get a job filming weddings or some crap like that."

The film cut again and restarted in the dark interior of a car. I squinted to make out the picture. All I heard was heavy panting. Then the screen switched to grainy, green-tinted night vision, and I was assaulted by the image of Kylie, her face bobbing up and down in Tony's lap.

"Oh my God! Fast forward it! I don't want to see it!" I screamed, covering my eyes.

We all laughed as Mikey fast forwarded the video. He paused and then rewound the footage.

"Here it is—check it out," he said.

I uncovered my eyes to see Tony on-screen, grabbing the camera and causing the picture to wobble crazily. I heard Kylie's voice off-camera.

"Hey! What about me? Time for my cookie," she purred.

"Yeah, right," said Tony.

Then we heard the sound of a car door opening, followed by a brief scuffle and a thump. Kylie's voice became a screech.

"You fucking asshole!" she screamed as Tony slammed the car door and gunned the engine.

The green-tinted picture next showed Tony's progress as he followed a good distance behind another car—and it was obviously Caroline's. We heard Tony dial three digits on his cell phone.

"Yeah, I just left a party, and there's this girl who was totally drunk off her ass—excuse me, drunk as a skunk—and she's driving away, and I'm behind her, and she's weaving all over the road. I think she's going to crash and kill somebody."

A span of several seconds passed.

"I'm on Ridge Canyon Road... Yes, just a mile past Gold Leaf Drive. Please hurry! I think her name is Caroline... Yeah, L-O-V-E-L-Y-1." That was Caroline's license plate number.

A few more seconds of silence, and the camera followed Caroline's progress. Her car was weaving, but only toward the center divider. It looked like she was talking to whoever was in the passenger seat.

"No," Tony continued, "I don't want to give you my name. My parents will kill me if they find out I went to this party. Look, she just turned right onto Arroyo... Yeah... We're at a red light."

The light turned green, and Caroline's car continued on for several minutes, then we saw red and blue pulsing lights reflecting off its rear window. Tony rolled down his window—I could tell by the hum of the motor—and said, "Right there, officer."

Tony veered off the road and onto a dark side street. He pulled the car to the curb and cut the engine and the lights. The picture trembled as he removed the camera from the dash and zoomed in on the scene with Caroline and the cop.

Slowly it came into focus. Caroline was standing at the rear of her Jetta, and the police officer was shining a flashlight in her face. She was agitated, speaking with her hands. I wished I could have heard the conversation.

"Too bad we didn't have a remote microphone for her car," Mikey said, mirroring my thoughts. "I would love to hear her try to charm her way out of this one."

Hillary and Tracy stood at the front of the car, where a second officer questioned them. Another police car pulled up.

"Must have been a slow night in the valley, huh?" Tanya asked.

The field sobriety test came next. It was hard to tell if Caroline passed or failed—the picture wasn't clear enough to see. Finally the officer held up a Breathalyzer for her to blow into…and then hand-cuffed her and put her in the back of his cruiser.

Mikey and Tanya cheered wildly, then cheered again when Tracy and Hillary were similarly detained, though they weren't handcuffed. Two of the officers poked around inside the Jetta, and the three of us watched raptly as they pulled out several items and placed them on the car's roof.

I swallowed audibly. I asked Mikey, "Did you decide on meth or X?"

"A little of both," he answered. "The dumb bitch didn't even lock her car this time. Can you believe it? And it still smells like fish!" He laughed. "If she had opened the glove box or reached under her seat for any reason, she would have found it."

"The stars aligned," Tanya said, her gaze never leaving the screen.

The video ended with both cruisers driving away and a tow truck hooking up the Jetta.

Mikey turned to us with a huge smile. "I'm going to edit it to just the highlights and upload it tonight. We'll post a bulletin on every student Web site in the valley. By noon tomorrow the whole town will see Caroline getting taken to the big house and Kylie smoking Tony's skin pipe."

Mikey and Tanya were amped, and their satisfaction should have been contagious. Instead fear crept into my heart. My burning need for vengeance had suddenly turned into a cold ball of ice, and though they say revenge is a dish best served cold, it festered in my stomach, the taste like bitter ashes on my tongue.

9

Portents

Caroline didn't show up for school on Monday, and everyone knew why. The video had gone viral, distributed by Tanya and Mikey and viewed by a countless number of people, including the police department. Information coming through the grapevine was still sketchy as to the outcome of the arrest: first there was talk of her parents sending her to an East Coast boarding school, but then the rumor was that all charges had been dropped and she would be back at Moss Ridge High the next day. By the time school let out most of the student body was convinced that Caroline was moving to Switzerland, Hillary would be home-schooled and Kylie would be sent to live with her grandparents in Korea.

By Wednesday Caroline and Kylie still had not returned to school, although Hillary had, and she set the record straight about Saturday night's events. She and Tracey were grounded by their parents until the end of the term, but both girls shrugged it off. Caroline's driver's license was suspended for three years; even though she had blown just under a 0.08 on the Breathalyzer, it was still illegal for a minor to consume any alcohol whatsoever. The drug possession charges were still pending. Caroline had, of course, vehemently denied any knowledge of how the drugs had gotten into her car or to whom they belonged. She had undergone all the drug tests the police demanded of her, and no traces of methamphetamine or ecstasy were found in her system.

On the legal front, her family's attorney picked up on the fact that her car had been unlocked that night and anyone could have put the drugs in it. In addition, the tape of the 911 call was brought into question. The attorney hypothesized that the caller was not a good, concerned citizen but the one who had set up Caroline.

Thankfully, no one recognized Tony's voice in the video. That had been an important part of the plan I'd hatched with Mikey and

Tanya—that he was not well-known to the student body and could remain anonymous behind the camera. We were pretty lucky that Kylie never put two and two together and came forward to identify him as the culprit. We speculated it was because she hadn't met Tony before that night and probably didn't even remember his name. Even if she did, she was probably too humiliated to say anything.

When rumor had it that Caroline would return to school the next day, I spent my lunch hour sitting in the captain's chair in the Stink Wagon, discussing the gossip with Mikey and Tanya. Mikey sat on the floor, lounging against the rear bench seat.

"That's too bad her drug tests came up negative," he said, absently rubbing the stubble on his chin. "I heard from a good source that she's done X on occasion, but I guess it was too long ago for any trace of it to be in her system."

"Who cares?" Tanya asked. She sat cross-legged next to Mikey, braiding her hair in thin strands that mixed with the rest of her loose locks. "She lost her wheels and, more important, her rep. Your laughing in her face was so perfect, Audrey. If you had gotten pissed and duked it out, it would have just been a big clusterfuck. But you made her look like an idiot—like the spoiled drama queen she is."

"Thanks," I said. "I thought I was going to kill her when she knocked me into the pool, but Kara really saved the day." Lately the thought of Kara and my friends diving into the pool to help me save face was the only thing that thawed the fear in my chest.

"I know!" Tanya said. "That worked out perfectly. Me and Mikey ditched the booze and made sure Tony was on track while everyone was in the pool." She snickered. "The film of Kylie's blow job was pure bonus. I gotta tell ya, Tony had a blast helping us out. He wants to know what we're doing next."

The ball of ice hardened painfully.

"Nothing," I said, gripping the arms of the captain's chair. "I am so done with this. I did what I set out to do—I humiliated Caroline and her group. Anything more would be pushing our luck to the brink."

"Oh come on!" Tanya said. "Things are just getting good! What about that idea you had of putting sulfoxide in their gym shoes?"

"Yeah, my grandma used that stuff for her arthritis. Made her smell funky," I said. "Like garlic."

Tanya laughed. "I love it. Stinky cheerleaders…yeah!"

Mikey lit a cigarette and took a deep drag. He smiled at Tanya.

"Yeah, Audrey," he said. "Let's really rip it up. I'm thinking some personal property damage, perhaps some vandalism… We already turned Caroline's car into the fish-mobile. Maybe we could do something interesting with the rest of the gang's vehicles. I think a spray-painted hard-on would be perfect for Kylie's Honda."

As Mikey and Tanya continued to bounce ideas around, reveling in the more outrageous and destructive plots, I felt a light click on in my head. They didn't care if we got caught. More importantly, they didn't care if I got caught. These were not true friends. They were coconspirators. They were drunk off the power they wielded, the pain they caused. I felt nauseous. The cigarette smoke and stale air of the van became overpowering.

"I gotta book," I said. I slid the panel door open and jumped out. "See you guys later."

"Wait!" Tanya called. "Don't forget to stop by the new shop later."

Shit. I had forgotten all about Tanya's store with her friend. I had promised to come see it while they were setting up.

"Okay," I said, knowing I couldn't get out of it. "Can I bring Kara with me?"

"Sure!" Tanya beamed. "Kara's awesome. I never knew the little munchkin had so much chutzpah."

Munchkin? I didn't like that. It felt like something Caroline would say. I knew Tanya didn't mean it in a hurtful way, but it doubled my worries about her and Mikey's motives.

I hurried into environmental science, barely making it to my desk before the second bell rang. Kara sat directly in front of me. She turned around.

"You smell like cigarettes," she whispered, wrinkling her nose.

Damn. I fished around in my handbag until I came up with a small bottle of perfume. I sprayed some on my hair and clothes.

At the front of the room the teacher began his lesson on Southern California's water tables, and I leaned forward to whisper in Kara's ear. "Wanna come with me to Tanya's new magic shop later?" I knew she would. She was fascinated by the occult and wanted to learn to read tarot cards.

"Yeah!" she responded, and I smiled. With her by my side, at least I would feel like I had a true ally with me, now that I was fearful of Tanya and Mikey.

Tanya's store, which was in one of the older shopping centers in town, was a small storefront surrounded by a supermarket, a pharmacy, and a row of smaller shops. Hers had tall glass windows in front and a beautiful new awning of dark-blue fabric embroidered with stars and crescent moons. The Sacred Tree was painted in gold lettering on the glass door.

Tanya spotted us and hurried to unlock the door. "Hey, come on in!" she said, waving us in. Smoky-sweet incense infused the air, and soft music drifted from unseen speakers, a melody of harps, chimes, and soft chants. The ceiling was draped with long, thin spans of the same fabric as the awning; fluorescent lights shone through the tiny stars and moons, giving the store the atmosphere of twilight. The walls were painted a very light shade of blue-gray. Unpacked boxes were stacked against one wall along with unassembled shelving and lights.

In the center of the store stood a magnificent tree that rose from floor to ceiling. Charms and other items hung from its branches, which disappeared into the draped fabric. I laid my hand against the trunk, which was at least four feet in diameter. Dark-green leaves with clusters of white flowers covered the tips of the branches. I gazed up through them, feeling for a moment as if I were standing in some ancient forest.

"Looks real, doesn't it?"

A woman stood in a doorway at the rear of the store. Dark red hair framed her long, thin face, its angles too sharp for her to be considered beautiful, and yet she was striking. Her eyebrows arched as she regarded me with eyes as green as summer grass.

"You must be Merry," I said as I stepped back from the tree.

She nodded and walked forward, stretching her hand out to grasp mine briefly. Her jeans and T-shirt caught me off guard; I had expected swirling shawls and lots of beads.

"And you must be Audrey," she said, never breaking eye contact. Her eyes were piercing.

I nodded and pushed my hands into my pockets. I looked up again into the tree. "It does look real," I said.

Merry nodded. "It's an accurate model of a rowan tree. They're sacred in ancient mythology and folklore, thought to protect against malevolent beings. Its wood was used for making wands and magician's staves. There are also many medicinal uses for its berries. Are you interested in mythology?"

"Well, I don't know much, really, except for fairy tales and stuff."

"Ah, but I bet you don't realize those fairy tales are based on true legends. Yes, they get twisted and embellished through the centuries, but they are based in fact."

"So there really was a Snow White who ate a poisoned apple?" I asked.

"The Walt Disney version of Snow White that everyone knows is just one of dozens of variations on that legend—from Germany's version by the brothers Grimm, to Russia's 'The Dead Princess and the Seven Knights,' to Scotland's Gold-Tree and Silver-Tree. But to answer your question, yes, I do believe the root of the story is true."

Kara and Tanya drifted over to join our conversation.

"See?" Tanya said. "That's why I went into business with Merry. She's the end-all when it comes to mythological knowledge. Did you tell them you're teaching me tarot?"

"No, I thought I'd let you do a reading for Kara, and I'll do one for Audrey. Follow me."

She led the way through the doorway at the back of the room. I followed her into a small hallway. To my right was a restroom, and to the left was an open doorway framed by a long curtain. I walked through that into a room that wasn't much larger than a walk-in closet. A round glass table sat in the center surrounded by four chairs.

An involuntary giggle escaped my lips. Merry turned to me, her eyebrows raised.

"I'm sorry," I apologized. "It's just so...Madam Zolta-ish." I shrugged my shoulders and felt myself blush.

Merry took a seat and gestured for me to sit across from her. "Don't be embarrassed. People want the kind of atmosphere they see in movies and on television. No one wants to have his or her fortune read in a setting that looks like a cafeteria. They want drama and mystery. Our store will provide that."

I nodded. "Just so you know, I don't really believe in this stuff. I mean, I have an open mind and everything, but I'm not a big believer in psychics or magic."

"That's okay," Merry said, smiling. "We'll just do this for fun then."

I returned her smile and relaxed in the soft chair. She handed me a large deck of cards. They felt heavy in my hands; their surface felt almost oily. I thumbed through the deck, looking at the pictures.

"These are beautiful," I said.

"I want you to hold the cards and mix them as you think of a question you would like answered or a problem you can't find a solution to. When you're done, hand them to me."

"How will I know when I'm done?" I asked.

"You'll simply feel it. The cards will be guided by Gaia, the earth mother, but they also have a force of their own. They will be guided by your subconscious. Together you will know when the cards are ready."

I had my doubts but continued to thumb randomly through the cards. I turned them over so I could no longer see the colorful pictures. I thought of Caroline and her friends. I had prevented myself from thinking of what would happen next—I was too frightened of the possibilities. Instead I had buried my worries in the back of my brain and had tried to go about my day-to-day business. I now brought those thoughts to the forefront of my mind and wondered if my revenge was finished—and if my good luck would hold.

I took several slow breaths and concentrated on the feel of the cards in my hands, on their smooth texture. They had the dusty-spicy smell of a very old book; it reminded me of Saturday afternoons I'd spent in the public library searching for new books. The corners of my mouth turned up as the pleasant memories washed over me. I looked down to see that I had stopped shuffling the cards without realizing it. Merry gently took the deck from my hands and began laying the cards face down on the table.

"This is a Celtic cross," she said as she spread five cards in the shape of a cross and four cards vertically beside it. She laid a final card at the top of the cross and then turned a card over at the heart of it. On that card was a red-winged angel pouring water from one chalice to another. The angel had one foot in a small pool of water surrounded by lilies, the other on land. The setting sun glowed brightly in the background.

"Temperance," Merry said calmly. "This is the significator, meaning this card represents you."

I was taken aback. "You mean I'm an angel?"

Merry smiled. "Temperance is a card of the underworld. It represents blood, life, the conscious and unconscious. You must be prepared for the deepest questions of who you are, who you think you are, and who you will become. It is telling you that you have reached a pinnacle of self-awareness."

Merry turned a second card over to cover the first: an armored warrior standing in a chariot pulled by two sphinxes, one black, one white.

"The Chariot," Merry said. "A conquest or external battle. It also symbolizes perseverance, turmoil, or vengeance. This card represents the conditions surrounding your question."

My pulse jumped as I listened to her words. I reminded myself that there were probably a zillion ways to interpret these cards.

Merry turned a third card, placing it above the first. It bore a picture of a man dressed like a pope. He sat on a throne with two monks below him.

"This card represents what you hope for in relation to your question. The Hierophant symbolizes a need to conform, to receive social approval. It is also a warning for you to reexamine your understanding of the meaning of things. You must beware of hypocrisy."

She turned over a fourth card and placed it below the first. On it a bright-yellow moon shone between two stone pillars. Two dogs howled at the moon while a crayfish crawled from the water.

Merry tilted her head slightly, studying the cards.

"The Moon. This card is what you have experienced in relation to your question. The Moon can be deception, trickery, or disgrace. It illuminates our animal nature, the tendencies of the savage beast. This is a card of bad dreams and ill health."

She turned the fifth card and placed it to the left of the first. This card was upside down, showing a crowned king sitting on a throne engraved with the heads of rams.

"The Emperor, inverted," Merry said. "The Emperor upright is accomplishment, confidence, and wealth. Reversed means indecision, petty emotions, and lack of strength. This card represents your past."

Merry turned a sixth card, placing it to the right of the first. I flinched as the image of the devil was revealed, a reversed pentagram etched above his horned head. A man and a woman, both nude, stood on either side of his cloven hooves, chains wrapped around their necks, securing them to the throne.

"The Devil," Merry said, barely audible. "Downfall, violence, disaster...an evil person. This card is the influence that will come in your future."

I wondered if I should stop her from turning over any more cards. I didn't want to know my future if it was full of bad news. But before I could say anything, Merry reached for the remaining four cards to the right of the cross. The first one showed a beautiful woman with a crown of stars, holding an orb in one hand. She was perched on a throne, surrounded by a field of flowers with a waterfall in the far background. This card was upside down as well.

"The Empress, inverted," Merry said. "This card is the attitude of the question being asked. Normally the Empress is a card of accomplishment, fertility, and the Goddess herself. Reversed, it symbolizes inaction, anxiety, fear, and infidelity."

Without pausing, Merry turned over an eighth card. A nude man and a nude woman reached for each other; a dazzling sun shone behind them while a red-winged angel looked on.

"The Lovers," Merry said with a lift in her voice. "Romance, a lover, is going to enter your life. This person will influence the question being asked."

I immediately thought of James. My pulse raced as I imagined him becoming my boyfriend.

The ninth card depicted lightning striking a stone tower. Two figures fell headfirst from its burning windows, terror on their faces.

"The Tower," Merry said. "A sudden change, downfall, the end of a friendship, abandonment of the past." She looked into my eyes, her face solemn. "Your life is going to change radically. This doesn't mean it will be for the worse. It just means that the change will be significant."

I was really starting to hate this fortune-telling stuff.

Merry turned over the tenth and final card. I looked down to see a nude woman kneeling with one foot in a pool of water, the other on land, a pitcher of water in each hand. She poured one pitcher into the pond, the other on land. A huge yellow star shone above her, surrounded by seven smaller white stars.

"The Star!" Merry said, her joy and relief apparent. "The Star is hope, serenity, inspiration, and generosity. It is also spiritual love and balance. This is your culmination card. It is the end result of all previous cards."

"So that's good, right?" I asked, not certain I wanted to hear the answer.

"That's very good," Merry replied. "I have to tell you, Audrey, this is a very powerful reading, and I was more than a little worried. The cards are showing a clear story."

She gestured toward the cards spread across the table.

"You're clearly in the midst of some kind of battle or challenge, and the choices you make will change your life. They will influence the person you become. According to the cards, you are already questioning who you are and who you want to be. You will be influenced by both good and evil people. It's up to you to choose the direction your life will take. Having the Star as your culmination card is a wonderful sign that all will come out well."

She reached out to grasp my hands. Hers were warm; mine were cold.

"Whatever struggle you're facing, you're going to be stronger for it," she said. "Make sure you follow your heart and always reach for the light, not the dark."

She gave my hands a final squeeze and released them.

I didn't ask her how I would know which decisions were right and which were wrong. I already knew. I didn't even need to consult my heart; my stomach was already telling me how sickening my actions had been. It was time for me to resign from the business of revenge.

A thought occurred to me. I rubbed my hands together, contemplating how to broach the subject with Merry, who was gathering the cards up and wrapping them in a satin cloth.

"Merry?"

"Yes, Audrey?"

"Thanks for the reading. It was really...amazing."

She smiled at me as she secured a ribbon around the cards. "But you have another question?"

"Um...yeah. It's just that, you seem so...wise. Mature, I mean." I stammered, trying to get my meaning across.

"You want to know why I'm in business with Tanya, who is not wise and mature."

"Yes." I sighed, relieved that she got my meaning so quickly.

"Tanya is a very young soul. She has much to learn about generosity and kindness. She is a good person, but she is like a shallow pool. In time she will deepen. On the practical side, she is also the source of our capital to start this business."

I nodded. "You needed Tanya's money for startup."

"Yes," Merry said. "And I needed a partner. When we met last year at the festival of Ostara, the spring equinox, I knew our acquaintance would be a fortuitous one."

She leaned back in her chair, stretching her arms over her head. "Have you ever heard the expression that whatever you do will come back to you times three?"

"Yes, I think I heard it in a movie once."

"This is the motto I live my life by. If you give kindness, it will be returned to you in triplicate. If you give cruelty, well…you know."

We got up, and Merry led the way back to the storefront, where Tanya and Kara were bent over their own cards spread across the countertop.

"Merry, help me with this, will you?" Tanya asked. "Is the Wheel of Fortune destiny or is it Harmony?"

Merry went to help, but I hung back, not wanting to intrude on Kara's reading in case it was as deeply personal as mine had been.

A few moments later, Kara was slinging her purse over her shoulder, ready to leave.

"Just a minute," Merry called as she walked to the tree in the center of the store. I watched as she scanned the branches and reached up to extract a necklace from one of them. She returned to the front of the store with the necklace dangling from her fingers.

"I want you to have this," she said, holding it up for me. It was a plain black cord on which hung a beautiful pewter star with seven points.

"This is the elven star. It represents the seven magical places: sun, moon, sea, sky, wood, wind, and spirit. I thought you would like it, to remind you of the Star in your reading."

I felt tears prick my eyes. I couldn't explain why I was so moved, but the charm felt like more than a gift—it felt like a talisman. With shaking fingers I put on the necklace. The pendant rested a few inches below the hollow of my throat.

I tried to thank Merry. For a few dreadful seconds I was afraid I was going to start bawling like a kid. I pulled her into a wordless embrace. At that moment I felt closer to her than to any other person in the world. This stranger who barely knew me had looked right into my soul and had seen the light that burned in the darkness.

10

Friends and Enemies

"I want to talk with you about Caroline Riggs' arrest and the party that occurred prior to it."

Mrs. White leaned back in her chair, absently turning a pencil in her fingers as she contemplated me across her desk.

Shit. So far I had managed to avoid any questions from parents or teachers about the events of that Friday. I needed to be exceedingly careful with my words.

"Yeah, that's really something, huh? I mean, I knew the Cheerleaders—I mean Caroline and her friends—partied, but I didn't know they were into drugs." I shrugged my shoulders, trying my best to look innocently shocked.

Mrs. White continued to stare at me. This was her tactic: she would keep silent and wait for me to spill my guts. I stared back at her, my face calmly neutral as time ticked by.

"I heard you and some of your friends were at the party. Is that correct?" she asked.

"Yes. We were invited."

Several more seconds of silence passed.

"And…was there some kind of confrontation that took place between you and Caroline?" The pencil continued to turn lazy circles in her fingers.

"She pushed me in the pool."

"Why did she do that?"

"That question's a bit obtuse, Mrs. White," I said, not able to suppress my irritation entirely. "She hates me. She's always hated me. And I was hanging out with her ex-boyfriend at the party. Why wouldn't she want to push me in the pool?"

"James Ridley?" she asked, sounding genuinely interested.

"Yes."

She nodded her head slightly. "James is a good kid... Decent grades, varsity basketball." She seemed to be talking more to herself than to me. "I also heard something about M&Ms with unflattering pictures on them?"

I clamped my lips tightly, trying to suppress the smile that wanted so badly to escape. Fearing I was about to have another laughing jag, I mimicked Mrs. White's long, silent pauses. I won the battle. She probed ahead.

"Did you have anything to do with those candies?"

"I did not order the candies. However, I did immensely enjoy seeing them."

"Uh huh. And was the purpose behind the candies to humiliate Caroline and her friends?"

My humor vanished like smoke. Breathe. Don't blow it.

"Mrs. White, I didn't force Caroline to drink booze at that party. I didn't even invite her. I didn't put her picture on M&Ms, and I didn't do anything except be the butt of her verbal abuse and get pushed into a swimming pool. I'm glad she got busted, but to be totally honest with you I wish I didn't have to hear her name ever again. I'm done with her. All I want to do is live my life and hang out with my friends. Caroline is a waste of my time."

I crossed my arms over my chest, waiting to hear whatever psychobabble she would dish out.

"Dating her ex-boyfriend probably isn't the best tactic for removing her influence from your life, don't you think?"

"We're not dating. We're just friends."

"You might want to consider keeping it that way," she said.

Megan leaned close to admire the star pendant on my neck.

"Cool! I'm so jealous that you got your fortunes told for free! Me, Lily, and Jane want to go get ours done too, but we'll have to pay twenty bucks a pop."

"Just make sure you have Merry do it, not Tanya," Kara said. "Audrey said her reading was awesome, but mine from Tanya sucked. All her interpretations were really vague and lame."

The five of us were gathered in Megan's room, sitting in a

semicircle and chatting. We'd piled up our textbooks in the middle like wood for a bonfire.

"What was your question?" asked Lily.

"I wanted to know when I would lose my virginity," Kara replied.

Megan and Jane cracked up, rolling onto their backs on the soft carpet.

Lily shook her head at Kara. "All the things you could ask, and you wanted to know when your cherry will be popped?"

Kara threw her hands in the air. "Well, I didn't know what to ask! It's not like I have more important issues to worry about! I was just… curious."

Megan sat up, wiping tears from her eyes. "So what did she say?"

Kara shrugged her shoulders. "Just stupid crap about traveling over water and new adventures."

"Maybe you have to go on a cruise to get laid," Jane said, and she and Megan burst into further gales of laughter.

Kara stuck up her middle finger at them, clearly not amused that her sex life—or lack thereof—was so humorous. "Well excuse me if I have interests other than arm wrestling and muscle shirts," she said, making fun of Megan's masculine hobbies and style of dress.

Megan exaggeratedly flexed her biceps, her smile never faltering.

"What about your question, Audrey?" Lily turned to me.

My discomfort rose at the thought of sharing any details about my reading. I had told very little to Kara and decided that was the best tack to take with the rest of my friends as well.

"I just wondered how the summer is going to turn out—you know, if James and I will hook up or something."

"Oh jeez! Another loss-of-virginity quest!" Megan cackled.

"Excuse me," I said, trying to sound indignant. "Dating and screwing are separate activities."

"Not if you know what you're doing," Megan replied. "So what was the verdict?"

"Just that something unexpected would happen. But romance is definitely in the cards, so to speak."

"Woohoo!" Megan cheered. "At least one of us will be kissing something other than her pillow." She grinned at Kara, who flapped her thumb against her forefinger, mimicking Megan's chatter. We all laughed—until the soft trill of a cell phone interrupted. All of us reached for our phones before I realized it was mine. I didn't recognize the number on the display.

"Hello?"

"Hi, Audrey?"

"Yeah, who's this?"

"It's James."

My heart leapt into my throat. I swallowed several times, trying to clear it as well as my panicking mind.

"Hi!" I said a little too enthusiastically.

"Hey," he replied, sounding like his usual relaxed self. "I hope you don't mind me calling your cell. I got the number from Susan in American lit."

"No! I don't mind. That's cool. I have study hall with Susan." I was babbling. I snapped my lips closed, desperately trying not to sound like an idiot.

"I'm calling to see if you have any plans this Saturday. If not, do you want to grab a bite and see a movie?"

"Yeah, that sounds great," I said.

"Cool. Text me your address and I'll pick you up at six."

"Sounds good."

"See you then," he said.

"Okay, bye."

I pressed the disconnect button feeling like I had just swallowed a very large amount of hot soup. My cheeks flamed as I looked to the expectant faces of my friends.

"Well?" Megan asked.

"That was James. He asked me out for Saturday."

The room erupted with cheering and oohing and aahing—it sounded like a boy-band concert. I laughed as my friends mussed my hair and congratulated me.

Megan high-fived me. "That was one freaking accurate fortune-telling!"

⁓⁓⁓

I awoke the next morning feeling far too elated for the run-of-the-mill Thursday that it was. I took extra time with my hair and makeup and hurried out the door with barely a word to my mother.

Kara was waiting in her car in my driveway, engine idling.

"Finally," she said when I climbed in next to her.

"I'm sorry, Kara. I'm just so nervous to see James today. What if he ignores me or takes one look at me and decides he doesn't want to go out on the date after all?"

"You're such a dork! Will you just relax for Christ's sake? I'm going to do another extreme makeover on you before your date. You'll look so good he'll eat you alive!"

We laughed. It felt lascivious. I couldn't help myself.

We rolled into the school's parking lot five minutes before the first bell. The good humor Kara had infused me with quickly evaporated as I saw a knot of girls conversing at the school's side entrance. Caroline was back, and like bees to honey her crew of obnoxious admirers hovered around her. Her arrest seemed to have made her an even bigger celebrity on campus. Now she had a bad-girl edge to her reputation.

She stood among her court of minions, ministering to them like a queen. Kara and I veered far to the right to skirt around them. Kara kept shooting sideways glances at me as we walked; I could tell she was afraid of another confrontation between them and us. Neither one of us spoke.

We reached our lockers, and I rifled through the untidy stack of books in mine, finding the ones I needed for my first two classes. I slammed the door and turned to see Caroline within kissing distance of my face.

Instinctively I dropped my book bag to the floor, ready for another punch to my chest. Caroline smiled down at me. I could see Kara in my peripheral vision. She was immobile, her mouth slightly agape, frantically trying to decide if she should run for a teacher or not.

Caroline turned her head lazily toward Kara. "Run away, little rabbit." She made shooing gestures with her hands.

Kara remained frozen in place as Caroline turned back to me. The other students around us had paused to watch. Someone pulled out a cell phone and started filming.

Caroline stepped closer, and I took an involuntary step back to avoid her face touching mine. My back bumped against my locker.

Caroline spoke through her teeth, her voice audible only to me. "You're going to pay, you ugly bitch. When you least expect it, I'm going to get you. Your skanky new friends won't be able to save you."

"Get to class!" Mr. Harris' deep voice boomed as he approached us. The crowd around us quickly dissolved, the students hurrying off.

Caroline narrowed her eyes and gave me a last cruel smile before she sauntered away. She strolled past Mr. Harris, who stood nearby with his hands on his hips. "Morning," she said to him in her sweetest voice.

The crowd effectively dispersed, and Mr. Harris left for his classroom. Kara and I followed in silence. She grasped my shaking hand as we walked, letting go only when we parted ways and headed for separate buildings.

When I arrived for second-period American lit, I was still on edge. I sat at my desk in the far left corner of the classroom, rubbing my hands together vigorously to try to warm them. One row over and two desks up, James turned in his seat to nod his head and smile at me. I tried to return the greeting but gave him more of a grimace than a smile.

After what felt like an endless class, the bell rang, and I gratefully gathered my books to head to my locker. Scared shitless that Caroline would be waiting for me, I gripped the strap of my book bag with white knuckles. A hand touched my shoulder and I jumped, letting out an involuntary "eek!" as I did so.

"Sorry!" James smiled as he caught up with me.

I laughed, unable to resist his easy charm and his beautiful blue-green eyes. "I guess I was daydreaming," I said, smiling up at him.

"I do that all the time," he said. "My little brother likes to sneak up on me when I'm not paying attention and scare the crap out of me."

We arrived at my locker, where I was intensely relieved to see no sign of Caroline. With James there it took me three tries to get my combination right. As I opened the door he leaned casually against Kara's locker, talking about the double feature playing that Saturday and casually removing a piece of lint from the shoulder of my blouse. There was no way I could follow what he was saying. His touch was like a defibrillator.

"So I know this is short notice," he said, "with prom being just a couple of weeks away, but do you think you'd want to go with me?"

Suddenly, I heard every word he was saying. "I... I... Yeah, sure!" Once again I found myself trying to suppress the idiot factor.

James smiled, revealing a gorgeous dimple on his left cheek. "Let me know what color you're going to wear so I can get your corsage, okay?"

"Okay," I said, giddy with delight.

"Gotta run." He stood up straight, smiling at me for a moment longer. "See you later."

I watched his tall frame as he walked toward the cafeteria. My legs were jelly. "Solidifying plans for your date?" Kara asked, approaching her locker with a smile on her face. She dialed her combination.

"He asked me to prom."

She slammed her locker door shut, her mouth agape.

"Oh…my…God. I'm starting to hate you. Let's hit the mall tomorrow after school for a dress." Clearly she was all business when it came to fashion.

I bounced on the balls on my feet, my only reply another high-pitched squeak.

11

Ice Blocking

By the end of the day the news of my prom date had made it outside my circle of friends. I had told only a few people, but apparently they couldn't resist passing it on to acquaintances. Apparently it was quite a buzzworthy topic.

After school I ran into Tanya near the admin building, where she had just picked up her cap and gown. Without so much as a hello she started ranting.

"What the hell are you going to dumbass prom for? And why are you going with Caroline's dumbass ex-boyfriend?"

"He's not dumb. And everyone makes mistakes. We all hang out with the wrong people sometimes." This statement seemed especially apt in light of my present company. I needed to break it off with Tanya and Mikey somehow; I just didn't know how. Part of me hoped they would just forget about me and all our schemes after graduation.

"He's another dumb jock. I thought you liked real people with real personalities."

"Tanya, it's just prom, okay? Can't you just let me go through the motions like all the rest of the boring conformists you disdain so much?"

"Whatever," she said. "Catch you later." She waved as she headed toward the parking lot.

I watched her go with relief.

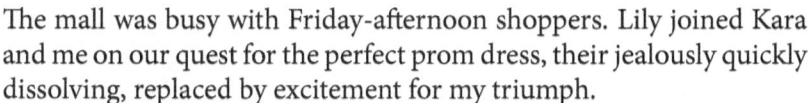

The mall was busy with Friday-afternoon shoppers. Lily joined Kara and me on our quest for the perfect prom dress, their jealously quickly dissolving, replaced by excitement for my triumph.

"God, I hate all this pink foofy shit," Kara said as she rummaged through a rack of formal wear.

"Well, I'm not wearing black or red, so just forget about that," I told her, crossing my arms.

Kara tsk-tsked me, disappointed that I didn't share her passion for sequins and satin.

"Girls, girls," Lily said. "Let's find a happy middle, shall we?"

"Easier said than done," Kara grumbled.

I was sick of shopping too. I'd never had any love for it to begin with, so two hours of looking at dresses was like torture for me.

"What about this?" Lily asked, holding up a dress on a hanger for our inspection.

I froze, taking it in from top to bottom. "It's perfect," I breathed. "Please tell me they've got my size."

I lounged on my bed, gazing at the delicious dress that hung on my open closet door, ensconced in a protective clear plastic bag.

A soft tap on my door interrupted my daydreaming.

"Come in."

My mom smiled as she entered the room. She stopped in front of the closet to examine my purchase.

"Wow," she said. "Very elegant." She lifted the skirt to examine the fabric more closely. "So this boy is coming to pick you up tomorrow?"

"Yeah, Mom. Please don't embarrass me."

She turned, looking piqued. "I'm not! I just want to meet the boy who's taking my only child out on a date."

I buried my face in the pillows of my bed. "It's no big deal, Mom," I said, my voice muffled. "Teenagers date all the time."

"I'm aware of that, Miss Smartypants. And I trust you to use your brain and not do anything stupid. It's him I don't trust."

As soon as she left the room I got up to change into my pajamas— a ratty wife-beater and oversized flannel boxer shorts. As I prepared to escape into the latest fantasy novel I was reading, I heard the low rumble of a van pulling up to the house. I darted to the window and my worst suspicions were confirmed: the Stink Wagon in all its back-firing glory idled out front.

Tanya nimbly jumped out of the van and trotted across the front lawn. She boosted herself up the sidewall to spring onto the over-hanging porch roof and walked on cat feet to my open window. She leaned her head in the window and smiled. Her long hair tickled my hands on the window frame.

"Come on. We're going ice blocking." She pulled on my wrist as she turned from the window.

"Who—huh—what? What the hell is ice blocking?"

"Come on, Audrey! Time's a-wastin'. Get your ass in gear."

"No! I've got plans for tomorrow," I said. "I'm going to bed in a few minutes."

Tanya gave me a withering look. "Don't—be—a—pussy."

I grunted and grabbed my tennis shoes under my bed. Whatever it was Tanya and Mikey wanted to do, I would have to get it over with as quickly as possible. I hesitated in the center of my room, thinking, then quickly scribbled a note on the pad on my desk: "Couldn't sleep. Went for a hot chocolate at Starbucks. Back in a jiff."

I left the note on my pillow just in case Mom discovered my absence, though there was no reason to think she would. I never snuck out of the house… Well, not until now. Anyway, the note might save me from a grounding if I was caught. I silently cursed Mikey and Tanya for making me risk my date the next day with James.

Tanya opened the van's sliding door, and I climbed in behind her. Mikey was behind the wheel, and Tony rode shotgun. Thirty minutes later Mikey was parking the Stink Wagon on the side of a maintenance road next to the country club golf course. A few scattered lights dimly illuminated the deserted hills of manicured grass.

Tony and Mikey opened the rear doors. Each grabbed an end of a huge tray bearing two enormous blocks of ice. Tanya grabbed two rolled-up beach towels and scurried to the chain-link fence that bordered the course. She squatted low to lift the gaping bottom of the fence high enough for the rest of us to crawl under. Tony and Mikey struggled with the heavy tray, dragging it under the fence after them.

I followed the group as they walked across the golf course, careful to keep their voices low as they talked and snickered. Just when I thought we were never going to stop walking, Mikey came to a halt at the top of a slope. Mikey and Tony grunted as they tipped the blocks out of the tray.

"Me first!" Tanya stage-whispered.

She folded one of the beach towels and spread it over the top of the ice, then crouched on top of it. Mikey gave the block a mighty heave over the edge of the hill. On the dew-covered grass it was like a Slip 'n Slide. Tanya squealed in delight as she raced down the hill in the dark, her brown hair streaming out behind her. Mikey got a running start to launch himself on the second towel-covered block. He rode the ice on his stomach, whooping all the way to the bottom.

"Those assholes better shut the fuck up," Tony said with his hands in his back pockets. "Security's gonna hear 'em." His bushy, long hair hid his face, and I couldn't read his expression in the darkness. He reached down to grab the tray in one hand and then stood up and slung his arm over my shoulders.

"Let's catch up so we can have our turn," he said, smiling at me.

"Great!" I said, feigning anticipation, then ran down the hill to escape his arm. God! The last thing I wanted was Tony coming on to me. I still couldn't get the image of him and Kylie out of my mind.

At the bottom of the hill Mikey and Tanya laid on the ground next to the ice blocks, laughing and kissing. Mikey looked up when we approached.

"Dude! My ice nailed Tanya before we hit bottom." He laughed. "She's so light, she doesn't slide nearly as fast as me."

"Come on, help me with this," Tony said, and with Mikey's help managed to wrestle the blocks back onto the tray—with much cursing. Tony strung a beach towel through the tray's handhold to pull it with, and the two of them trudged up the next incline, with Tanya and me in close pursuit.

"Your turn," Mikey said to me, laying a towel over the ice.

"No, that's okay. I'll probably fall off and break my ass or something."

Before I knew what was happening, Tony scooped me up in his arms and sat me on the block of ice. He gave my nose a tweak and then heaved the block over the edge. Too scared and shocked to jump off, I clung to the sides of the block with my hands and feet. It was like trying to ride a kid's toy horse that was way too small.

The wind rushed in my ears, and my eyes watered. It was too dark to see what was at the bottom of the hill, and I had a dreadful image of landing in one of the duck-scum water hazards that dotted the course.

But then the hill leveled out, and I slowly came to a halt. I heard Tony before I could see him: "Look out!"

I jumped off the ice and ran. Tony, atop the other ice block, raced past me. He came to a halt a few yards away.

"Whew! Thought I was going to hit you there for a minute," he said, climbing off the ice and grinning at me.

Before I could respond, Mikey and Tanya came running down the hill toward us. The panicked looks on their faces said that something was wrong.

"Go, go, go, go!" Mikey yelled, pulling the tray behind him.

Tony grabbed me by the hand, and we took off after them. I ran blindly, a painful stitch in my side. Finally we scrabbled back under the fence, but before we'd all made it into the van, a spotlight hit us. I turned to see a golf cart racing toward us, a security guard behind the wheel.

Mikey gunned the engine. The van farted and coughed as we scrambled to close the doors. Spraying dirt and gravel, Mikey charged the van forward, and we raced down the dirt access road. I gripped the back of the bench seat, panicked that we were about to be arrested for trespassing.

"Shit!" Mikey yelled as he saw the city's parks-and-recreation truck blocking the road ahead. Without slowing he made a hard right, plowing through the chain-link fence. The van flew across the golf course, ripping up great chunks of grass. I looked through the dirty back window to see the golf cart still in pursuit.

Tony whooped as we took a hillock at full speed and all four tires went airborne. I bounced off the bench, hit the van's floor, and screamed. Mikey cranked the steering wheel right and the van spun in crazy donuts. After three rotations he turned out and drove back through the gaping hole he had made in the fence. Flying down the dirt road in the opposite direction, we hit the paved road with a sickening scrape.

Mikey didn't slow down until he was parked in Tanya's garage. He cut the motor and the four of us sat in silence, listening to the ticking of the hot engine. Tanya turned to look at Mikey and brayed with laughter. Mikey and Tony soon joined her. I just sat there, thinking what a bunch of dumb shits they all were.

"Damn. Now I'm going to have to paint the Stink Wagon," Mikey said as he opened the door and climbed out.

Fifteen minutes later Tony was pulling up to the curb in front of my house. I hadn't wanted him to drive me home, but my only other choice would have been to walk. Mikey couldn't take the van out again until he'd disguised it with a fresh coat of paint, and Tanya didn't drive. Now I was sitting in the same seat Kylie had occupied when she'd blown Tony. For the short drive I leaned as far as I could against the passenger door and opened it almost before the car had come to a complete stop.

"Thanks for the ride, Tony."

He grabbed my wrist before I could get my feet out of the car.

"Hang on a sec." He pulled me back toward him.

I froze, horrified, as he leaned over to kiss me. I ducked back until my head was leaning out the open door.

"Tony… I'm seeing someone."

"Come on," he said softly, trying to pull me back over to him. "Let's just fool around a little."

"No thanks," I said, jerking my wrist out of his grasp and jumping out of the car.

He leaned out, calling after me. "You know, you're really not much fun for a girl with such great tits."

I kept walking, not turning as Tony sped away. God, what a douche bag. No more Tanya and Mikey or any of their friends.

12

First Date

I slept late the next morning. Kara woke me up by pouncing on my bed at noon.

"Wake up, Cinderella, time for the ball," she sang. "Or actually, I guess this is more like getting to know the prince before the ball."

I moaned as I pulled the pillow over my head.

Thirty minutes later I was freshly showered and telling Kara all about my misadventure with Mikey, Tanya, and Tony.

"Oh my God, Audrey!" she said.

"I know." I held my hand up before she could say anything else. "I'm not hanging with them anymore."

"Good, because I can tell you with absolute certainty that when we go to our ten-year reunion, Mikey and Tony will not be there. They'll be at Wayside Prison doing five to eight."

"You're probably right," I said.

"And what was with Tony's comment about your chest? Like big boobs automatically make a girl more fun?" She gestured toward her own small breasts. "I guess he'd consider me a stick in the mud, huh?"

I laughed. "Mrs. White would probably say he was weaned too early and it created an obsession with boobs."

"Speaking of the headshrinker, I forgot to ask how your last session went. Did she pull Caroline in to talk about the fight at Tanya's party?"

"Hardly." I shook my head and rolled my eyes. "All she could concentrate on was the stupid M&Ms." I wiggled my fingers in the air. "Ooooo!"

Kara laughed. "Really? I mean, what's the big deal about the candy anyway? I'm still scratching my head over why Caroline got so pissed about it. She could have just given handfuls of it to everyone and said, 'Eat me.'"

It took us five minutes to stop laughing.

We spent the afternoon snacking on grapes and crackers and watching reality TV. A flurry of butterflies exploded in my stomach as the hour of my date with James approached. Kara worked her magic, dolling me up, though I drew the line at body glitter. She settled instead for a bronzing powder, insisting that I needed a glow.

I examined my reflection in the closet mirrors. Kara and I had opted for casual chic: a pair of khaki short shorts and a white sleeveless blouse with a deeply scooped neckline. Kara styled my long hair in perfect loose curls, her specialty. My strappy wedge sandals completed the ensemble.

"You look hot," Kara said.

"I'm too nervous. I can't take a deep breath." I played with the star pendant around my neck, rubbing it as if a genie might pop out at any moment to grant me a wish.

"He already likes you, so just cool it," Kara said as she fluffed my hair a final time.

Both of us jumped at the sound of the doorbell.

"He's here!" I said as we ran to peek out the window. James' blue Bronco was parked at the curb.

Kara grabbed my elbows. "You look great. You'll be fine. Get going." She turned me around and gently pushed me toward the door.

I heard my mom in the hall talking to James.

"Here she is!" she said in a ridiculously chipper voice. I could tell she was trying hard to play the Cool Mom.

"Hi," James said, looking just a tiny bit shy. My mother's presence had diminished his self-coolness. He wore plaid board shorts and a polo shirt and looked like a Gap ad. My heart raced.

"Hey," I said with equal shyness. I turned to my mom. "So I'll be back about eleven thirty."

"Try to make it eleven, dear."

I gave her a pained expression.

"Okay. Well, have fun, kids," she said—one last attempt at being Cool Mom. It failed miserably.

"Your mom's pretty strict on curfew, huh?" James asked as we walked to his truck. He hit the unlock button on his key fob, and we climbed into the cab.

"Not really. I think she's just trying to fulfill her motherly obligations."

James nodded silently as we pulled away from the curb. "I thought we'd go to Pedro's for dinner, if that's okay with you."

"Yeah, sounds great," I replied.

Too nervous to make conversation, I occupied myself with looking around the Bronco's interior. The seats were worn but clean and smelled faintly of cologne. I wondered if he'd sprayed it on the fabric on purpose.

Pedro's was small and already crowded by the time we arrived. It was a popular spot with locals who choose to forgo the chain restaurants that dotted the valley. Our waitress found a table for us on the patio that faced the parking lot. She laid out some chips and salsa as we scooted our chairs in.

"Something to drink?" she asked.

"Coke, please," James responded.

"Me too."

She hurried off to get our drinks.

"So," James began, putting his elbows on the table and leaning toward me. "I'm finally on a date with the beautiful Audrey Kelly."

A sound escaped my lips—a cross between a raspberry and a hiss.

"No, really," he said leaning closer still. "I've had my eye on you since the start of term. I wanted to ask you out ever since I broke up with Caroline, but I didn't think you'd go out with me since I'd dated her. I mean, with the bad blood between you guys and all."

The waitress returned with our Cokes and asked us if we were ready to order. James grabbed his menu, giving it only a passing glance. "Carne asada burrito, please."

"And you, miss?"

I scanned the menu, trying to find something quickly. I finally settled on the chile relleno. It had no beans in it, so I wouldn't make the dreadful faux pas of farting later.

James resumed our conversation as soon as the waitress left with our order. "But you said yes, and here we are." He flashed his hundred-watt smile at me, showing off his irresistible dimple.

I took several swallows of my drink before I decided how to respond. "The thought of going out with you outweighed my reservations."

"So it does bother you that Caroline and I dated?"

"Yes. I can't lie—it does. She's...not only hard to live up to physically, but so different than me in personality. I'm not sure you and I will get along if she's your type."

James tensed. "Sometimes you don't really know what a person's about until you've dated them for a while, you know? It took me some time to see her dark side."

I relaxed. He had said exactly what I had wanted to hear.

"So you must have thought I was a real geek in junior high. And freshman year. And sophomore. Huh?" I asked.

He laughed, shaking his head. "To be totally honest, I don't even remember you during those years. I know that makes me sound like a dick, but I guess I was too preoccupied with other things."

"That's okay," I said. "I was pretty unnoticeable back then."

Our food arrived and I picked at mine nervously. James began to devour his burrito. I guessed a varsity basketball player burned a lot of calories. Thirty minutes later he was laying cash on the table and we left for the movie. In his truck I buckled my seatbelt and I turned my head to him. "Thanks for dinner. It was really good."

"No problem." He reached over to hold my hand as we drove down the parkway. His hand was big and warm and made my fingers tingle. This was as good as it gets.

13

The Pony Express

James didn't let go of my hand until we turned into the long driveway of the Pony Express Drive-in.

I gaped, momentarily confused. "I thought we were going to the Cineplex."

"The double feature is here, not the 'plex," he replied.

"Oh." I sounded stupid.

My friends and I rarely went to the drive-in anymore. When we were kids it was a weekend staple, with its cheap admission and double features. Now it was run-down—the sound sucked and the movies were always blurry, probably because of all the light surrounding the place. The valley had gone on a building spree in recent years and now the area was constantly lit up like a Christmas tree.

Still, inexplicably, the drive-in was known as a teen sex hotspot—hence its nickname, the Baloney Pony. As James drove up next to the glass booth to purchase our tickets, I thought of this and felt a sinking sense of dismay—which grew only worse when I read the marquee. It was a Jackie Chan double feature. I hated chopsocky movies unless Quentin Tarantino directed them.

We cruised the lot looking for a good spot. He chose one about two-thirds back, center screen.

"Let's go get some snacks," he said as he climbed out of the truck. Once again he held my hand as we walked toward the concession building at the rear of the drive-in.

"Hey, Ridley!" some guy called out to James as we approached the entrance. James released my hand and walked over to him and his crowd of buddies, bumping fists with several of them. They struck up a conversation about cars, motorcycles, and so and so's new sound system while I lingered a few steps back, ignored.

James seemed to realize this a few minutes later. He reached back to put his arm around my waist.

"Hey, you guys know Audrey, right?"

They all greeted me with "hey" and "hi."

"Hi." I gave a single, low wave to the group.

"Why don't you grab some drinks and popcorn while I talk to these gearheads?" James said, handing me a twenty. "I know this talk bores the hell out of chicks." He flashed me his winning smile.

I left for the concession building, not sure how I felt. Yes, he was paying for everything, but it irked me that he sent me off to get refreshments like a waitress or something.

I waited in line for what felt like hours before finally reaching the register. I ordered a large bucket of popcorn and two soft drinks, and I handed over the twenty. While waiting for my change I looked up from the food and found the guy at the register standing still, the twenty still clutched loosely in his fingers.

"Hey...you're that chick from the video. The one who brawled with her shirt open." His face broke into a wide smile.

"Yeah, that was me," I said.

"Hey, you wanna go out sometime?"

"I have a boyfriend," I answered quickly. That was a big lie—James could hardly be called my boyfriend, this being our first date and all. But what the hell? Maybe he would be my boyfriend by the time prom rolled around.

"Oh," the popcorn guy said, looking disappointed. "Okay."

He finally opened the register and handed me a small amount of change.

I left the building trying to balance the popcorn bucket and the drinks in their flimsy cardboard carrier. If I could just manage not to slip on the gravel I'd be okay.

James hurried to grab the tray from me. "Great! Thanks for getting this. Sorry my conversation took so long."

"That's okay," I told him, forgiving him instantly. "I've got your change."

"Just put it in my pocket, will you?"

I slipped the small wad of cash and coins into his shorts' pocket as quickly as I could, my face flaming crimson. James didn't seem disturbed in the slightest.

We settled into the Bronco's cab with the popcorn resting between us. He dialed in the proper radio frequency and the drive-in's prerecorded message began to play. I stared at the small playground directly below the giant movie screen. A few kids played on the swings, enjoying what would be the best part of the evening for them.

The movie started, and we watched in silence for the first fifteen minutes or so. Then James moved the popcorn tub to the backseat, scooted closer, and put his arm around me. I smiled at him, thinking how great it felt.

"So," he began, looking at me rather than the screen. "You and your friends hang out a lot, huh? I've seen you at a few games with them."

"Yeah, we try to catch most of the season, although we don't usually go to the away games."

"Not that big a fan?"

"No, it's not that. It's just you can't go see a game without seeing the Cheerleaders too." I immediately regretted bringing it up. Caroline just kept creeping into the conversation.

"Oh yeah... I didn't think of that," he said.

I quickly steered the subject back to my friends. "I've been best friends with Kara and Lily since grade school, and Jane and Megan since junior high."

"You guys will be inseparable next year then—all of you seniors together."

I looked down, feeling sad. "Actually, next term will be tough. Kara will be at school only half a day 'cause she's starting a regional occupational program for cosmetology, Lily's doing a semester in Belgium, and half of Jane's classes will be at the junior college." I kept looking down at my hands.

"That's a bummer," James said. "Your gang's shrinking."

"Yeah... Oh well... What're you gonna do?"

James seemed to sense my sadness and changed topics. "So I noticed you ride with Kara all the time. Do you drive?"

"I have my license, and I drive Kara's car sometimes, but I can't afford my own car right now. Actually, I could use my savings to buy a beater, but the insurance would kill me—and my mom."

"I hear you," he said, nodding his head. He thumped the Bronco's steering wheel lightly with his fist. "This beast gets only about twelve miles to the gallon. It's great for campouts, though. You should come with us next time we go to state beach."

The thought of car camping with James gave me a rush. Then I pictured him getting a good look at me in the morning with a monstrous case of bed-head.

He moved the arm that was across my shoulders and played with a strand of my hair. My neck broke out in goose bumps, and my voice shook ever so slightly. "So you're going to USC next year?"

"Yeah, but I'm taking a semester off first. Gonna do some traveling."

"Really?" I imagined him backpacking with a Eurail pass.

"Yeah, and my dad's still having shit-kittens over it. He thinks it's a waste of my time and his money. But my mom managed to persuade him to let me go. She did the whole European tour when she graduated."

"You're going to Europe?"

"No, me and my buddy Travis are going to Australia." His face lit up as he described his planned adventure, including planes, trains, and automobile tours of the land down under.

I tried to pay attention to his descriptions of the towns and national parks they would be visiting, but my mind was busy doing the math: he would be gone by early September and would not return until mid-December. If James really did want to be my steady it would be only a summer romance. But the summer hadn't officially started yet. We would have over three months to hang out, and that seemed like forever.

James snapped me out of my reverie. "What about you? What colleges are you applying to? Or are you going the occupational route?"

"Well, my mom's pretty insistent about college. I'm thinking about Washington State or maybe Berkeley, if I can get in."

James shivered. "Why do you want to go where it's cold and rainy?"

"I like the rain. It's so dry and brown here most of the time. Plus I think it would be nice just to go live somewhere new, you know?"

Of course he didn't know. James had been popular and well-liked his whole life. Why would he want to leave that behind?

We sat in silence for another minute or so before he brought his hand down to my neck. His other hand rose to trace the star pendant on my necklace. He leaned forward, paused, then gave me a gentle kiss. His lips were soft and slightly parted; his tongue probed mine. One of his hands pressed against the small of my back, turning me toward him and pulling me closer. He tasted like butter and popcorn salt.

I forgot everything in the world except the sensation of his mouth and his hand, which slowly wandered from my neck to my shoulder and then my upper arm. I wrapped my hands around his neck.

He broke away from my lips and kissed my neck, my ear, my collarbone. I shuddered. He pressed his body closer still, and I felt the hardness of him through the thin fabric of his shorts. My heart kicked into overdrive as I fought the urge to reach down and touch it.

A sigh escaped my lips as we sank down onto the bench seat. His kisses wandered down to the top of my bra and his hand came up under my blouse, squeezing my breast. I arched my back in pleasure as his thumb stroked the thin fabric covering my nipple.

His hard member pressed into my thigh as he lowered the shoulder of my shirt and bra strap and drew my nipple into his mouth. My eyes rolled back as my hands clutched at his thick, brown hair. I felt his hand wander up my leg, higher and higher, until he was reaching under the edge of my panties. I snapped back into focus, grabbing his wrist to stop him from going any farther.

He looked up. "What's wrong?"

"Nothing… It's just kind of fast, you know? First date and all?"

Now I felt like a prude. I wondered if he would get pissed.

He smiled and pulled my shirt back into place. "That's okay," he said, and we returned to our former upright positions.

Relief washed over me. It would have been so easy for me to go all the way, but the last thing I wanted was to be a one-night wonder. He probably thought we would do it after prom. That didn't sound like such a bad idea to me.

We settled back into a comfortable snuggle and watched the rest of the movie, which I paid no attention to at all. At one point I reached for my soda and noticed a wet stain on my shorts. I thought maybe I'd spilled some soda on it, or some butter had leaked through the popcorn tub. Then I saw a similar wet spot on the front of James' shorts. Realization dawned. I didn't say anything for fear of embarrassing him.

By the time the first feature ended, it was nearing ten thirty. The lights of the playground snapped on as the credits rolled down the screen.

"I guess we'd better hit the road if you want to make it home by eleven, huh?" James asked.

"I probably should, just to appease my mom. I'm sorry about missing the second movie."

"Ah, that's no biggie. I've already seen it anyway," he said with an easy smile.

Fifteen minutes before my curfew, James pulled the Bronco up to the curb in front of my house. I saw the living room curtain twitch—Mom was peeking.

"Thanks again," I said as I grabbed my purse and opened the door.

"You want to go swimming at my house tomorrow? The pool's finally warm enough."

"Yeah, that sounds like fun," I said. I was supposed to go to a hair stylist expo with Kara and Lily, but I didn't think they'd mind if I flaked for a swim date with James.

"I'll pick you up at noon," he said, then leaned over to kiss me goodbye. The kiss was brief, and I was hugely relieved it wasn't anything like our earlier liplock, since I knew that Mom had her eye on us. I checked to make sure the wet spot on my shorts was completely dry and then jumped out of the car and headed for the front door.

As soon as I closed it behind me, I heard the Bronco roar off. I wandered into the kitchen for a glass of water. Mom was perched at the table, a romance paperback in her hands.

"Don't even pretend you weren't looking out the front window a second ago," I told her as I filled a large glass from the dispenser in the fridge door.

She smiled guiltily. "I was just checking to see if it was you." She laid her open book down on the table. "So how did your date go?"

"It was fine," I said as casually as I could. I had no intention of elaborating for her. I was saving the juicy details for Kara.

"I saw him kiss you in the car," she said.

"Uh huh."

"How come he didn't walk you to the door? In my day a boy would always walk a girl to the door—and bring flowers for her."

"Mom, this isn't the nineteen fifties. People are more casual now."

"I know," she said, looking slightly irritated. "It just seems like the polite thing to do."

I wondered how impolite she would think James was if she knew about the wet spot. I covered my mouth to stifle a laugh before I turned from the fridge.

"James asked me to go swimming at his house tomorrow. Is that okay with you?"

"Will his parents be there?" she asked, looking at me over the tops of her glasses.

"Yes." I had no idea if this was true or not.

"I guess that's okay then."

Taking my water, I attempted to make a quick exit to the stairs. Mom called me back.

"Audrey, hang on a sec."

"Mom, I'm really tired, and I promised I'd give Kara a quick call."

She pulled out the chair next to her, indicating that I should have a seat. I groaned as I reluctantly collapsed onto it.

"Listen." She looked excruciatingly uncomfortable. She took off her glasses and began polishing them with the sash of her robe. "I know we had the whole sex talk when you were thirteen, but I feel like I need to reiterate some points with you now that you're dating someone seriously."

I felt the heat rise in my face. "Mom, really, you don't need to worry. I know how to be safe, and I'm not even at that point." Yet.

She held up her hand. "I know how smart you are, and I know you know what to do. I just wanted to tell you, if you want to go on the pill, I'll take you to the doctor myself."

I looked at her blank-faced.

"That doesn't mean I want you to have sex with this boy. I would really prefer if you waited until you were in college and in a long-term, committed relationship."

I felt an eye roll coming on and tried to stop it. She must have sensed it too.

"I know that particular hope might be an unrealistic one." She put her glasses back on and looked into my face with an earnestness I hardly ever saw. "Just promise me that you will protect yourself. Not just your body, but your heart too."

"I will, Mom. I promise."

As soon as the door to my room was firmly shut behind me, I was on the phone with Kara. I gave her a play-by-play of the entire evening and then told her about the swim date. She laughed when I told her about the wet spot but vowed not to tell anyone.

"I think you should frame those shorts and hang them over your bed," she told me.

"You are so twisted!" I laughed.

"And proud of it!" Kara replied. "Jeez, I hope this doesn't mean he's a premature ejaculator. That would suck."

"Ewww! Stop talking about it or I'll never dish for you again."

"Okay, now it's my turn to blow your mind with great news."

"What?" I asked, anxious to hear what was going on.

"Well… I was on Facebook and started chatting with Tommy Martinez."

"Really? Tom from yearbook staff?"

"Yeah, and we started talking about prom. Turns out he didn't have a date, and then he found I didn't have a date, and voila—we're going together."

"That's fantastic, Kara! Maybe we can all ride together—get a limo even."

"Yeah, that would be fun! I just wish the others were going, you know?"

"I know, but next year we'll all be seniors. It'll be a bigger deal. Besides, I think Megan would rather die than wear a prom dress."

We both laughed at the image of our butch friend in a satin gown.

"Anyway, I'm stoked we'll be there together," I told Kara.

"Me too, Aud."

14

Headfirst

I woke the next morning with the jitters, eager to prepare for my second date in two days with James. Without Mom there to bug me—she'd gone out with some friends for brunch—I took an especially long time shaving, making sure my body was perfectly smooth, then toweled off and applied generous amounts of coconut-scented sunscreen. In my bikini—coral pink, low rise, string ties—I stood in front of the mirror. A generous amount of cleavage stared back at me, and my flat stomach and long legs looked great. I turned to examine my backside. Not as pert as Caroline's, but it would do.

At least that was how I felt in the solitude of my bedroom. Being nearly naked in front of James would be tougher on my self-confidence.

I stepped into a white, strapless beach romper just as I heard the Bronco pulling up. I hurriedly scooped my hair into a ponytail, put on my flip-flops, and made it downstairs just as James was ringing the bell. I opened the door wide, smiling up at his gorgeous face. He wore board shorts with a large hibiscus pattern and a white button-down shirt that was completely open in front, giving me an eye-popping view of his defined stomach and chest.

I tore my eyes away from his delectable torso long enough to grab my straw tote bag from the stair rail. "Ready?" he asked with a chipper smile.

"Yeah!"

"Awesome," he said as I closed and locked the door behind us.

The Ridley house was another McMansion, on par with Caroline's Spanish colonial monstrosity. It was part of the same development, actually, but this particular model sported a Craftsman-style façade, moss-green shingles, large pillars, and a chimney.

Panic gripped me as I followed James into the foyer, anticipating the dreaded first meeting of the parents. James walked through to the great room, where he opened the French doors that led to the backyard.

"Where are your folks?" I asked as I set my bag on a patio chair.

"They're wine tasting in Sonoma. Left yesterday. Be home later tonight. My little brother's at my Aunt Sarah's. We've got the house to ourselves." He held his arms out wide, as if offering the entire place to me.

Relief washed over me at not having to meet his parents, who would probably judge me and compare me to Caroline.

The pool wasn't as elaborate as Tanya's, but it was still impressive. It had a square, Roman shape with a rectangular spa attached to the side. James kicked off his shoes and shrugged out of his shirt; he ran to the edge of the pool and dove in. Popping up a moment later, he shook his wet hair aside with one swift jerk of his head.

"Come on in," he said with a dimpled smile as he treaded water.

I stepped behind the patio chair my bag was on and pulled off my romper, then walked to the pool. Longest three yards of my life. Talk about excruciatingly self-conscious.

"Damn!" James said, his eyes widening as he watched me.

I smiled as I descended the steps into the water. It was cold, and I gasped slightly.

"You're better off just jumping in," he said. "You'll get used to the water a lot faster that way."

I braced myself and I dove in. I came up sputtering a few seconds later. "God, that's cold!"

"I'll warm you up," James whispered in my ear as he wrapped his arms around me under the water. Then we were kissing, and I was dizzy with excitement. Or maybe it was the aromas of sunscreen and chlorine. James' hands were everywhere at once: in my hair, on my back, sliding over my butt and legs. I kissed his neck, savoring the taste of his wet skin as he untied the string at my neck, baring my breasts. He cupped them in his hands and kissed them.

My back pressed against the pool steps. James' hands went to the ties on the sides of my bikini bottom.

"Do you have a condom?" I asked, my eyes closed, as he continued to devour my neck and lips.

He didn't pause as he answered, "Yeah, but they're up in my room. Aren't you on the pill?"

"No. Not yet."

Then he stopped. He looked at me. "Are you a virgin?"

I hesitated a second, then answered, "Yes."

His eyebrows moved up slightly. "Oh."

I looked up into his face, my hands resting on his biceps. "You seem disappointed."

"No, no!" he said, leading me by the hand out of the pool. "I just thought…well, you know, someone as hot as you would be more experienced." He wrapped a towel around my shoulders.

"My top!" I said, looking back at the pool. It was lying at the bottom of the deep end, resembling a lifeless squid.

James dove into the water and retrieved it in one smooth stroke. I waited for him at the pool's edge, thinking that our afternoon interlude had come to an end with the news of my inexperience.

Back on land, James shook the water out of his hair like a dog after a bath. I laughed as it sprayed everywhere. He handed me the bikini top and wrapped his towel around his waist.

Without a word he took my hand and led me inside the house, up the stairs and down the hall to his bedroom. My heart raced as I looked around. The room was huge, the walls decorated with posters, most from gangster movies.

"Big Scorsese fan, huh?" I asked.

"Yeah, his movies are the best. My dad's a gaffer, but mostly for TV, like reality shows. He's never done a film with him. I wish he would. I'd love to meet him. But enough about that." He took my hand and pulled me down onto the bed. The dampness of our swimsuits soaked into the bedspread as he kissed me with renewed energy.

My brain scrambled. Oh my God, am I really going to lose it right here and now? The mixture of excitement and nervousness was like electroshock therapy. I'd promised Mom I would wait until I was on the pill…but oh God this felt so good.

His hands kneaded and massaged me while his mouth moved from my breasts to my stomach to my thighs. I quivered as he quickly removed my bikini bottom and gently kissed my inner thigh, higher and higher until I felt his breath on my most sensitive part. I sighed as his tongue stroked and licked me. Warmth and delightful pressure mounted in my body until my toes were tingling. I clutched handfuls of bedspread, gazing down my naked body. The sight of his head between my legs suddenly put me over the edge, and I was nearly screaming in climax.

I reached down to push his head away, the tickling sensation too much to bear. He slid off the bed and retrieved a shoebox from underneath it. He placed it on his nightstand, removed the lid, and extracted a condom.

My bliss peaked as I watched him roll the condom onto himself. He was not small.

He finished putting the condom on and rolled back over to me. The kisses and caressing resumed as he guided himself inside me. I felt a terrible ripping, burning sensation, and he grunted with the effort of entering me slowly. I cried out, this time in pain rather than pleasure.

"I'm sorry I'm hurting you," he said softly, but then gave two final thrusts and shuddered. It was over. I lay under his weight, all sensations fading to a dull ache.

15

Confrontation

The next morning Kara and I sat hip to hip on the field bleachers during gym. I was too sore for running laps, and Kara had jumped at the chance to sit on the sidelines with me. We'd both used the "terrible cramps" excuse. Coach Cramer got the usual sick look on his face at the mere mention of our female cycle woes.

Kara was suitably awed by the details of my loss of innocence.

"I can't believe you had the big O your first time!" she whispered, giggling and clutching her hands together.

"Well, technically that happened before the actual, you know... deed."

"Yeah, but still."

Caroline, Tracy, and Hillary jogged past the bleachers on the track below, and I paused to look at them. Caroline's gaze remained straight ahead, but Tracy and Hillary glared at us.

"Watching my back is exhausting," I said, keeping an eye on Caroline. "I wish she would just give up."

Kara slung her arm over my shoulder. "I'd say that's pretty wishful thinking at this point, especially now that her old boyfriend is your new boyfriend."

"Good point."

The line at the soda machine was long. Kara chattered away about prom dresses and how black was going to be the it color this year. I patiently listened as the queue crept forward at a snail's pace.

A gentle kiss on my neck startled me. I turned to look up into James' smiling face. I beamed back, relishing his public display of affection.

"How's it going?" he asked, looking from my face to Kara's.

"Great! How are you?" Kara responded a little too enthusiastically.

"S'all good," he said, flashing his dimple.

It was our turn at the soda machine. "Here, I got it," James said. He hurried forward and pushed quarter after quarter into the coin slot. Kara and I thanked him as we retrieved our drinks from the dispenser.

"Awww, isn't that cute? The homecoming king and our school's mascot, the bulldog."

Caroline's voice was like ice water trickling down my back. I turned to see her standing there, hands on her hips as she surveyed us. James wrapped his arm around my waist and walked us closer to her. My feet didn't want to go in that direction, but I didn't want to lose his grip around me.

"Come on, Caroline," he said softly. "Being a green-eyed monster isn't flattering. You need to move on."

I held my breath, waiting for her reply. She flipped her hair off one shoulder, looking amused. "Hey, if you're going to slum it with the bush woman then you'd better be prepared for criticism from your real friends."

"You? A real friend? You cheated on me with my bud. Why don't you give Steve a call? Maybe he can cure that reek of desperation you carry around."

Her smile faltered and her eyes narrowed. "Fuck you, you loser asshole! I take it back—you two are perfect for each other. You can shave her pubes and use the trimmings to crochet doilies to sell at the swap meet!"

My hand twitched around the soda I was holding, rapidly shaking the can. Then I brought it forward, popping the top inches from Caroline's face. Caramel-colored foam sprayed everywhere and she staggered backward, rubbing the fizz from her eyes. My arm was soaked, and my white T-shirt was covered in cola polka dots.

James had jumped back to avoid my carbonated assault. I was too stunned to speak. I had acted out of rage, not thinking about the consequences. It was Proud's Mini-Mart all over again.

"You bitch!" Caroline hissed as she lunged at me. I braced for her attack, but the hit never came. James stepped in between us, his tall frame easily blocking Caroline's futile attempts to get at me. A huge circle of onlookers surrounded us. I saw a teacher headed our way at a run.

I spun, grabbing Kara by the hand. I bustled my way through the crowd toward our lockers. I felt so stupid. How could I get into a fight on campus? Like I didn't have enough trouble already with the school shrink halfway up my ass. My goddamn temper!

Kara kept quiet as I dialed open my locker and pulled out a hoodie. I quickly put it on, zipping it up to cover the worst of the stains on my shirt. From our vantage point we could see down to the quad below, where the crowd around the soda machine was breaking up. I tried to spot Caroline or James but couldn't make out either.

"I shouldn't have ditched James like that," I said, more to myself than to Kara. "I panicked."

Kara tried to be soothing. "It's okay, Audrey. I'm sure he understands you didn't want to get in trouble."

"Still, it was a chickenshit thing to do."

"Leave him a note in his locker."

I took her advice. I scribbled a quick apology on a sheet of paper I folded and squeezed through the crack in the edge of his locker door, pushing until it disappeared.

I hugged Kara and we separated for our third-period classes. Running down the breezeway, I nearly screamed when I felt a hand grip my upper arm. It was Tanya, her eyes alight and a wicked smile on her lips.

"I heard about your latest drive-by soaking. Sticky sweet beverages are your weapon of choice, huh?" She laughed.

"It was a knee-jerk reaction. I shouldn't have done it. It was stupid."

"No way! I'm sorry I missed it. I heard she's headed to the locker room to shower all the ick off."

I was almost at the classroom door and vainly tried to speed-walk away from Tanya. Unperturbed, she broke into a slow jog to keep pace.

"Hey, Mikey and I got a great idea. He's got these instant-melt vitamins and they're the perfect match for birth control pills. We're thinking maybe he could break into Caroline's house and switch 'em out with the real thing and—"

I stopped walking mid-stride. "Tanya, what the fuck? I told you I was done!" I grabbed her arm, leading her to the corner of the building, lowering my voice to an urgent whisper. "That is so—it's just so evil! I wouldn't do that to anyone. I mean, you're talking about involving an innocent baby. I—eeech!"

I couldn't keep the contempt from my voice. Tanya looked taken aback. She shrugged her shoulders, a defiant look on her face.

"Hey, no need to freak out on me. It was just a crazy idea. It probably wouldn't have worked anyway. Don't shit your pants or anything."

"I gotta go," I told her, releasing my grip on her arm. "Sorry I bit your head off."

"No biggie. Catch you later." She walked away without a backward glance.

I spent the rest of the day in a knot of anxiety, waiting for the inevitable note from the office. When none appeared by sixth period, the lump in my chest began to ease. It looked as if Caroline had decided to keep our little confrontation to herself. Which made sense when I thought about it—she didn't need trouble any more than I did.

However, I was sure this would only make her redouble her efforts to get back at me. The target on my back felt about the size of Rhode Island.

The weather grew warmer as prom approached, and the days flew by. The panic of finals overshadowed Caroline's possible revenge, and I spent every spare minute studying or hanging out with James.

I also fulfilled my promise to my mom and obtained a year's supply of birth control pills. I didn't have the guts to ask her to take me to the doctor, so I went to the county health clinic. It was fast, cheap, and, most importantly, private. With visions of Tanya and Mikey's devious pill-swapping plan echoing in my mind, I locked mine in a cashbox I had purchased just for them. Those days, paranoia was my constant companion.

On the day of the prom Kara arrived in the early afternoon. Our plan was to get ready and have the guys pick us up at my house so Mom could take pictures to her heart's content. Afterward we would drive separately to prom. The limo idea had been nixed when news that a blowout party was planned for after prom at the old Pinehaven Sanitarium. The old road leading up to it was well maintained but steep, so we'd all be carpooling with whoever had trucks and four-wheel drives.

Kara and I packed our knapsacks with changes of clothes for the party.

Butterflies bloomed and took flight in my stomach as Kara carefully applied my makeup. I again refused body glitter but made Kara happy by accepting false eyelashes. I worried I'd look clownish, but when I examined my finished face in the mirror, I was quite pleased. The lashes were lush but short enough to look natural.

"You're a genius, Kara."

"See? I told you. When are you going to learn to trust the master?"

"Masturbator," I mumbled, and we both laughed.

I sat on the closed lid of the toilet in my small bathroom and let Kara flat-iron my hair to a silky straightness and then texturize it, her fingers dabbing in and out of a small jar of wax and then twisting and separating strand after strand.

"Why'd you bother straightening my hair if you're just going to gunk it all up?" I asked.

"Just shut up and trust the master."

"Bator."

She gave an exasperated tsk and continued to play with my hair. Finally she gathered and twisted it into a loose knot at the base of my neck.

"Ta da!" she said, handing me a mirror to examine all sides of my head. The hairdo was impressive—elegant and sweeping but not overdone. I felt like a modern-day princess.

"I bow to the master," I said, flourishing my hand and doing a deep curtsy.

" 'Bout damn time," she said, smiling.

Kara put the finishing touches on her own hair, leaving it long and loose with soft curls, then zipped me into my dress. Its straps sat on the very edges of my shoulders; the bodice crisscrossed at the bust to create a sweetheart neckline. A quarter-sized, square broach was pinned in the center, encrusted with tiny, sparkling crystals. The skirt fell in a simple sheath to the floor. I twirled in front of the closet mirrors, thrilled with the way the dress' chocolate-brown satin gleamed in the setting sunlight coming in through the window of my room.

Kara stepped up behind me in Marilyn Monroe's halter dress from The Seven Year Itch, except that it was black. With her dark hair and pale skin, she looked fantastic.

Mom called us down to pose for pictures. She took around a million of them in the backyard, then another hundred thousand or so in the living room. I sighed with relief when I heard James pull up out front.

"Don't you want to go upstairs so you can make an entrance when he comes in?" Mom asked.

"Hell no! With my luck I'd trip and tumble down the stairs."

Mom and Kara both snickered, and neither argued with me. When James knocked, Mom opened the door, and he entered all smiles and holding a champagne-colored rose corsage in a clear plastic case.

"You look beautiful," he said, then kissed my cheek. I blushed and thanked him. He looked male-model gorgeous in a light-taupe three-piece suit with a chocolate-brown tie. He removed the corsage from its container and gently placed its elastic band around my wrist.

My mom snapped another zillion pictures as we waited for Kara's date. Tommy arrived in a black-on-black tuxedo, resembling a kid dressed as a mafioso on Halloween. Tommy and James exchanged brief heys and head nods.

The camera beeped and clicked as Mom photographed Tommy placing a corsage of white gardenias on Kara's wrist.

Elated that picture time was finally done, I climbed into the Bronco. I couldn't stop looking at James—he was so outrageously handsome in his suit. I pinched the underside of my forearm. Yep, I wasn't dreaming. This was really happening.

I glanced in the side mirror to spy on Kara and Tommy, who were driving behind us. I could see Kara's mouth moving a mile a minute while Tommy concentrated on operating his parents' Toyota. James kept the speed down so Tommy could follow.

"Are any of your other friends coming tonight?" James asked.

"No, just Kara and me. Dave Keppler asked Lily, but she turned him down."

"Not interested, huh?"

"I think her mind's already in Europe, so she really doesn't want to get anything started here. Plus I think she likes to play hard to get."

"I'm glad you're not like that," he said with a grin.

I paused, my brain firing in a million directions. Was he insinuating that I was easy?

He must have picked up on my uncertainty. "I mean... I'm saying... I'm glad you don't play head games," he said.

I breathed a sigh of relief, but then a familiar uneasiness stole over me as I thought of my recent deviousness. I tried in vain to push Caroline from my mind. I already knew she wouldn't be at prom—she was still banned from school events. But Hillary and Tracy would be there. Oh joy.

The air felt tainted by the thought of the Cheerleaders.

16

Threefold

The country club's largest ballroom was resplendent with light. The prom committee had foregone the usual balloons and streamers and gone with a Wish Upon a Star theme instead. Row after row of tiny white lights twinkled across the ceiling, punctuated by various-sized stars; dozens of potted ficus trees lined the edges of the room, each covered with more dancing lights. Round tables were dressed in silver and gold with huge, glowing star centerpieces.

Unconsciously I reached for my star pendant. It rarely left my neck, but now I felt only bare skin; it just hadn't gone with my outfit. I missed it. It had quickly become my personal talisman and I was used to grasping it like a cross or some other religious symbol.

I glanced at Kara and saw that she too was awed by the elaborate decor. She smiled at me. "Wow! I guess there's something to be said for living in a community of nouveau riche snobs."

The four of us made our way toward the circular, star-strewn tunnel where we would pose for pictures. The photographer was stationed at the tunnel's exit, where our classmates milled about, most of them watching the newcomers being photographed. Talk about being in the spotlight.

I concentrated on keeping my lips from trembling as James held my hands and we smiled for the camera. As soon as I heard the photographer say "got it" I practically ran to the other side of the tunnel, where we joined the gawking crowd and watched Kara and Tommy get their photo taken. It looked like they were being sucked into a starry vortex.

I giggled at the thought. James looked at me. "What's so funny?"

"It looks like they're getting sucked into a black hole. It's like The Twilight Zone."

He looked at the star arch and laughed. The whole year so far had been like one long episode of The Twilight Zone.

When Kara and Tommy joined us we made our way around the edges of the room, looking for a place to sit. A group of James' friends called him over, and we joined them at a table for ten. I hardly knew them; they were the real social elite. I slouched and ducked my head and turned to face Kara.

"I feel like I don't belong," I whispered.

"Me too," she whispered back. "I think me and Tommy are going to eat as fast as we can, then go mingle and dance."

"Sounds like a good plan."

James kept up a steady stream of conversation with his friends as we ate—limp salad, dry chicken, and tasteless pasta. I felt forgotten as I picked at my food.

True to her word, Kara pounded down her meal. She and Tommy got up from the table before dessert.

"See you later," she said, waving at me and taking Tommy by the hand. She practically dragged him to the dance floor, where they bumped and gyrated to a Pink song.

Feeling bored, I let my eyes wander around the room. I spotted Hillary wearing a skin-tight, red-sequined dress, and I couldn't decide if she looked more like a Miss America contestant or a high-priced hooker. She was leaning over a table, laughing and talking loudly to the others seated there.

Tracy went up behind her and whispered something in her ear, then they talked at length. I wondered what their secret was.

"So are you ready to dance?" James asked, interrupting my thoughts.

"Yeah, sure."

He took my hand and led me to the floor. I was a terrible dancer, so I hoped there would be enough other bodies out there to hide my imbecilic moves. James didn't seem to mind as he shimmed and jived; his moves were fluid and effortless. I wondered if there was anything Captain America couldn't do.

Soon the music shifted to a slow dance—"Open Arms" by Journey—and James wrapped his hands around my waist. I wound my arms around his neck, and we joined the swaying crowd around us. We looked like a bunch of ducks waddling this way and that.

When the music picked up again, we headed to the beverage table and stayed there while the DJ introduced the prom court. Though James was a shoo-in for it, he had already been on the homecoming court, so he wasn't eligible—the school always tried to spread the wealth. Tracy and Hillary were natural picks as well, but I was pleasantly surprised to see neither one made it. In fact, most of the prom court was made up of student council leaders.

Kara caught up with us, reaching around me for a bottle of water on the table. She spoke between gulps "Hey, guys! They're doing group pictures now. Do you want to get the four of us together?"

"Yeah, that sounds good," I said, looking at James for confirmation.

"Let's do it," he said.

We made our way around the Twilight Zone tunnel and lined up for the group shots in the lobby. The line was enormous but moved forward quickly as groups as large as ten huddled for pictures together. Kara and I chatted about the god-awful dinner as we waited.

As we talked, somewhere in the back of my mind I heard a commotion. Something near the door, but just not loud enough to get my full attention. Then something cold and wet splashed over my chest and arms. Kara screamed, and I gasped.

Looking up, I saw two people wearing black ski masks and holding brightly colored super-soaker water guns. Students shouted and scattered as the duo attacked me and Kara; within moments we were drenched. Then the odor hit me: whatever was in their guns smelled like an outhouse at the beach.

I turned, trying to step back from the foul jet, and the heel of my shoe caught the hem of my dress. I stumbled and fell to the floor. Sidespray peppered James' arm.

"What the fuck?" he yelled.

Tommy lunged for the gunmen, taking one down at the knees. The masked man kicked out viciously, battering Tommy's face. The second gunman grabbed his companion by the neck of his shirt, helping him to his feet. They were running through the door before the prom's confused chaperones had reached the front lobby.

James awoke from his shock and ran to help Tommy to his feet. Kara continued to sob, then bent to retch on the carpet. I climbed to my feet, trying to comprehend what had just happened. It was piss—rotten old piss. They had sprayed us with urine. My God… It was dripping from my hair and face… My dress was soaked with it.

Then everyone was yelling at once. A chaperone and a country club employee ran outside. Other chaperones were asking us who that was, what had happened, was there a fight? All of them flinched involuntarily as they got close enough to smell the urine.

Tommy held Kara as she wept. James paced back and forth, curses streaming from his mouth. My profound shock was finally broken when I saw Tracy busily snapping picture after picture, Hillary at her side. Hillary's eyes were alight with excitement and malice.

I had barely taken three steps in their direction when they both turned tail and exited the lobby. I wanted to chase after them. I wanted to smash that camera in their faces until it was in a million pieces—until their faces were bloody.

We sat, shivering and humiliated, in the lobby until police arrived, quickly followed by my mom and Kara's parents. Our classmates were herded back into the ballroom while we spent what felt like an eternity answering questions and giving statements.

When the final police photos were taken, a female chaperone grasped my arms, forcefully leading me from the lobby and down a back hallway to the women's locker room at the far side of the country club. She gave me towels and instructed me to take a shower. I stood under the steaming spray, lathering myself from head to toe over and over. I could hear Kara crying in the next stall; each sob was a stab to my heart. Guilt enveloped me, and I felt absolute desolation. Kara never would have been hurt like this if it hadn't been for me. This was all my fault. I tried to cry but couldn't. I felt utterly dead inside.

I stood with my head bent, watching my false eyelashes as they circled the shower drain like two drowned caterpillars.

Someone had gotten our overnight bags for us, and outside the showers Kara and I put on our after-party clothes and dried our hair with the dryers by the sinks. The chaperone silently gathered up our prom dresses and stuffed them into a large trash bag. Kara's face was red and swollen, her eyes puffed to mere slits. She turned off the dryer, her hair still damp and limp.

"I'm sorry, Kara," I said, looking at her reflection in the mirror as I stood next to her. "This is all my fault."

"No, it's not," she replied, not looking at me. "People are shit… It's not your fault."

"Yes it is."

"I just want to go home. I'll talk to you later, okay?" Still not looking at me, she hurried from the locker room.

I stood, staring at myself in the mirror. My face was plain as toast with no makeup. My elaborate hairdo was a distant memory.

The chaperone approached me. "You can go too, honey. Your date has already showered, and he can take you home." She put her arm around me and walked me out of the locker room. "The best thing to do now is get home as soon as possible."

I nodded numbly, thinking of the tetanus shot the police had instructed me to get. I let her lead me out the door until we were near the lobby exit. Inside the ballroom the DJ announced the last song—the party was winding down. A few students were still around, but most had left for the bonfire. A janitor rolled an industrial-sized carpet steamer over the soiled floor.

Once I left, it would be like it never happened—if it weren't for the photos. And possibly video. They would go out all over the world for everyone to laugh at.

James and my mother were waiting at the lobby doors. His face was cold and angry. He had changed into his after-party jeans and T-shirt.

"I'm sorry," I said as soon as I reached him.

"It's not your fault," he said, shaking his head.

"Mom, is it okay if I come home a little later? I want to ride home with James."

She hesitated, clearly not wanting to leave me, but she gave in. "Okay, sweetheart. I'll see you at home later." She kissed my cheek and gave James a brief hug. He thanked her.

James held my hand as we walked to his Bronco. I sat in the passenger seat, numb with guilt and humiliation. James buckled his seat belt and then unbuckled it to lean over and buckle mine. I had forgotten.

He began to drive. "Those bastards. I'm going to find out who did this and thump their skulls."

"James, pull over please. I need to talk to you."

He looked at me, a confused expression on his face, but then he pulled in to a deserted strip mall.

"What is it?" he asked as he cut the engine.

"I… I just wanted to tell you how sorry I am—"

"But—"

"Please let me finish," I said. "This is my fault. It's retaliation for everything I've done to Caroline. Dating you, the drink in her face, the M&Ms, the fish in her car—"

"That was you?"

"Yes."

James stared out the windshield, letting my words sink in. "But… all those things… Caroline had them coming. All the shit she's done to you… She deserved it!"

"I'm not arguing that, but I am saying that anyone who's my friend is going to be hurt. I'm poison."

James gripped the steering wheel. His jaw muscles worked as he clenched his teeth. "Fuck that. This is bullshit. If she wants to play games like this, then I'll have her shut out. She may keep her mob, but I'll make sure the rest of the school gives her a big dose of the cold shoulder."

I felt overcome by affection for him. I unbuckled my seat belt and scooted across the seat to kiss him—but quickly stopped.

"Let's go to the bonfire," I said.

"What? Are you nuts?"

"I know Caroline will be there. I have to confront her right now or I'm going to implode."

James stared at me, considering my words. "You know, you're right. If she did arrange this, then chances are those two masked dipshits will meet up with her at Pinehaven. All my buds will be there. We can do some righteous ass-kicking."

"As long as you leave Caroline for me," I said, re-buckling my seat belt.

17

The Bonfire

The number of vehicles parked at the reservoir was impressive. It looked like word of the party had spread to other schools. The Bronco rumbled past the lot of them as we slowly made our way up the winding dirt track.

James stopped and switched to four-wheel drive as we approached a steep incline. I gripped the door handle. The Bronco's tires grabbed and tore at the loose dirt, and James kept the speed steady. We cleared the hill and made the steep descent into the lower valley.

As we wound our way down the hairpin turns I could see the light of the bonfire glowing and flickering like a firefly. We parked just off the road, next to the other trucks and SUVs.

James hopped out of the cab and walked to the rear of the Bronco. When he noticed that I had not left the vehicle, he came around to the passenger door and opened it for me.

"You okay?" he asked.

"I'm scared," I answered. "Maybe this is a bad idea."

"I'll take you home right now if that's what you want."

I sat in silence, staring down at my clenched hands. Maybe I should take him up on the offer. Did I really want to face all these people tonight? Would they laugh and point their fingers at me? Then I heard the echo of Kara's hopeless sobs in my head and my anger ignited, incinerating my fear and uncertainty.

Walking hand in hand, we approached the bonfire and scanned the crowd of faces. No one seemed to notice us—too many people for any one to stand out. Music blasted from stereo equipment in the back of a truck parked near the fire. People were busy talking, drinking, and laughing. A long-haired boy grabbed a wooden pallet and threw it on the fire, and sparks burst upward. I squinted against the fire's light and heat.

I saw Tanya and Mikey sitting on the tailgate of a truck parked next to the pallets. Both were drinking from plastic cups. Tanya spotted me and handed Mikey her drink. She scooted off the tailgate and jogged over to me.

"Hey, how was the dance? Did it live up to your teen-movie expectations?"

I told her all about it in a monotone. Tanya's eyes grew to the size of saucers as I revealed the horrid details.

"What are you going to do?" she asked.

"I'm going to find Caroline."

Without another word, Tanya hurried back to Mikey. I watched her whispering in his ear. The relaxed expression on Mikey's face quickly morphed into barely suppressed fury, and his fists rapidly clenched and unclenched. I gripped James' hand more tightly.

As James and I headed toward the abandoned sanitarium, I heard Caroline's voice, her laughter like the low cackling of a witch. She sat on an empty windowsill of the building, her feet dangling a few inches from the ground, wearing shorts and a T-shirt. Tracy and Hillary, still in their prom dresses, flanked her along with a handful of guys, two of whom wore black pants and shirts. I knew in a split second that these were the super-soaker wielders.

Caroline turned her head to us as we approached. She hopped off the empty sill, her feet stirring up puffs of dust as she closed the distance between us.

"Hi guys!" she said in a cheery voice. "How was prom? I heard there were some unexpected golden showers."

James' hand gripped mine. He took a step toward her and spoke directly into her face. "I always knew you were spoiled, but I had no idea what a bitch you are too. Are you proud of yourself? Do you enjoy being an evil cunt?"

Caroline's face remained impassive. She crossed her arms over her chest and looked bored. "She fucked with me and mine. She got her payback."

I knew James wasn't done, but I could no longer hold my silence. "What did Kara ever do to you? You and your bitch posse have tormented me since seventh grade. We never did anything to deserve the shit you gave us."

"You exist!" she hissed at me, finally tearing her eyes from James' face to look at me. "You and your loser friends. Now you've gotten way above your station in life. It's my duty to put you back in your place—at the bottom."

I was astounded by her hatred. I tried to think of how to reply as people approached from all sides. Without warning James lunged for the nearest of the black-clad guys. They tumbled to the ground, scrabbling and punching while huge clouds of dust rose around them. A second guy ran forward to kick James in the rib cage; James made an oof sound as the kick landed. At that point his friends jumped into the fray.

Caroline's attention was focused on the fight, and I took the opportunity to pounce. I pulled back my fist and sucker punched her with all the force I could muster. It landed squarely on her cheek. She let out a high-pitched bark as she stumbled to one knee.

Hillary ran at me, her hands spread into claws. "You bitch!" she cried as she slapped, scratched, and kicked me, though with all the adrenaline in my system I barely felt any of it. Looking past her, I saw Tanya and Mikey in the melee and Caroline huddled near the wall of the sanitarium.

I gulped down air and screamed at the top of my lungs, "You chickenshit troll! You want me? Come on and fight me! Quit using your friends as a shield, you fish-dump whore!"

Her face exploded in a scream as she came at me. Twisting and writhing, we punched and kicked furiously. She drove me back with a series of vicious shoves until I felt a searing pain in my legs—we had stumbled our way onto the edge of the bonfire. Flames licked at my calves, and my feet lurched through red-hot embers. The pain was enormous. Every other sensation was blocked out as a scream built in my throat.

Someone grabbed me by the shirt collar and pulled. As my feet cleared the fire I saw it was Mikey. Warm wetness flowed down the side of my face. I reached up and came away with a bloody hand. How had my head gotten cut?

I spun, looking in all directions for James. Finally I saw him giving a final kick to a limp body on the ground. His lower lip was bloodied and he was covered in dust from head to toe.

I turned back to Mikey, trying to get my bearings. "Where's Caroline?"

"She ran that way," he said, pointing toward the road.

I scanned the road until I saw her, Tracy and Hillary climbing into an SUV. A huge plume of dust rose as the vehicle rooster-tailed up the road.

I was shaking. "I need to catch her. This will never be over until I kick her ass into the ground."

Mikey grabbed my hand and we ran for his van. On the way he yelled to Tanya and she quickly caught up with us. At first I thought we had the wrong car, but then I remembered he'd painted the Stink Wagon; the new gunmetal gray was worse than the previous beige. We scrambled in and slammed the doors. Partygoers jumped out of the way as we barreled down the road, leaving a trail of dust behind us.

I gripped the dashboard with both hands, trying to keep myself steady as the van swerved crazily. The skin on my lower legs began to tighten until it felt like it would split up the middle.

Mikey took the hairpin turns at frightening speed and caught up to the SUV in no time. Honking the horn, he charged the rear end, trying in vain to get them to pull over.

Tanya leaned forward between the two captain's chairs. "Get in front of them, Mikey."

"I can't. The road's too narrow."

"Right there!" Tanya yelled, pointing ahead. I looked to see a wide bend in the road.

Mikey gunned the van's engine, charging around the SUV. We were nearly in front of it when the road curved sharply. The van slid sideways, and the SUV plowed into us.

The sensation of falling filled my stomach. The last sounds I heard were the crunch of metal and shattering glass.

18

A Change of Scenery

A strange smell was bothering me. I wanted to keep sleeping, but the odor grew more and more powerful. It burned and tickled my nose. I pried my eyes open slowly, feeling like each eyelid had a ten-pound weight on top of it. My vision was badly blurred.

"Just be still, honey. Your mom is talking to the doctor. I'll go get her for you."

Was I dreaming? Where was I? My groggy mind reached for recollection. Memories came crashing into my head in a dizzying wave. Prom... Bonfire... In the van with Mikey and Tanya...

"Mom!" I called out.

A blurry shape hurried into the room. My mother's arms wrapped around me. The next voice I heard was my dad's.

"Hey, kiddo. You're going to be fine. You've got a concussion, some second-degree burns, and a lot of scrapes and scratches."

If Dad was there, it had to be bad.

"Where's Mikey and Tanya? I can't see anything without my contacts... Where's my glasses?"

Mom dug in her purse until she came up with them in their case. I put them on and finally saw the room in focus. My parents' faces looked so old under the fluorescent lights. Their expressions were pained.

"What happened? Are Mikey and Tanya okay? Did we roll the van?"

My mother and father exchanged silent looks.

"Yes, Audrey," my mother said while she gently eased me back against the pillows. "The van you were in rolled several times. Tanya's okay, but...Mikey was ejected from the vehicle."

"Is he okay?" My voice came out in a squeak.

"I'm sorry, love… He didn't make it."

All the air left the room. I lay still, stunned, holding my breath until her words sank in. My mother continued to talk, saying something about other injuries, but her voice was just background noise. I heard the words "seat belts" and "lucky."

I killed Mikey. I killed him. I'm a murderer. I'm going to hell. The words repeated in my mind over and over, a broken record of agony. I heard a high-pitched keening and realized it was coming from me. It turned into wailing. I brought my fist up, trying to shove it into my mouth to stop the horrid noise, but it didn't work. I felt a burning sensation enter my arm. Then I knew no more as I fell into blessed unconsciousness.

My room was stifling in the heat of the setting sun. Summer had arrived, end of term had come and gone, and I'd missed the last two weeks of school. Once I was back on my feet I'd gone to make up my finals in the administration building, but now I was confined here. I'd spent the majority of the last week secluded.

Friends had come and gone, keeping their visits short either by choice or because they sensed they were unwelcome. Kara was there the most, and she kept me updated: after filtering through dozens of eyewitness accounts, the police were able to nail the two assailants who had wielded the super soakers, and it hadn't taken much for them to roll on Caroline. She had convinced them to douche us at prom and was expelled for her efforts.

There were threats of lawsuits and much saber rattling, but only Mikey's parents followed through. They were suing the company that owned the property where the bonfire had taken place.

Tanya visited too, twice. She was quiet mostly. She blamed Caroline for everything that had happened, but there was no talk of vengeance. I was thankful she didn't blame me. No one did, apparently, judging by all the flowers and condolence cards I received.

My parents, however, blamed themselves. They were furious with the school for letting things get so out of hand at prom, but they were angrier at themselves for not protecting me more diligently. I was eternally grateful to them for refusing to let the school's shrink get ahold of me. They respected my wishes when I told them I didn't want anything more to do with Mrs. White.

James called nearly every day but rarely came by. He was busy preparing for his South Pacific trip. I asked him to come over for a last goodbye before he departed, and when he arrived I heard Mom letting him in downstairs. I remained immobile on the bed as he knocked softly on my door.

"Come in."

"Hey." James smiled as he flopped down next to me. "Whew! It's hot in here!"

He bounded off the bed to the thermostat near my door. He flicked the switch to "on" and a whoosh of air filled the room. He dove back onto the bed, landing on his stomach next to me.

"Still blue?" he asked, his head turned on the pillow so he could stare at me.

I turned and looked in his eyes, trying to discern his feelings for me. I braced myself, not knowing how he would react to my proposal.

"I want to go to Australia with you and Travis. It will take me a couple of months to get a passport, but I can meet up with you guys as soon as I do."

James looked surprised, then shocked. "Audrey, what brought this on?"

"I'm not going back to school. I've decided to get my GED instead. I want to get the hell out of this town and see the real world. We can travel together. It'll be great. We'll meet new people and have new adventures. It's just what I need to get out of my funk."

"Audrey I...I don't know what to say."

"Say, 'Yes, Audrey.' Say, 'That sounds great, Audrey!'"

"But Travis and me... We've had this planned for years. It's supposed to be a guy trip, you know?"

My bright flame of hope flickered and died. I had suspected this would be his answer. In my heart I knew James liked me but didn't love me, but I had deluded myself into thinking it was more. In fact our relationship had never progressed past the point of chemistry and lust.

I bit back my disappointed tears and tried for a small smile. "That's okay. I understand."

James looked uncertain for a moment, as if he were about to

change his mind. Instead he placed his hand against my face and kissed me. I broke away and got up, went to the bedroom door, and locked it. I returned to the bed to make love to James for what I knew would be the last time.

Two weeks later I sat at the dining room table having a rare dinner with both of my parents. My folks tended not to dine together, preferring to keep their relationship on a distant-friendly level, though they never quite succeeded in the way some divorced couples did.

They made small talk while I picked at my food. It was quiet for several minutes before I realized they had stopped talking. I looked up to see what had caused the awkward silence, and my eyes locked with my father's. He set down his fork, looking as if he were prepping for an unpleasant conversation. I felt my pulse quicken, wondering what horrible news he was going to drop on me.

"Audrey, I'm taking a job transfer in the South, and I want you to come live with me for a while."

"Huh? What?" I looked from him to Mom. Her calm face made it clear that she already knew all about this. "You mean San Diego or San Clemente?"

"No honey, southern Mississippi, on the Gulf of Mexico."

I sat, utterly stunned by his proposal. "Are you insane? Why the hell would I move to the armpit of the nation?"

My mother interrupted me. "Sweetheart, you're depressed. You need a change of scenery. I know you don't want to finish high school here. A move would be the best thing for you right now. We've talked to Mrs. White and she agrees. All we ask is that you give it a try for six months. If you don't like it, you can come home and finish up with home schooling."

My teeth clenched as I glared at them both. "So we're back to listening to the school shrink? You've all come up with the brilliant solution to ship me off to the wetlands and hide me away from the world?"

Shaking her head, Mom got up from the table and sat in the chair nearest me. She gently grasped my hand. "It's not like that, Audrey. Your aunt Tennison has lived there for over a decade and she says the town is absolutely charming. It's quaint and scenic, and you'll be only an hour from New Orleans. Your father and I aren't trying to hide you away... We just want you to spend some time in a new environment. You know, a change to help you get some perspective on the world."

I pushed off from the table without another word and went straight to my room, where I spent most of my time for the next two weeks.

My last day in California dawned hot and dry. I hadn't slept much during the night. I got dressed without bothering to shower and was out of the house just after Mom left for work. I set a fast pace walking to the bus stop, hardly noticing the people around me. I waited on the metal bench for the bus for an hour, or maybe it was ten minutes—I couldn't tell. I boarded the bus in a daze.

It was a short ride to Eternal Rest Cemetery. I knew the general area where Mikey was buried, but it still took me the better part of an hour to find his grave. When I finally found it I had to read the name four times before I was convinced it was the right one: Michael Woods, etched into a flat marker amidst hundreds of others that looked exactly the same. I don't know what I'd expected. Maybe I thought it would say "Mikey."

My legs began to shake as I stared down at the grave. When my knees started to give, I sat cross-legged on the grass. I had wanted to come to say goodbye, and now I couldn't think of any words. What could I say to someone whose life I had stolen? When my voice came out, it was barely above a whisper.

"I'm sorry, Mikey."

I got up and ran—through the cemetery, out the gates, and right past the bus stop. I kept running until a stitch tore at my side and my head pounded like someone was driving a railroad spike through my skull. I stopped, leaning my hands on my knees with my head down, gulping air in ragged gasps. I stayed that way until I was sure I wouldn't throw up. When the nausea passed, I returned to the house I would soon leave behind.

19

Welcome to Waveland

I pressed my forehead against the hot window, not caring if I left a greasy smudge. I barely noticed the scenery rushing past the rented truck's window. City had become desert, desert had turned to grassland, and grassland had become rolling hills. Now as we approached the Louisiana-Mississippi border, skinny pine trees stretched endlessly in all directions.

I could have fought to stay in California. My parents would have caved to my will eventually. But after two weeks of imagining a return to campus where every landmark would bring an unpleasant memory, running away had seemed like a better option.

Lily and Kara had tried to talk me into returning to school, reiterating the fact that most of the Cheerleaders were gone, either graduated or, in Caroline's case, expelled. Neither of them could understand that my reluctance to return to school had nothing to do with bullying or gossip. How could I explain to them how much I hated myself? Every time I looked in the mirror I saw a selfish, hateful murderer. Mikey was dead because of me. Couldn't they see the blood on my hands?

As far as I was concerned I deserved to be exiled to the swamps of Mississippi. Merry had warned me that my actions would return threefold upon me. I made my dish of revenge; now it was time to eat.

I lifted my forehead from the glass, stretching and glancing over at my dad. He had the grim expression of someone who was concentrating on not falling asleep. I had offered to drive several times but I could tell he didn't trust me behind the wheel of such a big truck with a trailer in tow.

"Dad?"

"Hmm?" he answered, not taking his eyes from the interstate.

"I need to ask you something important."

He pulled his eyes off the road briefly, looking at me with trepidation. "What's up, Audrey?"

"Dad, I want to use Mom's last name." I rushed my words, not wanting him to refuse before I could explain. "I don't mean it as an insult to you, and it has nothing to do with feeling closer to Mom or anything... It's just, well, if someone Googles my name..." I trailed off, not wanting to say it out loud.

"You don't want anyone to know about what happened this spring," he finished for me.

"Yes," I said, glad he had gotten it so quickly.

"Okay, hon. You can be Audrey Stevenson this year. Just promise me you'll go back to being a Kelly after all this...stuff is in the past."

"I promise. Thanks, Dad."

I turned to the window again, feeling enormously relieved as I leaned my head back. Before long the rumbling truck rocked me to sleep, slumped against the window. When I opened my eyes it was dark; occasional house lights glittered in the gloom. Dad guided the truck and trailer along a slender road with steady confidence, steering as if he'd driven it his whole life. A few minutes later we were turning in to a long driveway of crushed shells leading to an unlit house. I rubbed my eyes as Dad gestured toward it.

"Arrived at last." He opened his door, his back popping and cracking as he stepped out of the truck. The rush of humid heat overwhelmed the cab in seconds. I opened my door and climbed down.

The songs of crickets and other night insects were deafening. I had never heard so many chirping, whirring, singing bugs in all my life. I stood, slowly turning on the spot. I peered into the darkness in all directions, certain that I would see hopping insects everywhere, but there was only still, moist darkness. I took a deep breath, inhaling the strange scent of the place. I had expected it to smell muddy and stale, but it was like moss and cedar—woodsy and pleasant.

The house lights flicked on, momentarily blinding me. I looked up to see my dad gesturing from the front door. "It's nice and cool in here," he said, waving me forward.

I climbed the wide steps leading up to the screened porch that fronted the entire house. Going upstairs just to get into a house was weird for me; we didn't have that sort of thing back in California, where most houses were single-story ranches. Most houses out here,

Dad had explained on the ride out, were built up for when the water levels were high. At least all the ones near the coast.

On the porch I closed the screen door and went inside. In the narrow foyer, the air was cool; to the right was a small room with a fireplace and to the left a slightly larger room. I continued until I reached the combination kitchen-family room, where I opened a door expecting to find a broom closet but found a narrow stairway instead. I flicked the light switch and ascended the stairs into a long attic with a steeply slanted ceiling. It was stiflingly hot, but there was an air conditioner in one of the windows.

I scanned the walls until I found a switch for the globe light that hung at the center of the highest part of the ceiling. I turned it on, went over to the AC, and examined its buttons until I found the one that turned it on. Hot air blew out but it turned cool as I adjusted the thermostat to seventy-three degrees.

A second dormered window stood opposite the one with the air conditioner, and I went over to it. I pulled aside the dusty curtains and looked out at the dark landscape. I could see cars in the far distance, and beyond them was a vast expanse of blackness punctuated by a few specks of light.

I turned back to the room. Even with the low ceiling at the edges, it was twice the length of my bedroom back home. I wondered if my dad planned to use it as his office. Before I could go downstairs to ask him, I saw his head pop up from the stairs.

"I see you found the hideaway," he said, smiling.

"Yeah, it's awesome up here. Or will be, as soon as the AC cools it down."

"I knew you'd like it the moment I saw it," he said. "Even when I thought you'd just be visiting for holidays, I knew this would be the perfect retreat for a teenager."

A rush of love and gratitude overwhelmed me. Afraid of choking up, I went over to my dad and wrapped my arms around his waist.

"Hey," he said, clearly happy with my reaction. "It's just an attic. No need to get all mushy on me."

"It's great, Dad. Thanks."

We spent the rest of the evening unloading boxes and furniture from the truck. Working together, we lugged box after box to the small elevator that was on the ground level—really just a small cage with a folding door. A chain attached to a winch cranked it up to the

second-level walkway just off the screened porch. It made getting all
the boxes upstairs a snap.

However, the heavy furniture and mattresses were another story.
When we tried to get my full-size mattress up the stairs it flopped over
the rail and onto the gravel. Dad said to forget it until morning, when
he was expecting a couple of guys from his work to help him.

Sweaty and tired, I pulled out my hair dryer from my duffel bag
and used it to inflate a queen-sized air mattress. Dad and I sat on it,
surrounded by the detritus of our boxed belongings. We ate a dinner
of beef jerky, peanut butter crackers, and bananas that we washed
down with soda. Then I stretched out on the mattress, too tired to get
up and take a shower.

I woke up the next morning disoriented. I glanced over to see my
dad's back, still in his rumpled clothes. He was snoring softly. I lay still,
not wanting to wake him, watching the ceiling fan stirring the dust
motes that danced and floated in the morning sunshine. Finally the
need to use the bathroom forced me to get up.

My weight leaving the air mattress instantly woke my father. With
a final snort he turned over, looking as bleary-eyed as I felt.

"S'morning already." It was a statement rather than a question.

I grabbed my duffel bag and headed to the bathroom at the far end
of the house, next to the master bedroom. Another smaller bedroom
lay opposite. The bathroom was spacious, with a claw-foot tub in the
center. It was shiny and white, like it had been recently glazed. A tiled
shower stall took up one corner of the room, and the toilet sat across
from it. And then there was the vanity: the top a single piece of fake-
looking pink marble, the sink molded into the shape of a half seashell.

I relieved my grateful bladder and then rooted through my duffel
for my toiletries. I tried to leave room for dad's stuff as I put my many
bottles of soap, shampoo, and conditioner on the small shelf in the
shower. I took my time bathing but tried to save some hot water for
Dad, then I dressed in my last pair of clean shorts and a T-shirt. I
wrapped my wet hair in a towel and wandered barefoot to the kitchen.

While Dad took his turn in the bathroom I combed out my hair
and busied myself with searching for the coffeemaker in the many
boxes labeled "kitchen." I finally found it beneath a pile of pots and
pans. Good thing the carafe was stainless or it would have broken for
sure. Dad may have been a great driver, but he couldn't pack for shit.

He was showered and dressed before the coffeemaker had finished its chugging sounds. We had no milk, so I settled for a generous amount of sugar. We carried our steaming mugs out to the screened porch, the only room with furniture to sit on. We sipped our coffee in silence, both of us trying to wake our tired brains and ready ourselves for the long day of work ahead.

In the light of day the front yard was quite pretty, with three large oak trees spaced out across the green lawn, their low branches draped with moss, looking like something out of a postcard. The largest had a huge trunk that reminded me of the fake rowan tree in Tanya's magic shop. The moss looked like its hanging trinkets. I reached up to feel the star pendant that still never left my neck.

An old truck drove up our driveway, its tires crunching on the shells.

"Here are the guys from the plant," Dad said as he walked down the stairs to greet them.

I stayed on the porch and watched as he shook hands with the two men. One looked to be around fifty, bald with a stomach like a beach ball. The other looked like he was in his twenties. He had a stocky build and a shock of carrot-orange hair. The men followed my dad upstairs.

"This is my daughter, Audrey. Audrey, this is Jim and David. They're operators from the plant who're nice enough to help us out today."

"Hi," I said shyly, nodding to each.

The bald one, Jim, reached forward to shake my hand. "Hey there, little lady. So you've come to be a Mississippi belle, all right?"

I smiled, not sure how to respond. Before I could, David stepped forward to shake my hand as well. "Pleased to meetcha. Just call me Red—nobody calls me David. Davey or Red Dave, but mostly just Red."

"Okay," I said, trying not to stare at his lower lip. It bulged with a wad of chewing tobacco.

"Well let's get started on this stuff, guys," my dad said. "Audrey and I got the boxes already. I just need some strong backs for the furniture."

"Let's get to it!" Red said with more enthusiasm than I thought was warranted.

"Um, Dad? Can you help me get the car off the trailer so I can go to the grocery store?" I asked.

"I'll do it," Red said.

Looking uncertain, Dad dug in his pocket for his keys and handed them to me. "Do you want to wait a little while and we'll go together?"

"No, I can do it alone. And it can't wait. We need everything. I can't take another meal of road food."

"Okay," he conceded, rubbing his stomach in anticipation of a real meal. "Do you want to go to the local mart or one of the big ones?"

"Um, I think I'd better hit a super so we can stock up."

"Well, there's the Del in the Bay on ninety, the Vons in Diamond Head, or the Winn over in the Pass…" He trailed off, trying to think of more markets.

I stared at him. I had no idea what the Del, Bay, or Pass were. "Don't worry about it, Dad. I've got the handheld navigator. I'll just look up stores."

"Oh! Yeah, I forgot. Make sure you drive carefully. Unfamiliar streets and all."

I darted back in the house to grab my purse and GPS and headed down the stairs with Red close on my heels. He undid the tie-downs that secured the sedan to the trailer, turning to smile at me after each one as if to say, "Looky there, I got another one!" Feeling uncomfortable, I turned and pretended to examine the landscape around me.

"Ready for those keys now," he said, sounding like his mouth was full of marbles.

I handed the keys over and watched while he quickly backed the car off the trailer. I silently prayed he wouldn't run into a tree. Dad would be getting a company truck, and he'd agreed to let me have the seven-year-old sedan.

Red backed the car off the trailer without any trouble. He left it running and stepped out, then held the door open for me.

"Thanks," I said, quickly getting in.

Red shut the door and leaned down, his forearms resting on the open window. "If you get lost, just turn on around, and I'll be happy to drive you to the store and back."

I could smell the sour, spicy odor of the tobacco in his mouth. I swallowed, tried not to grimace, and smiled back. "That's okay. I'm sure I'll be fine."

20

Excursion

I put the car in gear, signaling the end of our conversation. Red stood up and spit a brown stream off to the side. This time there was no stopping my grimace. Oh, yuck. I drove away as fast as I dared while setting the air conditioning on full blast. I stopped at the end of the driveway, took a few steadying breaths, and fiddled with the navigation while the car cooled down. When the list of markets came up on the screen I chose one of the farthest ones, hoping to avoid Red for as long as possible.

I drove slowly, examining each house I passed. Most were tall and stately, many painted in soft pastel colors. Approaching Beach Boulevard at the end of my street, I gasped as the sea came into view in front of me. I'd had no idea we were so close to the water. The white sand was mostly empty, only a few people dotting it here and there, and the rippling water winked back sunlight. Someone was windsurfing in the distance.

A honking horn roused me from my sightseeing. I noticed the green light and quickly made a left turn, admiring the shore as I went. Finally I made a right and drove over a long bridge spanning a large bay and once again followed the shoreline.

Incredible mansions bordered the highway, set far back among clusters of oak trees, facing the gulf. Never in my life had I seen houses like these, except maybe in movies—neoclassical, antebellum, huge, white pillars, and porches that Scarlett O'Hara would have felt at home on. I drove as slowly as an old lady, barely keeping my eyes on the road as I ogled at the beautiful structures. Had I really called this place an armpit? What a dope I was.

The mansions eventually thinned, and multistoried townhomes appeared. I drove right past the market and had to double back at the next light. I found a good parking spot near the front. As I exited the car, the shock of the furnace-hot air stole my breath. The morning coolness had burned away and the heat of the sun combined with the humidity was stifling. It felt like God had forgotten to turn off his giant clothes dryer in the sky.

The grocery store, on the other hand, was nirvana. The frigid air cooled my skin and raised goose bumps on my arms. I grabbed a cart, flung my purse into the kiddy seat, and headed down the first aisle. There's something wonderfully comforting about supermarkets— they're the same no matter what town you're in. From sea to shining sea you can always count on a warehouse packed from floor to ceiling with anything you might need.

Halfway through my shopping expedition I stopped to examine shampoos and caught sight of the television screen suspended above the aisle. The black-and-white picture showed the back of a tall, blond girl. My heart fell into my shoes. For a split second I thought it was Caroline, but then I realized it was me. The store's security camera was showing my back as I stood in front of shelf after shelf of shampoo.

Don't cry, damn it. Get a grip, you wimp. I crossed my arms, grabbing my biceps in a painful clutch. I picked up my favorite mango-scented shampoo and conditioner and then spied boxes of hair color across the aisle. I took my time examining color after color, each with a delicious-sounding name: chocolate biscotti, caramel latte, cherry cordial. I finally settled on praline, thinking it was as close to my natural shade as I was going to get.

It took me a good hour before I headed to the checkout. My cart was filled to the point of overflowing. Only two cashiers were open, and I opted for the shorter line—only two people in front of me. I glanced at the racks of tabloids while I waited and glared as the cashier carried on an extensive conversation with the patron in front of me. The church picnic, the local booster club... Finally the woman waved goodbye and waddled away. I quickly unloaded my heaping cart and the cashier began scanning my items.

"Hi there, sweetheart. How are you today?"

"Fine, thanks," I said, not pausing in the process of transferring my stuff from cart to conveyer belt.

"I don't think I've seen you here before. Are you down here on vacation with your family?"

Jeez, how freakin' nosey could you be? "Um, no... I just moved here with my dad."

"Oh my! How exciting. Where y'all from?" She had stopped checking my groceries and was staring at me with her hands on her hips. My eyes twitched and I fought the urge to ask her why the hell she cared.

"California. Near LA."

"Oh…my…goodness! I'll bet you've seen all kinds of movie stars, huh?"

"No… Well, I did see John Stamos at Disneyland one time."

"Oh, I knew it! I would just love to go there some time. Me and Daryl went to Disneyworld in Orlando a few years back, but we sure would like to go to Disneyland someday. Daryl's my husband and he ain't never been further west than Houston, but we were talking about taking the kids camping in Yellowstone next year."

I stared at her, not knowing how to respond to the glut of information that spilled from her mouth. I just let her talk and nodded my head a few times with an "um" and an "aha" added in for emphasis. I focused my eyes on her nametag: Cheryl. She regaled me with tales of how nice this town was.

A tall, skinny boy with dark, wavy hair arrived and began bagging the groceries. He chimed in occasionally, adding tidbits about the coming fall's football lineup. "I play wide receiver," he told me, smiling shyly. "Are you going to Bay High or Hancock?"

There was no mistaking the hopeful look he gave me. "Actually, my dad's enrolling me at Our Lady Academy."

His face fell. It was obvious he had hoped to be the one who knew the new girl when school started. Maybe he even saw himself as a potential boyfriend. "Oh. Well, that's a good school. My cousin went to St. Stanislaus—that's the boys' school right next to Our Lady. They're kind of the same school."

"Yeah, my dad told me that."

The cart was finally loaded to the top. I hastily paid Cheryl.

"Here, let me help you out to your car," the boy said as he steadied the top bags in the cart. They threatened to fall off.

"Thanks," I mumbled, rooting in my purse for the car keys as I walked to the store's exit.

"Bye, sweetheart!" Cheryl called.

I gave her a quick wave over my shoulder, feeling supremely awkward about this total stranger calling me pet names.

Outside, the hot air once again blasted me as my feet hit the scorching pavement. I opened the trunk for the box boy and turned to help him unload.

"You'd better start your engine up to cool the car down," he said. "I'll put all the fridge stuff in your backseat so it won't melt."

"Good idea." I unlocked the door, started the engine, and turned on the AC to max.

"Thanks for your help," I said as he closed the trunk.

"My pleasure. My name's Randy, by the way."

"Hi, Randy. I'm Audrey."

"Nice to meet you, Audrey. That's a pretty name—like Audrey Hepburn."

I laughed. How little I resembled her. "Thanks. It's a family name, actually."

He nodded as he put the last few bags in the backseat. "Hey, listen, a bunch of us are going to hang out at the Mud Hut tomorrow afternoon after football practice. You should come." Randy's face turned beet red.

"The Mud Hut?" I asked.

"Yeah, it's kind of a legend in the Bay. It used to be a bait shop, then they added a bar and grill. During the day it's the best hangout in town. At night it's twenty-one and older."

"It sounds cool, but I've got like ten tons of unpacking to do."

"That's okay," he said a little too quickly. "If you change your mind, just take the highway to 603. Go north and it'll be on the right-hand side of the road, right after you cross the river. You can't miss it. It looks just like a big mud hut."

"Okay, thanks, Randy," I said, sliding into the cool interior of the car.

I drove home as slowly as I'd driven to the store, once again checking out the historic mansions. I wondered what they were like inside. Were they all modern, or were they filled with antiques?

Once home I made my way slowly up the gravel drive, and to my supreme relief I saw that Jim and Red's truck was gone. Looked like my shopping excursion had been just long enough. The thought of Red and his snuff-filled mouth was enough to make me gag.

I parked and popped the trunk. Dad came down the stairs. "Whew! Looks like you bought out the store," he said, eyeing the contents of the trunk.

"The backseat's full too," I told him with a grin.

"I'm surprised you had enough cash. I gave you only two hundred."

"I had some that Mom gave me before we left."

"Mmm." Mom had agreed to pay Dad child support now that he had full custody of me, but Dad wasn't comfortable with it. He'd continued to support our family even after the marriage had ended, and this was a blow to his pride. In the end he had agreed to let Mom send the money directly to me; I would use it for gas and groceries, and whatever was left would be mad money.

The two of us made short work of lugging the groceries to the lift. I unloaded the cold stuff into the fridge and freezer and then started on the cupboard items. This took me much longer as I tried to figure out how to organize the small pantry. When the last of the groceries was finally put away, I pulled out the deli sandwiches, pickles, and chips that I had gotten. We sat at the small kitchen counter and ate.

"Thanks for taking care of the shopping, Audrey."

"No problem. Thanks for doing all the heavy lifting."

He rumpled my hair as he stood up. "I'm going to get started on the office."

21

Shades of Change

I cleaned up from lunch and trudged upstairs to survey what tasks awaited me. My attic room was pleasantly cool, thanks to the AC I'd left on since the previous day. Our power bill would be enormous I thought as I stared around the large room.

My full-size mattress and box spring leaned against one wall. My dresser stood against another wall, its drawers pulled out and stacked near it. I spotted the metal bed frame nearby and maneuvered it directly below the center dormered window. Grunting and huffing, I managed to place the box spring and mattress upon it.

I methodically opened box after box, each labeled "Audrey's Room." Finally I found all my bed linens. Unzipping the compressed air bag they were stored in, I removed each piece and smelled it for freshness.

Starting with the bed skirt, I worked my way up until I was smoothing the pearly, blue-gray comforter into place. I added my huge body pillow to the head of the bed and layered on all of my throw pillows to create a sort of headboard.

I fell backward onto the bed, relishing its softness. I didn't feel like doing any more unpacking, so I headed for the bathroom, where the hair dye I'd bought awaited me. I ducked my head into the room opposite the bathroom to check on Dad's progress and found him organizing books on some shelves.

"Hey!" he said, looking over at me. "You all done with your room?"

"Not even close. I need a break."

"That's fine," he replied, looking back at the books in his hands. "No need to rush it."

"You need the bathroom?"

"No, go ahead," he said, not looking up this time.

I entered the bathroom and locked the door behind me. Pulling out the box of hair color from under the sink, I sat on the closed toilet lid and read the instructions. Twenty minutes later my head was completely lathered in what looked like melted milk chocolate. The bathroom was hot with the door closed, and the edges of the hair color began to foam slightly. I pulled the plastic shower cap over my sloppy hair and rinsed my hands in the sink, careful not to splash color anywhere.

I sat back on the closed toilet and waited for the color to set, reading a tabloid I had picked up at the store. When the time was up, I undressed and got in the shower. I kept my eyes closed tight and shampooed out all the color. My heart raced as I dried off and rubbed my head vigorously. Finally I looked in the mirror while combing out the tangles.

My hair looked dark, almost black, but it was hard to tell when it was still wet. I decided to dry it in my room, where it was cooler. I wrapped one towel around my head turban-style and a second around my body, then grabbed the hair dryer and made the dash to my room.

When I was finished, I laid the dryer aside and went to my dresser mirror. I stared in mild shock at the new me. The color on the box had shown a chocolate-brown color with strands of lighter caramel running through it. My hair had come out a rich chestnut with auburn highlights. I never would have chosen it, but I loved it.

I stared at myself in the mirror, tilting my head from one side to the other to examine all the color contrasts. Then I wondered if Randy would be disappointed if the cute blond he'd met today was now a brunette.

I stretched out on top of my bed with my hands behind my head. Thinking about my new town—amazing and different and weird all at the same time—I fell asleep to the soft hum of the air conditioner.

An enormous explosion woke me from a deep sleep. I sat up in the darkness and fumbled for my bedside lamp, cursing when I realized I hadn't even unpacked it yet. A brilliant flash of light illuminated the room for a second followed by the loudest clap of thunder I had ever heard. I screamed. I couldn't help it.

I stumbled off the bed and walked with my arms out until I found the light switch on the wall. Thank God the power wasn't out. Leaving the light on, I headed downstairs.

"Dad?" I called out as I entered the kitchen and then walked to the living room.

"Out here, Audrey."

I peered through the open front door to see him sitting on one of the rattan chairs on the front porch.

"Come on out here and see the fireworks."

Fireworks? What the hell was he talking about? There was another blinding flash of light followed by a loud boom, and I hurried to sit down next to him. Rain fell heavily on the porch roof, creating a loud, staccato beat. Cool air swirled and pulsed through the screened walls. I smelled fresh water and green things.

"Can you believe this storm?" I asked. "Is there going to be a tornado or a hurricane or something?"

"Oh no. This is just a little thunder shower. It will pass in an hour or so. It rains nearly every day in the summertime. It's nice, don't you think? Cools things off a bit."

"Yeah, I guess," I said. "It just seems so…violent. I mean, we get thunder like this at home maybe once a year. It's weird to think that it's going to rain every day."

"Big difference from the scrubby desert, huh?"

"Yeah, sure is." We sat in silence for a few moments, enjoying the sound of the rain. Over the patter of raindrops I heard a low grumble. It was Dad's stomach.

"Oh my gosh, what time is it?"

"A little after seven," he said. "I went up to see if you wanted to order pizza, but you were napping. It's on the kitchen counter whenever you're ready."

"Let's eat. I'm starving."

We left the porch and entered the brightly lit kitchen.

"Holy… What the hell happened to your hair?"

Oh, crap. I had totally forgotten about my hair, and in the dark of the front porch Dad hadn't noticed the color.

"Um…I was ready for a change?" I said, wondering how big a deal he was going to make of it.

He stared at me. "Wow, it's just…so different. You've always had blond or light-brown hair. But now..." He searched for the right words. "Now you sort of look like Natalie Wood in Splendor in the Grass. With your brown eyes and now that hair..."

"Thanks," I said, though I wasn't totally sure if the resemblance was a good thing or a bad thing.

We both grabbed pieces of the pepperoni pizza and ate in silence for a while. After I finished I went to the fridge and pulled out a head of lettuce and a tomato to make a quick salad.

"Not going to let me get away without eating my veggies, are you?" Dad asked.

I laughed. "Nope. And you can't leave until you've cleaned your plate, mister."

"Aye aye, captain."

I served him his salad; he poured way too much ranch dressing on it and dug in. "So what's on your agenda for tomorrow?" he asked.

"Well, I've got to finish unpacking, but other than that I'm not sure. What about you?"

"Red is bringing my new truck over, then I'll head over to the plant for a walk-through and to set up my office. I'll probably be there until pretty late, so feel free to take the sedan out exploring. Just make sure you take the navigator with you so you can find your way home if you get lost."

I contemplated checking out the Mud Hut but wasn't sure if I would be up for it. "I think I'll probably just hang out here," I told him.

"Okay. Once I'm settled in at work we'll go over to the school for a tour."

I loaded our plates into the dishwasher, put the leftover pizza in the fridge, and headed upstairs to my room. I stood with my hands on my hips, once again surveying the many boxes. I thought about calling Kara—it was only six in California—but really didn't want to. She'd want to talk about everything that was going on with the gang back home, and honestly I just didn't want to hear it. Thinking about my life in California was like putting on stale, dirty clothes straight from the hamper. I wanted to enjoy the freshness of my new life without tainting it with thoughts of the old.

I set about unpacking my boxes. By ten my room was pretty much finished. The two tiny closets that flanked the stairwell were filled, one with coats and jackets, the other with the few long dresses and skirts I owned. The rest of my clothes I carefully folded and put in my extra-large gentlemen's dresser.

I set my desk up at the far end of the room, directly in front of the window. It faced east, so the setting sun wouldn't bother me while I worked on my computer. I put my two narrow bookshelves on each side of the desk; their edges barely cleared the slanted ceiling. On their shelves I arranged all my books, pictures, and knickknacks.

Even with a bed, two nightstands, two bookshelves, a desk, and a huge dresser, a large portion of the room was still empty. I thought a low sofa with an ottoman would be perfect to fill the gap; I could probably get a cheap set at a thrift store. Then I could use the money Mom had given me to get a TV, a nice thirty-two inch.

With decorating ideas swimming through my head, I lay awake until nearly one. Finally a soft cloud of sleep settled over me.

22

The Jellyfish Shuffle

The sun was shining brightly when I opened my eyes. I stretched my body like a cat, relishing the summertime joy of sleeping in. I hadn't even heard Dad leave.

I got out of bed and walked to the window. Small sparks of sunlight winked at me from the dark-blue water in the distance, and I smiled, thinking a beach trip would be the perfect way to spend the day.

First, though, I would do a load of laundry so at least I could say I did something productive. I pulled down one set of curtains and set them in a heap on the floor, then stood on my desk and my unmade bed to gather up the rest. I took the dusty bundle downstairs to the old washer and dryer in the closet next to the attic door. I dumped the curtains in, added detergent, and set the machine to the gentle cycle.

In the kitchen I found a note in front of the coffeemaker: Hot coffee in thermos. Don't worry about dinner—I'll pick something up on my way home tonight. Love, Dad.

Two twenties lay underneath it.

"Dad, you're awesome," I said to the empty kitchen as I filled a mug and added cream and sugar.

An hour later I grabbed my beach bag and set out on the short walk to the shore. By the time I reached the boulevard I was sweating profusely. It seemed lazy and wasteful to drive my car little more than a block to the beach, but now I wished I had. I slipped off my flip-flops as soon as I reached the sand, which was hot too and had the exquisite texture of baby powder. I relished the feel of it on my feet as I walked closer to the water, looking for a good spot to lay my towel.

Settling on a spot, I laid out my towel and plopped my bag down. Pushing my sunglasses back up on my sweaty nose, I scanned the beach to my right and left. I could see a woman with a small child a long way off, and that was it. How odd it seemed to have an empty beach. At home all the beaches were packed elbow to elbow during the summer months.

I decided to go for a swim to cool down. I shrugged out of my beach romper, rolled it up, and tucked it into my bag. The water was flat as a lake, with the smallest ripples on its surface. I was surprised by its tepid temperature and burnished copper color; I could see my toes wiggling in the soft silt.

I walked out farther, looking for the cooler deep water to plunge in, but it never got above my knees. It was unreal: how could the entire gulf be only a foot deep? I spied a boat cruising by in the distance, so I knew the water had to be deep out there somewhere, but hell if I was going to walk for a mile and swim in a boating lane.

Giving up with a sigh, I lowered myself into the warm water and rested on my elbows. At least I could wash off the sweat. I stared down at my spangled bikini top, remembering the frigid water of James' pool. I wondered what he was doing just then. Were he and Travis in some club in Sydney? Or had they already left the city for the long drive up the coast? I thought I might cry, but instead a dull numbness filled my heart. I had cried my last tears over James.

I felt something soft brush my thigh and sat up, expecting to see some kelp floating past. Instead I spied a speckled jellyfish. I froze, not sure if this type stung. As carefully as I could, I stood up. Keeping my eyes trained on it, I walked back to the shore…and felt a piercing sting on my foot.

"Ouch!" I grimaced as I balanced on one foot to examine the damage, but I couldn't see anything. Walking double time back to the shore, I watched every step to avoid more jellyfish. That answered my question about why no one was enjoying the beach.

Feeling pissed off, I went back to my towel. As I sat down, a truck approached on the boulevard. I heard a honk and a loud wolf whistle—two guys in the cab and two in the bed ogled me as they sped past. I put my back to the road and ignored them.

Pulling out a cold bottle of water from my bag, I poured half of it on my aching foot. The water eased the sting into a dull throb. I downed the rest of it and reached back into my bag for my sunscreen. I lathered it on my face and body and lay back to soak up a few rays.

The pleasant sunshine soaked into my skin; the heat didn't feel so bad as long as I wasn't moving. I stretched my arms over my head and let my fingers and toes trail in the soft sand. But my repose was short-lived. I heard a radio blaring and turned to see that the truck had parked off the boulevard; the four guys had jumped out with drinks in hand.

Oh God, what do I do? I lay stock still on my towel, hoping they would simply walk by. No such luck.

"Hey! How ya doin'?" one of them said.

I turned my head to the side and saw them plopping down in the sand next to me. They looked to be in their late teens or early twenties. All four had deep suntans and were shirtless and barefoot.

"Fine, thanks," I said as nonchalantly as I could.

"We saw you out here and got you a Slush Puppy." He held out a large cup with a cartoon of a beagle on it. "I hope you like cherry." He grinned.

"Thanks, but I don't drink anything I haven't poured myself," I said, wondering how stupid he thought I was.

"Huh? What?" He cocked his head. Slowly, understanding dawned on his face. "Aw, man. You think I would spike your drink with a roofie or somethin'? I don't play that way." He pulled the plastic lid off the drink and took several large swallows. He stopped gulping and clutched his forehead suddenly.

"Argh...brain freeze!"

I started laughing, unable to help it. He took this as a positive sign and again offered the drink.

"See? It's harmless sugar and water."

"Yeah, but now you've probably tainted it with germs or herpes."

His friends laughed.

"Damn, there's just no pleasing you, huh?" He stuck out his hand. "I'm Max."

I leaned up on one elbow to take his hand. "Hi, I'm Audrey."

He shook my hand gently, smiling like he'd won a battle.

"Hey Audrey," he said. "This here's Kirk, Devon, and Rob." He pointed at each of his buddies in turn.

I gave a short wave to each, wondering how the hell I'd gotten myself surrounded by hormone-raging young men.

"You live 'roun' here, babe?" Max asked.

Here we go again with the pet names.

"Yes, and I need to get home to make lunch for my dad," I said as I stood up and began shaking the sand off my towel.

"Aw, don't leave, Audrey! C'mon, we'll take you over to Pop's Mart and I'll buy you a fresh Slush Puppy—roofie- and herpes-free."

I laughed again. "Thanks, but I really have to get going or my dad will freak out." That was a lie. I stepped into my beach romper as gracefully as possible, trying not to give them any cleavage or a butt shot. It wasn't easy.

"Well at least give me your phone number," Max said as I slung my bag over my shoulder and walked away.

I heard the guys laughing and mimicking the sound of a plane crashing.

23

The Mud Hut

It was just past one when I rehung the curtains in my room. The washer had transformed them from dusty moths into snowy-white butterflies.

I flopped back on the bed with the latest vampire novel I was reading, but it didn't hold my interest. Feeling bored, I let my mind wander back to my meeting at the beach. It was flattering to have so much male attention. Being an object of admiration had been a new thing for me back home and it seemed to have tripled since arriving here. Maybe there was just less competition. I didn't know for sure.

Feeling slightly swelled with feminine confidence anyway, I decided to make the trip to the Mud Hut. I took another shower to wash away the sunscreen and Gulf water, taking extra time on my hair. After it dried I used a large-barreled curling iron to make the loose waves Kara always did for me and put on makeup that was supposed to look like it wasn't makeup at all. Then I grabbed my purse and headed for the door.

I drove north on the highway before I realized I'd forgotten my navigator. Silently cursing, I slowed down and scanned the side of the road for the Mud Hut. I crossed a short bridge and there it was: a small, ugly building with a dirt parking lot in front. I pulled in and parked, checked my hair quickly in the mirror, and got out of the car.

Signs pointed me to the entrance in the back, where there was a large deck built over a river's edge. There were high, round tables with stools and a long bar across the inside wall. A dozen ceiling fans whirled at full speed. The place was crowded with people, and I stood toward the side as I looked for a place to sit. Could I sit at the bar? Was that allowed during the day?

A waitress approached a table carrying a huge tray heaped with steaming crabs, corn on the cob, and potatoes. She set the tray in the middle of the table, and the people around it began to dig in. The spicy smell of the seafood made my mouth water.

A bartender leaned toward me to ask me what I wanted.

"Um, a Coke please?"

He handed me a plastic cup with a picture of a muddy turtle on it. I paid and sipped the drink as I wandered the periphery of the deck, looking at the sea of faces. On the far side I came across a large group of teens occupying several tables, with a few boys sitting on the deck's rail. Among them was Randy, talking to the person sitting next to him. He looked up, saw me, and did a double take.

"Audrey?" he asked.

I smiled shyly. "Hey, Randy."

He jumped down from his perch. "Wow, you dyed your hair," he said.

"Yeah, I did." I ran my hand through a strand of it.

"It looks really good." He didn't sound too convincing.

The other kids had grown quiet, watching the exchange between us. Randy pivoted to face the group.

"Everybody, this is Audrey. She just moved here from LA. Audrey, this is Kaitlyn, Chris, Jessica, Billy, Josh, Ella, Mike, Austin, Hannah, Jake…"

The flood of names continued as Randy pointed to each of them in turn. They waved or nodded at me. I tried to act cool.

"That's the hot blond you met at the market?"

I looked toward the back of the crowd and saw a tall boy grinning from ear to ear. Randy blushed a startling shade of red.

"She changed her hair color, Jake. Shut the hell up."

Jake laughed but tried to cover his smile with one hand, knowing he had succeeded in thoroughly embarrassing Randy.

"What part of LA are you from?" asked a pretty girl with a round face and light-brown hair.

I took a small sip of cola, trying to calm my nerves. "I lived in the valley, about thirty miles north of downtown LA," I said.

"What grade are you in?" another girl asked.

"I'll be a senior in the fall."

"How come y'all moved here?" another asked.

"My dad works in water purification. He got a job transfer down here."

The rapid-fire questions continued, asked mostly by the girls. They were all so pert and pretty; I guessed my earlier theory about lack of competition was a bust.

"What school are you going to?" asked a girl with long dark hair and deeply tanned skin.

"Our Lady Academy."

Her faced darkened. "Oh. We all go to Bay High. No private-school silver spoons here."

"God, Jess, don't be so stuck up," another girl said.

The dark-haired girl looked over at her. "I'm not stuck up. It's the girls at that school who are stuck up."

"Yeah, but she hasn't even gone there yet. Give her a break."

Jess shrugged her shoulders and crossed her arms, her opinion of me seemingly set in stone.

Two waitresses carrying giant trays full of crawfish interrupted the conversation. They put them down on two tables.

"Mud bug time!" Jake said, rubbing his hands together.

I watched in barely concealed shock as they all grabbed up the shellfish, pinched and ripped off their tails, and took out the meat with their teeth. Many of them, even the girls, put the heads in their mouths and slurped down the juice. They threw the empty shells onto another tray.

Randy put one of the red beasties in my hand.

"Um, no thanks," I said as politely as I could. "I...already had lunch?"

"Oh come on! There's always room for crawfish."

I held the crawfish between my thumb and forefinger.

"Here," he said, taking it and pulling off the tail, then extracting the meat from it in the span of a nanosecond.

"Open up," he ordered, aiming it at my mouth.

I took the offer myself, rather than letting Randy feed me. I popped it into my mouth and chewed. I blinked in surprise. It did taste a lot like lobster, only spicier. Randy grabbed another crawfish and demonstrated how to remove the tail and suck the juice out of the head, but I refused to do it. Randy smiled, not offended.

Conversation was minimal while everyone ate. I sat on the deck's rail and accepted a few more nuggets of crawfish when Randy offered them. I spent most of the time sipping my Coke and watching the dynamics of the group.

A breeze blew gently at my back. I glanced up at the sky and saw a line of dark clouds moving in. Randy followed my line of sight.

"Looks like a squall's headed this way," he said. "We get a good soaking most every day in the summertime."

When the discard tray was heaped with shells, a blond boy with a peeling nose hopped off his stool. "Who's up for some doughnuts for dessert?"

All the guys in the group let out a low cheer.

"What do you say?" Randy asked me. "You want doughnuts?"

"Okay, yeah, I guess."

He smiled and pulled a ten-dollar bill out of his pocket, then tossed it onto one of the tables. Several others followed suit, scrounging around in their pockets, wallets, or purses for dollars and loose change. I grabbed my purse to throw in a few bucks but Randy pushed my hand away.

"I got it," he said.

I was starting to worry that I was leading him on. He seemed like such a nice guy, but as far as chemistry there was nothing there. I needed to play the friend card as fast as I could manage.

The group left the restaurant and jumped into their cars and trucks. Exiting the parking lot, they left clouds of dust behind them.

"C'mon. You can ride with me," Randy said as he led the way to a small pickup. He started it and adjusted a choke lever on the dash.

"She's a bit temperamental," he said as he shifted into first gear.

As he pulled out onto the highway I smiled and nodded, thinking the truck must have been at least twenty years old. Randy pointed out various landmarks as we drove north. Both of the truck's windows were rolled down, the humid air the only means of cooling. I gathered my hair in one hand to keep it from blowing in my face. The air actually felt nice as we sped over bridges and along vast stretches of pine and oak trees.

The highway crossed under the interstate and narrowed to two lanes. Buildings became scarce except for the occasional farmhouse, and a long stretch of reedy river appeared. I caught sight of a beautiful, long-necked white bird standing in the water among the grasses. Leaning back on the headrest, I gazed out the window and marveled at the sky. Back home it was like faded denim; here it was the deepest shade of forget-me-not blue. A column of puffy clouds lined the horizon, warning of an afternoon thunderstorm.

A short time later our caravan made a sharp left onto a hard-packed red-clay road. What doughnut shop was way back in the woods like this? We passed several properties with single-wide trailers, and a scruffy dog sprinted after the car in front of us, trying to bite its tire. He settled for barking at each passing car instead, his tail wagging furiously.

We drove at a steady pace until we reached a clearing with a rough dirt track in the middle of it. Rain began to fall hard and fast. Randy stuck his head out the window, allowing the rain to hit his face. He pulled back in and shook like a dog.

"Ah, perfect weather for doughnuts." He smiled.

Car after car went past us and onto the track. They raced around it, over hills, bumps, and berms. Realization dawned on me: We weren't going to eat doughnuts. This wasn't a Krispy Kreme run. It was a mud-whomping excursion.

Randy gunned the truck and fishtailed onto the course. I bounced, my mouth wide open, as the truck rocked, spun, and raced its way through the parade of vehicles. I gripped the door handle like a vise. He accelerated to overtake a small sedan, putting us behind a big Ford with a lift kit and knobby tires. It sped around a corner, spitting a fountain of mud onto Randy's windshield. Randy cackled with glee as he tried to get around the truck.

Mud and rain covered the windshield and came in through the open windows, but Randy seemed oblivious to it. He flicked on the wipers and tried to take the low side of a corner to pass the Ford but was blocked by the same sedan we had passed earlier, now hopelessly mired in the mud. The road was too narrow for two vehicles side by side.

Randy eased back and pulled off the course. The blond guy who had suggested the doughnut run drove the Ford; he pulled in front of the stranded sedan and got out to attach a rope to the bumper. He leaned his head into the window and kissed the driver—Jessica, the dark-haired girl who hated me. Blond Boy then hopped back into the Ford to tow the sedan out of the muck.

The rain continued to pound down. The rest of the drivers left the track and parked on the side.

Randy jumped out of the truck "Footrace time!"

Everyone got out of their vehicles and stood in the pouring rain, talking and laughing.

Oh, what the hell, I thought. I stepped out to join them and was soaked in a matter of seconds.

Barefoot and soaking wet, a dozen teenagers lined up on the muddy course. Pulling me by the hand, Randy led us to the far end of the line.

"On your mark!" a loud voice called out. "Get set! Go!"

We ran, gooey mud flying everywhere, bodies falling, splashing, and rolling. Randy and I were near the front when I began to run all-out. Grinning, I pumped my legs as hard as they would go while the cool rain whipped my face. Only two runners were ahead of me when I lost my footing and went down. Arms out, I slid on my stomach. I sat up laughing, trying to wipe the mud from my face.

Randy bent down next to me, breathing hard and asking me if I was all right.

"I'm fine." I laughed as he helped me up.

I gazed back to where the race had started and saw Jake jumping up and down, his arms raised in triumph. I looked at Randy, still laughing and trying to catch my breath.

"Just good clean fun, huh?"

He grinned from ear to ear. "Yep, just good clean fun."

Thankfully my beach bag was still in my car. I used the towel to protect the front seat from the muddy mess of my body. After waving goodbye to everyone and thanking Randy for the adventure, I eased into the car and made my way home.

My heart sank when I saw Dad's new company truck in the yard. Shit! I was hoping I would be showered and changed by the time he got home. I looked at the dash clock and was startled to discover it was after six.

The rain had abated, leaving scattered clouds in the sky. I rolled up my towel and tucked it back into my beach bag and took the front stairs two at a time, hoping to hightail it into the bathroom before Dad could see me.

I opened the screen door. He was sitting on the porch with a newspaper. He jumped to his feet before I was through the door.

"Audrey? What happened?" The look of concern on his face brought a rush of guilt.

"I'm fine, Dad. I went out to lunch with some new friends, and then it rained, and then they do this footrace thing on a mud track, and it was so much fun, and I promise I didn't get any mud in the car."

He looked relieved. He sat back down, and I told him all about the Mud Hut, the crawfish, and the footrace, careful to leave out the part about the car racing.

"Do you mean to tell me," he said, "that we've been here for barely three days and you're already running around with a gang of teenagers who like to sprint in the mud for fun? Should I be worried?"

"No, Dad. It was really all very simple. Just good clean fun," I said with a grin.

"Uh huh. Good clean fun. Maybe you should go look in the mirror, young lady."

"I'm just gonna go jump in the shower," I said, gesturing with my thumb over my shoulder, trying to ease my way through the front door.

"You do that." He sat down and picked up his newspaper again.

24

Fun on the Bayou

The following morning I sat on the front porch, sipping iced coffee and enjoying the coolest part of the day. Randy had called at eight thirty to invite me to a house party. After he assured me I was welcome and wouldn't be stepping on any toes, I agreed.

He wanted to pick me up at my house, but I insisted on driving myself. I would have to be home early—Dad had shortened my leash after I'd come home looking like the creature from the mud lagoon. Also, I reasoned to myself, it would make it a lot less like a date if Randy didn't pick me up.

It was obvious Dad had mixed feelings about my running around with a vivacious and possibly wild group of new friends. He was glad I was socializing, but I thought he might worry less if I had remained in my quiet shell for the rest of the summer. On the porch I rehearsed my conversation with him in my head, carefully rephrasing "house party" to "board games and pizza at a friend's house." After several run-throughs I picked up my phone to call him. He answered after two rings.

"Hey, Aud, what's up?"

"Hi, Dad. Some friends invited me to hang out at their house tonight for pizza and board games. Would it be alright with you if I go?"

"What friends?"

"Um…Randy, Jessica, and Jake," I replied, dredging up the few names I could remember.

"Whose house is it at?"

"Jessica's." That was the truth. I'd hesitated when Randy had told me.

"Will her parents be there?"

He was so much tougher than Mom. "Uh, I think so, yeah."

"I want to talk to them first."

Panic rose in my chest. "Dad, come on! I'm the new kid in town, and you want me to tell my friends I can't go play board games with them until my daddy talks to their mommy? You want them to think I'm a big dork?"

He sighed deeply. I held my breath, waiting for his response. I knew it was better to remain silent; if I begged and pleaded it would be all over for me.

"I want the address, the phone number, and you home by eleven."

I thought about asking for eleven thirty but decided not to push my luck. "Thanks, Dad. I'll leave all the info on the kitchen counter."

"I'm trusting you, Audrey. I don't want you around any drinking, drugs, or other craziness."

"I know you're worried, Dad, but I can't live my life under a rock."

"I know, I know." He emitted another deep sigh. "Eleven, got it?"

"Okay. Love you, Dad."

"Love you too, Aud."

I left the house at six wearing denim shorts and a white knit halter, with my hair in a ponytail and just a little lipstick and mascara. This time I refused to stress about hair and makeup and fashion—who knew? Maybe the kids out here partied in the mud too.

Even with my navigator, finding Jessica's house was a challenge. I missed the turn off the highway and had to double back and wind my way through narrow streets. Finally I found it—a small house perched on a black-water bayou. The front yard was full of cars. I managed to find a spot next to a large flagpole flying a white flag with a crimson border and a dark-blue corner with a white star. At the center was a beautiful magnolia flower.

A balcony ran along an entire side of the house. It was full of people in knots, in easy conversation. My nerves shifted into high gear as I made my way up the stairs, but no one paid any attention to me. I saw Jake at the far end with a group of people I'd never met. He glanced in my direction, and I waved at him.

"Hey, Audrey!" he called, grinning from ear to ear, waving me over with one hand.

I made my way through the crowd until I was standing next to him. Jake slung his arm over my shoulder.

"Audrey's new in town and she got baptized at the doughnut track yesterday," he said with a chuckle.

The boy standing across from us let out an ear-splitting whoop. "Baptism by mud! You a Mississippi girl now!"

I laughed, a warm feeling spreading to my core.

I saw Randy coming out of the sliding glass doors of the house, and I waved to him. He came over and joined in the conversation, giving the blow-by-blow of my face-first slip and slide.

"C'mon, I'll get you a drink," he said when the conversation ebbed.

We went back through the glass doors and into a dining room, then through to the kitchen.

"You want a soda, beer, hard lemonade?" Randy asked over his shoulder.

"Just soda, thanks."

Jessica was in the kitchen with a small group of people I'd met at the Mud Hut. Her dark hair was straight and gleaming.

"Hey," she said.

"Hi," I answered cautiously. "Your house is really nice."

"Thanks," she said, smiling. "My folks have threatened me with death if anything gets trashed, so this knucklehead is supposed to help keep order tonight."

She gestured to the blond driver of the Ford I had seen her kissing yesterday. She grabbed him in a headlock and gave him a half-hearted noogie. He ducked out of her grasp, laughing.

"Hey Randy," he said, playfully punching him on the shoulder.

"Hey Billy." Randy punched back a lot harder.

So the blond boy was Billy, and he was Jessica's boyfriend. I made mental notes. Randy grabbed two soft drinks from an ice-filled plastic tub in the corner and handed one to me.

We lingered in the kitchen for a few minutes then wandered onto the back deck, where people were mingling. I spent the next hour talking to people Randy introduced me to and answering the same questions over and over. Everyone seemed to think that since I was from California I knew how to surf, saw movie stars all the time, and drove a convertible. I shook my head at the absurdity of the stereotype but checked myself when I remembered how just a short while back I had thought all Mississippians were either toothless banjo players or hoop-skirted debutants.

A loud female voice erupted in the family room. "Where the hell is the beer?"

I stood on my tiptoes to try to get a look at the shouter. It was a petite blond surrounded by three other girls. She had a spiky, pixie haircut with pink highlights around her face. She was pretty in a doll-like way, with big, blue eyes and rosy cheeks.

"Heeeeyyyy!" she called to the assembled crowd.

A few people, mostly guys, walked over to talk to her. Someone put a cup of beer in her hand, and she and her friends began drinking and socializing loudly. Obviously they wanted to be the center of attention.

Randy leaned in to whisper in my ear. "That's Charlaine Harrington and her friends. Jess is not going to be happy. She hates Charlaine."

We left the deck to look for Jessica in the kitchen. She was leaning against the counter, her arms crossed in front of her while she stared daggers at Charlaine, who inched closer and closer to the kitchen. Charlaine set her empty beer cup on the counter and stopped in mid-laugh when she saw Jessica.

"Oh, hey, Jess. I didn't know you were gonna be at this party," she said in a sweetly innocent voice.

"It's my house, Charlaine. Where else would I be?" Her voice was steely.

"Oh, I didn't know you live here! I thought you live in the trailer park behind the Laundromat!"

Her soft, southern twang was both charming and sinister. I felt my heart pound. Why oh why did these girls have to be so fucking mean? I barely breathed as I watched for Jessica's reaction. Without uncrossing her arms, she left the kitchen and walked down the hallway at a fast clip.

Charlaine grinned like a shark, picking up her conversation where she had left off.

Randy blew a soft raspberry. "What a bitch," he muttered.

"What's going on?" I asked him, not sure if I really wanted to know.

"Charlaine is a cheerleader at OLA, and she loves to taunt Jessica whenever their teams compete. Jessica's a cheerleader at Bay, and our squads go head to head all the time."

"OLA?" I asked.

"Our Lady Academy," he said. "You know—your new school."

"Oh!"

"Anyway, since they're competitors, Charlaine likes to mess with Jessica all the time, and Jess has thin skin."

"No wonder she looked at me like I was dirt when she found out I was going there," I said. "She thinks I'm another Charlaine."

I suddenly felt sick to my stomach. Cheerleaders—Christ. I wanted to ignore the whole thing, tune out Charlaine and her friends and wall off the hateful emotions before the old wounds could rip open.

Randy and I headed outside, where I cleared my mind by skipping rocks across the bayou. We chatted easily; I told him what California was really like, and he let me in on his favorite things about Mississippi: the tremendous rainstorms, its amazing history, the mostly easygoing nature of most of its people. Before long I had forgotten all about Charlaine and any sort of cheerleader-induced drama.

Heading back into the house, it was time for a bathroom break. I waited on line in the hallway, looking at the pictures on the wall. One was a family portrait with Jessica at about seven, standing in front of her seated parents, two boys I assumed were her brothers standing in back. In another she held up freshly caught catfish. In another they all smiled on the deck of a boat.

At last I reached the bathroom door. I heard the muffled conversation of several girls inside. They were probably screwing around with their make up while my bladder was about to explode. I knocked on the door.

"Just a sec," someone called from within. It was Charlaine; her voice was unmistakable. I leaned close, trying to hear what she was saying.

"Who cares if it's her house? She's a skank and she can eat it."

I heard a trio of tittering laughter. A dark cloud drifted over me and I wondered how I should react. Blissful ignorance? Hardened indifference? I felt paralyzed. Then an idea struck me. Bracing myself, I grasped the doorknob and pushed my way into the bathroom. Four surprised faces turned to stare at me.

"Oh, sorry!" I said. "My brother just called and said the cops have DUI checkpoints set up out by the highway. I have to piss and get the hell out of here."

Charlaine frowned at me. "BFD. Just go out the back way."

"No, you don't get it," I said, my voice rising. "They're screening everybody coming in or going out. My brother's a deputy. He's on his way right now to set up a checkpoint on the back road. Says it's part of the department's crackdown on underage drinking."

Real concern spread across their faces. I looked from one to the other, breathless in anticipation.

"Shit! We better bail," Charlaine said.

They pushed past me and out of the bathroom. I leaned my head and watched them hurry toward the balcony. Smiling, I locked the door and used the bathroom at my leisure.

As soon as I opened the door, a voice startled me.

"You are so full of shit," Jessica said, grinning. "I can't believe they bought that lame-ass story."

I smiled back at her. "They've been drinking. Their judgment's impaired."

We both laughed, and the tension that had been between us broke.

"So why'd you do it?" she asked.

I paused, the events of the previous three months flashing through my head. "I just hate people like her. I've had to put up with her type a lot." I left it at that.

I spent the rest of the evening with Randy glued to my side while we hung out with Jessica and Billy. I laughed when Jess asked me if I would go out for cheerleading at OLA. I explained about my lack of coordination. Randy understood perfectly after witnessing my fall in the mud the previous day.

At ten thirty I hugged Jessica goodbye and waved to everyone else, and Randy walked me to my car. The front yard was significantly less crowded.

"Thanks again for inviting me, Randy. You and your friends are good people."

Even though I couldn't see his face clearly in the darkness, I could tell he was blushing.

"Ah, it's nothin'," he said with his head bowed.

I could tell he wanted to kiss me, so I rushed my next sentence. "I feel really lucky that I found such great friends here already. My boyfriend back home just dumped me before I moved out here, so it's great to meet people who just want to be my friends, you know?"

I fervently wished I could see his face better. He was quiet, processing what I had said, deciding what his next move should be. Before he could make one I slid into my car and started it up. I rolled down the window.

"Bye, Randy! Drive home safely, and watch out for those DUI checkpoints!"

He laughed and waved goodbye.

25

An Isle of Friendship

The next morning I took my latte upstairs and dedicated myself to catching up on e-mail. I wrote a long note to Mom, giving her the details of my new surroundings and all the great people I'd met. I knew she'd be happy to hear I was adjusting so well. Then, deciding to save myself some time, I copied and pasted what I'd written into an e-mail to Kara, Jane, Lily, and Megan. Bam—finished!

I spent the rest of the morning attacking the housework. I vacuumed, mopped, scrubbed, and polished until the entire house squeaked. I wanted my freedom more than ever this summer, and cleaning had to score me some brownie points with Dad. I wasn't disappointed when he arrived home from his golf game at the country club.

"Wow," he said as he surveyed the great room and kitchen. "You've been domestic today, I see."

"Yeah, I know I've been slacking, so I thought I'd catch up."

He smiled and kissed me on the top of my head.

I finished off the day by making a big pot of spaghetti, a loaf of garlic bread, and Dad's favorite kind of salad—antipasto. We ate on TV trays and watched a baseball game. I was loading the last plate into the dishwasher when my phone trilled in my pocket.

Looking at the readout, I was surprised to see it was Jessica calling. I flipped the phone open.

"Hi, Jess."

"Hey, Audrey. A bunch of us are taking a boat out to Ship Island this weekend. We want to go before the Fourth of July rush. You want to go?"

"Yeah, sure! What and where is Ship Island?"

"It's one of the Mississippi Barrier Islands. It's about a half hour boat ride from Pass Christian Harbor. It's a great place to swim and sun. The water's really pretty. Not too many jellies either."

"It sounds really cool," I said, thinking how nice it would be to go for a good swim with no slimy visitors. "Do we go on a charter boat or something?"

"No, my brother Jared promised to take me and a few friends out on our family's boat."

"Oh. That sounds cool. Who all is going?"

"Hmm, let's see—it's me, you, Billy, of course, Randy, Kaitlyn, and Josh."

Six people and a day on an island. Man oh man… I was so glad I'd buttered Dad up with chores and Italian food.

<hr/>

Saturday morning arrived. Jessica would be picking me up in twenty minutes. Out of the shower, I greased myself up with sunscreen, combed my wet hair into a tight ponytail, and brushed my teeth. As I finished applying a layer of waterproof mascara, Dad called out to me from the porch.

I went out and found him chatting with Jessica, Billy, and Randy and shaking their hands. Dad had agreed to let me go on the condition that he got to meet my friends. I watched silently, impressed by Billy and Randy's use of "yes, sir" and "no, sir." I was headed toward the steps with my straw bag on my shoulder when Dad kissed my cheek loudly in front of the others. How embarrassing.

"Make sure you're home by six," he said. "Don't forget, we've got Sunday brunch with Aunt Tennison tomorrow."

"I know, Dad." I smiled as I waved goodbye.

The four of us piled into Jessica's car. The day was a scorcher, without a cloud in the sky, and the car had barely cooled down by the time we parked at the harbor. Randy and Billy grabbed a soft-sided ice chest from the trunk and headed over to the mini-mart to buy drinks and snacks. Jessica and I walked down the ramp and across the dock.

We arrived at the stem of a large, shining-white boat. Two outboard motors glinted in the hot sun. Jessica climbed from the dock to the swim platform on the right side of the outboard. I waited for the rocking of the boat to abate before I stepped on. With my bad balance I'd be lucky not to take a header into the water.

"Hey, Jer! Where you at?" Jessica called as she walked under the center console roof. She disappeared down the steps of the boat's cabin.

"Hey, Jess! You're late."

She popped back out at the sound of her brother's voice. I turned to see a tall, broad-shouldered man walking down the dock toward the boat. I tried to watch him as discreetly as I could as he boarded the boat. Jess hugged him.

"Audrey, this is my brother Jared."

"Hey, Audrey," he said with a drawl that was deep and rich as molasses.

I stared up at him. His face was tanned, his square jaw peppered with stubble, his black hair slightly curled. He smiled, and his teeth were dazzling white. It changed his whole face, transforming it from sculpted Greek god into a friendly and inviting. His eyes, framed by dark lashes and thick brows, sparkled, a starburst of copper at the center, outside a ring of slate blue.

My brain ground its gears as I searched for words. Say something! I screamed inside my head.

"Hi," I said, my voice sounding timid and shy.

"I hear you just moved here from the West Coast." With his accent it sounded more like "Wes Coas."

"Yes, from LA." I tried to think of something else to say. "Your eyes look like the water." It was out of my mouth before I could stop it. Oh God, he was going to think I was a freak.

He paused, looking dumbfounded, then threw his head back and laughed wholeheartedly. "Well, I never heard that one before," he said, grinning from ear to ear. "Let's see what yours look like."

My heart thudded as he stepped forward and grasped my face in both his hands. He stared down into my eyes, looking serious as he peered this way and that. His fingers were work-rough, and my face felt as if it would melt like butter in his grip.

"Hmmm. I see a woodsy brown, with some green and gold specks in it. I'd have to say…oak tree. Yep, your eyes look like an oak."

He released my face. I could still feel his hands. "I never heard that one either," I said, smiling.

I darted my eyes sideways and saw Jessica looking at me, which made me blush even more.

"Yo!"

We all turned to see who was shouting. It was Josh, along with Kaitlyn, Randy, and Billy.

"Hey, bro!" Josh called as they reached the boat. Jared clasped his hand and pulled him onboard, followed by the others.

I leaned toward Jessica. "Does everyone call your brother 'bro'?"

She laughed softly, shaking her head. "No, it's Breaux." She spelled it out for me. "That's our last name."

"Oh! Is that French?"

"Yeah, with Welsh, Scots-Irish and some Choctaw Indian thrown in for good measure."

The guys stowed our bags below deck, and the six of us perched on seats around the boat. Randy sat under the canopy talking while Jared maneuvered the big boat out of the harbor. Soon the engines were accelerating with a loud roar as we raced over the water.

I stood just behind the canopy, grasping the chrome rails with fishing poles attached to them. The wind whipped my face and hair. I smiled. The sea air made me feel alive.

"C'mon, let's ride up front," Jessica said. She peeled off her shirt and shorts to reveal a bikini, brown with pink polka dots. Kaitlyn followed suit, stripping down to hot shorts and a white bikini top connected in the middle by a metallic peace symbol studded with a rainbow of rhinestones. They tossed their clothes down the cabin stairs and stepped onto the walk-around side of the boat, grasping the chrome railing as they made their way to the bow.

I was unnerved at the thought of undressing down to my bikini, not to mention creeping along the side of a speeding boat. Frozen with indecision, I just stood there. Jessica waved at me, gesturing me forward.

"C'mon!" she yelled, but it was nearly lost in the wind.

"Go ahead, Audrey," Jared said, looking over his shoulder from the driver's seat. "The water's glassy out there. You'll be okay."

Feeling compelled to act, I hurried below deck to step out of my sandals and beach romper. I ignored the ball of ice in my belly as I hurried back up the galley steps and onto the deck. I walked past all three guys to get to the walk-around. Jared's eyes were hidden by dark, wraparound shades, but Randy's eyes were about to pop out of his skull. I tried to pretend I didn't notice as I gripped the rails and hunch-walked my way to the front, aware that the guys were getting an eyeful of my backside.

I sat down next to Kaitlyn and gratefully leaned my back against the slope of the cabin. The groove of the walk-around anchored my rear in place, making me feel secure. I copied the other girls and stretched my legs out in front of me.

As the boat surged through the water, Kaitlyn and Jessica told me all about their past trips to the island—the sunburns, the beach parties, the hookups. Like all girls do, I silently compared my body to theirs. Kaitlyn was shorter than both Jessica and me; her figure was soft, with a small bust, and she had pale skin and ginger-blond hair. Jessica's was toned and muscular like a gymnast, her darkly tanned skin taut and well-defined. I felt a bit out of shape compared to her. Although my legs were long and slender and my stomach flat, my bust and hips gave me an hourglass shape.

Enough of that, I told myself. I closed my eyes and enjoyed the gentle surge of the boat over the rolling waves. Jared had been right— the ride up here was pretty good.

"Dolphins!" Kate cried.

I opened my eyes to see them on both sides of the boat, leaping in and out of the water and riding the boat's wake. I laughed and watched them play. They seemed to be smiling at us as they leapt and splashed. The whole trip was worth it just for this moment.

A while later, Jessica pointed to a vague shape up ahead.

"Look, Audrey, there's Fort Massachusetts."

I peered into the hazy distance. It looked like a long sand bar. I couldn't see much besides a curving brick wall that was overgrown with green shrubbery. I saw the shape of another barrier island.

"What's that?" I asked Jessica.

"That's Cat Island," she said. "There are a bunch of them out here. There's Ship, Cat, Petit Bois, Horn, and Deer Island."

Jared eased back on the throttle and the boat crept toward the south side of the island, where he cut the engine and dropped anchor. Everyone scrambled to grab bags and then leapt over the side of the boat. I watched as Jared peeled off his T-shirt and jumped into the waist-deep water. Josh handed him the ice bag then went in himself. Jess and Kate eased in from the swim platform, holding their beach bags on top of their heads.

I sat on the swim step, preparing to leap. Jared waded over to offer his hand and I took it, my heart in my throat. Even with his grip to steady me I managed to arch my feet too far back. I would have gone headfirst into the water, but instead my face landed on Jared's chest.

"Whoopsy daisy," he said as he grabbed my upper arms.

"Thanks," I said. He gave me another dazzling smile as he took my beach bag from the platform.

"That's okay. I'll carry it," I said, reaching for the bag.

"Nah, I got it. You just concentrate on keeping your feet under you. Watch out for spotted jellyfish. If you see one, just shuffle your feet sideways until you're around it. Their sting ain't too bad, but it still smarts."

"Yeah, I found that out earlier this week."

"Eh, you're probably immune to them now that you've gotten zapped."

I looked sideways at him and caught his mischievous smile. "Are you teasing me?"

He only laughed.

I tore my eyes off him and gazed into the water, looking for the dreaded jellies. The water was crystal clear and glinting all around me. Now this was my kind of beach.

26

Calm Waters

When we finally reached shore, I pulled on my swimsuit cover and a baseball cap. I tried to keep my eyes off of Jared but they wandered to him of their own accord. I decided to focus my eyes on Josh's back. He carried a Boogie board under one arm and was already looking pink around his shoulders. I tapped Kaitlyn and pointed to Josh's skin. Without breaking her stride she pulled a can of sunscreen out of her bag, shook it vigorously, and sprayed him like a pesky mosquito. He took it without complaint.

Taking a cue from Kaitlyn, I reapplied a generous coating of sunscreen, making sure to get the tops of my feet. She had told me on the boat about the time she got second-degree burns on hers on a trip to the island.

"Do you want to see the fort?" Jessica asked.

"Yeah, that would be cool," I said.

Josh looked concerned. I could tell he had no desire to see the fort. "Um, you gals go ahead," he said. "We're gonna stake out a good spot here before they're all taken."

Kaitlyn rolled her eyes. "Go ahead," she said. "I know you want to body board."

"Thanks Kitty-Kate," he said, kissing her cheek and rushing off.

"Kitty-Kate?" I asked.

Kaitlyn rolled her eyes. "That's his nickname for me. Most everybody else just calls me Kate."

I nodded, thinking the pet name was sweet.

"Thanks for offering to give me the tour," I said to her and Jess. "I know it's probably boring for you two."

"No problem," Jessica said. "There's not much to see, so it won't take us long. Besides, you can't have your first trip to Ship Island and not see the fort!"

The three of us made our way down the beach and walked along the half-mile dock that stretched the entire width of the island. We passed a snack bar and a canopied picnic area and clusters of people heading the opposite way, no doubt to claim prize spots on the south-side beach. Finally the dock was over a vast stretch of long grass that waved in the light breeze. Yellow, pink, and purple wildflowers dotted the grass, giving it an almost prairie-like appearance. I saw a copse of trees in the far distance, near the east side of the island.

By the time we reached the fort I was sticky with sweat and glad I'd worn a hat to keep the sun off my face. We walked through the large doorway leading into the center of the fort. The shaded interior was dark and cool. A park ranger was preparing to give a tour to a small group of people. We skipped that in favor of a quick look around.

While walking along the top of the fort, we stopped at a giant cannon so Kate could snap some pictures. The tour group was just getting started on the level below us. I listened as the ranger explained how the fort had been used to prevent a British invasion of New Orleans during the War of 1812 and as a prison for Confederate soldiers during the Civil War, after the Union had captured New Orleans in 1862.

"You like my brother, huh?"

Jessica's question caught me off guard. I wasn't sure how to answer. After a few seconds of contemplation I decided that honesty would work best.

"He's hot," I said.

"You know Randy's got it bad for you, right?"

"I know," I said. "And he's fantastic. I was lucky to meet him on my first day here, but—"

"But he just doesn't do it for you, right?" Kaitlyn said.

"Exactly. I wish he did—I really do—but there's just no spark there."

"And there is a spark with Jared?" Jessica asked.

"I'm attracted to him. I don't know him well enough to say anything else. Does he have a girlfriend?"

"No," Jessica answered. As we continued to talk, we made our way back to the dock for the long walk across the island. "He did a few months ago, but they broke up."

"How old is he?" I asked.

"Twenty-three. I can tell he likes you, but you're still in high school. That might put him off."

"I'll be eighteen in three months."

Both Jessica and Kaitlyn looked surprised.

"Were you held back a year?" Jessica asked.

"In a matter of speaking, yes," I answered. "My mom enrolled me in preschool just before I turned four. I was a really clingy kid, and I guess I screamed bloody murder when she tried to leave. Anyway, since I was one of the youngest kids, she decided to wait a year before trying again."

Jessica and Kaitlyn nodded. "When's your birthday?" Jessica asked.

"October second."

"Mine's April seventeenth, and Kate's is June fourth."

We walked in silence for a time before Jessica spoke again. "Do you want me to give Jerry your number?"

"Jerry? Is that his nickname?"

"Yeah, that and Jer and sometimes Jerk." She laughed.

"Only if he asks for it," I replied. "Where does he work?"

"He and my brother Jackson, the oldest in our family, own two shrimping boats. Jared works one during the season and does carpentry work the rest of the year."

I processed the information as we walked. I thought he must have been making really good money to own a pleasure boat like the one we'd ridden there on. It had to be at least thirty feet long and the price of really expensive sports car or even a small house. But Jessica had said it was a family boat, so maybe he was a partial owner, or maybe it was his dad's boat. I wanted to ask Jessica about it, but I was afraid she would think I was materialistic. The truth was, I was interested in Jared, period. I didn't care if he had money or not.

I gazed at the horizon as we walked, taking in the breathtaking blue of the sky until it met the green and blue tones of the sea. I felt a world away from the smoggy skies of LA, and I felt happy. God, how long had it been since I felt this way? Not giddy or excited—just plain happy.

When we reached the south beach, the three of us needed drinks. We spotted Josh and Randy making running jumps onto their Boogie boards. My happy feeling ebbed slightly as I watched Randy and wrestled with my guilt. He was all thin, wiry muscles. He looked cute in his knee-length board shorts. I willed myself to like him more. Then my eyes landed on Jared as he waded a bit farther out. A chill ran up my spine when I looked at his tan, well-muscled arms and torso. I sighed. It was like comparing a water boy to a running back.

I couldn't wait to get in the water. This time I stepped out of my beach cover without any hesitation and joyfully splashed my way in. The water was wonderfully cool and clear. I swam farther out until it was up to my chest, then turned on my back to float. A tug on my foot brought my head up in an instant, and I saw Jared smiling at me. I laughed and splashed water in his face. A full-fledged water fight ensued until I was gasping for breath.

"Uncle!" I cried. Jared laughed and relented. I blinked several times to remove the stinging salt water then looked toward the beach where Jess and Kate pulled items out of the cold bag.

"Time for a drink," I told Jared, and I headed for the shore.

Jessica and Kaitlyn were arranging blue canvas beach chairs in the shade of three big umbrellas they had rented. My feet hit the dry sand and immediately began to sizzle. I ran to the shade of the umbrellas as if sprinting over red-hot coals.

Eventually the guys wandered out of the water and migrated toward the shade and food. Everyone found a chair, and Jessica passed out sandwiches and drinks. We filled our stomachs with ham and cheese, chips, water, and soda. Sated, I leaned back in my chair to lounge in the shade and listen to Jared tell a story about him and a group of friends secretly staying the night on the island—something that was strictly forbidden. I laughed as he talked about his friends scaring the crap out of each other by telling ghost stories about the Confederate soldiers who haunted the fort.

"It's too bad you missed the Ship Island Rendezvous, Audrey," Randy said. He sat next to me and seemed eager to divert my attention from Jared's story.

"What's that?" I asked.

Randy brushed crumbs from his hands. "It's a huge party—tons of boats and a big barge with a DJ. It's kinda like spring break in Fort Lauderdale."

"You just like the wet T-shirt contest, Randy," said Billy. Randy leaned over and punched him on the arm. Jess sat up on the other side and punched his other arm.

"Ow!" Billy rubbed his sore arms with a look of mock petulance.

"Anyway," Randy continued, "it's a great time."

"Well, there's always next year," I said with a happy heart.

I spent the ride home in the galley below deck with Kate and Jessica, enjoying the shade and the breeze that flowed through the sky hatch. The interior of Jared's boat was cared for just as much as the outside—it was immaculate. Soft bench seats surrounded a table; there were a mini-fridge and a tiny sink to the right of the ladder and a closet-sized head on the opposite side.

We made it back to the harbor by five. As we left the boat I tried to chip in for fuel and the beach rentals, but Jared brushed me off with a wave of his arm, telling me it was no problem—he always took his baby sister out to the island, and her friends were always welcome. I watched as Jessica gave him a quick hug.

The six of us trudged down the dock toward the parking lot. Despite my constant application of sunscreen, I felt utterly fried. I kept my hat firmly on my head, fearing the Medusa-like hairdo that waited underneath.

Once home, I turned from the porch stairs to wave to my new friends as they drove away. I clung to my happy feeling like a life preserver in a sea that had finally gone calm.

27

Old Town

Dad called up the stairs. "Audrey? Breakfast!"

Uh oh. It couldn't have been a good thing if he was cooking. I wandered downstairs groggily, combing my fingers through my sleep-ruffled hair. I found Dad at the stove, flipping a pancake into the air and catching it in the pan with ease.

"Holy shit!" It came out of my mouth before I realized what I was saying.

He turned his head and smiled at me with a look of utter satisfaction. "Didn't know your old man could flip flapjacks, huh?"

"I... No! When did you learn how to cook?"

"I can only do breakfast, so don't get too excited. I used to cook all the time for Tenni and me when we were kids, but once I married your mom, well, I guess I just fell out of the habit."

I tried to picture my dad and Aunt Tennison as little kids, and the only images I could conjure were the old photos I'd seen.

I sat at the counter and he handed me a plate of three hotcakes. "I could get used to this," I said as I added butter and syrup.

After we finished I started to load up the dishes. Dad told me to leave them for the evening. "Tenni's expecting us at her shop by eleven, so go get dressed."

I showered and returned to my room to get ready. I was looking forward to seeing my aunt Tenni. I hadn't seen her in five years. She rarely traveled; she was content to tend the souvenir shop she had acquired after her divorce several years earlier. She was five years older than my father, short, plump in a sexy way, and never bothered to color her prematurely silver hair. She was always sending me gifts—probably why, when I was little, she had seemed to me like a kindly, smiling Mrs. Claus.

When it was time to go I got in the passenger side of the car. I wanted Dad to drive since I was still unfamiliar with the streets. It took us only minutes to reach Tenni's shop in Old Town, Bay Saint Louis. I had driven right past Old Town on my first shopping excursion but didn't know at the time that I was so close to her shop.

We parallel parked off Beach Road and walked at a leisurely pace through town. We passed a tall theater with an old-fashioned marquee, followed by row after row of shop windows featuring everything from kites to artwork to ceramics. I peered at each display we passed, laughing when I saw a tea set shaped like a crab, crawfish, and shrimp. The shops were open, but few people were out on the street.

"How come it's not crowded, Dad?"

"Sunday morning, hon. Most everyone's at church."

I absorbed this information silently. I didn't know anyone who went to church back home even though there were plenty of houses of worship; our valley had Mormons and Muslims and everyone between. But I was in the Bible Belt now. I wondered if Jessica's family went to church and tried to picture Jared sitting in a pew in his T-shirt and cargo shorts. The image made me smile.

We cut down a side street and walked half a block until we came to a tiny, yellow cottage. A white picket fence surrounded the front yard, which was exploding with flowers. The colors and textures overwhelmed me. We walked under an arched arbor and up the steps onto the front porch. The front door was glass, with large windows set at either side. I looked in the door and saw Aunt Tennison waving and walking toward us.

"Teddy!" she cried as she flung the door open.

Dad scooped his sister into a bear hug, lifting her off her feet. "It's so good to see you, sis."

Still holding him around the waist, Tennison saw me standing shyly behind my father.

"Oh my God, Audrey! Is that you?" Her voice rose to a delighted soprano twitter. "You're so beautiful! My gosh, you look like one of those girls in the magazines!"

She reached forward and pulled me into an embrace. The sweet smell of coconut and vanilla drifted over me. I felt just like a kid again.

"Hi, Aunt Tenni," I said, hugging her back with true affection. Her warm embrace in this beautiful cottage felt like coming home.

I had to blink back tears as I admired her shop. What had once been a small parlor and dining area now showcased art and souvenirs. She'd arranged the merchandise with no form or formality, but somehow it worked—like the garden in front. Framed canvas paintings were stacked against a wall while various tables held trinkets and music boxes. Dozens of beautiful stained-glass art pieces hung in the light of every window.

I wandered slowly through the maze of objects, examining items at random. Dad and Tenni's conversation was a hum in the background as I knelt before the paintings. I thumbed each forward to view the one behind it. The fourth painting was a sunset landscape. The shoreline and gulf lay in the distance; a huge oak tree dominated the foreground. There was a silhouette of two people holding hands under the oak.

"That's a picture of the Friendship Oak, honey. It's just down the road a bit, off Highway Ninety. They say that those who stand in its shadow will remain friends for life."

"I love this painting," I said, not taking my eyes off of it. "It's beautiful."

"Then it's yours."

I looked up at her. "No! Aunt Tenni... I can't take this."

"You can and you will. I painted it myself, and if it speaks to you, that makes me happier than any check would."

"You painted this? It's incredible!"

Tennison actually blushed, a sweet smile curving her small mouth. "Well, I'm no Miss Alice, but I try."

I had no idea who Miss Alice was and was too thrilled with the painting even to ask. I thought about where I would hang it in my room, but I realized that my room wouldn't do it justice. It was going on the living room wall where everyone could admire it.

I waited with Dad while Tenni turned the shop keys over to a young woman whom she introduced as Becka. Tenni told her to lock up at five sharp.

"Okay," Tenni said as she grabbed a purse the size of a bowling bag. "Let's go get some lunch at Trapani's."

We walked along in the shade of the oaks, making our way back toward the shoreline. After a few minutes we arrived at a glass-fronted restaurant overlooking the beach and the Bay Bridge. With a name like Trapani's I was expecting Italian food; I was surprised when I opened the menu and found po' boys, hoppin' John, and boudin. Worried about the spiciness of a food with the word "hoppin'" in it, I decided on a shrimp po' boy.

After we placed our order, Tenni regaled us with descriptions of Cajun, Creole, and Lowcountry cooking. Her narrative of spices, herbs, and cured meats had my stomach grumbling and my mouth watering. By the time our food arrived I was starving. I dug into the po' boy. I had expected something like a shrimp salad sandwich, but this was nothing of the sort. The shrimp had been cooked scampi style, with a mixture of spices that I was unfamiliar with. The buttery sauce soaked into the bread, giving it a wonderful texture, soft and crusty. I ate every bite and tried Aunt Tenni's gravy fries. I had never heard of putting gravy on fries—chili and cheese, yes, but gravy? They were surprisingly awesome. I washed it all down with a glass of tea that was so sweet it hurt my teeth.

I sighed in contentment as well as gloom when I realized how much exercise it would take to burn off this amount of calories. It was no wonder so many people I saw around town were portly. This was some of the best food I'd ever had. I smiled as I thought of a typical lunch back in LA: tofu salad and a fruit plate.

"So what have you been up to since you've been here, Audrey?"

Before I could answer, Dad was leaning toward his sister. "Lemme tell you, Tenni. She's already got about a dozen friends she runs around with, taking trips to the Barrier Islands and doing crazy races in the mud. They seem like good enough kids though."

Tennison smiled at me with a sparkle in her blue eyes. "Now don't you worry, Teddy. Folks down here are good, God-fearing people." She gave me a wink. "What are the names of your new friends, honey?"

"Um, there's Randy Hoda, Jessica Breaux, Kaitlyn Necaise, and Josh Cuevas."

"I know the Breaux family," Tenni replied. "They've got a big place on the Jourdan River. David's a manager at DuPont. I think his wife Julie used to be a schoolteacher over in the Pass."

I listened intently, hoping she would have details about Jared.

"They're a good family, Teddy. Real nice people.

"Jessica's brother took us to Ship Island," I added. "His name's Jared, and he has this incredible boat."

Tennison nodded. "Oh, yes. I remember hearing about Jared and his brother Jackson getting into the shrimping business. Their daddy was fit to split when he found out his oldest wasn't going to use his college degree and his middle son wasn't even going to college. He's an Ole Miss boy hisself and had his heart set on his sons following in his footsteps. I think he's pinned his hopes on Jessica now. Personally I think he should be downright proud of those boys of his. They're making a fine living for themselves, both of them homeowners at such a young age. How many boys in their twenties can claim such a thing?"

So Jared owned his own house. I couldn't help being impressed.

Aunt Tenni seemed to have her finger on the pulse of the community. I guessed there weren't any secrets in a small town. I wondered how long it would be before the ugly skeletons in my closet came out to join the party. I shuddered at the thought.

"You okay, Audrey? Is the air conditioning giving you a chill?"

"I'm fine, Aunt Tenni."

"Well, I'd better get home to my goats before they decide to jump the fence," she said. "I'll expect to see you both for dinner at my house this week. Will Wednesday work for you, Teddy?"

"Wednesday's fine," he answered.

We rose from the table and left the restaurant for the steamy outdoors. Tenni wrapped me in another coconut-scented hug as we said our goodbyes. Dad and I traced our steps back to her shop, where my painting was wrapped in brown paper for me. I thanked Becka and cradled the painting in my arms like a sleeping child.

As soon as we were home I wasted no time unwrapping the canvas. I scanned the living room briefly, deciding on the perfect spot. I set it on the fireplace mantle and stepped back to admire it. Perfect.

I went to the kitchen to finish the dishes from the morning. I worked in silence and wondered when Jared would call.

As it turned out, I didn't have long to wait. I was propped against my bed pillows, reading about my favorite heroine battling vampires when I heard the trill of my cell phone. I grabbed it from my nightstand and looked at the unfamiliar number on the screen before answering.

"Hello?"

"Hey, Audrey. It's Jared Breaux. Jessica's brother."

Like I needed an explanation of who he was!

"Hi! Hey, thanks again for the great trip out to Ship Island." I was proud of the casual friendliness in my voice. I did better over the phone than in person.

"Don't mention it. I had a great time too." He paused. "Hey, you want to grab some food sometime? Maybe see a movie?"

"Yeah! That sounds great." My heart pulsed painfully.

"All right. How about Wednesday?"

My heart sank to my toes. "Oh, I'm supposed to have dinner at my aunt's house on Wednesday." I hoped he didn't think I was making excuses.

"Uh, Tuesday then?"

A rush of utter joy bounced my heart back into my chest. "Even better," I replied.

"Great. Pick you up at six?"

"Sure. Do you need my address?"

"Nah, Jess's got it. I'll see you Tuesday."

"See you then. Bye."

I closed my phone with numb fingers and placed it on the nightstand. Then a surge of endorphins had me on my feet, running in place on my bed as fast as I could go. I let out a delighted whoop as I jumped and landed on the floor with a loud thump.

"What's going on up there?" I heard Dad's faint voice.

I ran to the stair rail and leaned over. "Nothing, Dad. Sorry!"

28

Art Imitating Life

I was ready for my date a full hour early. Jessica had called about five times already. Once she got an inkling of how excited and nervous I was, she started in on the teasing. First it was a bogus story about Jared losing a testicle when he was twelve. Then how two of his previous girlfriends mysteriously disappeared. Then his debilitating groin rashes. At that point I threatened to hang up on her.

Jessica laughed and told me Jared deserved all the teasing. When she had gone on her very first date at fifteen, Jared had met the boy at the door, pretended to be her father, and grilled him until he was close to tears, all while cleaning a hunting rifle.

Her story had me cracking up. Apparently teasing ran in the blood of the Breaux family. I hung up feeling slightly more relaxed.

Glancing at the clock on my nightstand, I saw it was quarter to six. Butterflies surged to life in my belly. I walked to my closet door and opened it to see the mirror inside. I examined myself from head to toe, turning to look over my shoulder to ensure everything was in place: pale-yellow sundress cinched at the waist with a wide, cream belt, strappy wedge sandals, long and loose hair. My skin was golden brown and looked good against the color of the dress.

I went downstairs and stood at the kitchen sink to peer out the window and down the driveway. I hoped he wouldn't be late. I really hated when people were late. I had just decided a glass of water would do me good when a truck pulled in—a polished, white, heavy-duty Dodge Ram with a double cab, tinted windows, and very shiny chrome wheels. I was impressed. I thought back to Aunt Tennison's comments about the brothers' success. This was no high school kid. This was a man. With a real job, a home, a boat, and a truck. I felt like the ante had just been upped.

Jared cut the engine and stepped out of the truck. He looked positively gorgeous in dark-blue jeans and an open-collar, white, button-down shirt that didn't hide his powerful build. I felt the muscles in my lower back actually trembling.

"Dad, I'm getting ready to leave," I called down the hallway.

He had been hiding in his office since he had gotten home from work. Dad had never experienced seeing me off on a date, and I knew it was going to be torturous for him. I heard his desk chair squeak as he got up. He came out and looked me up and down silently with a grave look on his face.

"Do you need a sweater?"

"Not here, Dad. I think the night is nearly as hot as the day."

He nodded. I gave him a quick, reassuring hug around the waist, knowing he was feeling nervous. The doorbell chimed and I went to answer it. I wanted Jared to see me before my father confronted him.

Jared greeted me with a gorgeous smile. He looked even better up close. His face was clean-shaven, and the curl in his hair had been tamed into a slightly spiky wave.

"Come in," I said as I waved him forward.

Jared stepped in and offered his hand to my dad. They shook firmly. They were the same height, both about six foot two.

"Jared Breaux," he said.

"Ted Kelly," my father replied.

Jared paused, a fleeting look of confusion on his face.

"Oh, uh, Audrey uses her mother's last name, Stevenson," Dad explained. "We divorced when she was a kid, and..." He trailed off, looking to me for guidance.

Jared nodded. I was frozen, my tongue cemented to the roof of my mouth. Oh God, what if he Googled my name using Kelly instead of Stevenson? I had avoided the Internet like the plague, refusing to see what was linked to my prior infamy. I flicked my head to the side, struggling to push those thoughts away.

I picked up my purse from the table next to the front door, but apparently Dad wasn't done yet.

"So, Jared. I hear you're in the shrimping business."

"Yes, sir. My brother and I own two boats. We run them four to five months out of the year."

"Four or five months?"

"Yes, sir—the season differs a bit from year to year."

"That must leave you with a lot of free time."

Here we go, I thought. Dad was moving in for the kill.

"Yes, sir, it could, but I'm also a carpenter, so I keep fairly busy in the off season."

"Commercial construction or residential?"

"Residential, Mr. Kelly. I do mostly finish carpentry—cabinets, furniture, and such. But I've done just about all aspects of home construction as well."

I was impressed with Jared's responses. He seemed relaxed and confident. He didn't have that cocky coolness that James had.

"Ah. Maybe you could build me a bar cabinet. I always wanted one of those," Dad said with a half smile. He was teasing Jared but testing him as well.

"Sure, Mr. Kelly. I could do that."

I jumped in before Dad could start drawing up plans and haul Jared down to the tool shed. "Well, we better get going. Bye, Dad." I leaned in to kiss his cheek.

Dad raised one hand in a half salute as Jared followed me out the front door. I sucked in a great lungful of moist, woodsy air as I headed down the stairs. Once we hit the driveway, Jared stepped forward to open the truck's passenger door for me. I used the running board to boost myself in. The seats were leather, the interior plush. The cab still had that wonderful new-car smell.

Jared hopped behind the wheel and started the truck. The diesel engine let out a deep rumble. Soon we were crossing the Bay Bridge heading east.

"Your truck is really nice," I said.

"Thanks. I got it about six months back. I needed something big enough to tow the boat."

"The boat we went in on Saturday or your shrimping boat?"

He grinned. "No, the shrimping boats don't come out of the water. They're pretty much in there to stay."

"Oh." I suddenly felt dumb. I pictured his truck pulling a huge ship. It seemed cartoonish.

Jared drove like he'd been doing it his whole life, his left wrist resting on the top of the steering wheel, looking from me to the road as he spoke. His right arm relaxed on the seat's armrest. I took in his denim-clad thighs and long legs and listened as he pointed out certain homes where people he knew lived.

"You like seafood, right?" he asked.

"I love it," I said.

"Great." He grinned. "Then you'll love Shaggy's."

We pulled into Pass Christian and into the parking lot by the harbor, where a small restaurant perched high above the ground. I was halfway out of the truck before I realized Jared had hurried around to open the door for me. Walking into the restaurant, he held the door open for me. Boy, I could get used to this princess treatment.

Shaggy's was a good-sized space with open windows on all sides and a huge fireplace in the center. A middle-aged waitress with burgundy hair approached us. "Hey, Jerry! How you doin', sweetie?" She leaned in for a kiss on the cheek.

"Hey, Trudy," Jared said. "This is Audrey. She's never been to Shaggy's before, and this is our first date, so I'd appreciate it if you could make me seem really impressive, okay?"

Trudy cackled like a crow. "Sure, honey! We won't tell her that you usually stink like fish and pick your nose at the table!" She continued to laugh as she led us to the outdoor dining area.

"That's Trudy," he said, grinning. "Always in my corner."

I smiled back, loving the way Jared enjoyed her ribbing. As we followed Trudy to the deck, he put his hand on the small of my back, gently guiding me through the tables.

"We can eat inside if you prefer," he said.

"No, it's pretty out here," I said as I looked out over the water. It was just beginning to turn pink and orange in the setting sun.

Trudy gave us the best table on the deck—a corner spot with a panoramic view of the gulf. She handed us menus and Jared ordered a beer. She turned to me.

"You want to try the Rasta punch, hon?"

Before I could answer, Jared spoke up. "She's not twenty-one, Trudy."

"Robbing the cradle, are we, Jerry?"

"Don't make me feel old, Tru."

"I'm just playing with you!" She laughed, shaking his shoulder with one hand.

"Yeah, yeah, yeah. Just get the poor thing a drink, you harassing gypsy."

Trudy turned to me, looking infinitely pleased with herself. "I'll bring you the punch—virgin, of course." She walked off still smiling.

"She's like a second mom to me." Jared leaned forward. "I come here a lot with my brother and the crew, and Trudy's kind of adopted us."

I looked out to the harbor, at all the boat slips. There were a few huge shrimping boats with tangle-looking spires off in the distance. "So you guys come here to eat after you've shrimped for the day?"

"For the week, actually. We go out for a few days at a time. I'll be out again from Thursday until Saturday. I was glad you agreed to come out tonight, since I'll be working all weekend."

I smiled, thrilled that he wanted to go out with me as much as I wanted to date him.

I studied the menu, unable to decide whether to order the wasabi seared tuna or the southern-style barbeque shrimp. Before I could make a decision, Trudy was back with our drinks. She placed a bright-yellow plastic cup in front of me and set a tall cup in front of Jared.

"Your drink is on the house," she said. "To commemorate your first meal at Shaggy's." She leaned forward, holding her hand near her mouth. "And to wish you luck on your first date with Captain Morgan."

"Trudy!" Jared said.

Trudy's cackle was so loud several diners at nearby tables looked over to see what was so funny. "Now I've given you dinner conversation! No awkward silences here."

"Are you gonna take our orders or stand here embarrassing me all night? Jeez, I should have taken her to the Lookout."

Trudy sucked in an audible gasp. "Bite your tongue, Jared Breaux! There will be no blasphemy at this establishment."

I was still trying to figure out who Captain Morgan was when Trudy asked me what I'd like.

"Um, I'll try the wasabi seared tuna, please."

"Great choice, hon. Jared?"

"The blackened redfish, Tru."

She pinched Jared's cheek and off she went. Jared smiled, leaned back in his chair, and took a long swallow of his beer. I tried my drink. It was fruity and sweet.

"So who's Captain Morgan?"

Jared sighed deeply, leaning forward to rest an elbow on the table. "On my twenty-first birthday we had a big party here during one of their Reggae on the Roof celebrations. To make a long story short, I woke up cradling an empty bottle of Captain Morgan rum, wearing nothing but a Rasta hat and boxer briefs."

My mouth fell open. "Well, that's one way to celebrate the big two-one."

We laughed. The food arrived quickly and Trudy hurried off, as the restaurant was busy. My tuna was delicate, and the spicy seaweed salad was the perfect complement. Since I'd never tried Louisiana redfish or dirty rice, Jared insisted that I try a bite of each. In return I gave him a bite from my plate.

Our conversation flowed easily. I described Moss Ridge and my friends back home, surprised by how simple and good my life sounded. I told him about my aunt Tenni's shop and the beautiful painting she had given me.

Jared told me about all the fun he'd had growing up on the Gulf Coast, starting the business with his brother, and his passion for home restoration. He told me his plans for the continued expansion of his home. We talked about everything from hobbies to history, and he was happily surprised to hear that I loved Quentin Tarantino movies. He was a big fan too. We debated violence as an art form in film-making. I was surprised when I looked at my watch and it was nearly eight thirty.

Jared grabbed the bill Trudy had left, pulled out his wallet, and took out three twenties.

"Can I chip in for that?" I asked.

He looked up at me with a half grin. "No."

"Okay. I'll get the next one," I said.

"No you won't."

I hesitated, not sure if he meant we would never go Dutch or if there would not be further dates.

"I don't know how they do things in California," he went on, "but in Mississippi the man pays for the date." He smiled as he tucked his wallet back into his pocket. "It's a matter of pride and honor, don't you know."

"Well then, by all means," I said.

"C'mon, let's go downstairs and catch some music," he said. "No rum, I promise."

On the ground floor a live band was just warming up. We found two empty seats near the railing as they started playing. Jared leaned close to ask what I wanted to drink.

"A ginger ale," I said close to his ear, getting a whiff of his scent. He smelled like cinnamon and sun-warmed skin. I fought an urge to taste the skin on his neck just below his ear.

Jared passed the order on to a waitress, who returned with two ginger ales. Soon the band fired into an energetic, rockabilly version of an old country song. Jared pulled me to the dance floor. I panicked, my body stiff as sheetrock. I was feeble at dancing. Jared, on the other hand, had no such disability. With a firm hand on the small of my back and another grasping my hand, he led me into a rapid two-step that had me moving in ways I didn't know I could. I laughed as we twirled our way around the crowded floor.

By the time the song finished I felt giddy and out of breath. A slow song started and I leaned close to Jared, inhaling his scent as we moved on the dance floor. I gazed out at the harbor; the boats were rocking in the water, seeming to dance with us under the canopy of stars.

Once on the highway, Jared reached over to hold my hand. I liked the feel of his rough, warm hand in mine. We drove east for several minutes before he slowed the truck and pulled off to the left.

"There's the Friendship Oak," he said. "You've got the painting. Now you can see the real thing." He slowed further and parked the truck on a side street. This time I waited for him to open the door for me. We held hands as we walked. I could see the distant lights of the University of Southern Mississippi. Crickets whirred and chirped in the warm air, the only sound aside from the occasional car passing by on the highway.

We approached the enormous tree, its branches dipping to the ground. Once under the canopy I craned my neck to look up through the branches.

"Holy cow," I said as I took in the expanse. In the darkness the branches above us resembled a leafy ceiling. A few scattered lightning bugs glinted, flitting in and out of the hanging moss like living Christmas tree lights.

"The trunk is over eighteen feet in diameter," Jared said. "This tree has been here since before Christopher Columbus set foot in the New World."

He lifted my hand to his mouth and placed a feather-soft kiss on my knuckles. "Friends forever," he said.

"Friends forever," I replied.

He bent his head to mine, our lips touching and gently lingering. My world tilted. He broke the kiss, smiling and stroking my jaw line with his thumb.

"I'll be back in town to unload on Sunday. Are you up for a trip to New Orleans on Monday?"

"Yeah! I'd love it. I've always wanted to see the French Quarter and the Garden District."

"Okay, N'awlins it is."

Arriving home, I was relieved to see an empty porch—Dad was not waiting for me. Jared walked me up the stairs to the front door.

"Thank you for coming out with me," he said.

"Thank you for dinner and the dancing, and the tree was just… breathtaking."

And so was the kiss, I said in my head. He kissed my cheek, his warm breath brushing against my neck and ear, making me quiver.

"Good night."

"Night," I replied and stepped inside.

I watched from the kitchen window as he drove away, the truck's taillights flashing briefly at the end of the driveway.

I drifted around the house on the world's most plush cloud. Dad was on the living room couch, watching a basketball game. He turned to look at me over the back of the sofa.

"Hey, how was your date?"

"Dreamy," I said. It was the first word that popped into my head. Dad's expression was blank. He was probably trying to decide how much trouble this dreamy man was going to cause his only daughter.

29

Care Forgotten

My life took on a comfortable rhythm that week. A steady rain hit the coast and lasted for three days. I kept myself busy with light housework, shopping, and cooking simple meals for Dad and me. Aside from dealing with lecherous glances from Red whenever he and Jim stopped by the house, life was going swimmingly. I enjoyed my summer reading and kept up on my phone calls to Mom and e-mails with the old gang.

Lily called from Bruges with stories of castles, canals, and language barriers. She oozed enthusiasm, and I was truly happy for my friend's accomplishments in the world but when she asked about my new start, I felt reluctant to share. I didn't want any cross-contamination between my old and new lives. My existence in Mississippi was like a delicate glass ornament that I cradled in my hands, wary of anyone who might manhandle it.

So I limited my descriptions to geography, weather, and food. Before we hung up, Lily promised to come for a visit at the end of the year, and I agreed excitedly. I wasn't sure I really wanted her to, but I didn't want to hurt her feelings.

In those days I wasn't seeing Jessica too much; she was busy judging cheerleader tryouts at her school. As part of the senior squad, duties and practices ate up a good amount of her summer. We spoke or texted each other daily but didn't have plans to see each other until the Fourth of July at a barbeque at her house. Her whole family would be there; her parents even invited my dad. He was thrilled that he would get to scope out Jared's family. I was excited too but also anxious, with a healthy dash of dread mixed in.

As promised, Jared called on Sunday night after he returned from his three-day shrimping run. He told me about their excellent haul, and the sound of his deep, rich voice spread through me like warm honey. I couldn't wait for our trip to New Orleans.

On Monday we were on the interstate by eight, heading toward the City that Care Forgot. We managed to miss most of the commuter traffic until we crossed the bridge spanning Lake Pontchartrain. I listened to the steady thump thump thump of the tires as we crossed the vast length of it.

Our conversation during the past hour had been comfortable and easy. Jared was still cheery about his shrimping trip and explained to me that they always seemed to have the best luck on rainy runs— something about the sea churning up the shrimp.

Soon he was navigating his way through the heavy traffic of the city, following his own internal compass. He drove up an overpass and then under and around high walls. I was hopelessly disoriented by the time we parked on a gravel patch near a railroad track.

Equipped with my camera and sunglasses, I hopped out. We left the truck there and walked a short distance to an extensive park. Beyond it was the most beautiful church I had ever seen.

"That's Saint Louis Cathedral," Jared said. "We're standing in Jackson Square."

I admired the park with its grand oak trees, royal palms, and abundance of flowers. I snapped a few pictures of the cathedral, pushing aside my embarrassment of acting like a typical camera-happy tourist. Jared was relaxed and patient; he didn't seem to mind the photo delay a bit.

"Smile!" I clicked a picture of him with the cathedral in the background. He gave a small smile and looked like a rugged male model. When I was done he snapped a few photos of me.

We held hands and walked to the far side of the park to find the mule-drawn carriages. We stood in a short line behind a family of four and another couple. I read the ticket prices while we waited and was a bit taken aback, though I knew it would do no good to say anything to Jared. He'd already made it clear that he would take the lead in all financial aspects of our relationship. How did I feel about that? Well, I liked it. My mother had always harped on me about being independent and able to support myself, yet it felt really great to be taken care of by a man. Was that wrong?

When we reached the head of the line, Jared bought tickets. We climbed into an open-air carriage and settled onto its comfortable leather seats. The mule pulling our carriage was a beautiful, gleaming fawn color with a palomino gold mane and tail. A bright-pink plume jutted from her halter.

Our driver looked cruise-ship ready in his Hawaiian shirt, Bermuda shorts, and baseball cap. He swiveled on his perch above us and smiled. "Hey there! Do we have ourselves a couple of honeymooners here?"

My face flushed scarlet. Jared laughed softly. "No, man, just a second date."

"Second date?" he said. "Well shoot and Shinola, you kids look like you were made for each other. Why, I'll probably be couriering you two away from this church after y'alls' wedding in a year or two."

I thought I might just die. I had a momentary vision of pulling the driver's cap off his head and cramming it into his mouth. Jared looked over at me, saw the embarrassment on my face, and cracked up. My distress melted away.

Jared turned back to him. "Get going, you coot, before you lose your tip!"

The driver turned forward and snapped the reins. "Ha!" he shouted, and off we went, bells jingling as if it were Christmas Eve. "My name's Benny, folks. I'll be telling you lots of fun facts about The Big Easy today, but just pipe right up if you have any questions. In fact, I bet I know the answer to any question you can think up about our fair town and its history."

Jared rested his arm on the seat back, relaxed and calm. I tried to take in everything around me at once. The cornflower-blue sky was dotted with downy white clouds, giving us intermittent shade and sun. A soft breeze ruffled my hair as we traveled down narrow streets lined with wrought-iron balconies and colorful awnings. Flags fluttered in the warm breeze as we passed hotels and shops.

Benny kept up a continuous monologue about the city's long history. It was one of the oldest in America. We passed a building with a wooden sign hanging out front in the shape of a bicorn hat, and Benny told us that the top floor was once a refuge for Napoleon Bonaparte. He pointed out sunburst ornaments on many of the buildings, tributes to Louis XIV, the Sun King.

We passed a cemetery that was like nothing I had ever seen

outside of the movies. Huge crypts, stone angels, and spires stretching high into the air. For the first time I understood why so many vampire novels were set in New Orleans. The city was so different, so old and European yet vibrant and unique at the same time. I couldn't help but compare it to the towering glass and endless stucco sprawl of Los Angeles. The cities were truly a world apart.

Benny pulled the carriage to a stop in front of Café Du Monde. "Okay, folks, we'll do a fifteen-minute break here."

Jared stepped down from the carriage and offered his hand to help me. Benny pointed out a table on the patio that was reserved for his tour company.

"You drink coffee, Audrey?" Jared asked.

"Does a bear—" I stopped. "Yes, I adore coffee."

He ordered us two cafés au lait and something called beignets. While we waited I went on and on about how much I loved the city, and in fact the whole Gulf Coast. "I mean, it's so different than I thought it was going to be."

Jared smiled, his copper eyes intent on mine. "Did you think it was going to be all swamps and rednecks?"

"Yeah, I did. I really had no idea what life was like down here. It makes me feel so stupid—like I've been living in a bubble."

"You're not stupid, Audrey. You sound like a college graduate when you talk, or like one of those chicks on the evening news. Sometimes I forget how young you are. You don't seem like a seventeen-year-old."

"Almost eighteen," I said. "Thanks for saying that. But why do you think I sound like a news reporter?" I worried that he thought I sounded like I was reading a teleprompter.

"Mmm, just the words you use, I guess. You've got a larger vocabulary than most people I know. And your accent sounds so prim and proper."

"I don't have an accent!" I said, laughing. "You do!"

"Well, whatever—regional dialect, if you like." He waved his hand.

"Ohhh, now who's got the big vocabulary?"

Jared laughed and leaned forward to thump my nose lightly.

Our waiter returned with two oversized mugs, both topped with foam, and a plateful of what appeared to be flour.

"What's that?" I asked, pointing to it.

"Those, my dear, are beignets," Jared answered. "A treat you won't soon forget." He plucked a small ball of fried dough from the powder. He tapped some of the dust off and took a bite. I followed suit and bit in, closing my eyes and enjoying the rich, sweet flavor and crisp texture.

"Mmmm. These are delicious," I said as I wiped powdered sugar from my lips and fingers.

We enjoyed our coffee and beignets until it was time to get back in our carriage. We rode down more streets, past a brewery, a slew of bars, jazz clubs, and even a voodoo shop. I took dozens of pictures and listened to Benny's descriptions of the madness of Mardi Gras. We rode along the Mississippi River at a quick trot. Old-fashioned paddle steamers churned past huge cargo ships going the opposite way upriver.

We reached the Garden District, with its stately neoclassical and Greek revival homes and tree-lined streets. We passed houses belonging to musician Harry Connick, Jr. and Anne Rice, one of my favorite writers. Our tour ended on Saint Charles Avenue, near a stop on the streetcar line.

Benny turned to us as he set the carriage break. "I hope y'all enjoyed your tour today. Now don't you forget my wedding invitation when the time comes."

I rolled my eyes at him, no longer embarrassed by his taunting. We climbed out of the carriage. Jared shook Benny's hand, thanked him for the nice ride and handed him a twenty. I silently tallied our spending on this date—over one hundred dollars already and we hadn't even had lunch yet.

We set off down the shady street, heading for a Creole restaurant that was a favorite of Jared's. My eyes trailing over the many flower gardens and my hand in Jared's warm clasp, I marveled at the sensation of falling in love with both a city and a man.

30

Jared's House

Saturday arrived in a blaze of hot sun. Jared picked me up for a swim and for a jambalaya dinner he had promised to cook. I had offered to drive to his house, but ever the gentleman, he had insisted on picking me up.

It was a short ride from Waveland to Jared's place in Pass Christian Isles. As soon as we crossed the Bay Bridge we made a left onto a winding, park-like street and then into the gravel drive of a country house set high up on pillars. We parked under the house. Once out of the truck, I looked around the spacious yard: banana trees, a few palms, and a large oak near the mailbox. Tall pine trees created a barrier between his property and the neighbor's. Jared's home was a stone's throw from the water.

He took my hand as we walked up the long, wide stairway to the open-air porch. A canopy strung with shrimp-shaped party lights covered a wooden table on one side. On the other was a cabana-style bar with stools. A second set of stairs lay just beyond that. I glanced over the rail and saw a pool surrounded by a deck down below.

"Nice!" I said.

"Thanks," he said. "It took me a year and two tries to get it right. I made the deck too small the first time and had to expand."

"You built this yourself?"

"Of course. I'm a carpenter after all. C'mon, I'll show you the house."

"Did you build that too?" I asked.

"Nah, just remodeled the shit out of it."

Jared unlocked the door and held it open for me. I stepped into a large, airy great room with a high, open ceiling. Tall windows dotted the walls, giving the room a light, bright feeling. A large fireplace lay to my left, and a dining area and kitchen were at the back. In the center of the kitchen was a large island with several barstools. The counters were gleaming black granite, and the appliances were all stainless steel. Jared's house had a clean, masculine feel to it.

I couldn't hide how impressed I was.

"Jared, this is a fan-flipping-tastic house!"

He gave me one of his thousand-watt smiles. "Thanks. It's been a labor of love."

"How did you... I mean... The house, the boat, your truck, your business..."

"How can I afford so much stuff at twenty-three?"

"Yes!" I said.

"My grandma passed six years ago—my mom's mom—and she left her money to me, Jack, and Jess. Lots of stocks and bonds that we sold in ninety-nine, when the market was through the roof. Jack and I combined our cash to buy the business from a guy we worked for during summers in high school. With my profits from that and my carpentry I bought the house and my truck. The boat is actually split three ways between me, Jack, and our dad."

"Sounds like you made a good investment."

"Psh. Tell that to my dad. He was so pissed when Jack dropped out of Tulane to become a shrimper. Then when I told him I wasn't going to college he just about had kittens. He's determined that Jess uses her money for school even if it kills him."

I moved closer to him. "Isn't your dad proud of you guys? I mean, your business is successful enough that you own a home and boat and stuff."

"Yeah, I guess he is. Don't get me wrong—my dad's a great guy. He helped me out with my deck, and sometimes he even goes out with us on the ship. He just wanted us to be like him, and it was hard for him to accept that we didn't want white-collar jobs."

I nodded, thinking how much my parents were counting on my following their chosen path: college and career.

"Did you make this?" I asked, walking over to a wall of book-shelves that sat behind a tired-looking sofa.

"Yep," he replied. "I made all the wood stuff."

I walked around the couch to examine the coffee table—plain, solid wood with an amazing grain. I ran my hand along its smooth surface.

"Can I see the rest of the house?" I asked.

"Yeah, sure."

My pulse raced as I walked into his bedroom, wondering if, like James, he would take advantage and make a move. But, ever the gentleman, Jared simply waited by the door while I looked at the pictures on top of his dresser. There was a snapshot of him and someone who must have been his brother, Jackson—they looked startlingly alike—shaking hands at the stem of a huge ship. "Whistler" was painted on the back of the ship in white lettering.

"Is this your brother?" I asked.

"Yeah, that's him. My partner, my buddy, and my pain in the ass."

"Why's that?"

"Nah, he's a good guy. We just like to bug each other every chance we get." He shrugged and ran a hand through his thick hair. I fought the urge to run my fingers through it as well.

"Why is the boat called Whistler?" I asked.

"Captain Rick named it a decade ago. It's his nickname. He's always whistling a tune."

"Ah." I walked back to the doorway.

"You wanna go for a swim now?" he asked.

"Yeah, sounds great."

I tried to push away the image of my first swim with James and what it had led to. On one hand I couldn't wait to get physical with Jared. On the other I was enjoying the old-fashioned romance. At the time I hadn't regretted the fast pace of my relationship with James, but now that I had a taste of letting things build, I realized what I had been missing. The conversation, the laughter, and the anticipation made everything that much sweeter.

We walked down to the pool. Adirondack chairs and loungers and two enormous sun umbrellas were spaced around the deck. I pulled off my white-cotton smock and stepped out of my navy-blue shorts and tossed them on a chair. I slipped off my sandals and jumped feet first into the pool, shooting down like an arrow and pushing off the bottom to resurface. Jared was cranking open an umbrella that was wedged into a large, Baja-style platform at the shallow end of the pool. I swam over to join him.

We lay in the shade for a good half hour, just talking: favorite foods, TV shows, books. Then we delved into sticky subjects like religion, politics, and world affairs and discovered that we could agree to disagree with no resentment. When we got into a debate over censorship, Jared put me in a playful headlock and gave me a noogie. I used the opportunity to wrap myself around his body like an octopus, pressing my chest against his. He grasped my face with both hands and kissed me.

I thought my brain might fry. All thoughts of taking it slow were gone, and I yearned for him to take me. I could feel the response of his body against my thigh, letting me know he felt the same.

"You're killing me, you know that?" he asked.

"Right back at you," I said, then leaned in to taste his neck.

I moaned as he cupped my breasts and squeezed gently, his thumbs fondling my hard nipples. Then he stopped, pulling away slightly to look into my eyes. "I want it to be special with us," he said seriously. "Not just a hookup."

"I want that too," I replied.

"I need... I don't have any... It's up in my room." His words were a tangle.

"I'm on the pill," I said. "I have no STDs, and I've been with only one person before."

He whispered into my ear. "I'm clean."

"Do it," I said, my eyes half closed against his wet face.

He didn't need any further urging. He pulled my top aside and devoured my breasts. I arched my back, pushing him to take more and more into his mouth. I reached down, feeling the hard length of him as I pulled at his swim trunks. He pushed aside my bikini bottom and slid into me. I raked my hands through his hair, and he gripped my buttocks, holding me firmly as he pushed with long, slow strokes. My head rolled back as waves of pleasure rocked me. He gasped as his pleasure met mine.

As if on cue, an explosion of thunder split the sky overhead, bringing us back to reality. We got out of the pool. Jared wrapped a towel around me, and we hurried back up the stairs and into the house. We spent the rest of the afternoon and early evening watching Reservoir Dogs and Pulp Fiction and enjoying the incredibly tasty shrimp jambalaya that Jared cooked. Outside, rain pelted the windows as we made love on the couch, in the bedroom, and on the kitchen floor. My flesh, heart, and mind seemed to align with the universe as I clasped my body to his, staring into his whiskey-and-slate eyes.

31

Crab Fest

I spent much of the following morning thinking about Jared's house. It needed a woman's touch—upholstery in seaside colors, a beach theme. I imagined us married, sharing the beautiful house, making it into a home.

Aunt Tenni was going with us to the Bay Saint Louis Crab Festival that day. Being July third, it was bound to be bustling. I was looking forward to the carnival but had a hard time taking my mind off the next day's barbeque at the Breaux family home. I wondered if Jessica would know that Jared and I had gone from dating to full-fledged couple.

I dressed and put on my new necklace—a gift from Jared after one of our marathon sessions in his bed. It had been dangling on the headboard. It was a chrome lug nut, about a half inch thick, hanging from a simple black cord. He said it was his lucky charm; it had fallen off a stripped gear on his boat and he had cancelled his outing that day to buy replacement parts. A squall had hit the area he would have been boating in, and two unlucky boaters had been lost at sea.

Aunt Tenni arrived fifteen minutes early, and off we went to the festival. We parked near her shop and made the short walk to the park where the carnival was. A Ferris wheel churned alongside the zipper, a topsy-turvy cylinder of spinning cages—a barf-tastic ride if ever there was one. We made a beeline for a cotton candy stand, where Tenni and I indulged and Dad looked bored. We walked slowly, looking at the game gallery, then spied a large tent where there was a beer tasting. That was the last we saw of Dad. He waved to us and disappeared inside.

Tenni and I continued on, stopping only for hush puppies, shrimp kabobs, and shaved ice. Eventually we came upon a gold-and-white striped tent with a sign out front with a large, blue hand on it.

"Oooh, let's get our palms read!" said Aunt Tenni. I hesitated, thinking about my tarot reading. It had foretold events both tragic and wonderful, and every bit had come to pass. Maybe I didn't want to know any more.

"Um… I don't want to, but I'll go with you while you do," I said.

"Okay," Tenni said. She poked her head in the tent's flap and called out, "Hellooo?"

"Please. Come in," a voice replied.

Inside the tent a woman—olive-skinned, a tangle of bushy, black hair—sat at a small table, a purple-silk scarf tied around her head like some kind of half-assed pirate. Strings of beads and baubles were draped around her neck. I pressed my lips in a tight line to keep from laughing out loud. I thought of the unpresumptuous Merry and imagined she could banish this creature with a twitch of her nose.

"Please, have a seat," the woman said, gesturing grandly with her hand. Tenni took the chair directly across from her; I sat behind her. "Please, I ask donation of twenty dollars for a reading for you."

She had a slight accent—Eastern European or perhaps Armenian. It was probably fake, for dramatic effect. Tenni quickly pulled a twenty out of her purse and held it out to the woman. She wouldn't touch it; she held out a silk pouch instead and instructed Tenni to place the twenty in there. That done, she laid her hands palms up on the table, directly in a shaft of sunlight that came in through an opening in the tent's ceiling. "Please. Place your hands palm up in mine."

Tenni obeyed. She looked expectant, like someone checking lotto numbers. The woman leaned forward to peer closely at her hands. She used her thumbs to trace the lines, examining her right palm and then the left.

"Your element is fire. You have had a very fortunate life. Your girdle of Venus and Apollo lines are quite defined." She pointed out each line in turn. "You have been successful in business but not so successful in love, yes?"

"You could say that," Tenni answered.

The woman stopped and looked over at me, her eyes narrowing. I froze. She turned back to Tenni's hands. "You keep yourself busy to hide that you are lonely. You have not found true love, no. You must make a change in your life. You have a travel line that is long and deep.

You must take the adventure and find your mate." She folded Tenni's hands together, squeezing them between her own.

"Now you," she said, gesturing to me.

"No, not me, thanks." I said.

She waved, an irritated look on her face, as if shooing a bothersome fly. "Yes, yes. You must. Phil tells me you must."

"Who?" I asked.

"Phil! Phil is my spirit guide. He is standing right behind you, impatient as a child waiting for cake."

Tenni and I glanced at each other. This woman was a couple of sandwiches short of a picnic. She saw our silent exchange and squirmed in her seat. "No charge. I give you for free. Please."

Not wanting to upset a possibly loopy woman further, I shrugged and switched seats with Tenni. I laid my hands palms up, and the woman placed her hands on the table.

"Hmmm… Yes, yes, yes, yes." She made noises as she ran her fingers over the lines of my hands. "You are in love. This love is good—it is a good match." She closed my palms together quickly. I thought it was a good thing she hadn't charged me, since her reading was so brief. I began to draw away, but she clenched my wrist to hold me there. I frowned, ready to tell her to let me go.

"Phil say you are in danger. He say you are hiding. He say you cannot hide in the attic."

I froze at her words, angry and scared simultaneously. "I'm not hiding from anybody," I said a bit too loudly, pulling my wrist from her grasp. I left the tent in three long strides, angry that this gypsy had made me feel vulnerable and dispelled the cloud of bliss I had been living on.

"Stay out of the attic!" she called after me. I didn't turn around.

Tenni had to trot to keep up with me. "Hey, Audrey, hey! Stop."

I stopped, crossing my arms over my chest.

"What is it, honey? What did she say that upset you?"

"How'd she know my room is in an attic?"

Tenni looked confused. Her brow creased. "An attic? Oh, your room! I forgot all about it being upstairs. Oh, honey, you can't let that silliness bother you. I should never have suggested getting our palms read. It's all my fault you're so upset."

I felt guilty. "No, Aunt Tenni, it's okay. She just spooked me is all." I gave her a hug and she hugged me hard in return.

"C'mon," she said, holding me at arm's length. "Let's go ride that vomit comet over there." She pointed to the zipper. "That'll get us rebooted!"

Tenni was right. Several terrifying revolutions on that sadistic ride were enough to chase my spooky feelings away. We rode the Ferris wheel twice, lost seven dollars trying to win a ridiculously huge teddy bear, then gave up and went in search of Dad. He was right where we'd left him, sipping beer in the air-conditioned tent. When we told him we were ready to leave he gave a last, longing look to the many glasses of beer lined up on the bar.

The three of us spent the rest of the afternoon and evening at home playing cards, eating pizza, and laughing at the stories Aunt Tenni told about the many ways she'd tortured little Teddy when they were growing up. My favorite was when she convinced him to suspend himself with bungee cords from a beam in the garage. She told him he could fly like Superman. Once he was up in place she removed his pants and then opened the garage door for all the kids walking home from school to see.

When Grandma Mae heard my dad screaming she ran out to the garage, saw him hanging with his pants around his ankles, and proceeded to pull him down and spank him. I laughed so hard my stomach ached. Chuckling and wiping his eyes, my Dad looked at me and pointed. "See? Aren't you glad you're an only child?" I nodded my head enthusiastically.

Later that night, as I lay in bed in the dark, I listened to the high-pitched whistles and bangs of fireworks being set off by kids too eager to wait until the next night. I thought about what Dad had said. For all the complaining he did about his sister and her mean tricks when they were kids, he had changed since their reunion here in Mississippi. He didn't seem as lonely as he had back in California. Their camaraderie seemed to rejuvenate him.

I also thought about what it would be like when I was forty-seven, the same age as my dad. I had no sibling to reminisce with. I fell asleep feeling a little bit sad.

32

Fireworks

The barbeque at the Breaux house didn't start until three, leaving me with most of the day to myself. Unable and unwilling to keep my new life secret any longer, I e-mailed a long letter to Kara and attached several photos of Jared and me on our New Orleans trip. Almost as soon as I sent it my phone rang, and it made me jump. I ran to my nightstand to grab it. Kara's smiling face glowed at me from the screen.

"Hi!" I said.

"What the fuck did you do to your hair?" she screamed.

"Oh yeah! I decided to go back to my natural color, and um, that's how it came out. Do you hate it?" I didn't really care if she did.

"No! Not at all, it's just…so different. You've been blond or blondish for so long, I just never pictured you with that shade. It looks really pretty."

I breathed a small sigh of relief. Maybe I did care what she thought.

"And Jared!" she went on, not waiting for my response. "Oh my God. He is masterful! Jeez, you always get the hunks. It's so not fair that you're getting all the demigods while I'm stuck with the scrawny gamers with fake online girlfriends!"

I laughed. "What about Tommy Martinez?"

Kara did a loud raspberry. "He took a trip down to Rosarito Beach and came back with a girlfriend named Sylvia."

"Oh, Kara, I'm so sorry."

"Don't be. He was a candy-ass. Every time I tried to get him to do it with me he would get all nervous and stuttery, saying it wasn't the right time or some shit like that."

"Maybe he's gay," I said.

"Maybe. So what about you and King Creole? Is he hot in the sack?"

"It's not polite to kiss and tell," I said, trying to keep the glee out of my voice.

"Yeah, right. Spill it, bitch."

"Let's just say he's a beast and I'm the prey."

Kara breathed out audibly. "Oh my. You are a lucky girl."

"Yes I am. Yes…I…am."

Four outfits, two hairstyles, and one deep-breathing exercise later, I was putting the cooler in the car. Dad had filled it with microbrewed beer he'd bought at the carnival as well as two bottles of wine. I'd added the Jell-O mold—in the shape of a flag, blueberries, strawberries, and whipped cream forming the stars and stripes—in a casserole dish on the top.

Getting into the car, I smoothed my navy-blue shorts to keep them from creasing. I had planned to wear a sundress or skirt—something that would look sweet to Jared's folks—but when I came downstairs and saw my Dad in his favorite Hawaiian shirt and Bermuda shorts, I ran back up to change into something more casual: the shorts and a white T with an American flag decal.

Once on the highway I directed Dad so he wouldn't miss the turnoff to Jessica's house. My pulse pounded in my neck as I spied it up ahead. Cars filled the front yard, but not nearly as many as on the night of Jessica's party. I saw Jared's and Billy's trucks. We pulled into the driveway and parked near the fence.

A group of people sat on the porch, and a middle-aged man stood at a grill, spatula in hand. By the time we were out of the car and ready to unload the trunk, Jared had come down the stairs to lend a hand. He shook hands with my dad and reached for the cooler.

"Hang on a sec," I said. I opened the cooler and took out my Jell-O creation.

Jared leaned close and whispered, "You look gorgeous." His breath on my neck gave me goose bumps. I smiled up at him, afraid to say anything Dad might overhear.

We followed Jared up the stairs. He set down the cooler and put my Jell-O on a table, then made the introductions.

"This is my mom, Julie, and my dad, David. This is Ted and

Audrey," he said. His parents looked like nice people. They stood side by side near the barbeque. David was the same height as Jared, with a lot of salt-and-pepper hair and deep laugh lines etched around his eyes. Julie was a full head shorter, with a plump build that reminded me of Aunt Tenni. Her eyes were the same as Jared's, deep amber with blue edging.

"How nice to meet you," Julie said, stepping forward to give me a hug. I hugged back, pleased by her friendliness.

David shook hands with Ted. "So, I hear you're the new plant manager out at Port Bienville. How you like it so far?"

"Well, there's a lot of work that needs to be done, but I guess I'm up for the challenge."

Julie shook Dad's hand and turned to her husband. "Now don't you talk shop all afternoon."

"Nag, nag, nag," he replied.

"You're burning the burgers, David."

Jared's dad spun around. Smoke billowed from the grill.

"Shoot!" He grabbed a beer and doused the burgers with it. There was a loud hiss and then a cloud of white steam.

"Now that's the way to make a perfect burger," my dad said. He opened our cooler, took out a beer, and tossed it to David. "A good marinade makes all the difference."

"That's the way!" David replied. He examined the beer's label. "Nice. You get this at the festival yesterday?"

"Yep. They've got quite a microbrewery."

David popped the top off with the handle of his spatula. He took a long pull and swallowed. "Ahhh. Not bad," he said, looking at the label again. "Not bad at all. Although it ain't Dixie."

"Hey, y'all, I'm Jack," said a voice behind me, and I turned to see Jared's brother. He shook Dad's hand and then mine. "You'll have to excuse my dad's taste. He's loyal to the core to Dixie beer, though it ain't much better than your average cutting-the-grass brew."

David pointed his spatula at Jackson. "You just mind your manners, boy, b'fore I have to take you out to the woodshed."

Jared and Jackson both burst out laughing. David pushed past them and grabbed a dark-brown, long-necked bottle from a tub of ice. "Here," he said, handing it to my dad. "That's Dixie Blackened Voodoo Lager, and there ain't a better beer in town."

Dad took it and admired the label for a moment before popping the cap.

Jared slung his arm over my shoulder. "They'll be talking beer all night long. C'mon. Jess and everybody else is out on the back patio."

We walked through the living room to the back deck.

"Hey!" Jessica said, standing up from her seat. She walked over and hugged me. "I like your shirt." She stepped back to admire the flag decal.

"Thanks," I replied. I waved to Kaitlyn and Josh, who sat nearby, and Randy, who sat on the deck railing just like he'd been that day at the Mud Hut. He flicked his hand in return, giving me a weak salute. He looked from me to Jared with a sullen expression on his face.

A very pretty girl with long, brown hair and a round face approached. Jack put his arm over her shoulder. "Audrey, this is my wife, Miranda."

"Hi," I said. I had forgotten Jack was married. He was only twenty-five, which seemed young. Maybe people got hitched at a younger age down here. Tenni was only eighteen when she'd married her husband...but then again, she was an eccentric hippie. Uncle Rex hadn't been much older than her at the time anyway.

"It's very nice to meet you, Audrey," Miranda said. "You're just as beautiful as Jerry said."

"Thank you," I replied, a little embarrassed. Jared looked even more embarrassed.

"C'mon over and sit down," Miranda said in her lovely, soft voice.

I sat in a comfortable patio chair at the table. Jared sat down next to me, one hand holding a beer, the other reaching for my fingers. He grasped them loosely and traced small circles on my thigh with his thumb.

Randy jumped down from his perch on the railing, looking agitated. "Josh, let's go get those bottle rockets from your truck. Don't need to be dark for those."

"'Kay," Josh said as he got up.

Randy gave me one last baleful look and then took the back stairs two at a time. I exchanged a silent look with Jessica. She shrugged, communicating what I already knew—that hurt feelings were inevitable. There was nothing to be done except give him time to get over it. Still, I was sad to think there would be no more mud-whomping rides with Randy in my future. He would never be satisfied just being friends.

Soon Julie was calling us to the front porch for chow—burgers, potato and macaroni salads, and boiled peanuts, which I'd never had. I took a little bit of everything. By the time I reached the end of the table, my plate was close to overflowing. I'd have to make a second trip for dessert, which included my Jell-O flag, apple pie, and homemade ice cream.

Dad stayed on the front porch to eat with Mr. and Mrs. Breaux, along with Jack and Miranda. The rest of us returned to the back deck. Randy and Josh ignored the food, instead shooting bottle rockets off the deck railing.

I bit in to my burger and groaned. The meat was juicy, with a hint of spice. "My gosh… Does everything in Mississippi just taste better?"

That got a laugh from everyone at the table.

"It does! Trust me," said Josh as he lifted his shirt, puffed out his stomach, and rubbed it.

By the time I was done, I was so full I had to refuse dessert. I regretted it when I saw Jessica returning to the table with a large slice of apple pie with a glob of ice cream melting over it. She also had a small square of my flag on her plate.

"That looks so good, Jess," I said.

"You have to try some later when you've got room. I made the pie myself from a recipe I learned in home ec. Our cooking class at Bay High is the best. The teacher is a real chef—Cordon Bleu alum and everything. I'm so bummed you won't be at Bay next year."

"Me too."

"Maybe you can switch. I mean, you're in the right area and all."

That gave me a spark of hope. Maybe I could switch and go to Bay with Jessica and Kate and the others. I'd have to ask Dad about it.

Randy and Josh finished off the bottle rockets and moved on to fizzing flowers. I gathered up paper plates and cans and headed into the kitchen to help clean up. Jared's mom was already at the sink, washing pots and pans and handing them off to Miranda for drying.

"Can I help?" I asked.

"Sure, honey," Julie said with a smile. "Can you gather up the rest of the food from the front porch for me?"

I did as she asked, making three trips to bring in the abundance of leftovers. She handed me a set of plastic containers so I could store the remainder of the food. I set to it.

"So, Audrey," Mrs. Breaux said, "Jared tells me you'll be eighteen in a couple of months."

"Yes ma'am."

"And you're at OLA for the year. What colleges are you applying to, dear?"

I hadn't applied to any colleges yet—I hadn't even taken the SAT. My chest tightened at the thought of the enormous tasks that awaited me in the next few months. Couldn't the summer just last forever? Nothing to do but go boating with Jared and have fun?

"My dad wants me to apply to Tulane, Loyola, and maybe Duke. My mom wants me to go to UCLA or USC…maybe Pepperdine."

"Ahh. So your daddy wants you in the South, and your momma wants you back on the West Coast. That's a difficult situation you're in," she said. "What do you want to do?"

Both Mrs. Breaux and Miranda had stopped doing dishes and were waiting for my answer. I looked down at the floor, really thinking hard about what I wanted to do. I'd been thinking of nothing else for the past few weeks, but I hadn't faced the question head on until now. I missed my friends back in California, and I missed my mom more than I ever thought I would, but did I want to go back? The answer was simple: not yet.

"I think I'll apply in both areas just to make my folks happy and see where I get accepted, but I'm pretty sure I want to stay here, at Tulane or USM."

Mrs. Breaux looked pleased. "That sounds like a good plan." She turned back to the sink to finish up the empty bowls. "And your people. Where were they during the War of Northern Aggression?"

Jared had warned me about this question. It had taken him an hour to explain what the Daughters of the Confederacy were and how proud his mother was to be one. She didn't have a racist bone in her body; she just took pride in her heritage and the honor and dignity of her people fighting for their home state. I wasn't sure I understood, but I was grateful that he had prepared me in advance.

"My mother's family was from Texas. They served in the cavalry—for the South," I said. "My dad's family was in Virginia, and I believe he has ancestors who fought on both sides."

"Mmmm, a true brother against brother then. I'm pleased you're aware of your family's history. So many young people these days don't know and don't care."

I smiled, quietly thrilled that I had met her approval.

The sunset was nearly done, a blazing display of red and pink, as our group piled into the Breauxs' boat. Miranda stayed behind for fear of motion sickness—as I learned, she was expecting a baby in six months. I asked Jared if he was excited about becoming an uncle.

"Yeah, that'll be cool," he said.

Everyone sat hip to hip on the boat. Jessica, Kate, and I took our previous seats at the front, and Jared piloted us slowly through the curving bayou and out onto the Jourdan River. We joined the flow of boats making their way into the bay for the fireworks show put on by the local casino. We dropped anchor near the bridge and waited for full dark.

Josh talked about shooting off more of the fireworks he'd brought, but Mr. Breaux threatened him with death if he used his boat as a launching platform. Dad seemed to get along great with Mr. Breaux; they never seemed to run out of things to talk about, from the mechanics of running a manufacturing plant to football, NASCAR, and local property values. I was happy and relieved that Dad seemed to like the Breauxs so much.

Just after nine the first brilliant sparkles lit the air with a burst of red and blue, followed by an enormous, concussive boom. I joined Jared at the rear of the boat, leaning back against his chest as we both gazed up at the dazzling show. He wrapped his arms around my waist, nestling me close against his body. I tilted my head back against his shoulder and felt his lips graze my ear.

He whispered, "I love you."

Fireworks ignited in my soul, and I snuggled deeper into his warm embrace.

33

Dispute With Dad

The next few days had me confined indoors while a storm raged along the coast. Dad was always watching the Weather Channel to catch the latest updates on what was brewing. It seemed like one tropical storm or hurricane after another, but they always veered north or slanted south as they tore their way across the gulf.

Jared took advantage of the downtime to catch up on building furniture in his shop at home. In less than a week he delivered the liquor cabinet my dad had requested. It was beautifully crafted out of cherrywood, and Dad was hugely impressed with it although he tried not to let it show too much. It was undeniably the finest piece of furniture we had.

Aside from the lousy weather, the days and weeks following the Fourth of July were full of happiness for me. On the odd sunny days Jared and I took boat trips to the Barrier Islands and road trips to the aquarium and zoo in the city. On rainy days we spent hours talking, laughing, and making love.

Dad and I made the ten-mile drive north to Aunt Tenni's house at least once a week for one of her unique dinners. She was always trying out new recipes she found on the Internet. Some, like the tamale pie, were great successes; others, like the chipped beef on toast, didn't quite measure up. She always let me feed the two goats that roamed her fenced-in side yard, which stretched from the road back to the Jourdan River behind her property.

One day Aunt Tenni took me to a salvage shop to buy a sofa for my room. We settled on a futon-style loveseat that could fit up the narrow attic stairway. And Jared ran cable up to my room for a TV and then surprised me with a twenty-seven-inch flat screen. I showered his face with kisses; my dad looked embarrassed and left. Once Dad was safely downstairs I resumed kissing Jared until we were both out of breath. Dad never said a word about the razor burn I frequently sported on my face.

As the end of July approached and the beginning of the school year loomed, my bubble of bliss was ruthlessly popped. Dad and I were scheduled for a campus tour, and I had not yet told him about my desire to switch schools. I'd been so preoccupied with my social life I had simply pushed it to the back burner of my brain. But the tour was three days away; I couldn't delay it any longer. I made our usual Sunday breakfast—French toast and sausage—and served it on the screened-in porch. I waited until he'd had a chance to finish his coffee before I made my request.

"Dad?"

"Hmm?" he said, his cup cradled in his hands as he stared out at nothing in particular.

"What do you think about me maybe going to Bay High instead of Our Lady?"

His face said it all. His arms slumped into his lap. "What—the—hell—are—you—talking—about?"

"Well, it's just, you know..." I struggled to find the right words and to stop my panicking brain. "I've made some really great friends, and they all go to Bay. It would be so much easier for me to fit in there."

His face remained stony. "You can see your friends after school and on the weekends."

"Daaaad." I couldn't keep the whine out of my voice. "It's not the same. I'm not going to know anybody at Our Lady. Pleeease?"

He stood up and walked to the edge of the porch, running his hands through his thin hair. "Do you have any idea how many strings I had to pull to get you into that school? They don't accept new students as seniors. I busted my ass to get you into the best college prep in the area, and now you want to just toss it all away so you can be with your friends!"

He paced, shooting irritated glances at me and waving his hands as he spoke. "When's it enough, Audrey? You've got your own car, a five-hundred-dollar-a-month allowance, a boyfriend who takes you boating and buys you expensive gifts..."

I had been slouched in my seat, feeling intensely guilty, but his last sentence cut through me like a knife. I stood up, mad as hell.

"My five-hundred-dollar allowance, as you call it, pays for gas, insurance, and groceries every month! I never have more than a few bucks left at month's end! And if you want your stupid car back, then take it!"

"Oh that's easy for you to say, since you've got Jared to chauffer you around."

"Are you jealous, Dad? Are you upset that I have someone who loves me and who I love back while you're alone? That's your choice, not mine."

For a few terrible seconds I thought he was going to hit me. His face was a terrific shade of red, and his fists were clenched. He turned, stormed through the front door, then stormed back out with his keys and wallet. I stood on the porch as he got in his truck and sped out of the driveway.

I stormed up to my room, leaving the dishes untouched. Curling up on my bed, I was too mad to cry and just stewed in my own bitter juices until I finally fell asleep.

When I woke up it was after one, and I was thirsty and hungry. I walked to my window and looked down at the driveway. Dad's truck was back, parked in its usual spot. I went downstairs and looked around cautiously. The kitchen was clean; all the breakfast mess had been cleared away. I grabbed a glass from the cabinet and filled it from the dispenser on the refrigerator. The water was cold, and I gulped it down.

En route to the bathroom I saw Dad in his office, sitting in his chair, looking tired. I leaned against the doorway, the half-empty glass in my hand.

"Dad, I'm sorry about what I said. I'll go to OLA. It's just one year anyway."

He let out a long sigh, staring down at the floor. "I'm sorry too, Audrey," he said. He looked up at me. "I had no right to badger you about your money or your boyfriend. I was just mad and disappointed that you want to switch schools. The car is yours—I gave it to you, and you're right—you pay for all the costs associated with it anyway."

I nodded, accepting his apology. "I was thinking maybe I should get a job. Jared's out of town four or five days a week anyway, so I might as well do something productive with my time. Then I could make payments on the car and start saving for college next year."

"Audrey, no. That's the last thing you need to do right now. This summer was supposed to be a break for you, and this year you'll need to focus on your studies. You don't need to spread yourself too thin by putting in hours at a minimum-wage job. I wouldn't take payments on the car anyway—I told you, it's yours. As for college, your mom and I have been saving for that since you were five. If that fund runs dry, then we'll get a good loan."

"Okay." I knew that arguing would only get him agitated again. He had backtracked on all of his comments, but I wondered if he realized that I would always feel uncomfortable about taking money from him. I would feel just a little guilty whenever Jared picked me up for a date or gave me a gift. Dad's words had cut deep, just as I was sure mine had.

Dad and I took our campus tour at OLA and met the senior coun-selor, Mr. DeLisle. He was a very nice gentleman who made me feel comfortable—even though he knew the grisly details of what had happened at my prom and my troubles with being bullied, he had the good grace not to ask me about any of it. He did talk about the school's rules of conduct and its new zero-tolerance policy concerning student harassment, defamation of character, and violence. Well, that was one way to word it. Sure sounded better than bullying.

Jared picked me up that afternoon for a lunch he'd been promising me at the Fire Dog Saloon in Old Town. We stopped by for a quick visit with Aunt Tenni at her shop and then walked along the shoreline until we reached the pub. The place was full—it was lunch hour. As we looked around for an empty booth, a voice called out, "Hey, Jerry! Getchya ass ovah heah!"

The voice belonged to a man who looked like he'd just left a Jimmy Buffet concert. He wore a Hawaiian shirt with colors so bright they were practically glowing. He had a scraggly beard and a long, dirty-blond ponytail that was turning gray. On his feet he wore flip-flops that looked like they'd seen better days back in the 1970s.

Jared looked over, his face lighting up like a kid who just spotted Santa Claus on summer vacation. "Hey, Rick! How you doing, man?" He pulled me by the hand until we reached Rick's perch at the bar.

The two of them exchanged quick man-hugs. So this was the famous Captain Rick.

Jared put his arm over my shoulder, pulling me forward. "Rick, this is my girlfriend, Audrey."

"Hi," I said with a wave of my hand.

"You got yourself a new girlfriend, Jerry? She's a beauty. Way prettier than that other girl you were seeing last summer."

I laughed, not sure how to react to this crazy-looking pirate.

"Yep. She's a keeper!" Jared said. It surprised me.

We sat down next to Rick and ordered lunch. They both had oyster shooters and calamari rings while I enjoyed a salad topped with Cajun blackened shrimp. While we ate, Captain Rick told some stories about training the greenhorn Breaux brothers and how he was sure one or both would lose some fingers while learning to shrimp. Before we left the Fire Dog, Rick insisted we go to his house the next day for a barbeque.

Outside, Jared leaned close and asked, "Is it okay that I said yes?"

"Yeah," I answered. "I like him. He's crazy."

"You have no idea," Jared replied.

34

Captain Rick

Captain Rick lived at the far end of a neighborhood known as Shore-line Park, and I knew which house was his before Jared pointed it out. It was big, two stories, and made of concrete blocks painted a deep nautical blue. Bright-white storm shutters framed each window, and on the wall in the middle of second story was an enormous ship's wheel. Life preservers hung along the white-wood railing of the front porch, some with ship names on them. Others simply said "Welcome Aboard."

As we got out of the truck, Rick stuck his head out an open window on the second floor. "Hey! Come on in—the door's open."

Jared led the way. Inside the house, nautical tchotchkes covered the walls—shark jawbones, "No Swimming" signs, spyglasses, row-boat oars, Jolly Rogers, and pirate swords. Rick came clomping down the stairs, his bare feet making slapping sounds as he went.

"Hey, man," he said to Jared as they shook hands. He turned to me with a big smile. "Beautiful, bodacious Audrey," he said as he hugged me.

"Hey, get your hands off my girl, you old pirate," Jared said with a grin.

Rick put his fists on his hips. "I will admire beauty where I find it."

"Admire all you want—just keep your hands off," Jared said. He laughed and pulled me against him. I laughed at the two of them.

Rick raised his hands. "Welcome to Whistler Cove, Audrey my dear!"

He led me around the first floor. "Now, I know it's a bit dark down here," he said, "but that's because I built this house to withstand a Camille-style hurricane." He crossed himself.

"What's Camille-style?" I asked.

Rick stopped dead in his tracks. He looked at me like I was some sort of circus freak. Then he turned to Jared. "Do you mean to tell me this girl doesn't know about Hurricane Camille?"

A light bulb clicked on over my head. "Oh yeah! That was the one that hit back in the fifties, right?"

"Nineteen sixty-nine, young miss. It was only the strongest Atlantic hurricane on record, and the bitch's eye came right up the bay not five miles from where you're standing." He shook himself. "I built this house in nineteen seventy-seven, and I built it to withstand any more Camilles that might come this way. It's got eighteen-inch-thick, rebar-reinforced concrete walls. This baby ain't going nowhere." He patted the wall with his hand.

"Your house is fantastic, Rick," I said. "A home worthy of the most prestigious pirate!"

He gave me another hug. I looked at Jared to see if he would complain again, but I stopped. An ear-piercing squawk made me jump.

"Ah, shut up, you jealous wench!" Rick went to a large birdcage on a stand in the family room. In it was a green bird as big as a cat, with long, bright-blue tail feathers and a spot of brilliant red just above its beak. Rick opened the cage and put in his arm, and the bird climbed on it. He whispered and rubbed the bird as he brought her over to us.

"This is Maggie," he said. "She's an eight-year-old military macaw. I've had her since she was a baby."

Maggie turned her head to stare at me with one eye and held one foot in the air, reaching it toward me.

"She wants you to hold her," Rick said, bringing her closer. I stepped back, feeling nervous. "It's okay, she's gentle, and smart as a three-year-old." He sounded proud of her. "Just hold your arm out like this." He held his arm out, bent at the elbow.

I did as instructed, and Maggie stepped nimbly onto my arm. She walked to my elbow and reached toward my necklace. She took the chrome nut in her beak and chewed on it. I giggled as she worked the necklace back and forth, trying to pull it from my neck.

Rick stepped forward and took her back. "Now Maggie, that's not for you," he said. He took her back to her cage and she climbed on top of it.

"Not for you, Maggie," the bird repeated in a high singsong.

Rick went to the fridge in the kitchen, pulled out a bag of chopped vegetables, and filled Maggie's bowl in her cage. She happily began munching away.

"That's so cool that she talks!" I said. "How many words can she say?"

"Oh, about fifty or so. And she's really good at screeching. Even the neighbors can hear her when she does her kraaaak in the mornings." Rick did an amazingly accurate mimic of the bird's squawk.

"Well, that's the tour. Where's my nickel?" he asked. Jared gave him a soft kick on the rear end. Rick laughed and gestured for us to follow him out the side door of the kitchen. A long stairway led down to a covered patio at the rear of the house. Rick had a complete outdoor kitchen set up on the concrete, complete with cabinets and a small refrigerator. He fired up the barbeque and retrieved skewered shrimp and pineapple from the fridge. He placed them on the barbeque to cook.

When the food was done, Jared and I carried it to a gazebo at the edge of the bulkhead; Rick followed with two steel buckets of ice and beer. The three of us sat in the shade and watched the sunset while Rick told more stories about his early days—all his shrimping, partying, and whoring around.

After we ate, Rick went upstairs and got Maggie. She climbed over everything and everyone until she settled herself on the railing near Rick's shoulder. He'd saved a few pieces of pineapple and fed them to her one by one.

When we left in the evening, I kissed both Rick and Maggie on the cheek.

Jared and I arrived at my house just after ten. He parked near the end of the driveway, behind a large oak so my dad couldn't see us from the house, and Jared kissed my lips, my ears, and my neck.

"We should have stopped by your house before you brought me home," I said as he kissed his way up my jaw line.

"I know," he said, "but your dad's gonna get pissed if you start missing curfew."

I sighed. He was right. I mustered my willpower to full force and pushed him away with both hands. My fingers found the silky tuft of hair just behind his shirt collar. "I've got to get out of this cab right now or I'm not going to be able to control myself."

His teeth flashed in the dim shadows of the truck's cab. "I like the sound of that." He laughed and grabbed my waist, pulling until he was half on top of me, tickling me until I squealed. His hands became entangled in my hair as he kissed me again.

The house's floodlights came on, casting harsh light down the driveway. We scrambled upright, quickly fixing our clothing, which had come askew. We got out of the truck and walked to the house, looking like children who'd been caught with our hands in the candy jar.

"Are you coming over tomorrow?" I asked, not daring to stand too close for fear of an uncontrollable make-out session.

"Yeah, but I've got to wash my truck. It's a disgrace."

"But it's going to rain tomorrow," I said.

"Perfect. The soft water will do the rinsing for me."

"Can you wash mine too?" A mischievous grin spread across my face.

He put his arms around my waist, and I pressed my hands against his chest, only vaguely worried about what my dad would see. He was probably peeking out the kitchen window.

"You wear your pink-and-white bikini and I'll wash you and the car."

35

Emerging Skeletons

The next afternoon the air was still and hot as a furnace. A line of thunderheads in the west loomed like gray dust preceding an army's approach. If the rain didn't arrive soon we would end up having to use the hose after all.

I changed into my bikini, slipped on my flip-flops, and headed downstairs to scrounge up buckets, sponges, and old towels in the utility room. I grabbed Dad's portable stereo out of the shop, set it on the bottom stair, and tuned in to the local rock station. Gwen Stefani's "Cool" played as I filled the bucket with soap and added water from the hose.

I was swinging my hips and singing along when Jared pulled up in his Ram. He cut the engine and climbed out with a huge grin on his face.

"Hey," I told him, "you better lose the shirt pretty quick or it's gonna get wet." I gave him a quick squirt with the hose.

"Ay!" he yelled, laughing and running forward to scoop me up and swing me around. I dropped the hose. "I've got bad news," he said, still holding me in his arms. He kissed my nose.

"Lemme guess. You're going to sit in a lawn chair and drink beer while I wash both cars."

"No, but that's a damn good idea." He laughed. "I've got to run over to Jack's and help him move the bed out of his guest bedroom—I mean the nursery. Miranda wants to paint, and Jack refuses to let her move any of the furniture in her delicate condition."

"But he's going to let her paint and inhale all those fumes?"

"Nah, she's got this fancy-schmancy eco-friendly stuff that cost a fortune and is guaranteed not to kill any brain cells. Nothing too expensive for Cletus the Fetus."

He set me back on my feet. "Excuse me?" I asked. "Please tell me they're not naming the baby Cletus."

"That's just what I call the little walnut. Besides, Jack has to keep our J-name streak going. We've got Jack's all the way back to Stonewall Jackson, so the legend goes. But don't worry, babe—when we have our kids, you can name them whatever you want."

"Shut up," I said, hitting him lightly on the arm, trying to hide the little thrill his words sent through me.

"I'll be gone an hour, tops." He wrapped me up in another bear hug, lifting me off my feet and kissing me before returning me to earth.

"Oh, okay. I guess I can't be selfish and keep you all to myself. But be forewarned—I won't be washing your truck and my car."

He gave me a last, long look from my toes to my eyes. "I can't believe I have to leave this heavenly body to do some heavy lifting."

"Yeah, yeah, yeah. Get going before Miranda's hormones kick in and she decides to flail you."

He climbed back into his truck, gave me a wave, and honked the horn as he left. Thunder rumbled in the distance, but the clouds still hadn't moved closer. Maybe the storm would only skirt the gulf after all and leave us dry.

A Coldplay song came on the radio as I set to hosing down the Malibu. I'd finished soaping the majority of the car when Dad pulled up in his work truck, followed by Jim and Red in their trucks. My neck stiffened unpleasantly at the sight of him. I watched as the three men climbed out of their vehicles.

Dad approached, looking a little guilty. "Hi, honey. I invited the guys over to watch the fight tonight. Don't worry about dinner. I'll order some pizzas."

"Okay," I said, thinking that after we finished with the cars, Jared and I would go hang out at his place.

Dad gave me a quick pinch on the chin, then he and Jim headed up the stairs, stepping over the boom box as they climbed. Red was at the back of his truck, grabbing a small cooler. I went back to sudsing the car. When I looked up, Red was standing at the Malibu's trunk, one finger tracing lazy circles in the suds.

"I saw the weirdest thing the other day," he began.

I took a step back, trying to put more of the car between us. I didn't want to know about anything weird he might have seen. He looked at me, waiting for a reply I wasn't about to give.

"It was a picture of you on the Internet, but it didn't really look like you at all."

I felt like I'd been doused with ice water. Black spots swam in my vision for a few seconds, and I laid a hand on the car's roof to steady myself. "I don't know what you're talking about." My voice shook.

He went on like he hadn't heard me. "Yeah, it was you all right. I saw your name and the town where you used to live…Moss Ridge? But either that photo was doctored or you've had one of them Hollywood makeovers—you know, the ones that those plastic surgeons do—because your body don't look nothin' like the one in that photo." He stared at my breasts and stomach.

I swallowed hard. "Whatever you saw, Red, was some cruel practical joke someone nasty played. I'd appreciate it if you would just drop it."

He smirked. "Yeah, I found all kinds of interesting stuff on the Internet. Course, y'all never know what's true and what's bullshit. But it was interesting stuff, lemme tell you."

He spoke to my breasts, not even bothering to hide it. I grabbed a towel from the ground and wrapped it around myself.

"I'll just let you get back to your car washin'," he said as he slowly walked to the stairs. "You don't need to be all wrapped up in that towel." He smiled bigger than ever. "You remind me of that scene in Cool Hand Luke, where the prisoners are all working on a road gang and that buxom chick is washing her car and smearing her tits all over the windows. Mmm, mmm, mmm! I think I'm gonna call you Lucille from now on, Audrey. Yeah, Lucille!" He chuckled as he climbed the stairs.

I watched him until he was out of sight, then bent over and dry heaved. On shaking legs I went to sit on the bottom step. Hot tears fell from my unblinking eyes. I was still sitting there with the old towel wrapped around me when Jared returned. His smile quickly faded when he got close enough to see my face.

"Audrey? What's going on?"

I jumped to my feet and threw myself into his arms. I sobbed into his shirt.

"What?" he shouted. "What the hell happened?"

I took several hiccupping breaths. All the work I'd done to keep my dirty little secrets, to pretend it all had never happened, had been for nothing. The cat was out of the bag now. I looked up into Jared's frowning face. If I was going to tell him, I had to do it while looking him straight in the eye.

"Back in California, a girl who hated me took a picture while I was changing in the locker room. She used software to make it look all gross, with sagging boobs and bushy pubes, and she posted it on the Internet. It was supposed to have been taken off, but it still must be out there in cyberspace, and Red saw it, and he was saying all this stuff to me about how he knew it was fake or that I'd had plastic surgery—"

"So Red was Googling your name and he saw this bogus photo of you and started making comments about your body?" He gripped my upper arms with his trembling hands.

"Y-yes, and he was talking about how I looked like the car-washing girl in Cool Hand Luke, and he just kept staring at me, and I felt so... so dirty."

Jared's pressed his lips together until they disappeared. He ground his teeth. His grip became painful.

"Ow." I began to squirm. He released me and charged up the stairs two at a time. I ran up after him, scared out of my mind. He hit the front door so hard it bounced off the inside wall and swung back toward him. My dad was on the couch, and he jumped to his feet. Jim rose too, a startled expression on his face. Red remained on the sofa, casting a bored look over his shoulder at us.

"I need to speak to you outside, Red." Jared's voice was deadly.

Dad stepped forward, looking confused and upset. "Jared? What's going on?"

"Mr. Kelly, this man has been harassing your daughter, and I would like to have words with him outside."

Dad looked back to the sofa. "Red? What's he talking about?"

"Ted, I didn't do nothin'. I just made a comment about the movie Cool Hand Luke to Audrey while she was washing her car. If I offended her, I'm sorry."

Dad looked back at me, still confused, but seeming slightly less alarmed. "Is that it, Audrey?"

"No, Dad, that's not it. He saw the picture on the Internet. The one Caroline did in the locker room."

The blood drained from his face. His neck practically creaked as he slowly turned back to Red. "Did you look up pictures of my daughter on the Internet?"

Red finally stood up. "You guys are gettin' yourselves all worked up over nothin'. All I did was ask her about a photo I knew wasn't her anyways, and now everybody's freaking out."

My dad stared at his feet and breathed heavily. He was ready to blow. When he spoke his words were slow and careful. "Red, you're a good man to work with, and I hope that won't change, but if you approach, speak to, or look at my daughter again, I will have you arrested, or worse, I'll let this young man do what he so badly wants to do right now." He gestured with his thumb toward Jared.

Looking thoroughly shaken, Jim stepped between Jared and Red. "C'mon, Red. Let's hit the road." He headed for the door.

Jared stepped aside to let him pass. Red followed at a leisurely pace, a small smile playing across his face, and I stepped farther behind Jared as he passed. Jared followed them down the stairs, Dad and I right behind him. Dad stopped at the foot of the stairs, but I continued walking until I reached Jared's side. I wrapped my arm in his in a feeble attempt to keep him tethered to me.

On the way to his truck, Red paused. "You like 'em young, huh, Jerry?" he said, his voice so low only Jared and I could hear it. "She tighter than a ten-year-old?"

In a flash Jared's arm tore out of my grip, and his fist connected with Red's cheek. I screamed as the two men lunged at each other, their punches landing with meaty thuds.

Dad and Jim ran forward and pulled them apart. Red brought his elbow backward, hitting Jim in the chest and knocking him to the ground.

"Enough!" Dad yelled so loud it hurt my ears. "Red, get your ass off my property and don't come back! You got that?"

Red spit a stream of blood onto the driveway and charged to his truck. My Dad helped Jim to his feet and checked to see if he was okay.

The tires on Red's truck spewed gravel as he gunned the engine and tore out in a half circle. He aimed his truck like a missile, crashing squarely into the side of Jared's Dodge.

Jared ran toward his truck. Red threw his into reverse and nearly hit Jared, but he dodged out of the way before it clipped him. Jared reached the crushed door of his truck and yelled when it refused to open.

Red tore out of the driveway, tires screaming angrily on the asphalt. Jared headed for the Ram's passenger door. I ran as fast as I could and grabbed him by his waistband just as he was climbing into the cab. I pulled as hard as I could until he tumbled out.

"Audrey, let go!"

"No! You are not going after him!"

"Audrey, that son of a bitch just smashed the hell out of my truck. What the hell do you want me to do?"

"Let him go!" I was crying and shaking. I held on to his shirt. Images of Mikey's gravestone flashed through my mind. I couldn't be responsible for another death. I would rather die myself.

"She's right, Jared," my dad said. "We'll call the police and file a report."

I hadn't seen Dad approach. He had his hands on Jared's shoulders and was gently pulling him away from the truck. Jim was still standing where Dad had helped him to his feet, his face anxious as he rubbed the spot on his chest that Red had hit.

Jared looked at his feet and breathed hard. Gradually he calmed down. "Okay. Let's call the cops."

"What'd he say to you, anyway? What made you hit him?" my dad asked.

Jared looked into my father's face. "Something that no man should ever say."

Dad looked confused again, but he didn't question Jared any further.

"What are you going to say?" I asked, my breathing still rapid and uneven. "I don't want the Internet photo mentioned to the police. Why do we have to call them?" I was becoming hysterical again.

Dad wrapped his arms around me, smoothing my hair with one hand. "It's okay, Audrey. Everything's going to be all right. No one's going to say anything about the Internet. We have to file a police report for Jared's insurance and for my paperwork at the plant. That was a company truck Red was driving. I'm going to fire his ass."

Dad and Jared supported me on either side as we walked to the lift and rode it up to the house. They led me to the couch, helped me into my terrycloth robe, and handed me a steaming mug of tea. Time became fuzzy; moments seemed like hours, and hours seemed to pass in seconds.

The police arrived and took a detailed report of the afternoon's events. They interviewed Jared, Dad, and Jim. The story boiled down to a jealous man making a pass at his boss' daughter, resulting in a fight and property damage. I worried when the cops asked Jared who had thrown the first punch and wondered if Red could press charges against Jared, though he seemed unconcerned. The police asked Jared if he wanted to file battery charges against Red; he hesitated but answered "no." He just wanted a malicious property damage charge.

When Jim was done with his interview, he apologized to my father about a million times—he felt guilty about inviting Red over to watch the fight. He'd known Red a long time and knew he could be a bit ornery at times.

Jim finally left, and Jared and Dad agreed that I should go to bed. Jared laid a gentle kiss on my forehead, then Dad walked me up to my room. I mutely climbed into bed and he tucked the covers around me. He turned off the light. I knew no more.

36

Purge

It was nearly noon by the time I shuffled into the kitchen feeling tired and weak. I feigned a smile for Dad as I sat at the counter.

"How you doing today, hon?" he asked.

"Okay, I guess."

He handed me a cup of coffee. "Light and sweet, just the way you like it."

"Thanks, Dad."

"I talked to your mom. I told her everything, and she wants you to call her as soon as you're feeling up to it."

I felt numb as I sipped the coffee. Dad gave my arm a gentle squeeze and left the kitchen. After finishing the coffee I took a long, hot shower, got dressed, applied makeup, and dried my hair until it hung silky and straight over my back and shoulders.

In the kitchen I made myself some toast and drank some juice, and my energy slowly returned. I grabbed my keys and headed toward the door.

"Dad, I'm going over to Jared's for a while. I won't be long," I called.

He came out of his office. He looked me over, saw I looked calm and put together, and kissed my cheek. I hugged him tightly.

I drove slowly to Jared's house. His battered truck was parked in the driveway. I was barely out of my car before he was down the front stairs, and he ran over to embrace me. We held each other for a long time before I spoke.

"I need to talk to you. I haven't been honest with you, and I need to explain some things."

He looked into my eyes, a slight frown creasing his forehead. "Okay. Let's go inside." He turned toward the stairs.

"Can we go by the water instead?" I asked. "I just really feel like being out in the open right now."

He shrugged. "Sure, but we'd better take your car."

"Of course," I said as I looked at his poor truck.

We drove to the west side of the bay and parked near a small fishing pier. We walked along the sea wall hand in hand until we found a good spot to sit, our legs hanging over its edge. The sun had passed its zenith, and the calm waters of the bay glimmered with reflected light.

I took a deep breath and looked him in the eyes. "The girl I told you about—the one who posted the altered picture of me on the Internet—her name is Caroline, and she first began to bully me when we were in junior high."

Jared listened without interruption as my tale unfolded. I told him about the pranks and teasing and their escalation until the Internet photo and the fight at the mini-mart. I told him about my plot for revenge against Caroline and her friends, and my friendship with Tanya and Mikey. I told him about the sardines, the party at Tanya's, the video of Kylie, and how we had planted drugs in Caroline's car. I revealed every ugly, humiliating detail of what happened at prom and the horrible fight at Pinehaven. Finally I told him about the car accident and Mikey's death.

"I moved here hoping to erase the past few months from my life and start over. But I'll never be able to do that. What happened is a part of me." Tears fell from my eyes. "I'm not proud of it, but I can't hide from it anymore."

Jared was quiet. He looked at the dark water below our feet. I could only imagine what he must have thought of me: his new girlfriend, a vengeful plotter who had done such horrible things.

"I understand if you don't want to see me anymore," I said. "I wouldn't blame you."

He looked up, startled. "Are you breaking up with me?"

"W-well, no…but I thought you wouldn't want to go out with me anymore."

"Why would you think that?"

"Because I'm such a horrible person!"

"Why? Because you defended yourself? Because you fought back? Okay, planting drugs was pretty severe, but that was your friends' idea, wasn't it?"

"Well, yes, Mikey and Tanya thought of it. But I went along with everything. And it's my fault Mikey's dead."

"Bullshit, Audrey!"

I was shocked.

"Mikey and Tanya sought you out, not the other way around. They chased after Caroline. You are not responsible for what happened. It was a horrible accident. Sure, the whole thing was messed up to begin with, but you can't carry the blame for everything."

I tried to see it from his point of view. Maybe he was right—maybe I wasn't entirely to blame, but I would always carry guilt for Mikey's death.

"What happened is awful," he went on, "and I know it seems like the biggest thing in the universe to you right now, but as lame as it sounds, it will fade. Let me tell you something about me." He laced his fingers in mine. "When I was in high school I stressed, and I mean I stressed hard, all the time. I had to maintain at least a three-point-six GPA, had to play varsity ball, had to run for student council, had to apply to the right colleges. I did all of it because that's what my folks expected. And not just that—it's what I expected of myself. I made myself absolutely miserable by trying to be someone I wasn't. I didn't want to be popular, or a school leader, but I told myself that I did.

"The day Jack said he was going to buy Rick's business was the day he saved my life. That was the day I let all the bullshit go, just tossed it all aside, and finally became my own person. Without that decision I would still be following a checklist, doing all the things I was convinced I had to do. In a few years you'll realize just how small a blip on the radar high school is. It's just a stepping stone. And your enemies can hurt you only if you let them."

I let his words soak in. "So you still want to be my boyfriend?"

He kissed me, soft and lingering. "Of course I do."

Relief and happiness washed over me, cleansing the dark corners of my soul. I wrapped my arms around his waist, snuggling close. "I thought once I told you about everything you'd want to get rid of all the drama. I carry so much bad karma and baggage with me."

"Audrey, you see where we're sitting? This is called a sea wall. When a storm rages and the water level rises, the wall holds it back. Your sea wall is right here." He tapped my chest. "It's your heart, your willpower, your friends, and the people who love you."

37

The New School

After the incident with Red, my mom tried to convince me to come home. I told her there was no way in hell I would leave Jared, and she got even more worried, thinking I was going to run off and get married and start popping out babies. After an hour of assurances that I was still going to college, she gradually accepted my choice. However, I had to promise to be home for two weeks for Christmas. It was a small price to pay for being able to stay in Mississippi. Besides, it would give me a chance to see all my old friends on their turf without any intrusions into mine.

After talking to a personnel manager at his workplace, Dad offered Red a transfer to the Houston branch of his company. Red balked at the offer initially but changed his mind when he realized my dad wasn't kidding about suing him. In the end he packed and left.

Jared and I decided to give his family a heavily edited version of the fight with Red. We left out the Internet photo and mentioned nothing of my past troubles. Maybe we could tell them later, when it was further behind me, but not just then.

Shortly before school was to start, Mom sent me an early birthday present—a beautiful leather book bag. I didn't tell her I wouldn't be able to use it during our frequent rainstorms because I didn't want to hurt her feelings. I spent my last week of freedom shopping for new folders, notebooks, pens, and pencils, and the Sunday before start of term I drove west to Slidell to go to the mall. I figured some new clothes would distract me from my worries.

Each time I felt my heart begin to thud frantically in my chest, I replayed Jared's words in my head: It's just a blip on the radar. In nine months I would leave high school behind forever.

I came home with four new outfits and the determination to slog through the school year without worrying about the social aspects. I didn't know if it would hold if my past came out, but I did know that no matter what, I would survive.

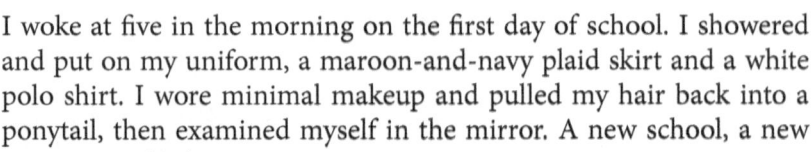

I woke at five in the morning on the first day of school. I showered and put on my uniform, a maroon-and-navy plaid skirt and a white polo shirt. I wore minimal makeup and pulled my hair back into a ponytail, then examined myself in the mirror. A new school, a new town, a new look.

During the five-minute drive to campus I did some deep-breathing exercises. I was early and found a good spot in the student parking lot. I grabbed my book bag and walked slowly toward the building where I'd have my first-period class—marine and environmental science. It was an elective, since I'd already finished my science requirements at my old school, and one of the few coed classes in my schedule. I was surprised when I'd first learned the boys from St. Stanislaus shared some classes with the girls at Our Lady Academy. I wondered why they hadn't simply combined the two schools into one.

I found a bench under a shady oak in the courtyard near the building. I sat down and pulled out a notebook and doodled to pass the time. Teachers walked along the breezeway, cups of coffee in their hands as they made their way to their classrooms. I glanced at them nervously as they passed, reminding myself to call the nuns "Sister" instead of "Mrs."

Students began to come into the yard, migrating to the low brick building. Church bells pealed loud and melodious from the tower of the huge Our Lady of the Gulf cathedral. Slinging my bag over my shoulder, I took another deep breath and set off for class. In the room I took a seat in the middle of a side row and looked around at the posters on the walls—the Gulf Islands National Seashore, the Natchez Trace Scenic Trail, and the Russell Cave National Monument. I wondered if we would be taking any field trips.

Other students filed in in twos and threes. A few gave me curious looks, but most were too busy socializing and trying to decide where to sit. The teacher came in too—Dr. Wiggins, a slight man with thinning blond hair and a beard.

"Okay, everyone stand up, and when I call your name take the first desk on the end. Work your way down the aisle until everyone is seated alphabetically." His voice was deceptively deep given his slight frame.

Everyone groaned.

"All right, none of that," he said. "The sooner we get seated, the sooner the fun can begin!"

He called names, and students took their seats. When I heard "Stevenson, Audrey" I moved to my desk. Only two kids were behind me: Tucker, Zach, and Williams, Matthew.

I scrunched down in my seat, trying to remain as inconspicuous as possible, hoping Dr. Wiggins would not bring me up in front for an introduction.

"Okay, class," he said. "We're going to do a little memory exercise. You'll love it. Trust me—you'll thank me for this one day."

He took a few steps closer to the first desk on the far right, pointed to the boy seated there, and said, "Stand up and tell us your first name and one thing that you like to do. For example, my name is Dr. Wiggins, and I like to paddleboard."

There were a few giggles; even I laughed a little, picturing him in a pair of loud board shorts, paddling along the Gulf on a huge surfboard.

"Go ahead," he said to the boy, gesturing for him to stand up.

The boy slowly rose, his face as red as a pickled egg. "Uh… Um… I'm Kirk…and…um…I like to fish." He dropped back into his seat.

"Now you," Dr. Wiggins said, pointing to the girl seated behind Kirk. The girl was a tall brunette. She stood up smiling confidently. "Kirk likes to fish. I'm Brenda, and I like to text."

The rest of the students took their turns, repeating the names and hobbies of the students who had gone before them. When my turn arrived I repeated each flawlessly but hesitated before introducing myself. What was my hobby? What should I say? I gulped, urging my brain to think of something fast.

"I'm Audrey…and I…like to read vampire novels."

Oh my God, did I really just say that? I sat and stared at my desk while the student behind me rattled off everyone's names and hobbies. My face burned when he got to me.

"Audrey likes to read vampire novels. I'm Zach. I like to watch vampire movies."

I looked back at him. He smiled and winked at me. I smiled back, not sure how to react to his flirting.

When Matthew, seated at the last desk, repeated all thirty names and hobbies without a single miss, Dr. Wiggins led the class in a round of applause.

For the rest of the period we received our books and went over the course requirements. Dr. Wiggins handed out a calendar, and I noted several Fridays that would be spent on the beach doing field work. I hoped every class would be as good as this one.

But second period was not nearly as fun—religious studies, which was completely foreign to me. I was hopelessly lost. I sat near the back of the room and listened quietly, wondering how I would ever pass. I'd seen The Ten Commandments and The Passion of the Christ, but other than that my religious knowledge was nonexistent. I silently cursed my dad for not letting me go to Bay High.

During first break I went back to the bench under the oak and munched on a granola bar. I looked over my schedule—I had AP English next, followed by economics. After lunch I had psychology and finally sailing as an elective. How cool was that?

English was pretty much as I imagined it would be—boring—but at least the reading list was good. Pygmalion, Washington Square, The Optimist's Daughter—I'd never read any of them, and they were of a higher caliber than anything I'd been assigned back at Moss Ridge High. I was thinking about spending the lunch hour in the library, checking them out to get a head start, when the girl sitting next to me spoke up. She was pretty, with blond, ironed hair framing her face. She had pale-green eyes that complemented her fair skin.

"Hi! I'm Dahlia. Are you a new student this year?"

"Yes. I moved here a couple of months ago."

"Really? Where from?"

I'd been dreading the inquisition but knew it was inevitable. "From LA."

"Wow. How come you moved here?"

"My dad got transferred."

"That's cool. You want to sit with me and my friends at lunch?"

"Um, okay," I said, pleased by the invitation.

The bell rang and we headed toward the commons. Dahlia told me about her friends, family, and favorite teachers and was disappointed to learn that we had no other classes together. We lined up at the cafeteria counter, selecting our food: chicken rotel, green beans, corn bread, and salad. We paid with our prepaid lunch cards, then walked to a round table near a window overlooking the courtyard. Two other girls joined us soon after. One I recognized from religious studies. The other was new to me.

"This is Ember and Cory," Dahlia said. "This is Audrey. She just moved here from LA."

They each said "hello" to me.

"Hi," I said, smiling at them timidly.

Why did I move to Mississippi? How did I like it there? Did I miss LA? They wanted to know everything about me.

"Did you have a boyfriend back in LA?" Cory asked.

"Yeah," I said, "but we broke up before I moved here."

"Really? Was it because you were moving?"

"No, he was a senior, and he left on a trip to Australia. So we just kind of, um, parted ways."

"Well, I'm sure you'll get asked out by a bunch of guys here," Dahlia said.

"Actually, I have a boyfriend already."

All three of them looked at me. I blushed.

"Who is it?" Cory asked. "Does he go to Stanislaus?"

"No, he, uh, used to go to Bay High. His name's Jared."

"How old is he?" she asked.

"Twenty-three."

"Whoa," Dahlia said. "That's a lot...older. Can we see a picture?"

"Um, sure," I answered. I pulled my cell phone out of my bag and fumbled through the contact list until I found him. "Here he is." I handed the phone to Dahlia.

"Cute!" she said.

Cory and Ember leaned forward to get a look. I resumed eating my salad, wondering if I would be ostracized now that they knew I was seeing an older man. I smiled. What they would think if they knew how intimate Jared and I were?

Dahlia handed the phone back, and as I stashed it in my bag I heard a familiar laugh behind me. I turned and saw Charlaine Harrington and several other girls in cheerleader outfits at a nearby table. As Charlaine talked she teased her short hair this way and that. There was just something about her I didn't trust. Whatever friends I made or didn't make, one thing was certain: I was going to stay as far away from her as possible.

I ate in silence, listening to my new acquaintances talk about who was seeing whom, likely homecoming candidates, and college applications. I glanced around the cafeteria, studying the rest of the girls. OLA had a good-sized student body, ranging in age from twelve to eighteen. But when separated by year, the groups became smaller: there were only forty-eight of us in the senior class.

The bell rang, signaling the end of lunch. I bid farewell to Dahlia, Ember, and Cory and walked to fifth-period psychology. Dahlia was off to her Latin class while Ember and Cory went to calculus. My curriculum felt a bit inferior compared to theirs, and I wondered if I would be able to keep up with my classmates.

I picked a seat near the back of the class, then listened and made notes as our instructor reviewed the outline and requirements. I could barely wait for it to end so I could go to my sailing class. When the bell rang, I gathered my books and bag and made a beeline for the door. I stowed my bag in my car and speed-walked to Beach Boulevard, falling in step with several others headed in the same direction.

We crossed the beach and made our way down a long pier where several pint-sized sailboats awaited us. We sat on wooden benches and waited for the instructor to appear. My heart sank into my shoes when I spotted Charlaine walking my way, her arm linked with a boy's. They sat on a bench near the end, and I was glad for the buffer between us. I would have liked to stay invisible to her for the entire school year.

Finally Mr. Jones showed up and began handing out our instruction manuals. We reviewed the first few pages together and watched as Mr. Jones hopped into one of the boats and pointed out parts for us to name. By the time he was finished the bell burred in the distance, signaling the end of class. I felt cheated out of a ride on the water, but I was sure we'd get to that next time.

I lingered, pretending to study the manual while I waited for Charlaine to get off the pier. I walked slowly back to the student parking lot, enjoying the soft breeze coming off the water. How fun it was to go to a school on the beach!

38

Good for the Soul

"How was school?" Dad asked as soon as he walked in the front door, carrying his laptop bag.

I sat at the kitchen counter, my English homework laid out in front of me. "Challenging," I said.

"Oh?" He took a seat next to me. "Academically or socially?"

"Academically, mostly. Also, I'm going to a Catholic school and know nothing about religion."

"Don't worry about all that stuff. I know you. You'll pull all As and Bs. And as for the religious stuff, it's all just gobbledygook anyway. A lot of the girls who go there aren't Catholic. Lots of them are Baptist and Pentecostal and so on and so forth. Don't sweat it. Just pretend to fear God and feel guilty, and you're practically Catholic."

He laughed; I gave a tight smile. I had already been christened in the waters of fear and guilt many times over.

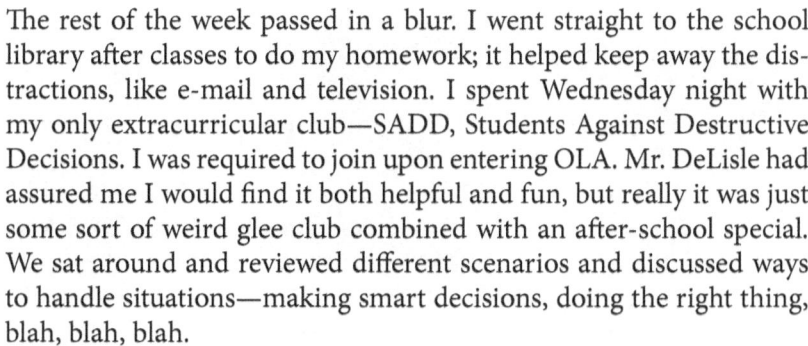

The rest of the week passed in a blur. I went straight to the school library after classes to do my homework; it helped keep away the distractions, like e-mail and television. I spent Wednesday night with my only extracurricular club—SADD, Students Against Destructive Decisions. I was required to join upon entering OLA. Mr. DeLisle had assured me I would find it both helpful and fun, but really it was just some sort of weird glee club combined with an after-school special. We sat around and reviewed different scenarios and discussed ways to handle situations—making smart decisions, doing the right thing, blah, blah, blah.

In the club we were encouraged to share real-life stories about confrontations and incidents we had dealt with. During other kids' declarations I would slide as low as possible in my seat, trying to become the invisible woman. Sharing my destructive decisions was the last thing I wanted to do.

When Friday arrived I felt a whole new nervousness at the prospect of my first Mass at Our Lady of the Gulf. I was grateful to have Dahlia as my guide. Lines of students filed into the cathedral like animals entering Noah's ark. I remained glued to Dahlia's side as we entered the dim, cool church, grateful for the break from the humidity outside. I watched other students dip their fingers in holy water and cross themselves, many kneeling slightly at their aisles' entrances.

Mass was not due to start for a while, giving students time to confess before services began. I followed Dahlia to the far edge of the cathedral. She waved at me and disappeared into a dark, wooden booth.

Oh, sweet Jesus! Cold sweat popped out on my neck and forehead. Okay; don't panic. You've seen this on TV a million times. You know the words. Just fake it.

A nearby confessional opened, and a girl came out. I looked to my left and right, seeing if someone else was going to enter. When no one did, I stepped up, nearly tripping over the threshold. I closed the door and sat on the tiny seat. I hyperventilated.

The small screen slid open with a snap, making me jump. I saw the vague outline of a priest on the other side. I tried to think of what to say.

"B-b-bless me, Father, for I have sinned. It's been… It… This is my first confession."

I waited for his response, breathing hard and sweating.

"Are you a Catholic?" he asked.

"No, sir," I replied.

"Well, in that case we can't consider this a regular confession. Would you like just to talk instead?"

I sat quietly for a moment, wondering what I could say. Should I talk about sins had I committed? According to whom? Me? God? And whose God, the priest's or mine? Maybe I should start with the lies or the coveting or perhaps the fact that I was not a virgin. I knew I could say anything to this man anonymously, but would I really do it?

I leaned close to the screen. "I've done bad things," I whispered. "I've hurt people. I've enacted vengeance on people who hurt me."

I stopped, waiting to hear his reply.

"And do you regret these acts? Do you feel badly about them?"

"Yes," I whispered.

"Do you have hatred in your heart for the people who hurt you?"

I paused, considering his question. Did I still hate Caroline? And what about Hillary, Tracy, and Kylie?

"I'm not sure," I said. "I'm still suffering the effects of what they did. But I wish I hadn't done anything to them."

"Then it sounds as if you are truly remorseful for your actions. You will be able to forgive yourself completely only when you forgive your enemies."

I chewed on this thought, wondering if it were possible. Caroline seemed so far away and long ago. Could I forgive her? Truly forgive her?

"Is there anything else you'd like to talk about?" the priest asked.

"Where should I start?" It was out of my mouth before I realized what I was saying. I clapped a hand over my mouth, my eyes tearing up.

"Start with the small things and work your way up from there." His voice was so serene. What kinds of confessions had he heard? Probably everything from "I took my brother's candy bar" and "I stole twenty bucks out of my mom's wallet" to "I shot heroin last weekend."

"I'm not pure," I went on. "I've had—I mean I am having sexual relations with my boyfriend, who I love."

"Don't you think it's important to save yourself for marriage? Sex is meant to be between a husband and a wife. Do you regret that you have given away such an intimate and important part of yourself?"

I paused, again considering his questions. "I do regret it with my first boyfriend, because I knew he wasn't the one from the very beginning, but I don't regret it with my boyfriend now. He's… Well, he's the one."

"If he were, don't you think he would wait until you were both joined in holy matrimony before engaging in these acts with you?"

"I… Um… I'm not sure." I regretted opening this can of worms. I contemplated what to do next. Part of me wanted to end the session, do whatever prayers or contrition the priest gave me, and move on. Another part of me wanted desperately to spill my guts, giving every detail of every bad thing I'd done since April. I wanted to expel it all from my system the way I had with Jared on the sea wall. Perhaps by confessing it all to this servant of God I could be forgiven for the things I had done.

I took a deep breath, leaned close to the screen, and began with the photo that had been posted on the Internet. A half hour later my throat was dry, and my body felt like an empty shell. The gallons of black bile that had been churning through my body were gone. They'd been diluted by the briny waters of the gulf since my arrival, and now the final dregs of were sluiced from my soul.

I left the confessional and looked around. I spotted Dahlia in a nearby pew and took a seat next to her.

A middle-aged priest walked up to the altar and began to recite prayers in both English and Latin. I knelt, sat, and stood, trying to stay in sync with the rest of the crowd. I watched while Dahlia entered the center aisle to take communion.

When Mass was over, I walked to the long rows of candles, lit one, and silently said a quick prayer. I took a Bible from the stack near the exit, prepared to do every bit of reading and prayer the priest had assigned me, and walked out into the bright daylight.

I gave Dahlia a hug and said goodbye, then practically skipped to my car, feeling light as a feather. I skidded to a stop when I saw Zach Tucker leaning against the door. When he saw me, he hurried to stand up straight.

"Hey, Audrey," he said.

"Hi, Zach. What's up?" I opened the back door of the Malibu and tossed in my bag.

He looked nervous, bouncing on the balls of his feet. "I, uh, was just wondering if you're coming to the game tonight."

"Game?" I asked.

"Yeah, um, the football game tonight against Hancock. I was going to ask you in marine science today, but since we were digging around in the sand all period I didn't get the chance."

"Oh, yeah, yeah...the football game." I searched for the right words to let him down easily. Not only did I have a date with Jared, but I hated football—which I had to keep a secret or I might get kicked out of the state. "I'm sorry, I'm going to miss the game tonight. My boyfriend and I are going to see The Skeleton Key at the Grand."

Zach looked crestfallen. "Oh, that's cool. I heard that's a good movie. See you Monday." He made a quick exit.

"Bye!" I called, but he was almost out of earshot.

I snuggled close to Jared as we sat in the dark theater, watching Kate Hudson battle a hoodoo priest in the swamps of Terrebonne Parish. On our drive home I asked him dozens of questions about hoodoo and voodoo, and he promised to take me on this tour called The Dark Side of New Orleans. It took place at night in the haunted parts of the city, including St. Louis Cemetery and Madame Laveau's House of Voodoo. I bounced up and down like a happy child.

"You're certainly chipper tonight," Jared said. "You must really like your new school, huh?"

"You know, I do! It's so different from my old one. I doubt I'll be getting a scholarship like ninety percent of the rest of my class, but I think I'll have a shot at getting accepted to Tulane or Loyola."

"Loyola, huh? I think you have to be a confirmed Catholic to go there."

"Well, I did have my first sort-of confession today, and to be honest I really like the idea of being forgiven for all my sins."

Jared held my hand. "You know, you don't need a priest to ask for forgiveness. You can just ask God directly."

"I know. It's just the whole ritual of it was…comforting." His forehead creased. "What?" I asked, suddenly nervous. "What's bothering you?"

He shrugged. "Nothing, really. I was just wondering if you're gonna go all religious on me and change our, um, relationship."

I smiled. I leaned closer to him, blowing a soft kiss against his neck. I whispered in his ear, "You mean am I going to stop doing this?" I kissed his earlobe while my hand slowly traveled up his thigh.

"Stop that or you'll make me crash," he said, smiling.

"I love you, Jared Breaux."

He looked me, his eyes communicating more love than I ever could have hoped to find. He brought my hand to his lips and kissed the top of each finger.

We decided to stop at his house before he took me home. We barely made it through the front door before we ripped each other's clothes off.

Later, on the short drive from his house to mine, we decided to take that tour of New Orleans for my birthday in early October, when the nights began to cool down. Little did I know that long before October arrived, my world would lay in utter devastation.

39

The Storm

As the second week of school started, my newfound feeling of lightness persisted. I even managed to feel eager about the upcoming SATs.

After classes finished on Tuesday I spent over an hour with my class counselor, going over my college applications. She was not as optimistic as I was and pointed out my lack of extracurriculars—no sports, no student leadership, no academic clubs. I shrugged it off, saying I would be okay with a year or two of junior college.

She studied my transcripts. "You need to rock your SATs," she said. "You get a great score and it'll make up for your lack of extracurriculars, okay?"

"I'll do my best, Sister Margaret."

"That's all I can ask, Audrey."

I endeavored to keep my promise by studying hard all week—two hours at the library doing my regular classwork, then another two at home prepping for the SATs. On Wednesday I drove to Biloxi to pick up a computer program that gave practice tests. I planned to do a practice run that weekend just to see how well I scored and focus my studies from there.

Jared called that night to tell me he'd gotten tickets to see Dwight Yoakam at the Grand. "How about taking a break from the books and going out for some music?"

I agreed wholeheartedly, happy for the break even though I wasn't a huge country music fan. I hurried downstairs to tell Dad only to find him glued to the hurricane watch on the evening news.

He glanced over his shoulder at me. "Looks like a big one's coming. I sure as hell hope it veers east."

"Dad, Jared has tickets for Dwight Yoakam on Friday night. Can I go?"

"Yeah, sure, as long as we're not evacuated."

I laughed, thinking how unlikely that was.

At school the next morning a portion of each class was devoted to storm preparations and checklists. I joined Dahlia, Ember, and Cory at our usual table for lunch.

"Have you guys ever been through a hurricane?" I asked.

"Oh yeah, lots of times," Cory answered. "It's no big deal. You board up the windows and go stay with a friend or relative who has a brick house on high ground. I think we've gone through two or three hurricanes and tropical storms. I don't know why everybody gets so jazzed up about it."

"Well, my mom went through Camille," Dahlia said. "And that was a very big deal. Her grandma got killed."

"Yeah, that was a bad one," Cory said. "I'm sorry, Dally, I forgot about your granny."

"That's okay." Dahlia looked at me. "Don't worry, Audrey. Camille was a once-in-a-generation storm. That kind is really rare."

I pushed my salad around with my fork, suddenly not hungry. "But it's been a generation since Camille, hasn't it?"

All three girls looked at me, silent and solemn as my words sunk in.

When Friday arrived, all anyone could talk about was the storm. Some students were leaving after school; others watched the news to see where the storm would arc. If it hit west of New Orleans we would get a high surge.

As soon as classes ended I raced home and called Dad. He said he would be stuck at work all night to help button down the plant in preparation for the storm. Then I called Jared—he and Jackson were on their way to the docks to secure the boats.

"Can't you move them east, to Alabama or something?" I asked.

"Babe, those boats just don't move that fast. Besides, there's no way to tell until the last minute exactly where the storm will hit. We'd have to take them all the way to the panhandle or farther. Don't worry. I'm insured." He laughed nervously.

"I don't know what to do," I said, panic edging into my voice.

"First thing, just calm down. Then get yourself a box and fill it with your photos and important papers—the stuff that's irreplaceable. Don't worry about any of the big stuff. I'll be there to pick you up for the concert in an hour."

"We're still going?" I asked.

"Hell yes we're going. It's Dwight Yoakam!"

I laughed and said goodbye, then got busy doing exactly as Jared had instructed. I filled three large boxes and labeled them. As I was taping them shut, the phone rang again. I thought it would be Jared telling me he was on his way, but it was Mom.

"What's going on with this hurricane?" she shouted.

"Mom, Mom, Mom!" I had to yell to get through her panicked jabbering. "Everything is fine. We'll have plenty of time to evacuate if we have to, and we probably won't even have to."

I went on to spoon-feed her every soothing line I'd been told over the past two days. It took forever, but I managed to calm her down a little. In the meantime, Jared arrived. He waited impatiently as I gently ended the conversation with my mother.

The mood at the concert was jovial. Lots of people were making plans for hurricane parties, and I struggled to understand their optimism. I felt guilty just being there while my father worked and while Jared tried so hard to hide his worry from me.

When he dropped me off at my house later, I felt physically and emotionally exhausted. I went inside and checked the answering machine—the light was flashing. It was Dad, telling me he'd be sleeping on the couch in his office so he could finish prepping the plant the next day. He promised to be home by three at the latest.

I collapsed in bed and fell asleep with the TV tuned in to the local news channel.

———

Saturday dawned gray and ominous. I zeroed in on the scroll at the bottom of the television screen: evacuations from Mobile to New Orleans ordered for those who lived within ten miles of the coast. The picture above it showed congested highways and people heading for the Superdome.

In a daze I went downstairs to the bathroom. I showered, dressed, dried my hair, and ate a bowl of cereal all on autopilot. Tenni called me with reassurances, telling me that Dad and I should pack our bags and head up to her house as soon as he got home from work.

"Okay, Aunt Tenni. Lemme just call Jared and see where he's going."

"Audrey, honey, you sound funny. Are you okay?"

"Yeah, I'm just, uh, trying to be cool, you know?"

"I see. Well, whatever works for you. Call me right back after you talk to Jerry. Tell him he and his family are welcome at my place too."

"Okay, Tenni. Call you right back."

I speed dialed Jared's number. It took five rings; the smooth surface of my calmness shattered to pieces.

"Hello?" he finally answered.

"Jerry, where are you?" I shouted.

"I'm covering my windows with plywood," he said. "I'll be done in a couple of hours, then I'll come over, okay?"

"I think we're going to Tenni's house. She said to tell you that you and your family can stay there too."

"Everybody's going up to Jack's place in Poplarville. He and Miranda have a cabin up there. You and Tenni and your dad can come too."

I wondered what to do. "But Tenni's got the goats, and she says she's far enough from the coast for the evacuation. She's north of I-10."

"Yeah, I know. It's up to you guys if you want to come up to Poplarville. If you're going to Tenni's, I'll go with you."

Relief washed over me. "Ah, good. I was hoping you'd say that."

"Rick called a couple of hours ago and offered his place for us to camp out at too."

"But he's too close to the coast!" A wave of worry crashed over me.

"He'll be okay. His house is eight feet above sea level, plus another fifteen feet from bare earth to the second floor, so he's got a good twenty-three feet of clearance. The storm surge is supposed to be around twenty feet, so he'll be high and dry."

"But what about the wind?"

"Well, if the eye hits east of New Orleans, then it shouldn't be too bad, plus he'll have all the windows buttoned up, and the house has eighteen-inch concrete walls."

After I hung up I walked the house again, looking for anything imperative that should be packed up. I found a shelf of knickknacks I'd made for Dad from the time I was in kindergarten. I picked up a porcelain rabbit that I had made in first grade and ran my fingers over it. I wrapped each item in newspaper and added them all to the box of documents. I wrestled the three boxes to the lift and lowered them downstairs.

Jared and Dad arrived at nearly the same time. The back of Dad's truck was filled with plywood, which they hauled upstairs and screwed over the windows and doors. As the sky darkened I went to the kitchen to forage for dinner. Knowing the power was likely to go out, I emptied the freezer and cooked a huge array of food that could later be packed into the ice chest.

The three of us spent the rest of the evening eating, making and answering phone calls, and watching the news. Close to midnight I left Jared sleeping on the couch and went to my room to sleep. All night I was tortured by nightmares of wind and flying debris.

On Sunday morning I woke feeling completely unrested. I quickly turned on the TV, praying the storm had veered southeast. My heart sank; the hurricane was a monster, its swirling mass of clouds blocking out nearly the entire Gulf of Mexico. The projected path showed it moving directly over New Orleans.

I hurried downstairs to see if Jared and Dad were watching but found them both loading boxes into the backs of their trucks. I ran back upstairs and stuffed clothes into my largest duffel bag, then put my laptop and schoolbooks into my leather book bag. I struggled to zip it closed.

At noon we locked the front door and secured the final piece of plywood over it. We got into three separate vehicles and joined the caravan headed north on highways 603 and 43, creeping northward a few feet at a time in single file. Every now and then a car would rush past on the other side, heading south. I pounded the steering wheel in frustration. Why was the only northbound evacuation route one stinking lane?

Irritated, I hit the scan button on the radio until I found a station playing classical music. I practiced deep breathing until my pulse slowed and my nerves calmed.

At long last we made the left turn off the highway and drove the short distance to Aunt Tenni's home. She met us downstairs to help lug the boxes into the house. With that done, Tenni and I went inside to heat up the leftovers I'd brought for dinner while Dad and Jared secured the storm shutters on all the windows.

After dinner I followed Aunt Tenni around the house as she pulled flashlights, candles, and matches out of drawers. She filled her bathtub to the brim with cold water and checked the gas level on her generator. By the time we went to secure the goats, the wind had begun to gust. The goats were already huddled in their small house, snug and secure for the night. Tenni patted their backs and scratched under their chins.

We took turns showering. Everyone wanted to be fresh and clean in case we didn't have water in the morning. Dad retired to the guest room around ten, looking utterly exhausted. Tenni went to her room soon after, leaving Jared and me in the living room, watching television as the storm got closer and closer.

Jared lay on his side, and I spooned against him. When I woke, it felt like I had just fallen asleep moments before. Rain pelted the roof and walls, sounding like pebbles smacking the house. I looked around the dim living room. Jared sat in a rocking chair in the corner, tying the laces on his work boots.

"What's happening?" I asked.

"Nothin', babe. I'm just going outside to take a look."

He stood and carefully opened the front door, and I followed him. Wet gusts of wind hit my face, making me squint. Dad and Tenni were at the railing.

"Power's out already?" Jared asked my father.

"Yeah, it went out just a few minutes ago," he answered. "We've been monitoring the radio. The eye hit at state line. We're going to get hammered."

"Are we far enough?" Jared asked.

"I don't know. Tenni's house is brick, so it should hold up okay. We might lose the roof, though."

I listened to their conversation with growing horror. How could they be so calm? I bit my lower lip, concentrating on remaining calm.

It wouldn't do any good to fall apart. If the three of them could maintain their calm, then so could I.

We went in and out of the house for the next few hours, watching the storm, monitoring the goat house, and pacing. We drank a lot of coffee, but none of us ate anything. My stomach grumbled and I went to the kitchen to make sandwiches by flashlight, mostly to distract myself.

I carried the stack of sandwiches on a plate out to the front porch. The wind had died down.

"Is it over?" I asked.

"No, honey, it's the eye of the hurricane," Tenni said. "It will be calm for a while, and then the second half of the storm will hit."

"Oh," I said. Aside from some scattered branches and roof tiles, it hadn't been bad at all.

Then I heard something. What was it? Where was it coming from? It crackled and popped, like a hot fire or cooking popcorn. I scanned the horizon for smoke, thinking a nearby house nearby must have been on fire.

"Do you hear that?" I asked Jared.

He walked to the railing, and the look on his face made my blood run cold.

"It's the surge. It's the water coming this way."

And he was right. Water oozed from under the front door.

"Tenni!" I yelled, pointing to it.

"Oh my God," she cried. She pulled the door open, releasing an ankle-high flood.

In the living room, the grate over the floor furnace bubbled dark water like a fountain. We were all knee-deep in a matter of seconds.

"We've got to get on the roof!" Tenni yelled.

"No! We can't. The second half of the storm will blow us right off!" Jared said.

"What do we do?" I yelled.

"Tenni, do you have a boat?" Jared asked.

"No, but Jimmy next door does."

We ran out the back door but stopped dead in our tracks: the river had risen and overflowed. Trees and large chunks of homes flowed past. Jared grabbed my hand and we ran through the water, toward the back of the house next door. Out of breath, I turned to check on

Dad and Tenni, but there was no one behind me. I saw them pulling the goats out of the shed, which was flooding with frightening speed.

Before Jared could grab the knob on the back door, it flew open. A large, bearded man and a woman with a screaming baby came stumbling out.

"We need to get everyone into your boat," Jared said.

The man nodded and we sloshed into the water, heading toward a carport at the rear of the house. The boat was there; it was a pitiful-looking thing, small and aluminum with very little room.

The bearded man held the infant while his wife climbed into the boat, then he handed the baby back to her.

"Get in," Jared told me.

"We have to get Dad and Tenni," I said, pointing to them. They were leading the goats toward us.

"Goddamnit!" Jared hissed. He went back through the water to them. I could hear them arguing, Dad and Jared telling Tenni to leave the damn goats and her refusing to.

"Put 'em on the roof, Tennison," Jimmy said. "They won't fall off. They've got the feet for it!"

Tenni paused. She was sobbing. "Help me," she said to Jared.

Dad took came over to the boat and steadied it. The water was now waist deep. Jimmy and Jared hurried to set an aluminum ladder against the side of Jimmy's house, and Jared lifted the first baying goat onto Jimmy's shoulders. Jimmy climbed halfway up and hoisted the goat onto the porch roof. It stood there, looking dumbfounded.

The second goat went up much more easily, seeming eager to join its friend. Jared lifted her up, and before Jimmy could grab her, she scrambled up the ladder herself.

Exhausted, Jimmy and Jared walked back to the carport. They and Dad gathered around the boat as Tennison climbed in.

"Tenni," Jimmy said, "if one or both of those goats decides to jump down, they're on their own. My wife and baby are more important, and so is your family here."

Tenni looked abashed. "I know that, James Donnelly. But they deserve a fighting chance. I can't just leave them to drown."

"All right then," he said, and that was the end of it.

Jimmy's wife draped a rain slicker over her head and shoulders to keep herself and her baby dry. The carport kept the worst of the rain off of us, and we prayed the wind would not take it away. Jimmy assured us that he had anchored it in concrete.

The men stood in the water, holding the boat steady while the wind tore at our hair, faces, and clothes. A deep vibration reached my chest, and I heard a low roar in the distance.

"It's a tornado," Jared said. "They sound like freight trains."

"Will it hit us?" I asked.

"No way to tell."

"How high is the water going to get?" I asked.

"I'm not sure. It was never supposed to get this high. The surge has to be at least thirty feet to get this far inland. It was supposed to be only twenty-three tops. We should have been high and dry."

I nodded and leaned my head forward until it was resting against his chest. I could feel his heart beating steady and fast and the heat of his skin through his wet T-shirt. I closed my eyes and prayed that this life that had just begun would not end. I prayed for Jimmy and his wife and their tiny baby. I prayed for my father and aunt, for Jessica and the rest of Jared's family. Oh please, God…please…let us live.

40

The Aftermath

For six hours my father and boyfriend held the boat with Tenni's neighbor. For six hours I prayed silently to a god I hoped was listening. When the storm finally passed, darkness fell once again.

Jimmy had been right—the goats were just where we left them on the roof. The water had receded to ankle height by the time we got them down and returned to Tennison's house. Tenni led them to the back porch, filled a large bucket from the grain bin, and set it out for them to eat.

We opened the back door and entered the house. The water was gone, but it had left behind plenty of evidence of its passing: a dark scum coated the walls where the water had reached its high mark, area rugs squished underfoot, furniture lay wherever the receding water had left it. Dad had put our boxes from home on top of the washer and dryer, and they had been safe from the water. Likewise my purse and duffel bag.

I walked the rest of the house, surveying the damage. Out front, our vehicles were where we'd left them, although they were now useless. I stared out to the south, imagining how much worse the damage must have been there. I was alive. Jared, Dad, and Tenni were alive. That was what mattered.

In the dark we walked four blocks that felt like four miles, fighting our way through brush and tree branches and past stranded vehicles, jagged pieces of wood, furniture, mattresses, and appliances. We arrived at a two-story home that sat high above the ground. It was full of people. Every neighbor with a ground-level home had come to find a dry place to rest here. Tenni barely knew the owners, but they took us in with no hesitation. We spread out the dry blankets and towels we had salvaged from Tenni's house on the back deck where some space was still available. Finally we slept, exhausted and heartsick, surrounded by strangers who were now our brothers and sisters in tragedy.

A sunbeam warmed my face, painting light across my closed eyes and waking me slowly. I hoped to escape back into nothingness, but my mind refused.

I sat up, stretching my aching body and looking around groggily. The house was alive with activity. People were milling about, talking, folding up bedding, and making plans. I wandered into the living room where dozens of people sat around a television tuned to CNN. The news showed New Orleans flooded, with people stranded on rooftops. Boats and helicopters rescued survivors. The city had remained nearly undamaged until the levees had failed. The news showed the Superdome, where evacuees were housed, and looters in the streets, stealing everything from shirts and shoes to food and water. I leaned close to a woman standing next to me.

"Why aren't they showing us? When are they going to show Mississippi?"

"Who knows?" the woman answered. She looked disgusted. "All they seem to care about is the city. And those dumb niggers are shooting at the rescue crews!"

I cringed and went to find Jared. He was downstairs, helping siphon gas out of someone's car to use in the house's generator. A barbeque was set up nearby and someone was cooking eggs and bacon. I thought about the food back in the ice chests at Tenni's house. The ice was probably melted, but maybe the food was cold enough to keep. We needed to get back there and salvage what we could.

Jared finished filling the generator and came over to hug me.

"Hey, babe," he said. "How you holding up?"

"I'm fine. Where are Dad and Tenni?"

"Tenni's upstairs, waiting in line for the toilet. Your dad's walking around here somewhere, trying to get a phone signal."

"Has anyone been able to call out?" I asked.

"Not so far. All the lines are crashed. Listen." He took me gently by the shoulders. "Jack or my dad will be looking for us, so I need to get back over to Tenni's house. Once they get here, I want you to go up to Poplarville and stay with Jess and my mom, okay?"

"You're coming too, then?"

"I can't. I've got to check on Rick and my house."

"Then I'm going with you."

"Audrey," he said, putting his hands on his hips and looking up at the sky. "I need to know you're safe. Can you understand that?"

"I need to know that you're safe. Can you understand that?" I was stubborn and determined—dangerous qualities in a teenager.

Jared rubbed his temples. I hurried to soothe him before his frustration turned into anger.

"Look, Jerry, when your dad or Jack gets here, we'll go check on Rick and your house. Then, if you want me to, I'll go to Poplarville with them. Deal?"

He scratched at his beard stubble. "Okay."

With that settled, I wrapped my arms around him. I felt like I could not get enough contact with him. I wanted to tie my arm to his and keep him in my grasp permanently. We were still hugging each other when Dad came around the corner.

"Any luck?" Jared asked Dad as he released me.

"Nothing," Dad said.

"I'm heading back over to Tenni's house to wait for my family," Jared told him.

"Okay, let's all go. I'll get Tennison."

"Yeah," I said. "I saw a bunch of looters on TV, and I don't think we locked the house when we left last night."

"That's not likely to happen here," Jared said. "They do that shit in the city, but people here know better."

I nodded, hoping he was right.

We reached Tenni's house with mud caked on our feet and legs. The house looked much the same from the outside, but I knew what kind of mess waited on the inside. She and Dad discussed plans to gut the bottom three feet of the structure, and all the furniture would have to go. Tenni would need a trailer to live in until the repairs were done. On TV they'd said the Red Cross was coming, but the nearest station was in Baton Rouge, a two-hour drive under the best conditions. Who knew how long it would take with all the damage to the roads and huge sections of the interstate shut down.

We spent the rest of the morning and most of the afternoon salvaging what we could. We gathered up all the dry clothing and food and placed them in the back of Dad's and Jared's trucks. I helped load the photo albums and paintings, all the while hoping the one Aunt Tenni had given me had made it—if our house had made it. I also wondered if Jared's and Jessica's homes were okay.

The sun was nearly set when Jack's truck churned the mud up in the driveway and David leapt from the cab. Jared and his father embraced, and Jack wrapped his arms around both of them. Jared sobbed until his shoulders shook; I watched with tears in my eyes, as did Dad and Tenni. Our loved ones had lived. Our homes had been destroyed. But most of all, there was still the unknown. How many friends had been lost? How many years would it take to rebuild? Could we ever regain our beautiful life here?

Jack and David slept in the back of Jack's truck. The rest of us resumed our places on the deck at Tennison's neighbors' house. I learned that their names were Bobby and Grace Lind; they were middle-aged, with two kids who were away at college. They housed forty-eight souls that first night and forty-two the second; those who had working cars had headed out of town to stay with family or at hotels. The Linds created a bathroom roster, giving everyone time to use the toilet and shower, and set up tables for salvaged food in what had become a communal dining room. Everyone was more than willing to share, and my heart ached with love for these strangers. They would give you the shirts off their backs if you asked.

In the evening all power in the Linds' house was shut down except for the television, which we all watched. We were dying for news of our own neighborhoods. The next morning we finally saw a lone CNN reporter standing on what was left of Beach Road in what was once Waveland: piles of splintered debris, the Bay Bridge in pieces, bodies in the streets, sheets hastily draped over some of them.

We tried to stifle our sobs. But it wasn't easy.

Cell phone signals came back in, but they were sporadic. David was able to call home to assure Julie everyone was okay. Dad was finally able to reach Mom; I could hear her screaming from a few feet away. Dad tried to calm her down before he put me on, but it was no use. She needed to hear my voice before she could accept that I wasn't dead.

Mom wanted to fly out immediately to pick me up. It took both Dad and me twenty minutes to convince her that would be impossible. She calmed once we told her I would be headed out of town in a day or so to stay with the Breaux family.

An hour later we set out for the coast, a ragtag group of a dozen people who needed to check on their properties and find friends and family. Tenni decided to make the trip north with Grace and a few others to the nearest FEMA location to start the paperwork process while Dad and I went with the Breauxs in Jack's truck. We made it halfway before we had to turn around and come back. The roads, covered with mud and debris, were impassable, and emergency crews blocked off other sections.

We returned to Tenni's house and got Jimmy, her neighbor, to loan us his boat. Jared siphoned gas from his truck to get it going, and I sat in the center with him and my father behind me, Jack and David in front. We navigated our way south from the Kiln down to Shoreline Park. Jared did his best to avoid all the debris in the water, but the hull of the boat still bumped against objects almost constantly.

I scanned the shoreline and saw only pilings where homes once stood. Power poles tilted at crazy angles where houses and cars had crashed into them. A riding lawn mower dangled by its rear wheels from a power line, suspended in the air like a pair of tennis shoes looped over the wires, and torn fabric and trash hung like macabre Christmas decorations. A naked body hung limply from one tree branch. I stared, paralyzed by horror, as bugs swarmed the corpse's head.

We were in front of the Breauxs' property for a minute before we realized we were in the right place. All that was left was the roof of the house, which lay forty feet to the north, mired in mud.

David sighed and stared at his property. "Well...that, as they say...is that."

"I don't think there's much point in trying to get out into the bay to check on our houses, Ted," Jared said. "If Shoreline Park is leveled, then there's no hope for Pass Christian Isles or anything that's a block from the beach."

"I know," my father answered. "Let's check on your friend and then head back."

Jared turned the boat around, steered out of the bayou, and emerged back on the Jourdan River. We crossed under Highway 603 at a still-intact bridge and passed the Mud Hut, which was in pieces. Jared maneuvered the boat slowly around the tail end of a car that protruded from the water. Close to the bank I saw the carcass of a dog half buried in mud. Farther along I saw what was appeared to be a horse that had survived the storm. When we got closer I realized that it was wrapped, still standing, between two tree trunks, its body bent and broken but still upright. I closed my eyes and covered them with my hands, determined not to see any more.

We pulled up to the jagged ruins of Captain Rick's dock. My heart filled with happiness when I saw the blue house still standing, looking as solid as ever…but then it sank when I saw a boat resting on the roof.

We climbed out of the boat, slipping and sliding in the mud as we scrambled up the slope.

"Did Rick hoist a boat onto his roof?" I asked Jared, pointing up to it.

Jared went ash pale. "Oh no." He took off at a dead run for the side stairs that led up to Rick's kitchen.

"What's wrong?" I shouted.

"It's the surge," David said. "The water went over the roof. Left that boat there."

My blood ran cold as I bolted for the stairs. They creaked and sagged as the rest of us caught up to Jared. Jack used a crowbar to remove the plywood from the door, and we all went inside.

I gagged and retched as the odor hit me, a wet, rotten stench like nothing I had ever smelled. Furniture lay everywhere, overturned and scattered by the floodwaters.

"Rick! Rick!" Jared shouted as he kicked objects out of his way, tearing through the house. The rest of us followed.

"Look!" Jack pointed to a ladder hanging down from a hatch in the bedroom ceiling.

Jared climbed up it into the attic. He cried out. I pushed Jack aside and climbed up too.

"Audrey, don't!" Dad said as he tried to grasp my ankle.

I stopped as soon as my head cleared the hatch. Three feet in front of me, Jared sat with his shoulders hunched, crying. Lying next to him was Rick, an axe clutched in his hand, Maggie cradled under his arm. Chunks of the low ceiling were missing. He had tried to chop his way through. I guessed the water had come too fast.

If Jared and I had stayed in Rick's hurricane-proof house like he'd invited us to, we would have drowned with him. The voice of the gypsy at the carnival echoed in my ears: "Phil say you are in danger. He say you are hiding. He say you cannot hide in the attic."

It was too much for me—the destruction, the death, the smell of decay. I swooned and tried to bite down on reality, but it was too late. My knees gave, and I tumbled backward down the ladder. Luckily, there were three men below me to break my fall.

When I came to, I was outside the house with my dad and David on either side of me. They were dragging me back to the boat. I took in great gulps of air, trying to clear the dizziness from my head, and looked around for Jared. He was behind me, Jack supporting him. I wanted to go to him, to hold him and comfort him, but I didn't know how he would react. Was he ashamed that I'd seen him break down and cry during the last two days? His grief only made me love him more. He had to know that. I wrenched myself free and stumbled to him, falling into his arms. He hugged me, his head burrowed into my shoulder, and we cried together.

In that moment I knew that nothing would ever be the same again.

41

Poplarville Cabin

We left that night, the five of us piled into Jack's truck. We towed Jared's truck behind us with its cargo of salvaged belongings.

David had made the necessary calls to the authorities about Rick's body. Aunt Tennison stayed behind with the Linds, to be near her property and stick with her friends and neighbors. She and Grace were knee-deep in FEMA paperwork and had plans to wait in line at the closest Red Cross station to get vouchers for new mattresses. They had already managed to acquire a huge stockpile of MREs and had sent some along with us. They were a novelty, but I couldn't survive on them for long. I missed decadent Southern food...but also felt guilty about how many others might have been going hungry just then.

Jared's family greeted us at their secluded cabin. They were desperate for news and wanted to know every detail of what we had seen. David relayed the events of the past two days while Jared went to take a shower. I couldn't listen to the story either, so I quietly excused myself and asked Jessica where I could sleep.

She took me to the small bedroom she was staying in. We sat and talked for a while. She told me about how Josh's father, a deputy sheriff, had stood on the roof of the dispatch center at the Sea Bee base when the storm surge hit and had seen people carried away by the floodwaters. His sister, a 911 operator, got a ton of calls from frantic people begging for rescue. She found out later that a lot of them drowned in their homes. One desperate mother had asked her which child she should save. She could hold on to only one.

Jess also peppered me with questions. I was exhausted and numb and just wanted to shut down.

"I can't," I told her. "I'm just not ready to talk right now." My voice cracked on the last word.

"Oh, hey, sure," she said. "Later, then."

I unrolled my blankets on the wood floor, set down my pillow, and within seconds was in a deep sleep. I didn't wake until late the following morning, when bright light streamed through the window. Jessica's bed was neatly made. I was alone. I wanted to turn over and go back to sleep, to escape the horrible images of the day before, but I was too hungry and thirsty. I forced myself up, stretching my aching back, and opened the bedroom door. I heard voices near the front of the house but tiptoed in the other direction, to the bathroom. I closed and locked the door behind me and took a long shower, soaping myself three times, trying to wash away the memories. Each time I closed my eyes I saw Rick cradling Maggie in his dead arms, and finally I couldn't hold it in any longer. I sat in the tub while the water poured down on me, crying until I was spent.

I left the bathroom wrapped in a towel, feeling empty but better. Back in the bedroom I realized I had no clean clothes. I poked my head out the door.

"Jessica? Can I borrow some clothes?"

She came pattering down the hallway, her feet bare. "Sure! Hang on a sec." She rummaged through her suitcase and found me shorts and a T-shirt.

"Thanks," I said, taking them from her.

She sat on the bed while I got dressed. I knew Jessica's clothes would never fit me. The shirt was tight; without a bra I looked way too alluring. She looked at the shirt on me. "Whoa, hello, Mother Jugs."

I blushed and hunched my shoulders. "I know, I need to wash all my clothes. Everything smells like mold and death."

"C'mon. I'll show you where the washer is. We're so lucky this place still has power. The wind knocked half of Poplarville's electricity out."

We gathered my clothes and bedding and stuffed it into my duffel bag. I followed Jess to a small shed at the rear of the property. The sandy soil of the yard was hard-packed and glaringly bright in the sunlight; all the crepe myrtle trees were denuded of all their bright blossoms. The southern pines were scruffy and sad looking.

"This used to be the old well house," she said as we approached a small building made out of concrete blocks. "Jack converted it into a laundry room a couple of months ago."

She opened the door, revealing a small, windowless room with a concrete floor and a skylight. A new washer and dryer stood against one wall, a deep utility sink and a folding table on the other. I separated my whites from my colors and stuffed the washer until it was full.

"Oh yeah," Jessica said, her face lighting up. "Mom's going to make beignets. She says that everyone needs a treat about now. I'm supposed to go help her."

"Go ahead, Jess. I think I can figure out how to do laundry." I laughed.

"'Kay." She skipped toward the door, came back to give me a hug, then trotted off again. I smiled at her sweetness.

I measured the detergent and set the load size and temperature. The washer filled with water and began to agitate. Just when I decided I'd better go back to the house to help with the doughnuts, the door opened and Jared came in.

"Hi!" I said.

"Hey, I was looking for you. Jess said you were out here. Thought I'd check on you."

"Gee, thanks. So much confidence in my ability to work a washing machine." I hoped a little friendly sarcasm would ease the sadness in his face.

He smiled and stepped forward. He put his arms around me, and I snuggled into his chest.

"Is everything going to be okay, Jared?" I held him close, waiting for his answer.

"It'll be okay, babe. It's gonna take a lot of time and even more money…but it's going to be okay. I promise."

He stepped back and placed his hands on my face. His eyes took in my shirt. "Good Lord, woman. You look like you're ready to report for work at an X-rated Hooters."

I laughed, hunching my shoulders. "I know, but all my bras are dirty. Look." I pointed to the glass front of the washer and the swirling mass of clothes and suds. "There goes one now."

Jared grabbed my shirt and pulled it up over my breasts. He grasped them, plunging his head down to kiss and suck them. My surprise turned to desire as he lifted me onto the folding table. Feeling the joy of being alive, we tore at each other's clothes and coupled furiously. My heart pounded. When I came I thought my head would explode.

We were locked together, panting and still when the door suddenly opened. Jessica stood there, staring at Jared's naked ass and my legs wrapped around his back. She looked like she didn't know whether to laugh or cry. She slammed the door and stood outside, laughing hysterically.

"I…am…mortified," I said as Jared and I pulled apart and grabbed for our clothes.

"You and me both," he said. "Christ, my baby sister."

Jared dressed, gave me one last kiss, then quickly vanished. Jessica waited for me at the back door, still laughing as I did my walk of shame back into house for another shower. To her credit she never said a word to me or anyone else about the incident, but the smirk didn't leave her face for quite a while.

———

The next few days passed quickly as we fell into the work of maintaining a household crowded with people. Family and friends of the Breauxs sought shelter with us while they figured out where they would live. Shopping trips to towns farther north yielded new clothes and bedding as well as an air mattress for me to sleep on.

We soon found out that the FEMA trailers would take weeks if not longer to arrive. All of the schools had been wiped out, flooded and broken by the storm's fury. The entire Mississippi Gulf Coast lay in ruins. There was nothing to return to.

David and Julie decided to stay in Poplarville with Jack and Miranda until they could rebuild. Miranda seemed happy enough about it, since Julie would help when the baby came. Jessica would enroll at Poplarville High the following week. I thought my dad and I would follow the same route, but he told me his company was going to scrap the plant. The damage was too extensive; it would cost too much to restore.

"Does that mean you're out of a job?" I asked, panic gripping me. If he lost his job, where would we live?

"No, not right away. I'll be overseeing the dismantling. I'll be pulling a paycheck for at least six months. After that... Well..."

I began to hyperventilate, wondering what kind of bombshell he was about to drop on me.

"I'm going up to Jackson to buy a travel trailer. We'll stay in it on Tennison's property while we get her house fixed up."

I breathed a sigh of relief, but Dad still looked anxious. I knew he had not told me everything.

"OLA is really bad off," he continued. "So are the rest of the schools. They're not going to be ready for students for months, Audrey."

I knew what he was going to say next before the words left his mouth.

"The best place for you would be back with your mom."

I took a deep breath, ready to launch into my legitimate and logical reasons why this was a bad idea, but he held his hand up to stop me.

"I know what you're going to say, but just listen, okay? It makes no sense for you to stay here, living in a small trailer in a ruined town with no school when you've got your room at home waiting for you. You've missed only a couple weeks of school, so you can re-enroll with hardly a hiccup. I've talked to your mom and she agrees."

He paused, placing his hands on my shoulders. "Jared agrees too. He doesn't want your life and education affected by this mess any more than the rest of us."

Blood pulsed from my feet to my face. I imagined steam coming out of my ears. Without saying another word I stormed out of the house, slamming the door behind me. I looked for Jared and found him under the carport with Jack. They were draining all the fluids from Jared's truck's engine.

"What the fuck, Jared?" I stormed over to him. "You told my dad it's okay to ship me back to California? You want to get rid of me?" My voice crackled and shook as I choked back my tears.

Jared grabbed a rag and scrubbed at his hands, trying to remove the grease while he led me away from Jack. We went under a copse of trees at the rear of the property.

"Audrey, you know it's not like that," he said. "Things here are a fucking disaster. You don't need to be living like this when you've got your mom chomping at the bit for you to come home. Besides, it's just temporary until school starts up again out here."

"Uh huh," I said, my anger rising again. "And did my father mention to you that he'll be out of a job in six months? I doubt he'll find a new one anywhere around here! You said it yourself—the town is trashed. Once I go back to LA there's no coming back!"

He looked concerned now, and I felt vindicated. He frowned as he thought the whole thing through.

"No. That won't happen," he said. "I'm sure your aunt will let you live with her once the school's back up and running. Her place will be fixed up before then."

"Why can't I stay with your family now? Why can't I stay with you? I'll be eighteen in a month!"

His voice softened. "My dad already offered to let you stay here in Poplarville, but your mom and dad want you back home. Besides, it's going to suck here." He rubbed his forehead with his still-greasy hand, leaving a smudge. "The boats are gone, my business is gone, my house is gone... Getting the insurance companies to pay up is going to be a nightmare. I'm not going to be fit company for any human being for the next few months."

I was about to argue that, but he stopped me. "Just until OLA reopens, okay?" he said. "I'm sure it'll be back on its feet by Christmas break. I swear to God, Audrey, I will come out to California and bring you back myself if you're not in Mississippi by then."

I looked into his eyes and knew he was telling the truth. I began to cry. "Long-distance relationships never work. What happens when you fall out of love with me?"

"That's not gonna happen. Don't even think it. You're mine, and I'm yours. You have to have faith in that."

He pulled me close, wrapping his arms around me. I rested my ear against his heart, listening to its steady beating.

42

Full Circle

I looked at my reflection in the bathroom mirror, a feeling of deep resignation washing over me. I'd given my hair color a boost as soon as I'd returned to California; I was still very tan and I'd lost weight since the storm, so my face was more angular. I looked fine—except for my eyes. They were disturbing. They looked…old. I put on some shadow and eyeliner and brushed on a layer of mascara. I surveyed them again.

Oh, who cares? I thought. Who am I trying to look good for?

I plodded down the stairs to the kitchen and hung my book bag over the chair at the counter. I trailed my fingers over the bag's soft leather, happy that it had survived the storm. Mom was busy at the stove, flipping pancakes—another one of her attempts to suck up for bringing me back here. I hated her and Dad for it, but I didn't take out my anger on them. Instead I existed in a fog of depression, fulfilling my obligations but determined not to find any joy in them.

Jared called me every day, sometimes twice. He told me every detail of everything going on back in Mississippi, from paperwork he filed to the flood of construction jobs coming in to news of my friends left behind. I missed him so badly my chest ached, as if my heart were being squeezed in a vise.

Kara, Jane, and Megan all came by to welcome me home. I half listened as they filled me in on all the happenings around town. Only one revelation broke through my haze: Caroline Riggs was pregnant. She and Steve Schubert planned to get married in the spring, after the baby was born. Apparently Caroline was really jazzed about the pregnancy and couldn't wait to be a mother. I was shocked.

I lay awake in bed for hours after that, chewing over the thought of mean, spiteful Caroline being all gaga over a baby. When I talked to Jared about it the next day he wasn't surprised at all. He said Caroline had probably gotten pregnant on purpose, because she so desperately wanted and needed someone to love her unconditionally. His theory gave me food for thought. The more I considered it, the more plausible it seemed. I almost felt sorry for her…almost.

"Thanks, Mom," I said as she sat a plate of three hotcakes in front of me. She leaned against the sink and watched as I added butter and syrup.

"Mmmm," I said. "Yummy."

"You know, Audrey, it's not too late for you to back out. You don't have to go to Moss Ridge High. You can go to The Learning Center instead—do online schooling."

"Mom, I thought we already hashed this out. I don't care what anybody at school thinks of me or heard about me. I don't care if they all saw that fake picture. It doesn't matter anymore."

"I know, honey. But it's one thing to say it. It'll be something else if someone starts harassing you again. I know that Hillary girl is still at the school—"

"Mom, look at me. I've seen families walking down the road with nothing but a shopping cart of food. I've seen dead people and animals lying around like garbage. Do you think I care what a bunch of stupid teenagers think or talk about?"

She went pale. I hadn't told her about the horrible things I had seen. Dad and I had both tried to protect her from the heinous details. Her face crumpled, and she began to cry. I pushed my chair back and went to hold her. I soothed my mother the way she had soothed me so many times, gently stroking her hair and back.

Starting school two weeks into the semester was an odd experience. By third period I was used to all the stares and whispers. Kara was in two of my classes and Jane and Megan in one each, so I had near-constant companionship until lunchtime. Many people—some I knew, some I didn't—approached me to ask about the hurricane. They had seen the coverage on TV and were disappointed when I explained that I hadn't been in New Orleans, even though I'd been in an area that had gotten hit even worse. They had never heard of Waveland, Bay St. Louis, Pass Christian, or any of the other towns that had been knocked flat.

Three days into school, I literally ran into Hillary when I was opening the door to the school's library.

"Sorry!" she said, stepping back. She did a double take and realized it was me. "Oh…Audrey."

It was the first time she had ever said my name without a derogatory term attached to it.

"Hi, Hillary," I said, trying to act nonchalant. The truth was I didn't need to act—I really didn't care.

"I heard you were back from out of state," she said.

"Yes, temporarily. I'm moving back at Christmas."

"Really? How come?"

How strange it was to have a cordial conversation with a former sworn enemy. "Well, as soon as my school reopens, I'll be going back. I've already applied to a couple of colleges there as well."

"So…you really like it…in the South, I mean." She was careful to keep the conversation exceedingly polite.

"I love it," I said.

"That's cool. Well, see ya." She turned to leave but then turned back. "Hey, Audrey?"

"Yeah?"

"Listen…about last spring…I'm sorry about what we did. I don't even know why I went along with it. It all seems so stupid now. I know my apology probably doesn't mean much—"

"It means a lot, Hillary. I'm sorry too."

She nodded twice, then turned and left. I walked into the library, my sense of awe leading the way.

―――

I returned home from school to find a bouquet of huge, white magnolias from Jared. I stroked their waxy, dark-green leaves and pulled out the card: The Magnolia State is not the same without you. This place with no flowers will bloom again when you return. I love you. Jared.

Tears welled in my eyes and fell down my cheeks. My heart ached for him, and my soul ached for my green, flowered Mississippi.

―――

Slowly I fell into the routine of school. I studied often with Kara, Jane, and Megan, and all of us bemoaned the absence of Lily, who was by far the best academically in our little group. She wouldn't be home from Belgium until Christmas. In October we took the SATs. We wouldn't get the results back for a month.

I continued to talk to Jared, Jessica, and Dad as often as I could, even though every conversation left me frustrated. I couldn't believe how complicated the recovery was on the Gulf Coast. The scope of the work that needed to be done and the inept state and local government leaders made the cleanup and reconstruction maddeningly slow.

Jared and Jack jumped right into the contracting business but were stuck with little to no materials. Folks couldn't rebuild until they received insurance settlements, and even then their hands were tied as new building requirements were instituted. Work would be delayed indefinitely until debris could be cleared and basic infrastructure restored.

In the meantime rescue crews continued to fish bodies out of the mud and muck by the hundreds. No one could guess how many others would never be found—all the elderly and loners with no family to report them missing...

The heartbreaking stories were endless. Still, all I wanted was to return to Mississippi and help my family and friends restore their lives. I crossed each day off my calendar, counting down until Christmas. It seemed so far away.

My mom surprised me with breakfast in bed on the morning of my birthday though I had purposely tried to forget it. Kara had wanted to throw me a party, but I had refused. I couldn't take thinking about the New Orleans trip Jared and I had planned.

I sat up as Mom placed the breakfast tray on my knees. She sat at the foot of my bed, singing "Happy Birthday." I gave her a small smile and picked at the scrambled eggs on the plate. I had eaten only a few mouthfuls when she seemed to be overtaken with impatience.

"Come see your present!" she said, taking the tray away and pulling me to my feet.

I followed her downstairs, wondering what she had gotten me. I guessed jewelry—a diamond pendant or maybe opals, my birthstone. She led me through the kitchen to the door of the garage.

"Mom?" I asked warily.

She giggled as she opened the garage door and propelled me forward. Parked dead center was a cranberry-red Ford Mustang with a gigantic, white bow on the hood. A mishmash of emotions flared inside me: shock, then joy, then disbelief and denial.

"Mom, it's too much! We can't afford this. College tuition is going to be monstrous—"

"Honey, in case you've failed to notice, this has been the best year of my entire real estate career. I made enough money to pay cash for that car and for your first two years of college."

I stared at her. "You made that much?"

"Yes I did! The market is white-hot. Of course, the bubble is going to burst in a couple of years, but in the meantime I'm feathering the nest."

She looked so pleased with herself I couldn't help but be sucked in. I went to the car and ran my fingers over the bright paint. I opened the driver's door and sat down on the soft leather seat, inhaling the intoxicating new-car scent. I admired the dash and the stereo, then looked up to the sun roof. I was glad Mom hadn't gotten me a convertible. It was too buggy and wet on the Gulf Coast for that.

She disappeared into the house and came out holding our purses. She jumped into the passenger seat and handed me a set of keys.

"Let's go for a spin!" she said, buckling her seat belt.

"Mom, I've still got bed head."

"C'mon, just around the block!"

I sighed, smiling as I pushed the key into the ignition. The engine flared to life with a deep rumble.

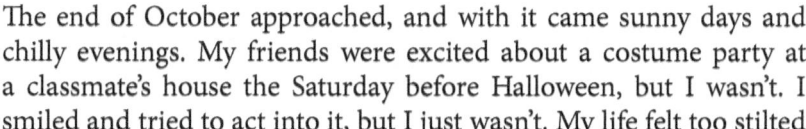

The end of October approached, and with it came sunny days and chilly evenings. My friends were excited about a costume party at a classmate's house the Saturday before Halloween, but I wasn't. I smiled and tried to act into it, but I just wasn't. My life felt too stilted and incomplete.

The day finally arrived when I could check my SAT scores online, but I chickened out and made Kara do it while I hid my face in my hands.

"Don't freak out so much, Audrey. You can always retake them."

She tapped the keyboard, bringing up the test scores. "Okay, what do you want first? Math, essay, critical reading?"

"Just give me the total." I knew I wasn't going to hit that magic twenty-four-hundred max, but how close had I come?

"Hang on a sec while I find it. Okay, you ready?"

"Tell me!" I yelled.

"Nineteen fifty."

I looked at her smiling face. "Are you sure?"

"See for yourself."

I added them up myself. "Oh my God." I was elated but panicked. "I've got only three weeks to get my college applications in!"

"Chill, baby," Kara said. "You've got the whole stack right here. One step at a time, okay?"

I took a breath. "Okay."

I spent the rest of the week filling them out and checking and double- checking them. I hoped they were good enough. I hoped I was good enough.

43

Halloween

The final bell of the day buzzed. Megan and I left our sixth-period keyboarding class and headed for the parking lot. We were discussing costumes for the party when a voice called out to me.

"Audrey!"

I looked around. Leaning against his Bronco, looking as model-gorgeous as ever, was James Ridley. I was surprised...and attracted.

"James! Hi!" I walked toward him. He met me and scooped me up in a bear hug, then swung me in a circle. He went in for a kiss, but I managed to tilt my head at the last second. It landed half on my lips and half on my cheek.

"Wow!" he said. "You look beautiful."

I disengaged myself from his grasp, stepped back, and pulled Megan over next to me. She looked unsure of what she was supposed to do.

"You remember my friend Megan?" I asked James.

"Yeah, of course. Hey, how's it going?"

"Good," she replied.

James bounced on his feet. He pushed his hands through his hair. "Oh man, it's so good to see you, Aud. I missed you so much."

I took a mental step back. He had missed me? That seemed unlikely since he'd dumped me. It wasn't like he'd pledged any love or fidelity to me before he'd left for Australia. I'd gotten only a single frickin' postcard for Christ's sake!

"What are you doing here?" I asked. "You were supposed to be in the South Pacific until the end of the year."

"Yeah, well, plans change. Everything was going great until Travis met a nurse from New Zealand and decided to go home with her. He really fucked everything up. I was stuck by myself, so I decided to change my ticket and come home."

"Travis just bailed on you?"

"Um, pretty much. I mean, he invited me to go with them, but who wants to be a third wheel? Listen, can I drive you home so we can talk?" He glanced over at Megan, making it obvious he wanted a private conversation.

"I have a car," I said.

"Really?"

"Yes, a Mustang. My birthday present."

"Sweet. So then let's just take a ride, and I'll bring you back to get your car, okay?"

"Uh, Megan, I guess I'll talk to you later?" I said.

She looked wary, as if she weren't entirely sure if she should leave me alone with him.

"Yeah, sure," she answered. "I'll call you later, 'kay?"

I hugged her then climbed into the Bronco next to James. The car's interior brought back memories of the ride out to Pinehaven on prom night. I shook my head, trying to dispel them. We started out of the parking lot and down the road, and James began talking nonstop about his travels down under. Didn't take much insight on my part to realize he had started missing me only after his buddy had abandoned him. I could only imagine how many girls he had hooked up with before then.

"Sounds like you had a really great time," I said as he pulled back in to the school's parking lot.

He cut the engine. "Yeah, but I screwed up, Audrey."

"What do you mean?"

"I never should have turned you down when you said you wanted to come with me. I didn't realize how much I cared about you until we were apart, you know?" He looked at me earnestly and took my hand. He caressed my fingers one by one. "What I'm trying to say is...I want you back. We were really good together, and I want that again."

I was stunned. He leaned forward, ready to kiss me, but I pushed him away. He looked hurt and confused.

"James, I love someone else now."

He frowned as if he couldn't believe I could care for anyone but him. "Well, that was fast," he said.

"Excuse me?" Anger flashed through me like lightning. "You dumped me last spring without a glance backward as you floated off overseas. I don't recall you ever telling me you loved me or to wait for you. We had a clean break and you know it."

He exhaled heavily, turning back to face the steering wheel. "You're right. I know you're right. I was just…hoping."

My anger dissipated as quickly as it had come. "It would never work with us anyway, James. I'll be back in Mississippi by Christmas. My life is there now. I'll be going to college there next fall."

"College, huh? That's great." His voice held no enthusiasm. "What are you going to major in?"

"Environmental science. I want to study the earth and the environment—geology, geography, all that. If I can handle the coursework, I might even pursue environmental engineering, but that's years away and God knows how much money in tuition. I'm just going to focus on getting my BS at this point."

"Why are you interested in that stuff?" He sounded so condescending.

"After the hurricane I knew I wanted to study the water and land of the Gulf Coast. Did you know that if the Mississippi Barrier Islands had been restored after Hurricane Camille they would have provided a major speed bump for the hurricanes that came after? I'm sure the government will approve funds to do that now, and I want to be a part of it."

"Why do you want to live in that redneck, hillbilly place anyway?" He didn't look at me; he just kept staring at his steering wheel. "You gonna become an ultraconservative and fight to resegregate schools?"

His words stung, but I knew there was no point in arguing with him. He was bitter because I'd rejected him and didn't want to hear about the virtues of the South and its people.

"Take care, James." I opened the door and got out of the Bronco.

I thought I would hear the sound of screeching tires as I walked to my car; instead I heard his door opening and closing.

"Audrey… Hey, Audrey, stop!" He ran up and grabbed me by the elbow. "I'm sorry I said that. I didn't mean it. What you want to do is awesome, really."

"Thanks," I said. "I appreciate that."

"This guy," he began, looking down at his feet then back up to me. "You think he's the real thing?"

"I know he is."

James looked back down. I reached up and placed my palm gently against his cheek. "You're a great guy, James. I'll never regret what we had."

He remained where he was while I walked away.

On the day of the Halloween party Kara and Jane came over to prepare our costumes. We'd decided to go as the three Fates—we'd wear togas and do our hair in ringlets and, at Kara's insistence, wear lots and lots of body glitter. She laughed as she sprayed it on me. Finally her deepest wish was fulfilled.

Megan just wore black from head to toe. "You know, if you die on Halloween, you go straight to hell," she told us.

"Shut up!" Jane said. "You are so full of shit."

Megan laughed, picked up a pillow from my bed, and threw it at Jane's head.

Mom took dozens of photos and we listened patiently as she gave the "no drinking, no drugs" speech. Then we piled into my Mustang (I had the coolest car, so I drove) and headed to the party. It was at Jose's; he was a varsity football player but none of us knew him very well. We parked several doors down and walked the rest of the way.

The front of the house looked like a rotting cemetery. The courtyard was covered in mist from a smoke machine and had a fountain that gurgled with blood-red water. Inside we edged our way past the game room where a bunch of kids were crowded around a Ouija board. I shuddered at the sight of it. No more spirits or fortune-telling for me—ever.

We found the kitchen, and I got a ginger ale. Kara, Jane, and Megan grabbed bottles of hard lemonade.

"You guys actually partake of the forbidden fruit now?" I asked.

Megan looked at me. "Now that you're driving, hell yes."

I laughed, shaking my head. So much for Mom's pep talk.

We took our drinks and went to the backyard, where there was a Jacuzzi full of red water and mannequin limbs. We people watched and laughed at others' costumes, especially all the sexy nurses, sexy witches, and sexy maids. Girls could sometimes be so predictable.

I caught up with some old friends and friends of friends until music began to thump and the courtyard became a dance floor. Kara and I sat on a bench at the side while Jane and Megan joined the throng of gyrating bodies.

A couple of guys I vaguely recognized from school stumbled up to us, drinks in hand. One of them, a short, stocky blond, pointed at Kara. "Lemme guess... Athena, right? You're Athena... And you." He pointed at me. "You're Venus. Am I right?"

"Close," Kara said, smiling. "We're the three Fates, but our third is somewhere out there." She pointed at the dance floor.

"Wuz a faaayt?" the second boy asked. He looked even drunker than his friend.

Before Kara could answer him, she froze, her eyes on the dance floor. I tried to find what she was looking at...and then I saw her. Near the center, dressed like Tinker Bell, was Caroline Riggs, dancing with Steve Schubert. Her long ponytail swung from side to side, her wings bumping and brushing other dancers in the face. Her midsection showed a small baby bump.

What should I do? Should I ignore her? Should I leave? Before I could decide, Caroline saw me and stopped dancing. She whispered something in Steve's ear, left the dance floor, and headed to the house.

"Should we leave?" Kara asked, shouting to be heard over the music.

"No. Give me a minute, okay?"

"What are you going to do?" she asked.

"Nothing bad," I said, squeezing her shoulder.

I walked into the house and went room to room, looking for Caroline. I found her in the kitchen.

"Caroline," I called out as I approached.

She turned, saw it was me, and turned her back to me. I stood next to her, my resolve solidifying.

"I just wanted to say that I'm sorry about everything that happened last spring," I said. "Things got way out of hand—for both of us, I think. I convinced myself that revenge was justified, but I never should have sunk that low."

Her silence lingered.

"I heard you were expecting. Congratulations. I hope everything turns out good for you." I waited, not sure if I should say anything else or just walk away.

"Are you finished?" she asked, still not looking at me.

"Yeah, I guess I am."

"Good, then get your ass away from me."

My hope for some sort of closure collapsed. The apology from Hillary had made me believe anything was possible, but now I realized that was not going to be the case with Caroline. What was that old saying? Some people you just can't reach?

I turned and went back to my friends. Kara breathed a sigh of relief. There would be no more fighting, no more revenge. That ship had sailed, burning like a Viking funeral pyre, and had sunk to the bottom of the ocean. Good riddance to it.

44

Farewell

Arriving home from school one afternoon I found not one but two thick envelopes in my mailbox, one from the University of Tulane and the other from the University of Southern Mississippi. I tore one open, then the other—both acceptances. I released of gush of air, my legs shaking. Now my return to Mississippi held the tang of reality. I would be going to college in the South. Loyola, LSU, U of M—whether they accepted me now didn't matter. One way or another I was going!

I thought about the Christmas holidays as I dressed for school. Winter break was fast approaching, and it was time to start shopping. It would have been fun to buy my family and friends unique gifts from Old Town had it still been standing. Kara would have loved a beach glass art piece, and Mom would've been tickled with a shrimp-themed tea set.

Downstairs, Mom stood at the sink, her back to me as she quietly sipped her coffee. "Mom, are you okay?"

She turned to face me, her mouth smiling but her eyes sad. "I'm fine honey. Just a little bit blue this morning."

I felt guilty. I'd been taking her for granted the past two months. I'd been so focused on getting back to Mississippi I'd hardly given her the appreciation she deserved.

I thought of what I could do to cheer her up. "Hey, how about I cook dinner tonight?" I asked. "Mrs. Breaux taught me how to make jambalaya. I could run by the store after school and pick up the ingredients."

"That's sweet of you, hon. Let's just play it by ear, okay?"

"Okay." I wondered what had triggered her mood. Maybe it was some kind of post-menopausal thing.

The school day crept by as I trudged my way from class to class. The sun was out but the air was so dry it made my nose hurt. I missed the rain of Mississippi.

Finally the school day ended. Megan had volleyball practice, so I walked to the parking lot alone.

"Audrey!" a deep, male voice called out.

I slowed down then faltered as I looked around. Was it James again? Man, that guy just wouldn't give up. Then I saw a muddy, bug-splattered truck. I blinked, positive it was a mirage. Then I heard a laugh, so hearty and carefree.

"Jared!" I ran at him full speed and nearly knocked him down. Then we kissed…and kissed…and kissed. When we came up for air, other students were lingering at their cars, watching with curiosity. I ignored them and gazed into Jared's eyes.

"What are you doing here?" I asked. "I can't believe it! Why didn't you tell me you were coming?"

"Whoa, slow down there, babe. Give me chance and I'll explain everything."

I laughed. I didn't really care how or why he was there. All I cared about was that he was there.

On the short drive home Jared told me that Our Lady Academy was restarting classes on a small portion of the campus—which meant that it was time for me to return. He had decided on the spur of the moment to drive out to get me, to help haul my furniture and tow the Mustang. He had talked to my dad, who had convinced Mom to let Jared surprise me. Now I understood Mom's sadness. She would be losing me again.

I was ready to pack my things and leave that evening, but Jared convinced me to wait a few days. This was his first trip to California and he wanted to look around before we left. I agreed, brightening at the thought of seeing the sights through his eyes.

I ditched school for the rest of the week and took Jared to Disney-land, Hollywood, Griffith Park, and hiking in the Angeles National Forest. He had a wonderful time. He loved the mountains and the low humidity.

Which made me anxious. Would he want to move to California?

I turned the thought over and over in my mind. I would go wherever he was; there was no doubt about that. I'd applied to two colleges in California and been accepted, and it wasn't too late to switch plans.

Finally I got up the courage to ask him. We were walking hand in hand on the beach in Malibu, the sand cool beneath the soft sunshine.

"Jerry?"

"Mmm?"

"You're not thinking of staying here in California, are you? I mean, that would be okay, I guess, if it's what you really want."

He stopped walking and took both my hands in his. "Is that what you want, Audrey?"

"I want what you want."

"That's not what I asked. What do you want?"

I searched my heart to ensure my answer was one hundred percent honest. "I want to go back to Mississippi."

"For sure?"

"Absolutely."

He exhaled a huge sigh and lifted me into a hug. "Whew. You had me worried there for a second."

"I was worried that you wanted to stay here!" I told him.

"Naw, babe! I am a child of the South. I may be able to travel around, but unless my feet are planted back in that muddy clay, I will wither and die!"

My friends and my mom threw me a small farewell party. With no time to prepare, they kept it simple—Christmas decorations and Mardi Gras beads on every light fixture as well as a huge king cake we made ourselves. Jane found the tiny plastic baby in her slice and was named queen of the day.

My friends loved Jared, especially Kara, who told me he looked like a cross between Clive Owen and Elvis. I think it was more than his good looks that won them over, though. It was his easygoing southern charm, his everyman quality. Their eyes sparkled when they looked at him. It didn't make me jealous—it made me love him more.

Twenty-four hours after the party we were speeding east through the desert. There had been no grand, weepy goodbyes, only simple farewells with promises to meet again soon. Mom would be out for Christmas come hell or high water, she said, no pun intended. Kara and Jane planned to visit during Mardi Gras. And I promised visits back west during breaks.

I gazed at the terrain rushing past the window, truly seeing it for the first time. I remembered my first drive east with Dad back in June. Had that really happened just over six months earlier? It seemed like a lifetime ago. Back then I'd been blind to the world and its potential. Now my eyes were wide open.

45

Redemption

Thanks to Jared and Jack, Aunt Tenni's house was fresh and dry. They'd rehabbed hers first, before starting all their other jobs, because at least she'd had a standing house to work on. There were new floors, dry-wall, and paint, new wiring and insulation, and a brand-new kitchen. The house looked better than it had been before the storm.

Aunt Tenni's shop, on the other hand, was no more, along with most of Old Town Bay St. Louis. With not much else to do, she immersed herself in painting like never before. She was a one-woman factory, churning out images of the landscapes around her as she remembered them: beautiful sunsets on the gulf, hazy sunbeams slanting through oak branches draped in Spanish moss, quaint shops dotting flower-lined streets. She even tried to duplicate the painting she had given me of the Friendship Oak. It was as beautiful as the original but not the same. This time the couple standing under the tree resembled Jared and me.

Dad was still living in the trailer on Aunt Tenni's property and intended to stay there until he figured out his next career move. He insisted, though, that I take the second bedroom in the house, and as soon as I arrived from California we moved my stuff in. Tenni was happy to have me and told me to stay as long as I wanted, but I planned to move into a dorm at Tulane in the fall.

I felt like I was standing on the edge of a precipice. My life had undergone a great shift, and it was about to change even more. The strings that tied me to my parents grew longer and thinner as I fol-lowed my own path.

I arrived at Our Lady a good hour ahead of schedule, glad that I'd left myself so much extra time—the main roads were clear, but the closer I got to the coast, the more detours I had to take. So many neighborhood streets still lay in ruin.

I was excited to be back on campus, though only a handful of students had returned. Many families had left town and had not come back. Some girls had transferred to other schools and had just decided to finish the semester where they were. Those of us who remained at OLA greeted each other with new warmth, feeling a lot more like a family. Our principal choked back tears as she welcomed us.

I didn't get much work done that first day. Everyone wanted to share a story of the storm, and each was compelling. We linked hands, our hearts in our throats as the tales unfolded, binding us together in a sisterhood of survival.

———

Volunteerism was new to me. I'd helped out at a couple of school carnivals and had passed out oranges and water at the LA Marathon, but that was it. Upon returning to the Gulf Coast, however, it was clear that I had to do more. I joined my classmates to recreate our town, our county, our state. We gutted homes that had been flooded, traveled far and wide to deliver needed supplies, and fundraised with religious fervor.

I spearheaded an effort to pair up with a sister Catholic school in California. The girls there got donations from their families and sent them to us—enough to provide a good Christmas to many who would have otherwise had none. We brought fresh trees to families living in FEMA trailers, and the looks on their faces were enough to move the most hardened heart. We handed out frozen turkeys too, along with canned and dried goods, clothing, and new toys. I felt like Father Christmas. Or Mother Christmas. Or something.

Until then I'd always been too selfish to give my time away, but once I started doing it I understood why people liked volunteering so much. It was a high of the purest sort, comprising kindness, love, and generosity. Whatever evil or ills I had committed in the past were absolved. I built my future from the ground up, day by day.

Eventually spring arrived. From the mud and brine came new

houses, bridges, buildings, and businesses. Dad took a job overseas, promising to come home every few months. Jared's and Jack's insurance payouts finally came, and the building began. Jared and I designed his new house together, making it bigger and better than it had been before the storm. The Breaux brothers had more construction contracts than they could handle and so hired as many local workers as they could. They even put their shrimping business on hold to tend to the more important work of reconstructing neighborhoods.

On the last day of school before spring break came, I headed east to meet Jared in Biloxi at a construction site. On impulse I pulled into the drive leading to the Friendship Oak. I parked and walked up to the tree. I laid my hand against its gnarled trunk and looked up into its branches. They teemed with leaf buds. The tree had weathered the storm and had made it through. So had I, and I had emerged renewed and filled with life.

www.leslieannkeatley.com